A CLASH OF TIDES

Chronicles of the Dolah

Book One

Alivia R. Maar

A Clash of Tides: Chronicles of the Dolah, Book One

First Edition

Copyright© 2024 Alivia Maar

ISBN 979-8-9894240-3-0

Dedicated to everyone who has no idea who they are or what they are going to do with their life. This one's for you.

Part 1 – Makoul

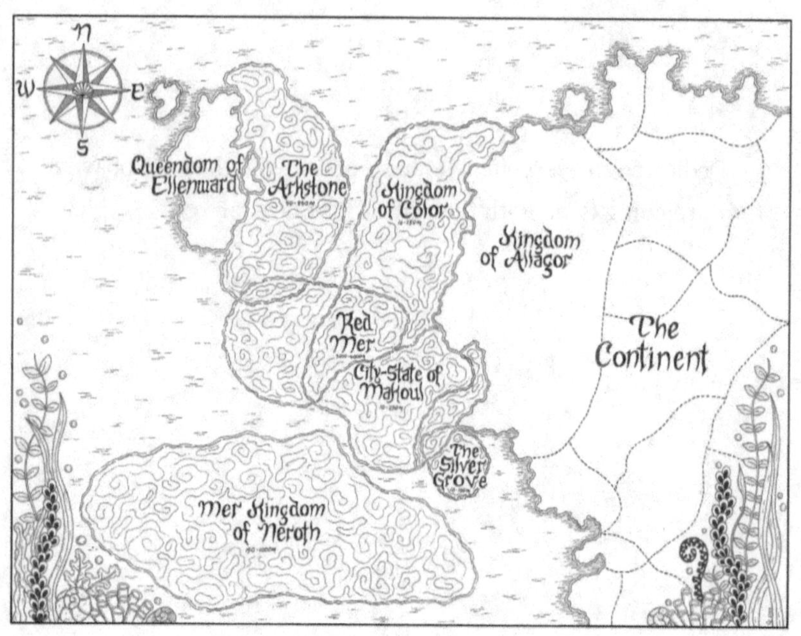

"But a mermaid has no tears, and therefore she suffers so much more."
Hans Christian Andersen

Prologue

Ivara (1602 A.D.)

Ivara stared up, looking through the darkness and meeting the dragon's gaze. He was angry with her. Even if his stern look had not given him away his gruff growl did. But there was something more in his huge golden eyes and scaly expression...pity and fear.

It is not too late to turn back. To stay. The great beast spoke in her mind. Ivara could feel a shiver run down her spine, from her neck to the tip of her tail. She was terrified. Terrified of leaving him. Terrified of what might happen to her if she went through with this. Terrified of what her freedom would *truly* cost her. Still, she nodded.

"It's all too much. The visions drive me mad, and the ghosts of all the lives I will never live haunt me in the night. If I stay much longer, I fear I will go insane." Ivara said by way of apology.

The Golden Dragon nodded and motioned for her to leave. In the distance she could see two mer girls waiting for her. Scyla the sea witch was among them. Ivara swam towards the party, eager and terrified all at once. This was it, after today everything would change. After today she would not even know who she was.

Chapter 1

To his lordship Neuros of Makoul, recent events have made it clear that the young mer known as Ivara Mare must be sent back home at once. This decision was determined by the Master and shall not be challenged. It should be noted that in her current state Ivara is prone to fits of hysteria, visions and volatile episodes. If any changes occur in the girl's personality the Master has asked that you alert him immediately.

A khipu sent from the Arkstone to Makoul (1602 A.D.)

Ivara (1603 A.D.)

A gentle shake of her shoulder pulled Ivara out of her slumber. A single glance around the room told her all she needed to know. Ka'I, her eldest sister slept restlessly on one side of their dome shaped bedroom. The twins Mele and Uhane curled up beside her deep in sleep, their tails curled around stalagmites to hold them in place against the tide. Only one sister was out of place, Ivara looked over to where Wyntir hovered above her. The mer girl's face was aflame with worry and anxiety.

"He's missing." Was all Wyntir said when Ivara gave her an irritated look. *He* being her little sister's sea serpent, they'd all advised little Wyntir against keeping. Unfortunately, the serpent was a gift from their mother, so none could bring themselves to push the mer girl when she decided to make it her pet. She'd named it Gar, and while she had tried to train it, Ivara wasn't convinced the thing could be trained at all. And so it was that every few days, Wyntir would find Ivara and ask her to help chase down her pet.

"When did you realize he was gone?" Ivara asked the albino mer girl. To which she received a disgruntled look.

"Just a moment ago. I knew something was wrong, and it woke me up I suppose." Wyntir's sweet young voice trembled with worry.

Ivara nodded and untangled herself from her stalagmite around which she'd been sleeping. Her little sister was convinced that she had some sort of bond with the serpent. Wyntir swore she could sense when the creature was hungry, sad, bored... on and on it went. Ivara wasn't so sure, but she'd been told by her father and sisters that her mother had a similar bond with her own serpent, so it was possible she supposed.

There were multiple thin stones that jutted up from the floor providing stability when water would push them around. The room resembled the inside of a cavern. Barnacles and small sea creatures ate at the grime on the walls and floor. A hole above them big enough for three, perhaps four led out. Her teal gills flared as she took a breath of the cool morning water.

Ivara's skin was pale but not nearly as much as her sisters Uhane and Wyntir. Her long straight hair was a less vibrant façade of something between blonde and brunette. And in her eyes, a pale grey storm cloud lingered. She was not beautiful, at least not by mer standards but still she did not dislike the mer girl that stared back at her through the mirror.

"Alright, let's go." Ivara gestured for her sister to lead on.

Wyntir took after their mother's people, known to all as the Red Mer, everything from her hair, skin, tail, even her eyes was as white as the giant glaciers in the far north. Ivara knew little of the Red Mer but she remembered her mother's skin being a vibrant crimson. It was her mother who had once explained to Ivara that the Red Mer gained their coloration from a secret ritual that involved their serpents but beyond that she would never elaborate.

Ivara on the other hand took after their father's side, ash blonde hair, grey eyes, teal tail and pale skin, she sported far more color than her younger sister but much less than any of her elder sisters. The thought made her turn towards her eldest sister Ka'I who was squirming in her sleep. Her tail wrapped tightly around her night stalagmite.

Ivara shook her gently and a sudden vision flashed across her mind's eye. She was in foreign waters surrounded by jellyfish, no, capillatas whose heads alone could fill her bedroom. Her pale tail was now a stark sea green just like her elder sister, and her brown hair was pulled back in a long, sleek braid. For just a moment Ivara was not herself. She was Ka'I, screaming in pain as their mother took a blade to her injured arm. Then as quickly as it had begun, the vision ended.

Ka'I startled awake, her gills flaring as she gasped.

"What-." Ka'I began but Ivara shushed her and motioned to the twins Mele and Uhane who were still asleep.

"You looked like you were having a nightmare. Are you alright?" Ivara whispered. Despite the constant spats she got into with her eldest sister, she did still care for Ka'I. Though Ivara couldn't help feeling that some part of Ka'I resented her for returning so soon from the west.

Ka'I bristled and slapped Ivara's hand away. "Fine, I'm fine. It was..." She glanced over at Wyntir grimacing. "...just a dream. Why are you up?"

"Gar is gone." Ivara answered before Wyntir could.

"Again?" Ka'I yawned. "Well, I'm sure he's fine. Happy hunting." Ka'I curled herself back around her stalagmite, yawned once more and waved them away before closing her eyes.

Wyntir grabbed Ivara's arm and the latter winced in pain. The long scar on her inner arm pulsed, a thinly veiled reminder that she was not whole. Ivara mastered herself and swam after her sister.

"She's still angry with me." Wyntir said once they were out of earshot.

"Let her be. Mother leaving wasn't anyone's fault, least of all yours."

"Perhaps." Wyntir answered shortly.

"Stop that. Mother was always going to leave. Stop blaming yourself. You know in a way, the only reason Uhane, Mele and I were even born is because of you. If Ka'I had been a Red Mer, who knows..."

"Thanks." Wyntir offered her a smile, but Ivara could tell her sister was hardly encouraged.

There was something wholesome about being able to help her family. Though she had no memories of all those years spent in the west she did remember the constant shame and frustration she felt when she returned to Makoul only to realize that she had nothing to offer. Perhaps she had been a politician, a scholar even. She would never know of course. The scar on her arm made sure of that. Along with denying her access to the last forty-six years of her life, it also took away her usefulness. She had left Makoul all those years ago a helpless tad. Now all these years later she returned a mer, nearly grown with nothing to show for all her time away save for a small mark.

A shadow passed over them and Ivara looked up. Above them a ship passed blocking the sunlight as it journeyed over their heads. And trailing behind it was a huge net, in it a white serpent about the width of her waist and twice the length of her arm. Ivara muttered curses before grabbing Wyntir and gesturing to the site.

"Gar!" Wyntir screamed and took off, but Ivara grabbed her wrist and held her still.

"Do you have a blade?"

Wyntir nodded. "I always keep one on me." The ship was going slow enough for her to recognize it. It was a walker fishing ship; she'd seen plenty of them on the outskirts of Makoul but never directly over the city-state. It was too deep here for the walkers to catch fish. She moved quietly below the hull of the ship pondering if they might somehow still be able to hear her. She doubted it. Wyntir followed with her small blade in hand, and they began taking turns cutting at the rope. Once Gar saw them, he too got excited and began squirming around in the net.

"Wyntir he needs to calm down, the walkers will notice his squirming! He's shaking the whole net!"

"I'm trying!"

A walker peeked his head over the ship, and she knew they'd been spotted. Ivara began muttering curses.

"Keep cutting, I'll be back."

"Wait where are you going?" Wyntir reached for her.

"Just keep cutting!" Ivara hissed in a low whisper to her sister. She swam to the front of the ship, thankfully it sat quite low in the water. Had they overloaded it? She waved away the thought, how the walkers loaded their fishing vessels was not her concern. And she would never truly understand how such large vessels were able to float on the surface of the sea. Ivara reached up and began to pull herself up into the gunwale. She'd meant to climb up gracefully but the effort of pulling her entire body weight up from an awkward angle forced an annoyed whimper out of her. Regardless, it did the job. A walker standing at the back of the boat spear in one raised hand turned toward her startled.

"They can climb?!" The walker man exclaimed, dropping his spear and stumbling backwards. She couldn't understand his words, but she could see his face. Ivara had not seen many walkers in her life but this one looked *horrified*. Another fell to his knees and began praying. All the commotion on the ship seemed to work in her favor. None of the walkers on the boat were paying any mind to their ill-fated net.

One of the walkers ordered the first to do something but the only word Ivara could make out was "Jensin." The rest of the speech was too strange and foreign for her to make out.

The one called Jensin, a young red headed male walker still at the threshold of youth and adulthood, with pale skin and freckles, pushed past the walker on his knees and grabbed for the spear. She struggled to unwrap her long teal tail from the side of the deck, the cramping of her muscles made her gasp. As quickly as she moved she was still too slow. The walker, Jensin, was unsure of himself as he pushed the spear up against her throat. He was just as scared of her as she was of him she realized.

"Jensin." His name felt strange and foreign in her mouth. His eyes widened and he stumbled back.

"It can *speak*?" Jensin yelled in a panic, never taking his eyes off her. She wasn't sure what his words meant but she could see the panic and surprise in his eyes.

Another command came from the fat bearded walker that had ordered Jensin to slay her. The bearded walker grumbled as he stomped over and took the spear out of Jensin's hand. Ivara had no idea what they were saying but she did not want to find out. Praying that her sister had freed her pet, she shifted her weight and fell back into the sea where Wyntir and Gar greeted her. They swam down a ways until they hovered right over the city, far from the ship before the two mer girls let their adrenaline take them over and began giggling like fools.

Chapter 2

Today we arrived back in Allagor. Even as I write this, I can see my kingdom's castle in the distance. Until now our trip has been a quiet one. But today we were attacked by the local mer. The creature did not seem as hostile as it did curious. The sailors say they saw another mer creature in the water around the boat but she never climbed up. The first though... it said my name. Despite my dislike for the creatures, I find myself enamored with her beauty...

An excerpt from Jensin's diary

Ivara (1603 A.D.)

The two mer girls swam together back towards Makoul once they'd mastered themselves. As much as Ivara preferred the warmth of the surface waters, there was no denying the danger that lurked above. However, spending most of her time in surface waters had its perks. Everyone had their preferred method of navigation. Some sirens preferred maps that were carved into the bones of large beasts, whales, dragons, and serpents. These maps were quite expensive as creatures of that size were few in number and hard to find as they rarely came to the surface. Even harder to take down. Other methods were readily available of course, many sirens who couldn't afford the pricey bone maps would carve their path into dead corals, the chiton of dead animals or old shells.

Those who were literate would simply link chains or create khipu and read their instructions rather than depending on visual assistance. There were some however who, like Ivara, preferred to navigate by the stars. She had learned to read them well as a small child when her family had taken a long journey. Ivara had been small then, a mere tad only thirty-five summers to her name. She could never remember where they were going or why, but the knowledge of her stars never left her even now at eighty three summers. Of all her sisters none could read the constellations as well as she could. Ka'I had even asked her on many occasions to join her on hunting outings in order to serve as the group's navigator.

Wyntir swam beside her and Gar along with them as they weaved around one another. Large sharks leered at their prey as they swam close to the sandy sea floor. Seagrass waved in the current, some bits of bloated seagrass floated past them. Below them a colorful haze of coral sat like a garden of flowers. By the time they made it back home Ivara's once iridescent teal green tale had faded in color to blend in with the blue of the sea around her. It was common at these depths to lose a bit of color, especially red hues, but Ivara didn't mind. When they entered the shared sleeping chamber their sisters had already begun their day.

"Wyntir sooner or later you are going to have to let that *thing* go. Either that or put it down." It was Ka'I who spoke, the eldest of her sisters. She could sense the jealousy and disapproval in her sister's tone. Gar, for his part, stayed beside Wyntir.

"Ka'I is right, Wyntir. I'm sure that mother meant well but we don't even know what Gar is." Mele said apologetically. Mele was perhaps the most mundanely colored of all the sisters. The honey haired siren sported a peach toned tail that ended in a near transparent flipper and eyes that were dark brown.

"No! We've discussed this! Papa said I could keep him so long as he's trained." Wyntir crossed her arms in frustration.

"Yes, well your *trained companion* just swam away... again." Ka'I gestured toward the creature mockingly. The entire room's attention was drawn toward the main entrance where sure enough the little white serpent was swimming away. Wyntir huffed and gave her eldest sister a childish look of frustration and spite. She covered the distance with three tail strokes and started herding him back to his reef within the room.

Once Wyntir had gotten out of range Ka'I turned. Ivara read the question in her deep green eyes before she asked.

"Where were you?" Ka'I asked without facing her. As the eldest of the five, Ka'I made it her sacred duty to manage how each of them spent their time. Ka'I may have felt she was doing them all a favor, though Ivara doubted it. Ivara just thought her sister was overbearing and nosy.

"I told you before we left, Gar had swum off. We went to find him. Last time I checked, neither myself nor Wyntir report to you." Ivara replied as she returned her older sister's steady gaze.

"Uhane?" Ka'I spoke now to their mute sister. Uhane was Mele's twin though the two couldn't look more different with her deep blue eyes and hair like the black sand of the north. Uhane had taken after their father with pale alabaster skin while Mele was the closest any of the sisters had come to their paternal aunt's darker complexion. Uhane just shrugged at Ka'I as she nearly always did when someone expected a verbal response from her. As intelligent as Uhane was, she was doubly mocking. The blue-eyed siren despised her condition and would rarely communicate with anyone other than her twin due to pure stubbornness alone despite the fact that nearly all the highborn in Makoul were fluent in the region's variety of sign language. Ka'I just sighed and looked back at Ivara.

"Do you truly think we couldn't see the ship from here? An explanation. Now." Ka'I could be just as stubborn as any of her sisters and once she was onto something, she was hard to throw off the scent.

"I told you. Gar was missing." Ivara responded shortly, not wishing to admit to her eldest sister that they had come into direct contact with walkers.

Ka'I narrowed her eyes but seemed to decide it wasn't worth it to push her little sisters. "I am going hunting tonight; you should join us."

"Thanks, but I'll pass." Ivara hated her sister's hunts. While most hunts yielded jellyfish, turtles or even large porpoises, the occasional sailor lost at sea would find his way to the group. The sight of the sailor's bodies being brought down to the city made her sick. They were too similar in look to herself, especially in the face.

"Got something better to do?" Ka'I said, her eyes narrowing to slits.

"No, but you do." Ivara said. She knew she'd hear no end if her sister found out that they'd interacted with walkers.

Ka'I raised her eyebrows. "Oh?"

"Oh indeed. Didn't the scouts report raiders from Neroth? Shouldn't you be seeing to the city's safety rather than wasting your time hunting?"

"How do you know about that?" Ka'I pressed.

"Relax I'm not spying on you. Word just gets around." Ivara shrugged secretly enjoying the fact that her comments were getting under Ka'I's skin.

Ka'I put a palm to her forehead and sighed. "You're right, I should go see about the city's defenses." With that she left.

"I should go as well; Papa asked me to see about our food storage." Mele said, pressing one final shell into her braid then gently slipping out after Ka'I.

When she left it was just Uhane that remained with Ivara in the sleeping room.

Chapter 3

"It was in my youth, as a freshman at university studying the art of prophecy that I saw them. The most breathtaking creatures I have seen in all my life. Colloquially referred to as 'Argentia Bestias' meaning silver beasts, these mer are dark of skin and hair while also silver of eye and tail. Those who have seen such mer count themselves lucky, both to be alive and to have seen such dazzling beauty."

The Prophecies of Northerners by Alec E. Kalith

Tallulah (1537 A.D.)

The morning was cool and quiet. The waters still held the coldness of the night while the first rays of sun struggled to find their home in the ever-moving ocean blue. Tallulah Dagny felt the gills along her neck flair with the rush of water. One breath in, one breath out. Slow and steady. The best way to start the morning her mother had said countless times. Tallulah quite enjoyed mornings like these. Before the day's work was to begin. No doubt a countless number of her peers were just waking up too. She began the arduous task of pinning her hair, which her mother insisted she keep long, and brushing off flaking scales. When she was finished her long tight curls were held together in a myriad of sea shells, all different colors. All of which Tallulah herself had collected.

Tallulah's village was a poor one. Once a bright sparkling jewel of the sea like that of Makoul, now the mer of the Silver Grove were such in name alone. Few lived here and even fewer hunted these waters. Gone were the fields of glittering purple vegetation and brightly colored schools of fish. In their place were humble caverns of old barnacle-covered rock and bare sand. Aside from the occasional drifter, or unlucky fish, that would soon be speared by the village watch, there was little life remaining in the Grove.

All that remained were the headstrong mer of the cool eastern waters. A solemn and stubborn people, the Silvers as they had been called for generations, prided themselves on being one of the few surviving lineages of the elder mer races. One of the only lineages to share ancestors with the likes of the Red Mer, the Atlanteans and the Dragons of the Arkstone. With dark ebony skin and silver scales, they were unique in the lack of variation amongst themselves. Few mer could boast such a thing especially in the east, but then few mer had been whittled down, village by village, to the last.

Such was to be expected as they were located too far south of the Kingdom of Colors to be considered of any value and even then, were still barely within their borders. Things like food and protection in times of war and famine rarely came. They didn't have a huge trade system like Makoul as they had nothing of value to sell.

Tallulah's father had once told her that long ago the waters in which they dwelled had been filled with color and life. Mer, animals, even the great beasts would make their homes here. The waters were fruitful back then her father said, though such times were before even his lifetime. The corals grew like a great rainbow on the sea floor and the members of all the regions would make frequent visits to look upon such beauty as was their home. The village, then a city-state, would grow rich in just one season and there would be such a surplus of food that they would have to throw it away at the end of each night! But the legacy of warring factions and shifting borders were places like this. Homes like hers, villages that prayed to a new god each night for safety and refuge.

Tallulah pondered on whether her father's stories had any merit. She had not lived in such a time of plenty. She was merely a tad and yet she knew hunger as a toxic spouse. Unwanted, but all too familiar. It had been a fortnight since her last proper meal. Then again, all proper meant these days was that she hadn't scavenged it herself.

Tallulah's father was with a hunting party searching for food, each time they left they took longer to return and came back with less. Tallulah didn't care much; the food wasn't for her. There was never enough to go around so it had to be given to the strongest, most able to work and most importantly reproduce. The mer lived far too long to waste resources on the weak. Many elders made it to eight hundred years or so her mother had told her. But Tallulah's mother was from a time before the reefs had bleached, and the fish had fled.

Tallulah, being only thirty years old, was still a child, a tad. Adults first, or anyone of breeding age. Then the male children. Then the healthy girls. The sickly came last but all too often, never. Tallulah's mother worked with the other village mer woman picking sea grass. The children weren't expected to work, too slow, too weak. Here on the outskirts children fended for themselves constantly scavenging. So, Tallulah got to wander about searching for food, only returning home once the light had escaped this part of the sea plunging it once more into darkness. That same darkness that invited the beasts of the deep to do their hunting.

Every now and again she would find some poor soul in a little dark body staring up at her with unseeing eyes. One who had not made it through the night. A reminder of what life in the Silver Grove had become. But by morning the child's body would be gone, disposed of by the village alderman. Tallulah wanted to cry every time she came upon one of the dead children, she sometimes recognized them but that was not what brought on her immense grief. The children were almost always her age. Each one might have one day been her friend had they had the chance to grow up, to live another day.

Tallulah began making her way towards the elder's cave. The village elder was fond of spinning tales of magic and prophecies. Dragons and witches. Warlocks that walked with legs just as the invaders did. Princesses dressed in finery. Damsels in distress. Tallulah had grown fond of the man. She would often come by the wreckage where he slept and offer him sea scum in exchange for a story well told. With a father who was never home and a mother who had never shown much interest in Tallulah, her heart would soften for the village alderman.

One such evening found Tallulah chasing crabs as they skittered through the sand. Once she had the crab in hand it was a matter of stunning it. The elder liked his food fresh so any offerings needed to be alive. Tallulah managed to dig her tiny hands into the beast's abdomen and gently tug on a small thin cord. The crab would go limp for a time. Tallulah found the practice soothing. Most of the other tads shied away from killing or maiming. But Tallulah watched what the adults did when they thought nobody was looking.

Though she was only thirty years old, still just a child, she was still old enough to watch and learn. She dreaded growing older, soon her tail would begin losing pigment and her fins would begin drooping. All signs of malnutrition, her scales had already begun to flake. She would watch the adults, they would kill anything that moved if it meant food, if it meant survival. But seeing as the old and sickly often starved to death, Tallulah's deal with the village elder was made that much sweeter. She came to him when the water was still cool with morning. Her silver tail swept against something smooth as she entered the wrecked ship, but she brushed it off and offered up her little crab with gusto.

"What'll it be today?" The elder's voice was soft and crackled with age. Some in the village said he was nearly four hundred years old.

"Another story, tell the one of the warrior queen, we never finished that one!"

He scratched at his greying beard. "Quite right. Hmmm, let's see where did we leave off?"

Tallulah thought for a minute. "The great war."

"Ah yes and do you remember the Mer Queen's name?"

Tallulah thought for a moment then shook her head. "No."

"Ella, that was her name. It is said that after the war the mer girl Ella fell in love with a walker and lived amongst them."

"Why? The walkers are awful, I thought you said Ella was a hero. You even said she knew magic! Why would she choose to leave her people? That doesn't seem very heroic to me."

"You're not the only one who thought so. It is said that her fellow mer were so angered by her betrayal that they sent a great dragon to burn her and her children alive in their castle on land as recompense for abandoning them. You see Ella was a fierce fighter and was said to be an incredible leader, if the mer couldn't have her then none could."

"But her children were innocent. They didn't betray anyone, why kill them? It doesn't make any sense."

"War rarely does and sometimes we are forced to do awful things for the greater good." The elder said sadly.

Tallulah mulled over his words, killing children was awful but she could hardly imagine how it could bring about good. It was quiet for a moment. Tallulah wasn't sure why but some part of her empathized with the warrior queen. "What happened next?" She asked softly.

The elder took a deep breath, his gills flaring. "It is said that she went to await the dragon in her highest tower. When the beast found her they spoke for a time and when they were finished all that remained of the queen and her children was ash. What was left of the queen was found by her close friend, a lady at court. It is said that seeing her beloved friend's ashes sent the woman into a terrible madness from which she never recovered." Above them the first rays of the morning were warming the surface. Tallulah's village was so close to the surface she could just barely feel it's warmth. "You should be going now."

"Just one more story please! That last one was so depressing. I'll bring you another crab!"

"No. I don't think so. Not today." The elder mer's face grew serious.

There was a shift then. Tallulah felt it though she couldn't well explain it at the time. For the first time she was actively being dismissed. She felt unwelcome. The water felt cold, all its warmth suddenly vanishing. Tallulah should have left then.

"Please? Just one more? I'll do anything!" Tallulah begged.

"No. Get out. Now! You can come back tomorrow." The alderman's voice held a certain ire to it that Tallulah had never heard before.

Tallulah was stunned by his words. By the harshness of her first and only friend.

"Sorry," she said in a small voice. Tallulah swallowed and wiped her eyes. She made to leave but her tail brushed against something smooth. Again. This time she looked down to see a tad, a boy about her age. His corpse was fresh. Too fresh. Tallulah began shaking with horror.

Surely the alderman had not meant to dispose of the child's body here. But then why was there a dead mer boy lying on the sand below her? No, it couldn't be. She'd assumed that the alderman was weighting them so that they could sink in peace to the depths. But this child was proof to the contrary. Tallulah turned the corner. There were two more, a boy and a girl staring up with sightless eyes. But these two were showing signs of decay. They'd been dead for a few days at least.

Tallulah felt bile rise up in her throat. Horror and terror mixed in the pit of her belly. She swam at the alderman, angry and confused.

"What have you done? Why haven't they been buried?" She screamed at him.

"I told you to leave, the walkers will be here soon. Get. Out!"

Suddenly everything began to click into place. The walker boats that visited every two weeks, the bodies, why none of the other mer wanted anything to do with them. It was the alderman. He was sacrificing their tads to the humans. She felt sick. Tallulah fell back against one of the smooth stone walls where her hands pressed against something sharp. A blade.

She should have left.

She *could* have left.

And perhaps it would have made all the difference if she had.

Chapter 4

"Now the mer folk are mysterious creatures filled with wonder. In my adventures in both Allagor and Ellenward I have often seen groups of mer venture just close enough to the beaches to be spotted at a safe distance. Though it is worth noting that these creatures are not entirely wholesome. Stray too far into the sea, and you will likely lose yourself to their enchanting call."

The Prejudice of the Mer Folk by *Willmont Anderson*

Ivara (1603 A.D.)

Ka'I was much faster than Ivara had anticipated and with her return from checking the city's defenses Ivara came to realize she would have to attend her sister's hunt. It was that or lose face. Ivara had never accompanied her eldest sister on one of her famed hunts, but she had seen the bloody aftermath. The bodies were always brought back and given to the poor. It was how they fed their hungry. Still, it made Ivara sick. She had no interest in taking these people's husbands and sons from them.

She wasn't sure what she was to bring or what they usually wore. Not that sirens wore much. Her indecisiveness nearly got the better of her, so she settled for putting her hair in a tight braid and left without much in the way of clothing aside from a tight band wrapped around her breasts. That was one of the biggest differences between her people and the land walkers. They had to cover everything. Their heads covered in wigs, faces dipped in white powder and their bodies completely covered in layers and layers of every assortment of fabric. The sirens did no such thing. For one, they were flawless, in body at least.

There wasn't a siren alive that was visually deficient. At least not at the depth in which they naturally lived. Even her younger sister Wyntir, who was far from the traditionally vibrant skin and scales of the locals, was utterly perfect. Wyntir was an albino, so she was widely regarded as one who in lack of pigmentation also lacked talent and skill, yet she did not lack in beauty. Lost in her thoughts, Ivara began her swim to the Red Harbor. The Red Harbor, as it was known to the sirens, was actually the kingdom of Allagor's main harbor. It bustled with men and women and children. Huge ships rose up on either side of her as she swam to where Ka'I and her maidens waited.

A chill wind swept over the water as Ivara surfaced next to her sister. "Nice of you to show up." Ivara shivered and pulled her tail in close.

"What do I do?"

"Sing to them and then... tear them apart." Ka'I said it as if it was a hobby, but Ivara felt sick. Ivara supposed that for her sister, it *was* a hobby. Swimming around in the nasty waters of the harbor calling out to the weak-minded humans. All the same Ivara was not here to raise suspicion so she did as she was told. The last thing she needed was Ka'I ratting her out to father, the less her elder sister knew of her morning trips to the surface the better.

She made sure to pick strangers and refused to look them in the eye. Most of the dockhands, sailors and others at the peer covered their ears or left to warn others. But slowly, ever slowly the few sailors too slow for their own good began to hear the mer's soft tunes. Entranced, they came one by one to watery deaths. Even as they watched their friends fall prey to the women that waited thirsty for blood they came. With each man the water became a darker crimson and Ivara found herself swimming in a pool of it.

She knew these humans would feed their poor and downtrodden. That it was unnatural for the walkers to traverse the water anyways. She ran through all the reasons that Ka'I had given her to justify the slaughter in her mind, but none could keep the bile from rising in her throat as she watched horrified.

"You know Ivara you don't need to feel scared or guilty. This is merely an indulgence no one is watching; you can take a bite." Ka'I said winking at her. She'd been so caught up in the sickening scene she hadn't even noticed her sister swim up next to her to watch.

Beside them there was a great splash and Ivara was thrown away from her sister. She looked and a large metal spear dove toward the sand, in the water where she had just been. Ivara looked around desperately for Ka'I, but the blood was too thick to see. The spear though, had found its mark, a male mer about her age purple in skin with navy blue scales lay unmoving in the sand below her, the spear jutting into his abdomen. The sight was scarcely revealed before another spear hit the water near her.

Ivara looked up to the spears thrower to see a familiar face. *Jensin.* His eyes were shot with adrenaline but also surprise. She knew he saw her but in all the confusion couldn't tell whether or not he recognized her. She gritted her teeth and grabbed the limp form of a walker; it was a female. An adult, but not very old. The walker's body twitched one last time before falling still as Ivara dragged her down towards Makoul. Unable to bring herself to look back at the carnage behind her, Ivara kept going.

Eventually the other mer in the pod caught up with her. Ka'I led them and Ivara followed the small pod back to Makoul. Though they tried to follow the warm drifts, their journey home was a cold one. Unlike Ka'I, Ivara did not care for the chill that came seeping into the water this time of year. Ivara was grateful when they finally hit Makoul's border. The sentries looked over their bloody cargo then ushered them in. They had just entered the city when they were greeted by Lord Neuros of Makoul. Leader and protector of the ancient city in which they lived, Ivara and Ka'I, however, knew him as father. He greeted both of his daughters with a huge grin and sent Ka'I's maidens off to begin giving out today's hunt.

"My girls! I trust you had an excellent trip?" Their father asked when the maidens were out of hearing range.

"Better than expected with the harsh weather of late." Ka'I replied, bowing her head in greeting. Not bothering to mention the walker retaliation.

Lord Neuros looked behind his eldest to Ivara, "and you? In all of my wisdom I never would have dreamt I would find you returning from one of your sister's hunts. Still, I'm glad you went. You could learn much from your sisters."

"I'm glad you agree. Though I thought it best to shadow and observe." Ivara answered, dipping her head. Her father chuckled.

"Come with me girls. I would like to speak with you." He took their hands, and they swam together toward the extensive rock formation that they called home. When they arrived, they found Uhane, Mele and Wyntir waiting in the entry hall. The three mer-sisters idly floated around, Mele occasionally whispering something to her twin Uhane who responded in silent fits of laughter. They were an odd group, from Ka'I's disgust with land walkers to Uhane's detached personality, to Mele's bubbly one, and Wyntir's curious mind. Each contrasted the other. They were each different from one another in so many ways. And yet they fit together like a puzzle. Ivara smiled at her family as they swam into the dining hall. Built from stone years ago the place had aged over time and was now covered in an impressive assortment of barnacles and colorful coral.

"Ah my dears, you have been scarce as of late; especially you Ivara." Her father said when they had taken their seats in the dining hall. Ivara smiled at her father just as the table's occupants all turned toward her. "Well, I have news regarding the southern raiders."

"Good or bad?" Ka'I asked, crossing her arms over her chest in a manner that let everyone know she was testy.

"A bit of both actually. Our informants in the south tell us that Neroth is in shambles, it would seem that the former king and queen didn't survive the uprising. As a result, the king's brother has taken over Neroth's government and the south has become quite dangerous since."

"Will they stay there; in the south I mean?" Ka'I asked.

"I doubt it." Her father replied. "We've already had reports of multiple attacks south of Makoul. Nearly all the other city-states in the Kingdom have advised us to prepare for an attack as Makoul will likely be hit the hardest seeing as any invaders will need to get through us to get to the rest of the kingdom."

"Couldn't they just go around us?" Ivara asked.

"Could they? Yes. Will they? No, the southerners have never been the gentle type. When they come North it will be a bloodbath. They have the advantage, and they know it. Which is why when the attack begins you all must flee."

"But father, we can help!" Ka'I struck her fist against the table. Her tail swung viciously, slapping the wall in her frustration. She winced.

"You can help by leading the people of Makoul northwards. I've ordered a mass evacuation. The women, children and elderly will swim northwards with you all at their head. Inform our neighboring city states of the emerging crisis. I'll stay here with the soldiers." Ka'I began to protest but their father held up his hand to silence her.

"You all are daughters of Makoul, and to this city you have taken sacred vows, now is the time to fulfill those vows and help those who need you." He waved his hand in dismissal and each left to prepare for the inevitable.

Chapter 5

Your people play with fire. The walkers are as demons, to make deals with them is akin to signing your own death warrant. One misstep, one failed trade and they will be upon you. Swarming you like a school of sharks.

A letter of advice from Lady Brizo of Makoul to the leaders of the Silver Grove. Sent in the year 1525 A.D.

Tallulah (1537 A.D)

"There's no chance the invaders will be here by dawn! Let's take our daughter and leave! We can flee to Neroth where it's safe." Tallulah listened to her father's rumbling voice through the stone walls.

"Flee to Neroth? It is a cesspool of liars and cut throats. We need to stay and fight for our home. We cannot abandon the Grove just because of a scuffle with some walkers." Tallulah's mother, ever the prideful mer retaliated.

"Isa this place is not the Silver Grove! It hasn't been for years. Perhaps it was once a home worth fighting for but look around. Bleached corals and bare sand, the hunters have been traveling to Makoul's borders for years just to find food. There is nothing here for us!" Her father, Biron, pleaded.

"Look at you! Tail tucked in like the coward of a merman that you are! Out of my way!" Her mother's voice, sharp, brittle and venomous, hardly the mothering type. Tallulah's mother was a warrior, and her father was soft. Father said she was too headstrong for her own good. Tallulah was inclined to agree. She could hear her mother's outrage as she burst through the entry to their home. Tallulah's mother saw her and suddenly she felt a sharp sting on her face. The slap was hard as her mother's hand connected with her face.

"A reward for your actions this day. Killing the alderman before he could make the trade! What were you thinking? The dead can give us nothing Tallulah, but they might have bought us protection. If not for you at least. But no, our deal with the walkers has been broken and we shall all suffer the consequences." Her mother grimaced. "Get a spear and come with me. Perhaps when you've skewered a few dozen of the walkers you'll have atoned for your actions."

Tallulah was a tad, young and naïve, but not stupid. "We should leave." She whispered. As she said it spears rained down all around them from the walker ship above. All around her mer were going to arms to defend their home in these shallow waters. Tallulah's mother didn't seem to notice, she was so lost in her own wrath that even the splashing and screaming of her neighbors didn't seem to fully register.

"Got that from your father, did you? Fine, go and hide. But don't come crawling to me once that father of yours has gone and gotten himself killed. Serves me right! How could I have borne such a cowardly little thing as you—" Her mothers words were cut off as a thick piece of wood accompanied at the top by something sharp and metal slid through her mother's back into her chest and halting inches from Tallulah's face. Tallulah screamed. The invaders had come, claiming their first victim.

Chapter 6

The girl is adjusting as well as can be expected to her former life. Visions and nightmares still haunt her but over the last year she has been attending more council meetings, which is a good sign. While the rune is holding, I believe the cracks are beginning to show themselves. Ivara may not know what or who she is, but she knows something is missing. Perhaps it is time for her to return?

Khipu from the Sea Witch to the Master of the Arkstone sent in the year 1603 A.D.

Ivara (1603 A.D.)

Ivara had left the council room when a slim webbed hand pulled her aside. Uhane, her sister, while being mute was certainly never afraid to interrupt.

"Not now Uhane, I have a few things to do before the evacuation."

Uhane kept her iron grip with one hand and with the other responded. It was no wonder that the travelers described Uhane as a storm made flesh. The mer girl's dark hair and pale blue eyes paired with her pale skin gave her an intimidating façade.

Ka'I has an idea, you should come, we are discussing it soon. Her sibling signed.

"An idea for what?" Ivara pulled away. "Father's instructions were clear. The city won't be safe, and the other leaders must be warned."

I know what father said; I was there, Ivara. I'm mute, not deaf. Let's just hear her out. Please? Uhane signed.

"Fine, when would she like to meet?"

Right now, actually. We planned it while you and Wyntir were out earlier. Come on, let's go.

"What about Wyntir?"

Mele went to fetch her. Now come on, let's go!

They swam back to their room together. The water was cool, and the light faded slowly the deeper they swam. When they had arrived back, Ka'I, Mele and Wyntir were waiting for them.

"Good of you to finally join us." Ka'I gestured to a stalagmite that rose from the ground. "Get settled, we have a lot to discuss."

"No, *you* have a lot to discuss." Mele countered.

"Excuse me?" Ka'I retorted.

"The rest of us are happy to follow father's plans. You just don't like being told what to do." Mele said.

She's right, remember the jellyfish incident. Uhane signed with one hand, the other hand trying to suppress a laugh.

"Firstly, it was a capillata, and second this isn't about taking orders," Ka'I's gills flared in frustration, "it's about how we can help defend the city."

Now it was Ivara's turn to interject. "You heard father! The city will fall regardless of what we do, we need to help the people get to a safe place! We need to leave!"

Ka'I raised her hand to silence Ivara and the rest of her sisters who had joined in to voice their objections. "I agree we need to warn the rest of the Kingdom. And I also agree that we have a duty to our people. But that duty is to defend them not to lead them into a foreign city state of which they have no prior knowledge."

"Our military is too small; we'd have no chance against the raiders. Yet you want us to face them head on?" Mele asked.

"No not us," Ka'I pointed downward towards the depths below, "*them.*"

"What? *That's* why you called us here? To try and convince us to seek out Mother and the rest of the Red Mer?" Mele asked.

"Think about it. No militia in the east is feared more than the Red Mer. Perhaps mother could persuade them to help us!" Ka'I threw her hands up to emphasize her own brilliance.

"Who's to say father hasn't *already* sent out a missive to the Red Mer?" Ivara chimed in.

Ka'I's smile faded. "Listen Ivara, I know you have only been back from the Arkstone for a couple of years but even *you* should know how much of a pacifist father is. The last thing he would do is ask mother to put herself into any sort of danger."

Ivara was silent. She wanted to throw Ka'I's words back at her, but her sister wasn't entirely wrong. Even with her amnesia she had been home far too long to be asking such questions.

Mele started. "Alright let's say we go along with this. How would we even find her? None of us could even see at those depths. All save for Wyntir, but she's never even been here before. How would she know where to go? And that's not even taking into account our timeframe Ka'I. For all we know the southern raiders will be here in a matter of days!" Mele shouted. "Can't you just once follow instructions and lead by example?"

"Surely you can see the wisdom in asking for help Mele? Perhaps we could ask the witch, she seems to know Ivara well enough." Ka'I countered.

"No, I don't see the wisdom in it! And the Sea Witch is dangerous. We will be in enough danger as is. We do not need to provoke the Witch."

Ka'I if you truly want to send for help then send a chain or khipu message to mother. Tell her the situation and that we are leaving. If we stay, we are likely to meet the same fate as the Silver Mer in the south.

"Fine, maybe you're right Uhane. I'll have to find a servant to send it though..." Ka'I trailed off and the group gave each other knowing nods. Anything to keep Ka'I occupied.

Chapter 7

"It has long been held that the people in the southernmost parts of Allagor have signed a treaty with the mer there. It is not surprising considering some of the best universities in all of the east are located in the south. Thus, knowing that the people there collect dead mer to study them is less surprising from a human perspective as it is when looked at from that of the mer perspective. Have we overfished, and drained these mer of their resources in such a manner that now they willingly give up their dead in an effort to recover it?"

The Prejudice of the Mer Folk by Willmont Anderson

Tallulah (1537 A.D.)

Tallulah was still screaming as a huge rough hand gripped her arm and pulled her down and away. Blood bloomed all around burning her eyes. Her father pulled her into the fray of the attack. She screamed until her voice left her. Tears spilled from her eyes and into the endless sea beyond. Salt mixing with salt. That of sea water mingling with the blood and tears of those she had known. The invaders were not of their realm. They'd come in huge wooden boats powered by sails and oars. Tallulah and her father swam down into the darkness away from the world that was being broken and remade before them. Away from her mother, away from the peaceful village life that could have been hers.

They swam on for a long time. When she became fatigued, she would grasp onto her father. His thick silver tail carried them long distances while she would sleep or rest. When neither could swim any further, they would lock their tails and let slumber take them. The open ocean was dangerous, there was little in the way of shelter and huge beasts often rose from the deep to greet them. One such beast greeted them mere weeks after they had set out. Tallulah could tell her father was exhausted, though he wouldn't admit it. All around them was open ocean as far as the eye could see. No sign of civilization, just an empty blue hell.

"We must be lost. Surely, we should be in Makoul by now." Tallulah whispered.

"It's further than you think."

So, they swam. They swam on and on, until a dark figure rose from the depths. Tallulah gasped but her father held her still. The whale was massive and grey, covered in scars. Its long skinny mouth sporting several thick sharp teeth. Tallulah had never seen anything so large. Terror and wonder gripped her in equal measure. Her breaths came in short uneven gasps.

"Papa?" She managed to get out. But her father was already moving toward the beast. It saw them and swam over to inspect them. Its eyes were the size of Tallulah's head. She gripped her father tightly and shut her eyes. *Had her father given up? Had he called the beast over to kill them lest they expire from exhaustion or starvation?* The thoughts swirled around in Tallulah's mind until she could no longer breathe. Then a series of clicking noises. She opened her eyes and looked at her father, a question in her eyes. He gestured to the whale. More clicking noises. Her father imitated the clicking fashion and Tallulah watched, fascinated as her father spoke to the beast in the strange clicking language. Finally, her father turned to her, exhausted but satisfied.

"He will help us. He is going north and he says that we may accompany him until he reaches his pod. But he says we must do as he says. When it is time to hunt, we hunt. When he wishes to sleep, we must sleep as well."

She did not know what to say. All logic told her to flee from the beast, but the whale's eyes held intelligence beyond her comprehension. This creature was sentient.

"Tallulah? Did you hear me?" Her father nudged her out of her reverie. She nodded and together the three of them set off northwards.

In the months that followed Tallulah often found herself searching for her mother in her own appearance. She had never realized how much she looked like her mother until she'd lost her. They were both dark of skin, Tallulah's father being of a slightly lighter complexion. Both her mother and her shared curls so tight they clung to her head like a crown. But she had her father's silver eyes. She clung to this as they swam on.

Hours became days and she forced herself to reimagine her mother. The image of a stern dark mer woman whose muscles were her most prominent feature slowly came to be replaced with a softer, kinder version. A mother that had loved her to the end. One that had embraced her and encouraged her. A lie and a fantasy but one that helped her sleep at night. Tallulah could sense her father's grief for her mother every time he looked at her but neither spoke of it.

Days turned to weeks, and weeks to months until before she knew it she was recounting to herself the panicked fleeing on the anniversary of her mother's death a year after it had happened. In those months her father grew more and more distant, and Tallulah likened him to a mer with a mission, he was searching for something. A safe harbor perhaps? One where the two of them could finally live in peace and forget the ghost that haunted them both.

Her father maintained that they were headed north then west towards the golden coast, he continuously said he had friends in the area. But Tallulah knew better. Biron, her father, had never ventured beyond their small village. No, despite her own fantasies

Tallulah knew the truth. They had no destination. They were running until something faster than either of them found them, caught them, and killed them.

Chapter 8

To my loving husband and beautiful daughters in Makoul,

Know that I miss you all dearly and that though I cannot return yet, I can offer something just as exciting. Though my dear Wyntir is still just a tad she will need increasing security as she grows. Thus, I have sent a regalec by the name of Gar, to accompany my khipu. The creature is intelligent and eager to form the bond. Just take care not to vex the creature as his bite is lethal.

With love, Mother

A khipu sent from Lady Brizo to her husband and children in Makoul in the year 1576.

Ivara (1603 A.D.)

Ivara Mare wasn't all that fond of Gar though she did admire the bond her pale albino sister seemed to have with the serpent. Whenever anyone got too close to her little sister Gar was always there. Her long pale scaly protector. Despite the beast being something of a pet, there was always a strange glint of intelligence in Gar's eyes far beyond what would have been attributed to any other serpent.

The creature seemed to understand conversations being had by Ivara and her sisters. Likewise, it showed far more emotion than Ivara had ever witnessed from a mundane pet, and it was wholly dedicated to its master. Wyntir was always trying to sneak the thing scraps and take it on swims. The siren never went anywhere without her pet, her friend. They were nearly inseparable except for those few times when Gar would swim off to gods only knew where. Even now, though Ivara racked her brain, she couldn't imagine what had made Gar bite Wyntir. So, it was with no small amount of horror that Ivara realized why her sister had looked so haggard.

Gar was gone... again. Wyntir became frantic. The two quietly searched under every rock and inside every crevice. Wyntir made to leave but Ivara grabbed her arm only now noticing that the pale white skin of her sister's arm was breaking out in hives and blisters. Inky black veins had begun to crawl up her arm from her palm consuming the healthy skin.

"Wyntir, what's this?" Ivara asked.

Her little sister jerked back in pain.

"He didn't mean to! It was an accident, that's all!" Wyntir squirmed away from her touch.

"Wyntir, did Gar do this to you?" Ivara whispered.

"He didn't *mean* to! I'm fine!"

"Wyntir he's a wild animal!" Ivara's gills flared as she took a deep breath. "You *need a healer*. Gar could be venomous."

"No, you're wrong. Mother wouldn't have sent him to me if he was dangerous... Besides any healer worth their salts has already fled Makoul." Wyntir's words were quietly defiant, but Ivara could hear the hint of worry trembling in her voice.

"You barely knew mother! Weren't you still just a tad when she left! This is exactly the kind of thing she would do. Probably some sort of awful trick or test. Believe me Wyntir she wasn't the loving sort." Ivara said. She regretted the words as soon as they were said. Her sisters looked up to her mother, it was true, but Wyntir practically worshiped her.

Wyntir jerked back her arm and cradled it to her chest. "It hardly even hurts. Please just help me find Gar, then I'll do whatever you say. I'll even tell father about the bite." Wyntir paused. "*Please* Ivara."

Ivara loved her sisters. Of all of them, she was closest with Wyntir. They were both strangers in one way or another amongst their siblings. So Ivara resigned herself, she would help Wyntir fetch her pet but first they needed a healer.

"Oh, you're telling father." She sighed. "Ok we'll go find Gar later. Right now, getting you to a healer is paramount." Wyntir opened her mouth to reply but only a hiss of pain came. The pale mer girl nodded though Ivara knew her sister was not happy.

They swam off in search of a healer. Hand in hand they swam downwards away from the sun and towards the sandy city below. The houses and shops at the bottom of the city were the first to have been built in Makoul, their color long gone save for vibrant coral and striped fish that swam all around. Over the years houses and hovels had been stacked one on top of the other. The closer one lived to the sun the more important they were. At least that was how it worked here in Makoul, Ivara wasn't sure about other kingdoms or city states. They kept swimming, passing home after home, most of them deserted by now but stopped when they bumped into Ka'I.

"What's that on her arm?" Ka'I asked, pointing to Wyntir's slowly creeping infection. "Why haven't you gotten her to a healer yet? The evacuation will begin in only a few days, she can't leave like this!" She said accusingly to Ivara.

"We were just on our way to a healer." Ivara replied before Wyntir could make the situation worse for either of them.

Ka'I scoffed and grabbed Wyntir by her good arm. She turned once more to Ivara. "I'll take her."

"If you hadn't stopped us, we'd likely already be there!" Ivara retorted, annoyed with her sister.

Ka'I slapped her and Ivara realized her sister was crying, whether out of anger or frustration Ivara did not know.

"*Don't* speak to me like that. While you were off living in your little fantasy realm in the west, *I was the one* who held this family together. Who do you think took care of mother when Wyntir was born? When father left to make negotiations with the Kingdom of Colors? Or did you just think that we were all sitting by waiting for your return for forty-six years? When mother left us because 'she had produced her heir' *I* took care of this family. I know you've only been back for a year and you're still getting used to things. But when things go astray you come to me. Understand?" Ka'I took a moment to master herself before turning to Wyntir. "When did this happen? Why didn't you seek me out?"

Wyntir looked away guiltily. "It was an accident. Gar didn't mean to."

Ka'I's mouth was agape. "Your beast did this to you? Where is he? A gift from mother or not, that *thing* should have been put down years ago."

"Good luck." Ivara said dryly. "He's missing again." She slapped her sister's hand away and took Wyntir. Before they took off, she turned back to her eldest sister. "Are you coming or not?"

Chapter 9

"The regalecs are not the only beasts of the sea. This place we call home holds many fantastical creatures of interest. One that is often overlooked is the leviathan. With their own languages, dialects and even regional accents these whales are far more intelligent than the average mer gives them credit for."

Toren's Bestiary, Volume 1: Creatures of the Sea by Toren Dagny

Tallulah (1538 A.D.)

They swam on, just the three of them. To pass the time Tallulah's father would teach her the clicks of the whale's language. As hard as she tried, she could never quite replicate the language. Still the whale seemed amused at her attempts.

"Keep practicing, you'll get it. The whale's tongue is ancient and no two pods speak quite the same. It can take years to speak it properly." Her father told her one day.

The water was getting warmer now and they'd often spot schools of colorful fish dart past them, some swarmed them, others feared coming close.

"Who taught you the language?" Tallulah asked.

"My grandfather, I was just a tad when he introduced me to the beast. Oh, I was terrified. But the beast was kind and inquisitive. Every few years it would come to the surface waters where we lived in search of my grandfather. The two had become friends over the years. It was important to my grandfather that I learn about the world through the eyes of others, even the beasts."

"You mean there are other beasts that speak in such a manner that we can understand?"

"More than you could fathom my dear. I'll teach you all of them in time but first you must master the whale's speech."

Encouraged by her father's words Tallulah began again, occasionally stopping to let the whale click in reply to what she was saying. Tallulah understood now what her father had meant. The Silver Grove *was* just a place. Home, her home at least was wherever her father was. She smiled at the thought. Even here on the outskirts of Makoul in the open ocean, she was home.

In the distance Tallulah could see the glitter of silver fish turn this way and that, the colorful reefs that lined the tall round buildings but that was not what made her gasp in wonder. It was the people. There were so many. Tallulah had learned as a girl that the Kingdom of Colors was the most diverse place in the world, even so she had always believed the rest of the Kingdom outside of the Grove looked somewhat similar to her. But these mer did not have glowing silver eyes and tails. Some had orange hair and dark striped, purple tails. Others had long pale flesh that mimicked seaweed jutting out from their head, arms and tails which ended in nubs rather than flippers. These mer reminded Tallulah of seahorses.

Others still, had hair made of flesh and long, thin, delicate tentacles sprouting from the head fell all around them. Tallulah was reminded of the jellyfish they had come across during their journey. Each one was unique and yet they all shared one thing, they were all dazzling to behold.

The whale made a series of clicking noises behind her. *Welcome to Makoul.*

Her father clicked back a response as Tallulah stared around dumbfounded. She listened as the two clicked back and forth until her father took her hand in his. "He says he must go. His pod is near."

Tallulah turned and for the first time spoke directly to the whale. *Thank you.* She clicked. The beast smiled in acknowledgement and swam off. She watched until he was a mere dot in the deep blue.

"What now?" Tallulah asked her father.

"Now we rest. Eat your fill tonight. Tomorrow we will discuss what comes next."

So, she did. And when sleep came, she did not see her mother, nor did she feel her grief. All she felt was happy and for the first time in a long time, she felt at peace.

Chapter 10

"While the Lord of Makoul is known for his kind heartedness and love for his family, Lady Brizo is often compared to the great kings of old. She is both witty and charming and though our Crimson Lady hails from the Red Mer, it is her overwhelming loyalty to Makoul that ultimately won over her the hearts and minds of her subjects."

A Beginners Guide to the Kingdom Colors by Nyra of Neroth

Tallulah (1538 A.D.)

When Tallulah awoke the next morning, it was not because of a hungry belly but rather to the warmth of the sun's rays. It took a moment for all the memories of the night before to hit her. They were finally here, the great city-state of Makoul. She found her father speaking with a dark haired mer woman just outside of the small spherical room they'd slept in the night before.

"Thank you again for your hospitality." Her father said to the mer.

"It was no problem at all." The mer woman speaking to her father said. "Did you need anything?"

"No, I'm just grateful for a place to sleep. We've been traveling for some time."

"You sure? Not even for the little one?" The mer woman said spotting Tallulah.

"Well, there is one thing. Do you know how we might get an audience with the Lord of these waters?"

The mer woman raised her eyebrows. "Their home is at the center of the city. You can request a meeting but there is no guarantee that they will see you."

"It's worth a try. Thank you again." Her father said, taking Tallulah's hand in his. Together they swam towards the inner city. Mer of all colors and patterns swam around them, the city was like a chest, its populace like gemstones.

"State your name and your purpose." A gruff looking guard said in a monotone voice when they reached the Lord's home.

"Biron, and this is my daughter Tallulah. We hail from the Silver Grove and have valuable information for the Lord of Makoul."

The guard looked them over. "Follow me."

He led them into the great hall where people were feasting, singing, and holding excited conversations. At the very back of the room sat a young couple. The male, Lord Neuros had pale skin and a long vibrant teal tail. He sported wavy brown hair and grey eyes. Beside him a mer woman with crimson eyes and skin. Such was her hair as well, the color of blood. And lurking behind them both was a giant crimson serpent with spots of white and grey. The serpent had to be at least twice as long as the whale and nearly as thick. Its eyes were hostile and intelligent, but not inquisitive. This beast was not her friend, but Tallulah could surmise that the beast being so close to the woman likely cared for her. Perhaps it was Lady Brizo's pet? It was the woman who spoke first, when she did the hall went silent.

"You were the two traveling with the leviathan just outside the city?" Lady Brizo asked them. She looked them over, curious yet stern.

Tallulah's father bowed his head. "It is true. The beast accompanied us here after we fled our home."

"It is rare to meet one from the epipelagic zone such as yourself who speaks the beast's tongue. Who taught you?" The Lady asked, leaning forward in anticipation of her father's answer.

"The skill has been passed down by the male members of my family for many generations, my lady."

Lady Brizo whispered something to her husband. Her husband, Lord Neuros nodded in agreement. The crimson mer untwisted her tail from her stalagmite seat and gestured for them to follow. As they left the great hall Tallulah could hear the laughter and conversation resume behind them. The Lady of Makoul led them into a far smaller, more private room.

"You say you fled your home?" She spoke now in a much more serious tone. All traces of formality gone, replaced now with concern.

"Yes, my daughter and I hail from the Silver Grove -."

The crimson mer woman raised a hand to silence her father. "I know where you're from. We don't get a lot of southerners this far north, much less any sporting silver eyes and tails. *Why* did you flee?"

Tallulah's father hesitated, looking unsure. She was about to tell the Lady when her father suddenly spoke. "I'll tell you but first I need guaranteed safety for myself and my daughter."

Lady Brizo sighed. "Ah yes, Silvers ever the diplomats. No doubt deals such as this were what got your people by for so long during the famine." She looked Tallulah over intently. "I cannot offer you the safety you seek here. Regardless of what befell the Silver Grove, there have been too many reports lately of walker interference on this side of the sea. Makoul has not taken the brunt of it, but I fear it is only a matter of time. Between the walkers on our coast, the increasing number of sick and the unrest in the south, I fear it will not be long before Makoul follows in the footsteps of our neighbors."

"Surely there is something you could do? We have been traveling for nearly a year in the open sea! We cannot –. I cannot go on like this. My daughter deserves a home. *Please.*"

"I sympathize Biron. I do, but unless you plan to go west, there is nothing I can do for you!"

"What's in the west?"

"It is said that there is a Dragon who dwells in the west, the Arkstone more specifically. Many say that the beast uses his scholars and magic to help those who seek him but Biron, the price is said to be very high. *Too high.*"

"Where can I find the Arkstone, have you a map?"

"Don't be ridiculous. If you are going to cross the sea, you will need an escort. I can provide you with one but be warned, this Dragon is not one to be toyed with. If it makes you an offer, you must take it, for your daughters' sake."

"I will. Thank you. And my Lady?"

"Yes?"

"We were fleeing the humans. It was just as you said. Be on your guard, it was a massacre." Biron whispered the last part, grief striking a chord in his voice.

They followed Lady Brizo out the back way to the edge of the city. Tallulah looked around for the leviathan, assuming that he would return to escort them. Instead, a huge serpent swam up from behind them. Its teeth were the length of Tallulah's arm. The creature looked at its master intently, and when Lady Brizo returned the glance Tallulah could have sworn the two were having a conversation in their minds.

The crimson Lady of Makoul turned back to Tallulah and her father. "My regalec will escort you to the Arkstone." Then the Lady reached out and put a gentle hand on Tallulah's face and kissed her forehead. "Good luck." She whispered.

Chapter 11

"...which brings us to the fantastical serpents known as regalecs. Often seen with their crimson counterparts, these sea serpents never abandon the red mer that they have bonded with. It is said that a regalecs venom is so potent that a single drop in the blood can melt an individual from the inside. Though while not entirely immune to said venom, it is worth noting that the red mer seem to have built up a certain resistance."

Toren's Bestiary, Volume I: Creatures of the Sea by Toren Dagny

Ivara (1603 A.D.)

Ivara and her sisters arrived at the small palace in Makoul to find absolute chaos. She could hardly see in front of her for all the movement. Seeing the look on Ivara's face Ka'I answered her silent question looking at her intently with her deep emerald eyes.

"It's the evacuation. Everyone's getting ready to leave. All the healers have likely already left with the first exodus." Her elder sister said, swishing her emerald tail.

They swam around, but there wasn't a healer in sight and their father was nowhere to be found so they decided to swim down into the city. Ivara could tell that Wyntir was growing exhausted from the pain. Finally, they found what or rather who they were looking for. A short stout healer with a matching tail greeted them. The sisters knew her as she worked at the palace, she was a kind old mer.

"Thaula? What are you doing here?" Ka'I asked angrily.

The mer woman turned to them to reveal a large woven bag filled with sea grass, living corals, and other assortments. "I heard of the evacuation. I expect there will be some bumps in the road so to speak. I'm just preparing."

Ka'I's gills flared in frustration, and she motioned to Wyntir. "Her regalec, the pale serpent. I'm sure you've seen my sister swimming alongside the pale beast."

The woman nodded her head. "It's bitten her. Can you help her?"

The old mer woman swam over and took Wyntir's hurt hand inspecting the inky blackness that was working its way up her arm. Wyntir winced at the healer's touch and began shaking with pain. Wyntir squeezed her eyes shut and began taking slow breaths in an effort to calm herself. Ivara hadn't realized how bad it was until now. It hurt her to see her little sister in such pain. She watched in vain frustration as her sister's pale tail tightened with stress. After a long moment of silence, the healer began shaking her head.

"What is it? What's wrong?" Ka'I blurted out.

"I cannot heal this. No healer can. You must get her to your mother as fast as possible. The Lady Brizo will know what to do with this."

"How? The evacuation has already begun, soon it will be in full flux. Besides our mother is in the deep with the rest of the Red Mer, it would be suicide to make such a journey without an escort." Ivara said. "Surely there is something you can do to help."

"I am sorry girls, but my wisdom is all that I may offer. Go now and seek your mother out. This is Red Mer magic. I dare not trifle with it."

Ivara turned to leave but Ka'I stopped her. "What are you doing?"

"You heard Thaula, we need to get her to mother. She'll know what to do." Ivara said.

Ka'I just huffed. "Fine, let's go. But we should leave now. The deep is at least a day's journey and the longer we stay here the more time we are losing."

They returned to their quarters to find their sisters nearly finished packing.

"Where have you three been? They've moved the timeline up; we are supposed to leave in less than an hour." Mele said anxiously, twirling her honey blond hair. The fair-haired twin's brown eyes spoke of worry.

They packed their things and Ka'I began tying a khipu to take to their mother. Ivara for her part kept watch outside the window. All around Makoul's soldiers swam past her at a great speed bearing large swords and spears. Their armor was aglow in the light of the sea. In the distance she could see a large shadow inching closer.

"They're here!" She shouted at her sisters. "Neroth's army is here!" In the distance she could see something else too. A great golden dragon as large as the entire palace of Makoul. Terrified and frozen, it wasn't until Mele grabbed her shoulder that she was able to look away. When she turned back to the window the vision of the beast was gone and only the shadow of the incoming army remained.

They left in a chaotic frenzy. Rushing out of the city's palace as quickly as they could. Neroth's army inched closer and closer, individual soldiers slowly coming into view though the army was too far away for Ivara to make out any faces yet. A scream in the distance and a series of wails made Ka'I turn.

"Don't stop!" Mele shouted among the chaos.

The mer from the city were gathering now in the largest exodus Ivara had ever seen. Mele and Uhane were trying their best to guide the crowds but there were just too many.

"This isn't right. We should be helping them!" Ka'I screamed.

"We are!" Ivara said, trying to calm her sister's bloodlust. "We have to help our people get out!"

"No!" Ka'I shook her head. "I'm going to help them; I'm going to fight." Ka'I shouted, haphazardly handing Ivara the khipu she'd made for their mother.

"Ka'I you're going to get yourself killed!" Mele screamed trying to grab at her as she passed. But Ka'I paid her no heed, instead swimming down and taking a trident from a fallen soldier and heading off towards the bloodshed. Ivara turned to her kin.

"What do we do?" Ivara looked around, the bloodshed and commotion was beginning to attract predators. Sharks of all types and other large fish circled them.

"We go north! We have to get out –." Meles' words were cut off when a panicked townsman smacked into her. The commotion became even worse and soon Ivara could see neither Mele nor Uhane for all the panicked mer trying to get away. Ivara grabbed Wyntir and they tried to swim away but a mer took Wyntir from behind and put a blade to her neck.

The mer man was one of their own. One from Makoul. Ivara could see the panic and desperation in his eyes. It made her hesitate despite herself. She'd never killed before. But before Ivara could finish her thought, Gar rose up from out of the chaos and bit the mer man in the neck. Immediately the mer's gills began to blacken as they rotted away. Panicked, he dropped his blade, released Wyntir and began clawing at his gills. The serpent did not relent, and its crimson eyes were an intense anger and bloodlust.

Gar tore into the panicked mer. Ivara could see the mer man's jugular being ripped away through the crimson haze that surrounded them. The two mer girls watched in horror as he choked on a mixture of seawater and his own blood. Ivara couldn't move for fear that Gar might rip into her as well. As for the serpent's current victim, he was already dead. Mere postmortem twitches were all that remained within the blackened rotting flesh.

Please stop! Stop! Please! Ivara wanted to scream the words, to sob them in a broken plea but her lips refused to move. She'd never been this afraid. Gar jerked his bloodied head away from his prey and gazed at her. She was shaking now. All she could do was grip Wyntir's hand and pray. But the serpents' blood lust was gone. Gar looked on at her as if investigating her. He reeled back his head as if to strike but suddenly went still. Then the serpent cocked its head and turned to Wyntir. Ivara looked over to see her younger sister splaying out her arms, putting herself between Ivara and Gar.

"No, not Ivara!" Wyntir said with surprising confidence. "Bad Gar, Ivara is not our foe. She would never hurt me." Ivara watched in astonishment as the serpent bowed its head to Wyntir. Her sister turned back to her. "Let's go. Something tells me it's only going to get worse." Ivara nodded in agreement, and they swam on with Gar in tow.

Chapter 12

"It is a widely held rumor that the Golden Mer, or rather their Master demands a blood sacrifice. However, I have spoken to those whom the Dragon has touched, and the offering required for such gifts as the Dragon can provide is far more valuable than blood."

The Golden Ones by Onyra Elron

Tallulah (1539 A.D.)

The journey to the Arkstone was long and arduous. Tallulah could not help but fear the serpent that accompanied them. Occasionally the creature would leave them usually only for a day or so, presumably to hunt. Sometimes it would bring back scraps but most of the time not. Though she had only known the wonder of Makoul for a night she missed it, almost as much than she did her own home. Perhaps it was the fact that her father could not speak to the beast. Or perhaps it was a culmination of all the change that had occurred around Tallulah in the past two years since her mother's death.

The more they traveled, the more the Silver Grove became a distant memory. Until one day, when the sea was cold and the day above them was cloudy, a light mist sitting on the waves of the surface waters. They reached Arkstone Reek two years after the attack that had claimed Tallulah's mother and countless others. Tallulah had no knowledge of the great kingdom that stood before them aside from the legends of dragons and magic that surrounded the kingdom's mythos. Legends, that was all they were, fantasies. Still the legends infiltrated Tallulah's imagination and offered her a distraction from the constant swimming as she and her father crossed the Great Sea making their way west. When they finally arrived, all Tallulah could see was rest, and perhaps an end to her misery.

Here surrounded by food and servants and more mer than she could count her mother wasn't dead just... gone. Here she wasn't a murderer she was just a young mer girl, excited and naïve. They were welcomed at the golden gates. Led by guards clothed in golden armor. A large muscular mer, his voice gruff bore a thin crown atop his head hooking itself under his ears, bore them to the heart of the Reek. A wide variety of caves large enough for hundreds, perhaps even thousands of mer to traverse surrounded a palace, the Arkstone. While the Reek was filled with traders and travelers, mundane individuals of no real renown, the gem at its center was the true beauty of the kingdom.

The *Arkstone*. Just the thought filled her with excitement. It was the centerpiece of a fantastical dream. A great palace with gates far too big for any mer. Stone that sparkled with gold and natural gems embedded in rock. All around bright vibrant corals grew along entryways. Their pink, orange and blue forms reached out for her. The water here was clear too, despite the immense amount of mer. More mer than Tallulah had ever seen in her life. She wondered to herself if this was what the Silver Grove once looked like, but the difference was too great for her to picture it.

Strangers passed her, each quite different from the last. Some were like her, dark coils atop their heads, eyes pale as the moon, skin a deep shade of cool brown. Tallulah's heart leapt with excitement at the thought of finding the familiar in this foreign place. But she felt it sink as one such mer woman approached her speaking a tongue that Tallulah could not recognize. These mer were just as foreign as the rest and Tallulah had the sinking feeling that no matter where they went, she'd always be an outsider.

Tallulah and her father were eventually led into a great hall where dwelt many of the guards Tallulah had seen around the city. She remembered the alderman telling her stories of the kingdom's famous hospitality. The Arkstone was said to be a land of opportunity where dwelt all who would start anew. Titles were few here and all were welcomed equally regardless of their status. Tallulah shook her head trying to forget the dead man's stories.

The burly guard that had accompanied them gestured for Tallulah to make herself scarce. She looked from the man to her father squeezing his hand in desperation. Her father offered her a smile and gently pulled away to follow the male guard deeper into the hall. She hadn't fully turned when a mer girl who looked to be only about ten years her senior grabbed her wrist, her smile beaming as she dragged Tallulah off.

Tallulah had never been on a "play date." The children in her village had never entertained such foolish ideas. The thought of wasting a whole day on the entertainment of an individual that had little to offer the community as a whole...it was ridiculous. And yet that was exactly what this girl wanted from her. To entertain her. To make her laugh, Tallulah realized as she watched the girl make silly faces at her. Tallulah offered her a smile, but she broke into a steady laughter as the girl became more and more of a nonsensical caricature.

"I'm Brina of Arkstone, used to be of Neroth but that was before," The girl said by way of introduction.

Her sparkling golden tail swept around gracefully as she spoke. The mer girl's voice was sprightly and sweet. The tad was brown of hair and eyes. Freckles covered her tanned skin. She wore her hair in two long braids that, had it not been for the sea water, would have fallen past her belly button. Her tail was that of solid gold. Her smile was one of pure joy.

"Tallulah of um... the Silver Grove." The thought of her mother being speared by the walkers sobered her up and she felt her smile fall. She could see the blood and her mother's face mere inches from hers. Brina looked at her and Tallulah could see the question in the tad's eyes. Gulping down her grief like old meat, Tallulah beckoned her smile back to her. "...or here I suppose."

Brina's eyes widened, "Here? Oh, that is so wonderful! Wait, how come we've never met?" The tad fixed Tallulah with faux suspicion.

"Oh I, um, just got here. So, I guess-."

"You mean you're an outworlder! From the outer banks? Or the big blue? Are you from the Kingdom of Colors? The city-states? Neroth?" Brina squealed with excitement. There was a nervous excitement about the tad like something observed in a seal pup.

"Well, my father and I, we-. Actually, it's a long story and we've been traveling for so long. Could we talk about other things?"

"Of course! Oh, I'm so excited to have a best friend!"

"Huh?" Tallulah's last friendship hadn't ended well and the thought of having another friend made her stomach turn.

"You will stay, won't you? Please? It's been so long since I've had anyone to play with around here and the master is terribly boring."

"Perhaps, but I make no reservations. I came here with my father; he is seeking the Dragons' favor."

Brina bristled at that. "Right of course. My family lives far south of the Arkstone."

"And you? Why aren't you with them?"

"Oh," Brina bit her lip and looked away. "I live here." She looked down and like a flash of lightning, so quick Tallulah nearly missed it, the tads smile dropped. Tallulah thought not to push.

"Right well, maybe I'll convince my father to have you live with us! It's like you said, we're friends now."

The tad said nothing, just buried herself in Tallulah as the two embraced. It was then that Tallulah felt the frame of the girl. She was rather small despite her attitude; she guessed that the tad was not much older than Tallulah.

Brina took her on a tour of the palace, if one could call it that. In truth it proved to be a series of large tunnels carved into the mountain beneath the sea. The palace was incredible. The hallways were large enough for a great beast to swim through.

Her new friend explained that she lived on the second floor from the top so she saw little of what went on in the larger part of the Arkstone. The mer girl's room was filthy, in the way of a child who had never before entertained guests. Fabric was unceremoniously tucked into the creases of shelves and walls and hair pins shoved into a sunken corner of the room. Forgotten crafts and projects lay piled on top of each other discarded in the corners of the room. On one side stone tablets lay and khipu floated inches above. Despite its faults it had its own sort of charm. Truly though her new friend lived quite a messy life, though a rich one it seemed.

Tallulah was so lost in taking in the mess around her that she almost failed to notice an older mer woman swimming in quietly. Without a word the mer woman began tidying up the room. When she reached the tablets, she took a few in her arms and looked over at Brina with a harsh gaze.

"These were to be returned to the library two days ago young lady." The older mer scolded Brina.

"But I haven't finished reading them yet." Brina brushed the mer woman off innocently.

"None of that, you can always go fetch the tablets when you need them once more. Honestly, I'd expect more from a golden mer such as yourself." The mer woman said harshly.

Brina huffed and let Tallulah out the way in which they'd come.

"Is that your mother?" Tallulah whispered once they'd left.

"Huh? Oh no. That's old Nan. She's *ancient. I've* no idea how she's still able to function."

"So your grandmother...or..?" All of Tallulah's grandparents had died long before she was born but she imagined they'd look about Nan's age were they to still be alive.

"Weren't you listening?" Brina waved her off. "Nan isn't related to anyone; she just works here. She cleans every now and again but she usually just bosses me around. It's awful." Brina put her hand to her temple and feigned dramaticism.

Tallulah smiled. "You're ridiculous. Where I come from children are hardly looked after by their own parents."

"Well just as soon as my mother comes to pick me up, we'll call it even, whaddya say? What do you think, should we give her a few hundred years?" Tallulah suspected that her bright expression and airy sarcasm hid something more. She wondered how long it had been since the mer girl had last seen her mother.

Tallulah just rolled her eyes. "Where *are* they? Your parents I mean?"

"I told you. They live in the south with my twin brother." She paused and seemed to size Tallulah up. "Can we just leave it at that please?"

Tallulah nodded and they swam on.

"So why here?" Brina said as they rounded the next turn.

"Hmm?"

"Well, you said earlier that you lived in the Kingdom of Colors, the Silver Grove wasn't it? It just seems like an awfully long way to swim just for a new place to live. Don't get me wrong, I'm very excited to finally have someone to talk to. I don't have many friends and the ones I do have, well I'm quite sure they only tolerate me because they've nobody else that *can* speak with them."

"But?"

"But well wouldn't it be simpler to just find a place in the kingdom you already lived in?"

Tallulah took a breath not wanting to relive the violent memories that had led her here. "My mother was killed. But even before that we knew it wasn't safe. In truth I think we only stayed for mothers' sake. We lived on the outskirts. Not much food, even less defense. When the raiders came, we just couldn't take them. Papa said the gentry of the Kingdom never cared about us poor folk. Said they'd just brush us off. That we needed to start over." Tallulah realized her voice was hitching with grief. She hadn't realized until now how much it truly hurt. Not just the loss of her mother but the realization that she too was alone and lost. Alone if not for her Papa.

There was a hand on her own. Brina squeezed. "I'm sorry." She breathed.

It was genuine. But it didn't make facing her fears any easier. So, she squeezed back politely and offered a small outward smile.

"I know what will cheer you up! Let's eavesdrop!" Brina said gleefully.

"On whom?"

"Your father and the Master of course."

And just like that Tallulah was being tugged down the hall and through a tight hole in the wall. "Is this safe?"

"Nope. That's what makes it fun!"

They half crawled; half swam through the hole until they reached a dip wide enough for them to reposition. "Where are they?" Tallulah whispered.

Brina put a single finger over her lips and pointed through a crack in the wall. They were above them. Brina's master, the Dragon was rather large and yet somehow smaller than Tallulah had imagined. His scales were a vibrant golden that shined even without light for them to reflect. He lay amongst walker riches that blinded Tallulah as they reflected from the dragon. Tallulah put her ear to the crack.

"...not safe without me!" It was her father. His voice cracked with panic. There was silence then her father spoke once more. "Please. *Please*. Anything else!"

There was no response, just silence.

"Who is he talking to?" Tallulah whispered.

"The Master." Tallulah gave her new friend a confused look. "The Master speaks in your mind. That's how most of the Dragon's servants receive his orders."

"Wait, did you say *dragon*?" Tallulah gulped. Brina nodded and hushed her, but Tallulah paid no mind. "Can you do that?"

"Not yet." The mer girl said. "Okay my turn!" Brina pushed her aside and put her head to the crack.

"Hey!"

Brina hushed her. "He's saying something about leaving the city."

"What did he say exactly Brina?"

Brina hushed her once more and listened again. Her face phased through many emotions. Worry then shock, sadness and anger then shock again. Personally, Tallulah couldn't understand why Brina would feel much of anything. Afterall they'd just met.

"He said...he said that he's leaving." Brina pursed her lips but the mer girl didn't seem surprised. Rather a mix of emotions settled onto her face.

"Oh, I thought we might stay a bit longer." A pang of sadness hit Tallulah in the chest. She'd grown fond of Brina in the short time since she'd met the mer girl.

"Well, that's the thing." Brina turned her head so as not to look Tallulah directly in the eye. "I think it's just him. Your father didn't say anything about you going with him."

"What? No. You must have heard wrong. Let me hear." She shoved Brina away a bit harder than she should've and pressed her ear to the crack beneath them. Silence. The conversation was over. The deal was made.

She was swimming as fast as her tail could carry her. Jetting out to intercede her father until she finally found him.

"What's happening?" The mer girl asked, "you're leaving?" Panic attacked her voice, and her questions came out in a cry as she desperately tried to hold back her tears.

Her father held her face in his hands and Tallulah saw that he too was crying. "The Dragon has offered us safety. It is as the Lady said, there is a price for such a life."

"Please don't leave me! You said we would find a home together; you can't leave me now." Suddenly like a broken dam all her grief and fear and rage came spilling out of her. She was screaming and crying at once. "Do not go where I cannot follow Papa! Please don't leave me!"

Her father tried to speak but choked on his words. So she gripped him with a ferocity that no beast could match. He returned the hug and smoothed her hair as he spoke in a sad whisper.

"One day you will understand. Someday someone will enter your life that you would do *anything* for. Even if it meant leaving them. The Dragon has promised you more than I could give you in a hundred lifetimes. If this is the price of your happiness, I will pay it willingly."

"I will never be happy without you Papa." Tallulah cried.

"Perhaps not immediately, but the hours will turn to days, and the days to months. Then one morning you will wake up and look around only to be surrounded by friends and maybe even a family of your own. And this day will be a distant memory." Her father kissed her forehead. "Remember, home is not a place. It is wherever your heart resides."

Tallulah nodded, when she had mastered her grief, she finally spoke. "Where will you go?"

She followed her father's gaze to the sunny waters above them. "There is a human kingdom nearby. I think I will go there."

One final hug. One final goodbye. Then he was gone, and Tallulah was left floating in the endless blue waters of the Arkstone.

Chapter 13

"I saw three queens rise from a burning pit. The first wore golden armor and a purple cloak. And in her sheath was a crystalline dagger. When the people saw her, they cried out.

'Kin killer!' They screamed."

An excerpt from the prophecy of the Dolah as it was first recorded by the mer of the Arkstone in the year 1207.

Tallulah (1539 A.D.)

Three days. It had been three days since her father had said his goodbyes to her. Since she had watched sobbing as he swam away. She had thought her father of all her family, surely, he had actually loved her. The idea of closure had become just that, an idea. Her reality was lonely, if it weren't for Brina and the multiple golden armored guards stationed all around the Arkstone Tallulah might have run away. Instead, she made her way to the gates of the outer ring every evening where she clung to the bars waiting and watching, just in case her father returned for her.

The Reek, that was the term the locals used to speak of the Arkstone's outermost ring. Magic was a secret few could afford to even dabble in. And the only thing golden about the outer ring was the guards in their armor. Thieves and whores swam about free of consequence and illegal trade offered a fruitful lifestyle for those who could keep closed lips. The alderman's stories had failed to mention this side of the Golden Kingdom. But the rabble of the Reek meant that none noticed little Tallulah as she spent her entire evening waiting, watching... hoping.

The evening was waning when Tallulah finally decided to turn in for the night. She had little confidence in her navigating skills at night, besides everyone knew that the predators came in droves at night. Not the pesky coral fish of the day but the great sharks, whales and capillatas that cast shadows over entire neighborhoods. The creatures that lurked in the darkness of this foreign sea terrified Tallulah. Reluctantly the mer girl swam to her new home. She passed mer of all sorts as she sought the safety of the room she shared with Brina.

Most of the mer homes in the Arkstone were built vertically one on top of the other. Architects would train different types of corals to form the bones of the home then fill in the rest with various substances. The richer one was in these parts the higher their home. Only the poor and sick lived in the sandy bottom of the Arkstone. Tallulah stayed high in the water mere feet from the waves above. From this height she could see the Arkstone in its full glory. It was quite enchanting, but before she could smile that familiar pang of loneliness would assault her heart.

Emotionally exhausted and thinking of her father, Tallulah curled herself around the spare stalagmite in the room she shared with Brina. In the back of her mind Tallulah could hear her mother telling her that she should be grateful. She was living as a princess, in a room in a castle, protected by a dragon...but none of that mattered to Tallulah without her father. She had traded one prison for another.

Tallulah did not know what time it was when two mer women robust in their old age, clad in golden scales and grey with wisdom and cunning, had found her sleeping curled around her stalagmite and taken her to a cavern far from the room her and Brina shared. The women would not give their names, they just gave her orders. At first Tallulah had thought them kidnappers but the golden diadems they wore clued her into their status as servants of the Golden Dragon. Still it did not take long for panic to set in on the young mer girl.

The taller of the two women, dark indigo of skin and green of eyes, was more quiet when she spoke. She seemed to read Tallulah's intentions before she even had the chance to speak. Tallulah found her to be the gentler of the two though. The other looked like Tallulah, more or less. They both had dark skin and tight curls. This mer however kept her hair cut close to her scalp for what reason she did not offer as both mer refused any attempts at conversation. Tallulah supposed it was none of her business but she did wish they would say *something*. Their silent stares unnerved her. The two mer women however seemed almost bored. They seemed to be speaking to one another in a language Tallulah could not hear.

Tallulah's eyes sprinted to every exit of the room in a desperate attempt to escape but when the women reached for her their grips were not harsh, rather they were gentle as they each took one of Tallulah's shoulders and arms in their own. Each was careful not to brush up against Tallulah's gills or irritate her scales. When she could not wrangle herself out of their grip Tallulah sighed and resigned herself to her fate. She let the two mer women lead her out of the room where she could still hear Brina snoring.

Together the Tallulah and the golden mer swam over the Arkstone. The inky darkness combined with the silence of the inner ring gave Tallulah an eerie feeling. Tallulah thought perhaps they were leading her to the outer ring, her father even. But they passed over the Reek just as swiftly as they had passed the inner ring. They kept swimming until eventually Tallulah could see an enormous cave in the distance.

Once inside the cave Tallulah was led to a small hole in the ground that seemed to funnel into another part of the cave, where Tallulah couldn't see but she could feel the flow and ebb of water around her. Wherever they were this part of the cave must have a much larger opening. The blue skinned one took Tallulah's hand gently in her own and squeezed, softly at first then harder. All the while giving Tallulah a reassuring smile. The gesture comforted Tallulah who had spent every minute up till now preparing for the worst and did *not* expect the other mer to be holding such a large blade. And yet when she looked over... In one foul swoop the mer cut into Tallulah's hand and the cavern began slowly filling with red blood.

"Again." The one holding Tallulah steady said in a thick accent all sense of comfort gone from her voice. Tallulah had the sense to try and pull away this time but the mer woman was much stronger than she looked. Tallulah screamed when the blade cut deeper into the already bleeding wound.

"Why are you doing this?!" She screamed again when the mer women shoved her hand down in the hole and squeezed at the wound.

Tallulah pulled with all her strength but the mer woman held her firmly. She spoke to the other in a language Tallulah did not recognize. Tallulah watched in horror and as her blood was squeezed from her hand in a small portion. When she finally managed to pull free she shot for the opening they had entered from, but a single word from the blue mer made her freeze. Panic rose in her chest as she found she could not move. The mer spoke again and Tallulah was swimming back against her will. It did not take a scholar to realize what was happening. Though she could not comprehend how, Tallulah realized that the blood the two mer had taken from her was now being used to control her. Her blood swirled in the water before her and something huge moved in the dark. As it came closer Tallulah could sense its towering height.

A sense of dread entombed her and Tallulah found herself struggling to breath. Tallulah's small head rose higher and higher. It was so *huge.* She had to reorient herself in order to see the creature's head. And when she did, she screamed. In that moment she was utterly terrified. The Great Golden Dragon brought his head closer to her until she had backed up against the cavern wall. Tallulah could feel her heart in chest, in her throat. *Bum. Bum. BUM.* She swallowed and ignored the tears that flowed from her eyes into the sea. She let out a silent cry then swallowed her fear and took a breath.

Are you scared girl? The massive Dragon smiled, his lips curling up revealing sharp teeth. The smallest of which was larger than her head. He was speaking in her mind. The Dragon was in her head. It was the most invasive thing she had ever experienced, and the most terrifying. Tallulah shook violently and clamored for something on the unbearably smooth cave wall to hold onto.

"Yes." She whispered aloud.

I can't hear you girl. The Dragon inched closer to her and she could feel a singular scale rub against her chest. The thing was massive, nearly the size of her own head. The incredible beast before her was made of pure gold, and even in the darkness of night it shone brightly. It's golden eyes shining with impossible intensity in the moonlight. The thing's claws were longer and thicker than her entire arm and grasped the rock below them leaving cracks and crevices in the creature's wake. She knew in an instant this dragon could shred her. One wrong move was all it would take. Tallulah could feel her chest closing up.

"Yes, please let me go." She tried desperately to raise her voice. To scream it but she could only produce a small squeak.

Speak up! The beast roared in her mind. Her head split with the feeling and she screamed again grasping at her head. For a moment she forgot her fear in the pain.

Get out! She screamed into her mind. *Get out of my head!* She roared it, let the words fill every piece of her mind and willed them forward. If she would die here it would be with some small amount of dignity. But the Dragon for his part just smiled and nodded at her in approval and... was that respect? She watched as the two older mer women made a small cut into the dragon. The ichor that rose out of the beast seemed to move with a life of its own and when it met Tallulah's in the water the two swirled in a bloody parade before the golden blood of the dragon shot into Tallulah's wound. The pressure slammed her into the wall and stunning her.

She felt the change immediately. Something bigger than herself lived in her now. The small, terrified tad who had once run from even the thought of fear was no more. In an instant the seed of something incredible had been planted in her blood and when she opened her eyes to see the dragon and his two maidens gazing at her with grins and pride she could feel it. It was like a fire and it burned in her chest. The world around her was no longer dark and drab but bursting with vivid color despite the lack of light. When she took a breath her gills flared with new life and she could almost taste the salt of the sea. The fire in her chest burned with new life.

It still burned there the next morning when she had awoken in the small room she shared with Brina and the morning after that. Again and again, morning after morning after morning she waited for the fire to burn out somehow. But it never left, for years it would stay with her. *Magic.* It lived within her every day, with every flare of her gills it made itself known. Now here she sat, a full two years since she had first become a true servant of the Dragon, since she had first tasted magic. Her gaze dropped to the undercity, to the Reek below still feeling the fire of magic burning within her.

Though she did not yet understand it, she knew that she was different now. Tallulah was no longer just mer. She was not just a simple silver. This was *dragon's blood.* And if the golden beast's blood now flowed through her veins... what did that make her?

Chapter 14

Dearest husband,

In just a few short years Wyntir will be fifty years of age. It is likely that her regalec will become restless in the coming years as the need to bond overcomes him. Should the two bond properly it is imperative that you send the girl to me immediately. Do not waste time on healers, the girl must be seen to by her kin.

Khipu sent from Lady Brizo to her husband Lord Nerous of Makoul in the year 1603

Ivara (1603 A.D.)

Ivara took her sister by the arm in a panic. She knew her mother had a similar beast when Ivara was a girl and so had always assumed Gar to be harmless. Thus the streak of fear that ran through her blood was all the more harsh. She tugged Wyntir along and together the two began to swim as fast as they could with Gar not far behind. Slowly the red water became blue again and the sounds of battle ebbed away. They swam on until nightfall. Exhausted and terrified they hid in a small dark cave. The few fish that were present fled upon their entry.

"How's your arm?" Ivara asked, looking over at her little sister.

Wyntir rubbed at the inky black but she no longer winced. "Better I think. I'm not sure how to explain it but I think it was Gar."

"Yes, well he's certainly proved himself to be a loyal companion." Ivara gave a nervous glance at the creature that had cuddled up next to her sister.

"No I mean when Gar bit the mer man I could *feel* it." Wyntir made to pet Gar but he was already asleep so she turned back to Ivara. "Are we getting close to mother?"

Ivara pursed her lips. "I'm not sure. I've never been to mother's home. And when that mer grabbed you... I'm sorry Wyntir I panicked. Honestly, I don't know where we are."

"Don't apologize. We're safe aren't we?"

"I hope so." Ivara replied. In truth though she did not feel safe at all. Had her sister not been so attached to the beast she might have already sent it away. But even a blind mer could see that Gar was protective of the mer girl. Then there was the uncertainty surrounding her other sisters. Anyone who was foolish enough to challenge Ka'I to a duel deserved the brutal death that would accompany such a challenge. But Mele and Uhane? Mele was a gentle soul and Uhane could hardly scream for help if she tried. Were they still alive? When Ivara finally did fall asleep it was due to sheer exhaustion from praying for her kin.

When they awoke the next morning they could faintly see bits of sunlight swirling through the calm water. Still they decided to stay in the cave until they knew what to do next. Gar remained with them. Despite her nervousness around the creature it was somewhat heartening to know that the regalec stood between them and any that would harm them.

"It's calm out." Wyntir said optimistically.

"Too calm." Ivara could feel the pressure drop. "There's a storm coming."

Wyntir swam over to her, khipu in hand. "Do you really think the Red Mer will come to Makoul's aid?"

"I don't know but I do think they can help you heal your arm."

Wyntir was silent as she twirled the khipu absently between her fingers. Finally the mer girl's gills flared and she took a deep breath before replying. "I'll take the khipu to mother. You go ask Scyla for help."

"What? No, you can't go into the deep alone! It's too dangerous."

"I'll have Gar. You saw how he protected me yesterday. I'll be safe with Gar."

"I've also seen your arm after he bit you, Wyntir!"

"And you saw what happened to that mer. It was like his neck was dissolving. Why am I recovering but that mer died before our eyes? You always said that mother had a regalec too. Maybe her kind, *my kind*, are meant to have such beasts."

"Wyntir I admire your affinity for Gar but there's no guarantee that he can protect you. And if anything happens to you I could never forgive myself for letting you go alone."

Wyntir smiled sadly. "I know, which is why I'm not asking. I need to see mother; I have questions that no one but her can answer. And Makoul needs the help of its allies more than ever. Both that of the Red Mer and the Witch. I know you know this is what's best for Makoul, you just don't want to admit it."

Ivara's face crumpled. "Of course I don't want to admit it." She began to cry. "What happens when all that's left of Makoul is rubble and corpses and you've gone where I cannot follow?" She took her sister in a fierce hug. "Stay safe, don't linger in any one place for long. And stay close to Gar." Ivara turned to the regalec, addressing him directly for the first time and praying he could understand her. "I don't care if you have to kill half the sea. You keep her safe, understand me?" The beast did not respond, he just inched closer to Wyntir in a protective manner. When they separated she looked at her sister to see that her white eyes had become blood red.

"What is it?" Wyntir asked, seeing her puzzled expression.

"Nothing." Ivara shook her head. "I love you." She watched Wyntir and Gar swim down into the inky depths of the sea until they faded to black. It wasn't until they had left her sight completely that she let herself begin to cry. Slowly at first, then it all came crashing down upon her and she was sobbing to herself all alone with not but darkness below and the vastness of the sea all around her. Steeling herself she surfaced, she could tell that she was near the coast slowly she made her way towards the witch's den with only the stars to guide her.

Chapter 15

"It is widely thought that the mer folk are quite vain, though the roots of such an idea come not from direct interactions with the mer. Rather it comes from an old wives tale of a maiden who looked upon the heavenly bodies of the folk of the sea and could not bear the knowledge that there lived a whole race of creatures that were more beautiful than herself. Perhaps we are the vain ones."

Prejudice of the Mer Folk by Willmont Anderson

Tallulah (1554 A.D.)

"Well?"

"Well what?" Tallulah looked in dismay at the strange attire she had donned for Brina's enjoyment. Her brunette friend had been becoming more and more withdrawn these past few years. Though she would never say it aloud, Tallulah suspected it was a result of her constant training with the Master. Thus Tallulah found herself doing her best to cheer her up.

"What do you think? I made it just for you!" Brina squealed. It was the first time Tallulah had seen her friend genuinely smile in days.

Tallulah choked. It was so, *so* ugly. A brazier made of two large green clam shells that had been awkwardly jammed together with an uneven hole speared through them to provide room for an itchy rope. The rope fit loosely around Tallulah's sides and tied in the back though it rubbed and gave her a blister. A dozen or so small pieces of what looked like bright pink scrap fabric were tied to the rope in the front to provide more modesty around the midriff. Though it seemed Brina had forgotten the backside of her new piece. To add insult to injury the rope had no halter so Tallulah had to keep swirling the water with her tail so that the shells stayed on her chest, without letting Brina on to what she was doing.

She could hardly bring herself to offend Brina. It wasn't a matter of the gift itself but rather of friendship. In the fifteen years since she had come to the Arkstone it had been Brina that had stood by her on both good and bad days, through thick and thin. The two mer girls had become fast friends. Were it not for Brina, Tallulah doubted she would still be sane.

"It's um... nice." At first she was afraid Brina wouldn't buy the obvious lie but then a beautiful smile bloomed on her face that lit up the whole room. She wrapped her arms about Tallulah and squeezed.

"I'm so glad you love it! Oh this is just the beginning! I bought some extra materials. If I plan it out maybe I can make you another one in purple!" Without taking a breath she was off, speeding away into the rush of the inner Arkstone and Tallulah was left alone with the only other mer in their shared room. A mocking snicker sounded beside Tallulah.

"You really must stop with these boorish lies. You look quite foolish you know." A slim mer girl with pale skin and long green hair so dark it was nearly black said from the edge of the room. The mer girl was her age, and was ethereally beautiful despite her missing eye. One eye was a beautiful emerald green, the other was a scarred hole. The remnants of a terrible infection from the mer girls' youth.

Corvena had a green orb painted to resemble her true eye but she rarely wore it in close quarters. Only in public did she don it, to save face and reaffirm her narcissistic pride. Were it not for the mer girl's missing mutilated eye and intense scarring she might have been a fantastic beauty. The type that artisans sang about, a mer who's appearance alone could lure men to their graves. Tallulah didn't respond or even acknowledge Corvena's remark.

"Besides," Corvena continued, "one day she's going to ask you to wear that *ridiculous* excuse for clothing out and judging from how you've reacted today, you won't have the heart to turn her down."

"Must you always be so rude?" Tallulah countered. Earning her only an uninterested shrug in return.

Corvena was the newest addition to their little group. For a while it had just been Tallulah and Brina. Tallulah's father had traded her to the Dragon and left for the surface. She remembered the heartbreak and bitter goodbyes they had exchanged. Now she lived like a lord's daughter save for a father or mother. Brina had introduced her to their Nan, an older mer who was awfully stern. Nan served as their mother, and the Dragon as their master. They had no father. Nan watched over them rather closely, doing their hair and teaching them manners. The Dragon in contrast had hardly any interactions with them.

By the time Corvena arrived Tallulah was finally beginning to cement herself as a member of the household and was even excited to have a new surrogate sister. However Corvena's arrival was anything but warm. Her father, a high ranking Lord from the upper Arkstone, accompanied by his wife, came in swiftly and without ceremony. Within a few days they were gone and Corvena was left behind as if forgotten in the haste. Which perhaps explained how oddly bitter the mer girl was for her age though outwardly at least, very tough.

Tallulah took the costume off and began re-dressing.

"Why *don't* you tell her the truth?" Corvena asked, her usually mocking tone showing unusual curiosity.

Tallulah fixed Corvena with a harsh glare. "Usually when someone is kind to you, you show appreciation."

Corvena sat up giving Tallulah an inquisitive look but said nothing. In a rush of cool water Brina burst through the tunnel leading to their common room. Corvena's hair swept up with the push of the water as if caught in a breeze and Tallulah stifled a laugh.

"Guess what I found?" Brina's voice raised multiple octaves before finally escaping as a squeak.

"What?" Corvena said flatly.

Brina grabbed each of them by the arms and tugged them. They swam out of the tunnels, water cutting through Tallulah's gills at a rapid pace that made her sputter. Brina swam hard, dragging the rest of her company with her. They swam out of the Inner ring and over the Outer ring. Corvena's hair was plastered to her face and Tallulah giggled as she watched her peer struggle to tie it back with one hand. "Gah. Stop, stop. *Stop!*" Corvena sputtered. Brina halted and they began floating with the current.

"I'm sorry, I –." Brina's voice was apologetic.

Corvena ripped away from Brina. "Don't touch me! Ugh! Where are we?"

Brina pursed her lips. "We're here." It was hardly a whisper. Brina had led the trio beyond the Outer Ring of the Arkstone to a place with no mer, no fish, no coral, no life, just bones. Enormous grey bones that stuck out of the sand. Corvena was silent as she let herself sink into the sand and slowly reached out to touch one of the smoothed bones. Some were as large as mountains. Corvena's hand made contact and she jerked back just as soon.

"Argh! It burns!"

"Very funny Corvena." Tallulah chastised in a dry tone as she reached towards the bone to pull herself up.

"No wait! Don't touch it!" Corvena pushed her away and yelped when her tail swept around hitting another piece of bone protruding from the sand.

Tallulah swam back. "Corvena, they're *bones*. Spooky, yes. Burning, no." Her frustration was beginning to build.

"I know that stupid." Corvena pushed off wincing as she rose back to where Brina and Tallulah swam. "They are bones and they burn."

Tallulah rolled her eyes and swam down to the sand scooping up a handful of pieces that had chipped off. The moment they made contact with her skin, a pain like none she had ever felt surged up her arm and she screamed. Tallulah's hand spasmed and the bones fell back into the sand. Corvena caught her and together with Brina they pulled her back up to level.

"Anyone else wanna try their luck in the creepy graveyard?" Corvena said, only annoying Tallulah further.

Tallulah pursed her lips and the urge to smack Corvena came upon her with a swiftness that surprised her. "Have you ever considered sewing your mouth shut?"

"Oh did I hit a *nerve*? Good. We shouldn't even be here."

"Hey guys." Brina squeezed Tallulah's hand.

But Tallulah ignored her. "Dammit Corvena, how are you so *toxic*? It's draining just being around you."

"Oh I'm sorry. Did I hurt the poor tad's feelings? Are you going to tattle to mommy? No, mommy got run through by the walkers. That's ok. There's always daddy-."

"Stop it."

"But your papa left too didn't he. Who can blame him? I've only just moved in and I already can't stand either of you. No wonder he left you at a stranger's archway." Corvena smirked. There it was. The killing blow. Not because it was rude or mean-spirited, but because it was true. Mere days after arriving at the Arkstone, Tallulah's father had departed for good. A teary goodbye was all that was afforded to her. And worse, even then they had both known he wasn't coming back. She was pulled back to the present by Corvena's voice like venom. "No rebuttal?"

"Tals." Brina squeezed harder.

Tallulah turned away, waving Corvena off. At first she just saw Brina staring out towards the bones, her olive skin made pale from fear. But it wasn't until she really looked around that she saw it. The bones weren't just large, they were organized. Tallulah grabbed Corvena's arm and pulled the trio towards the surface. The higher they got the more obvious it was becoming. Bones for miles and miles. An endless wasteland.

"It's a graveyard, a *dragon* graveyard." Tallulah whispered.

"C'mon. We shouldn't be here." Corvena countered tugging them back the way they came.

No. You shouldn't. A deep voice rumbled in Tallulah's mind. Tallulah spun and found herself face to face with a massive creature of glittering gold. The great golden dragon that seemed to take up the entire ocean as far as she could see.

Chapter 16

"Then I saw another emerge from the pit. She wore armor made of golden scales, and her crown shown like gold in the sun. In her eyes burned the fire of grief and death. And when the people saw her they cried out.

'Mother! Oh mother of death! Friend of the fallen, we beckon you to us.' But she neither saw nor heard them."

An excerpt from the prophecy of the Dolah as it was first recorded by the mer of the Arkstone in the year 1207

Tallulah (1554 A.D.)

The Golden Dragon stared down at them with unwavering eyes that glowed in the darkness. Tallulah was utterly still. As if that might help hide her here in the open ocean. Beside her even *Corvena* was shaking. Not Brina though. Tallulah watched as something passed between the mer girl and the Dragon. Finally, her friend lowered her head in defeat.

"Sorry." She whispered.

The Master scrutinized them each in turn before taking a deep rumbling breath. This is the grave site of many ancient dragons; it is no place for young mer such as yourself. Raw chaos lived here, amongst the broken bodies of the dead. Again, the Dragon took a moment to calm himself. He gazed with intense grief upon his kin. Tallulah recognized his expression; she could feel the heartbreak that lingered inside him. This place was more than just sand and bones to him. Finally after taking another breath, the Dragons gills flared and he began again.

This place used to be a warzone. Many great Sources perished here. Corvena furrowed her brows in question. *Come.* The words echoed into their minds and Tallulah's head shook with the intensity of the command. She would never get used to such a feeling. Their Master turned away and it took Tallulah a moment to realize his offer.

It was Brina who first grappled a huge spike, one of many that jutted from the Dragons back and beckoned them come. Tallulah and Corvena exchanged nervous glances before following suit. In an instant they were plunged back down into the depths. Corvena's long hair blew back into Tallulah's face but Tallulah feared letting go at such a speed. The Dragon landed and the graveyard shook. They scrambled off. In her hurry Tallulah's tail swept a bone and she cried out in surprise. *Chaos magic. And yet you are connected to it. We all are.*

"Nan said there was only sourced and unsourced magic." Corvena said.

Magic is chaos. Chaos is very dangerous. He paused and looked around mournfully at his dead kin as if seeing them when they still lived. Every bone here, every skeleton was once a dragon, a source. Some large, some small. Each of them Made by the chaos. But what is taken must eventually be given back.

"You mean these," she gestured to the huge grey bones sticking up out of the sand beside her, "are chaos *solidified.*" It wasn't a question. Brina's eyes widened in realization.

"Which means there's more sources... or at least there were."

Yes. I know of two such factions that use Sourced magic, ours and the Red Mer.

"What happened to them?" Corvena whispered, turning her attention back to the bones before them. She didn't elaborate but they all knew she meant, the dragons. What happened to the dragons that had died here.

War mostly, many who died here were young, in their prime. Fighting for their loves, their homes, the penmanship of war may change but the story never does. And neither does its ending.

Chapter 17

Scyla, I have received your missives regarding Ivara. Keep the girl safe, in this at least you must not falter. Concerning signs regarding the Dolah have been cropping up recently and the girl must be alive if she is to play her part in the war to come. I will reach out with further instructions soon.

Khipu from the Master of the Arkstone to Scyla

Ivara (1603 A.D.)

Ivara had been swimming all evening when the storm finally caught up with her. She could feel the pressure dropping further. Ivara swam deeper to avoid getting shoved around by the waves, but the storm blurred the water all around her with debris. With no place to wait it out she found herself swimming in circles, disoriented by it all. Still, she swam on, going deeper searching for signs that she was nearing the sea witch's cave.

She could still remember the Sea Witch leading her home when they had left the west. Her gentle words and kindness had calmed Ivara's nerves when faced with the reality of meeting her family again after so many years apart. The mermaid had few memories of her mother from when she was younger but she would always remember her mother's harshness. The Sea Witch though... Scyla had been a sort of mother to her as well. At least for the time it took them to travel east. Ivara always looked back on that time with a smile.

After many hours, the sea eventually returned to form and the water began to clear. Exhausted, Ivara once more swam to the surface to find that a full day had passed. The sun sat high in the sky and she could hear walker voices in the distance. Far off she could see the walkers going about their tasks on the harbor. She only now realized just how far the storm had taken her from her destination. Around her were various fishing vessels, the walkers in them throwing out their nets. The water was shallow here, so she swam slowly so as to not disrupt the water above her. She liked to imagine that from above her pale skin, dirty blond hair, and iridescent teal tail would be stunning. It was tempting to go near one of the ships but as much as she'd liked to let her mind wander into her curiosity about the walkers, there was always that voice in the back of her mind reminding her of her mission.

She thought back on the day she had returned to Makoul with the sea witch. Scyla had been gentle with her the entire trip back. And when they'd arrived, she'd allowed her to stay at her cave near the coast to rest before meeting her family for the first time in years. She never became frustrated with Ivara when her memory had failed her. She found herself wishing that she was approaching the witch under better circumstances rather than to just ask for another favor, though part of her was happy to see her friend and mentor once more.

Ivara spotted it then, purple sea grass. While it wasn't entirely uncommon in the east to see such, it was rather rare to see so much of it. Exhausted but happy to have finally reached her destination she swam through the long purple strips of vegetation that swayed with the current. Behind them lay the entrance to the witch's cave. It was dark but she could still see her friend waiting for her. Scyla was a large but fit mer. Her skin was green marred by black and red symbols that had been carved into her body. She had no tail but rather a dozen large thick tentacles, a marking of her ancient age. Scyla was the last of her kind, where modern mer had only one tail, reminiscent of a fish, the witch came from a sea people that hardly even resembled the mer at all. At her hip was the crystal athame which she used for her spells. At first glance one might think her a sea devil. But when she saw Ivara her scarred face turned into a great smile, and she swam over to greet the mer girl.

"Are you alright Ivara? You look exhausted." Scyla asked, hugging Ivara close.

Now that she was finally here Ivara could hardly get the words out. "It's Makoul. Neroth has attacked Makoul."

The Sea Witch's pale green eyes widened and Ivara could see the blacks of her eyes. Her green tentacles swirled as she swam closer to inspect Ivara. There was a maternal worry in the Witch's eyes. For a brief moment Ivara wondered if this was how her mother must have looked her over when she was young, before her mother had left them. The thought passed just as quickly as it had come when the Witch began speaking to her. Her words pulled Ivara out of her reverie.

"Are you hurt?" Scyla asked, worriedly looking her over.

"No, no I don't think so." Ivara looked down, trying not to stare at the many runes carved into the Witches green skin. They were not unlike the single rune carved into Ivara's own forearm.

"Neroth's come then? The southerners have finally made their move." Scyla's expression crumpled in sadness. "I should have known. The war mongering fool!" Her gills flared with frustration. "If only the girl had taken Neroth's throne. I do sympathize, poor Princess was so young when her brother died. Only a fool would attempt to thrust the authority of running an entire kingdom on one so young all caught up in grief. Still though... perhaps it would have made a difference. Now her fool of an uncle is going to set the whole sea ablaze." She looked at Ivara. "Has the attack already begun?"

Ivara didn't bother to inquire about Scyla's ramblings, she neither understood politics nor did she take much interest in them.

She just nodded and did her best to answer Scyla's questions as they came.

"When I left they'd made it into the city. We tried to get people out but..." Suddenly all the stress of the events that led her here came crashing down on her at once. Ivara felt as though her gills were stuck together, she couldn't breathe. Her breathing came in short quick bursts. "It was a bloodbath."

Scyla rubbed Ivara's back. "Shh, take your time. It's alright."

The Witch held her until the panic attack subsided. When Ivara was finally able to breath once more Scyla began speaking to herself. "You will have to flee. The south is of course out of question, far too dangerous, perhaps the north? No, there are too many smaller kingdoms to pass through." Scyla thought aloud. Her gills flared in frustration. "Damn it all!" She took Ivara by the hands. "Don't worry dear, I'll get you out of here. Far, far away from all this bloodshed."

Ivara pulled away. "No, you can't. I need your help; I need my memories back. Not a place to hide! You must come help us fight."

The Sea Witch gave her a sympathetic look. "I'm afraid there's not much I could do to help Makoul. But I can help you get away from here. It won't be pretty, but it will work."

"What about my sisters? Can you save them too?" Ivara asked, already fearing she knew the answer.

Scyla kissed the girl's forehead. "Do you remember when we left the west to come back to Makoul? Do you remember why I was sent to bring you back?"

Ivara shook her head. She'd always assumed her father had hired Scyla.

"It was to protect you. You were very sick back then; you were losing yourself and you were brought back so that you might recover in a safe place." Scyla pursed her lips. "But with war and plague the sea it is no longer safe for you."

"What do you mean?" Ivara asked, growing more anxious by the minute.

"Ivara those who seek you are more numerous than you know. Makoul's enemies may very well suspect what I already know. You are a danger, to yourself and others, especially if you do not finish your recovery." Scyla reached out and gently rubbed the rune on Ivara's arm, lost in thought.

"All those who would harm you live in the sea; thus you cannot stay here, Ivara. I must send you away. Just for a short time, just to keep you safe. Then I shall come find you and bring you home just as I did in the west."

Ivara jerked away stunned. "What do you mean I'm a danger? What do you know that I don't?"

"Ivara I -."

"Is it something to do with my dreams? My nightmares? You said on the journey to Makoul that the nightmares would go away but they only got worse!" Ivara couldn't help the suspicion that crawled into her voice. Tears welled up in her eyes.

"Your dreams?" Scyla asked. Ivara could sense her genuine curiosity.

"Yes in my daydreams, my nightmares even, I see things. Things that shouldn't exist, or things that aren't real. But they *feel* real...sometimes...sometimes I can't tell what's real and what's not." Ivara finished in a disheartening whisper. She looked down at her webbed hands which were shaking. "What's wrong with me?"

She felt the Witch's arms pull her into a comforting hug. Then Scyla took Ivara's face in her hands and gently brought her chin up so they were eye to eye.

"Nothing is wrong with you. Had we the time I might ask you about these dreams. But we do not have the time, and every second we linger here, those who would harm you creep closer. You must leave, for a time, and live on land. I will contact your allies in the west and when they are ready I will find you and bring you back to them."

Ivara was quiet. She could see no way out of this. Compliance was her only option. She could feel her heart beating faster and faster. "Will it hurt?" Strained by fear her voice sounded like that of a tad.

Scyla smiled at her sadly and unsheathed her athame. Ivara began to feel the pull of exhaustion come over her. She struggled to keep her eyes open. Finally, when she could no longer resist, she succumbed to the deep and dreamless sleep.

Chapter 18

"It has long been theorized that one must possess true dragon bones, or the dust thereof to perform any real magic. That was until the study of runes grew in popularity. How odd to think that there was once a time when humans had no knowledge of such things. Now it is not uncommon to find a university student turning their parent's gold coin into lead for drawing runes. As the saying goes, 'you can pay your way through life with gold, but you can pave your way through the *realm* with magic.'"

Practical Magic by Daniel E. Simmons

Tallulah (1554 A.D.)

Tallulah stared at Corvena, her mouth agape with shock. They'd returned from the mournful dragon graveyard.

"You can't be serious. It's forbidden!" she said. Was Corvena insane? Likely. But *this*?

"Oh come on! Tal it's a *dragon graveyard*! I know you felt it, that buzz of chaos. That *high*. I want to feel that again."

"Absolutely not."

They both glanced down at Corvena's palm where in the time since their last trip, a light scar had formed where her friend had touched the bone. Tallulah grabbed her hand and held it in front of her.

"This is what happens when you go against the Dragon's commands, Corv. And this is *mild*. We should have never been there in the first place. Have you even considered what might happen if we were to actively draw on that chaos magic? We could get hurt or worse! No, the answer is no. Find some other less dangerous way to break the rules."

Corvena yanked her hand from Tallulah's hard grasp.

"I wasn't asking your permission, dim wit! I was asking if you wanted to come along." The young mer girl's voice whipped through the water with annoyance.

"And I said *no.*"

"Fine then. I'll go by myself." Corvena's tail flickered with annoyance but in her eyes, Tallulah saw a different emotion. Mingled with frustration there was fear or perhaps anticipation of what she might find.

It struck Tallulah that though Corvena was still quite rough around the edges she was also still a child, just as Tallulah was. After all, they were the same age. Could she really expect someone their age to fully cope with magic and dragons and all while being raised by strangers? Tallulah herself still reminisced on her father and mother. On the life she might have led, had the string of fate not led her here.

As for Corvena, as much as the dark haired mer girl wanted this, Tallulah could see that she didn't want to go alone. Tallulah realized with some surprise that she didn't want the mer girl to go alone either. It surprised her how much she cared for the mer girl. Despite their constant bickering Corvena and Brina had become like sisters to her here. They were the only real family she had, and she didn't wish to see either of them in danger.

Though Tallulah was still a child, her time at the Arkstone had changed her. For all her bickering with Corvena, the dark haired mer was family. She had lost her family once; she would not make the same mistake again. Despite the ridiculousness of Corvena's request, Tallulah would be remiss if anything happened to the mer girl.

"Wait!" She sighed, rubbing her temple. "Alright I'll come but not now, not today. We have other commitments this evening so there wouldn't be time anyways. Later. We'll go later."

Corvena's ensuing smile was grateful and relieved. "Thank you, sister," she said. Tallulah was sure it was the first time the mer girl had ever said such words.

Part 2 – Allagor

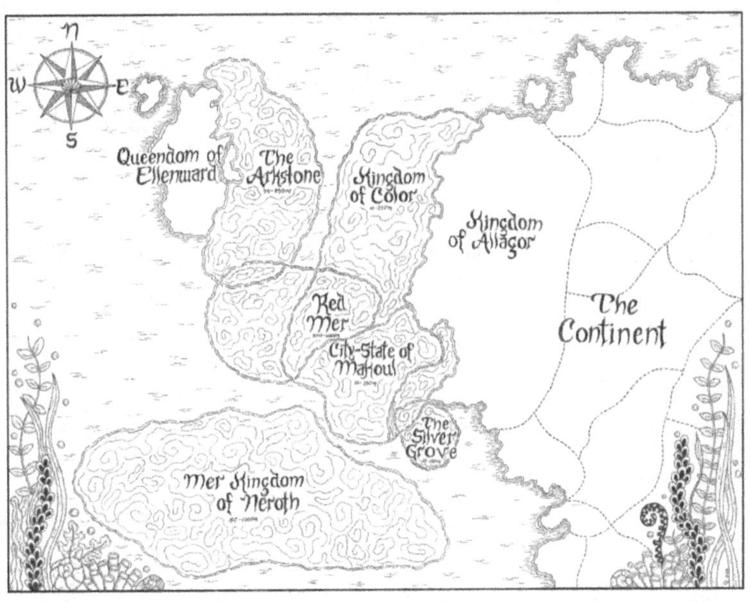

"Your tail will disappear, and shrink up into what mankind calls legs, and you will feel great pain, as if a sword were passing through you."
Hans Christian Anderson

Chapter 19

"Finally I saw the third queen rise from the pit. She was covered in scars. And her hair was like snow. She wore no armor, only an elaborate gown and a crown inlaid with amethysts and rubies. And when the people saw her. They said nothing but bowed silently."

An excerpt from the prophecy of the Dolah as it was first recorded by the mer of the Arkstone in the year 1207

Ivara (1603 A.D.)

Ivara was pulled out of her deep sleep by a choking sensation. Her lungs were ablaze with what felt like an unquenchable fire. She coughed, gasping for the familiar water to dulling the burning sensation. Something was off, the water wasn't coming into her lungs, it was leaving them... It was painful. Fear gripped Ivara as she opened her eyes, she was somewhere dark and cold. When she tried to swim up for a better view a heavy weight seemed to hold her down. She tried again. And again. Ivara could feel the panic rising in her chest. Her breaths became short, quick and shallow. She looked around but it was too dark to see. A bout of hysteria over took her and she laughed. She was mer. She could navigate by the stars alone. That calmed her but not by much.

Ivara looked up but there were no stars out tonight, or at least, if there were she could not find them. So she felt around. Beneath her hands was a rough, hard texture and it was dry. So that explained the choking. She was out of the water. Which meant she needed to get back in the water and quickly. The mer were odd creatures, they could breathe air but not for very long. And she had no idea how long she had been asleep.

"Scyla!" She called out for the witch but only a haunting echo greeted her. Ivara felt around for anything that lacked the dryness of the dirt around her. She felt it then. A small puddle about the size of her fist and half as deep. She felt around and found more puddles, but it wouldn't be enough. As she methodically worked her way around the small space where she had awoken her breathing began to even out. Each breath becoming stronger. She could feel the puddles getting closer together now.

Her hand missed the ground and she felt her arm plunge into the water. It was cold. Colder than she had ever thought water could get. Her other hand slipped on the slick rock and Ivara felt herself tumble into the icy water. She let out a yelp of panic. She tried to breathe slowly to calm herself but when she did the burning sensation returned to her lungs. Terrified, Ivara reached an arm out for the rock. She found it and heaved herself coughing and sputtering out of the icy water. Exhausted and confused she lay in the mud. Every time she tried to move her tail it felt odd. Not numb or hurt just...strange. It was hours before her prison finally came alight with the warm light of day.

When the sun's small rays finally did show their faces, much too late, Ivara could see that she was in a cove. Not unlike the one she had hidden in during the storm. The cove was small and had only two openings that she could see. A small opening in the rocky structure led out to a beach made of sand and small stones. The other opening led to the sea.

The light also revealed another detail Ivara had failed to notice. Her long teal tail had been replaced with two pale legs. They were shaped like those of the sailors and ended in small feet each with five toes. She wriggled those toes or tried to. She managed to twitch one of the big ones. Ivara supposed she should have been surprised but she wasn't. More than anything Ivara was scared. How would she get home? What would happen to her if she couldn't get back to her family? A shiver went through her spine that had nothing to do with the chill breeze against her wet skin. So Ivara Mare, the fourth daughter of the Lord and Lady of Makoul leaned back against the cold rock wall and sobbed.

It was a while before Ivara realized the reality of her situation. While she was sitting here drowning in her own self-pity the day was slipping away. And with it the light. She would need that light. So she resolved to find a way out. Despite all her efforts it was an hour before she managed to wiggle all ten toes. As the day went on, she made some progress and by early evening she could just barely stand. She was, of course, leaning ever heavily on the dark stone wall but it was progress. She would leave swimming for another day.

With her weight propped up against the wall Ivara limped towards the light that beamed in through a small exit at the edge of the cove. Once outside the light nearly blinded her. There was rarely a surplus of light in Makoul so Ivara had grown up used to the semi-darkness. This bright light, however, was something new. Ivara found that she didn't completely detest it. On those rare occasions that she would visit the surface she would bathe in that light. But this felt different. The light didn't just shine on her. It surrounded her. It lit up her soul.

Despite her fear and regret Ivara found herself smiling in the face of that light. As she walked on through the chilly wind the temperature began to drop. She could feel her smooth skin prickle with little bumps. They covered her and she began to shiver beneath the thin snow-white dress that she had awoken in. Another gift from the Sea Witch Ivara guessed. What made matters worse was that thanks to her little debacle earlier the pale white rags were now sopping even as they made way for the wind that blew against her. *What in the sea could have been so dangerous as to convince Scyla to send her here?*

Cold, terrified, and sopping wet, Ivara walked on. She had expected to find a harbor by now but her luck had long since left her. As the sun began to set she stumbled upon a path where the snow was thinner and turning dark. She'd seen snow before but only from a distance. Somehow she'd never imagined it to be this cold. Her whole body ached now and it was with agony that she continued to walk barefoot along the road. She tried using the stars to guide her but eventually decided that on land the road would be more reliable. Ivara was not dense. She had watched these people from afar. Seen glimpses of their world. She knew how they took to carriages when their legs failed them and ships when their carriages failed.

Her feet had long since gone numb and her legs were ice cold. Ivara felt warm tears prickle down her face as she walked on. She managed to stay on that icy road for another hour before her hopelessness consumed her. Her whole body ached. Every movement was agony made even worse by the fact that she had nowhere to go. So Ivara gave up. In every direction all she saw was snow. Just snow. No harbors, just an icy shore.

She found herself trembling as she stumbled and finally fell into that white powder. She could feel everything all at once. Feel the icy wind as it howled in her ear. The cold soft dirt as it caught her fall. And the vibrations in the ground as she began to hear the soft clomps of a large land beast. Hesitantly she opened her eyes to see a small dark dot approaching her by way of the road. At this distance it was too large to be a man and ran much too fast.

It approached at a steady speed though paying her no heed which made Ivara assume that whatever it was, it was not after her. All the same she went still and let the snow cover her. Pale as she was, it wasn't too hard to blend in. The dot grew into focus. Ivara could soon make out the faint outline of a man sitting in a horse drawn wagon. As the company came closer Ivara realized that the man had not yet noticed her. In an act of recklessness driven by the cold, she stood. The man gave her a surprised look. He was an older gentleman. From his lack of cosmetic care and his extensive number of years Ivara assumed him to be an elder of the land. Then he spoke.

"What a you be doin' out in this weather dressin' like that?" He asked once he made it close enough that she could hear him. His voice was scratchy and dry. Ivara couldn't help but think that it matched his appearance. She didn't know man's language well enough to speak it but she had spent enough time visiting sailors and singing to them that she could understand them. This particular man however had an accent thicker than the weather and Ivara crinkled her face in confusion. "Ye best be headin' home m'lady. Lest the weather get the best of ya."

Ivara shook her head. She was unsure how to put the words together to ask for help but tried her best. The old man just returned her confused look.

"Can ye understand me?"

She nodded furiously.

"Alright..." He scratched at his dirty yellow beard. "Well I can't very well leave ya in the cold. But ya see I'm not no rich royal ya see. Ye got any money."

She just shook her head.

"Thas alright we'll make do. Hop on now. Let's just say you owe me a favor alright?" He patted the seat beside him. That was good enough for Ivara. She hopped on. The old man gave her an itchy blanket to wrap herself in and the wagon began to jostle her this way and that. They rode on and the ocean's crashing waves turned into a distant murmur. The chatter of a bustling harbor city soon replaced it. The road took them to a small harbor manned by a village guard, despite the cold. The elderly man escorted her into a small building packed with people that like her were owners of not one but two legs. Ivara couldn't help but wrinkle her nose at the foul smells coming from the building and its rather haggard-looking inhabitants.

"Peace be with ya Hubert." A plump woman greeted them as they walked toward the bar.

"You as well Martha." The scrawny old man laid down a small pouch that made a tinkling sound as it hit the dirty table.

"And what'd this be for?" The heavy set innkeeper, Martha, took the pouch of coins. Leaning in she said, "I done told ya Hubert. Ya can't be goin round spendin money like this. Not in this part of town. The crooks will track yeh down before yeh can saddle yeh horse."

Hubert put up his old gnarly hands in surrender. "Not for me." He gestured to Ivara. "Found the lass a few miles from here. Had but a wee dress on. Poor thing was all alone in the storm. Thought yeh might could find her somethin' to keep warm in."

Martha looked skeptically at Ivara. "Now I don't want no trouble yeh hear?"

Ivara nodded. Her tongue simply wouldn't produce the words in the way these people managed so she just kept silent.

Martha screwed up her face in thought. "Alright." She said finally. Pushing the small coin purse back to Hubert she spoke. "We're friends, Hubert. I don't want yer money. We're gonna do this the right way." She pointed to the far wall where sat dirty brown dresses and dark green aprons to accompany them. "Whatcha waitin for lass? Get to work!" So Ivara changed into the considerably warmer and considerably less filthy tavern uniform and began to help as best she could.

Chapter 20

"...then I saw five creatures rise from the sea. Like harpies they were human, dragon and mer all at once.

I saw the first standing amongst the dead. She spoke to them as their friend, and as their queen. The second figure stood much taller than I, and in her hands she held the largest shield I had ever seen. The third was hardly visible to me as he or she was cloaked in darkness. The fourth, looked at me as I looked at him. As though he could see through time, and I knew we were of similar stock. And finally I saw a girl, her head cracked open and millions of lives spilled out before me. Hundreds of heartbreaks, deaths, love stories all laid bare.

This is what I saw. These were the five tenants to proceed the Dolah."

An excerpt from the prophecy of the Dolah as it was first recorded by the mer of the Arkstone in the year 1207

Tallulah (1554 A.D.)

Tallulah's nerves were on fire as they swam through the massive ribcage of what had once been a large Dragon. She wondered absently if the beast had been Golden like her master or if it was such of another color. She could feel the grains of the black sand beneath her tail as she swept her fins back and forth. Corvena swam just in front of her, the two weaved their way through skeletons thrice as thick as Tallulah and skulls large enough to fit a party of four or five for supper. Far above them the sun was just beginning its slow traverse from the east.

Corvena stopped suddenly and Tallulah, distracted by her wandering thoughts, crashed into her.

"Here should do well." Corvena said pleasantly.

"What's so special about this place?" Tallulah asked, trying not to sound bored. The remark earned her a glare from her friend. "I just meant as opposed to anywhere else in the graveyard. It's all the same isn't it? Just sand and bones."

Her pale friend gave an exasperated sigh. "*Technically* yes it is all the same but we are floating in the center. To be honest, I've no idea if it will make a difference but why not experiment and find out right?"

"You're worse than Brina sometimes." Tallulah slapped a palm to her forehead. "Fine. What do you want to try first?"

Corvena thought for a moment. Then she began. Tallulah watched anxiously as Corvena seemed to reach for something on either side of herself that Tallulah couldn't see. She closed her eyes, breathing deeply. Tallulah had only ever seen Corvena practice her magic once and the attempt had been far from successful.

The Shadow, as the Dragon had come to call her lately, could hardly conjure a wisp of darkness. Still here, surrounded by the bones of ancient beasts, Tallulah felt as though she was gazing upon a goddess.

So it surprised Tallulah when she felt an itching sensation and she could hear a soft hum but couldn't tell from where. Corvena's brows furrowed and at the tips of her fingers an inky blackness the size of a coin formed. Corvena opened her eyes and looked down at the shadows that swirled in between her fingertips and around her palms. It was small, yet much more than Corvena had ever managed to conjure in the past as evidenced from the dark-haired mer girl's grin and sheer amazement.

"I did it." Corvena whispered to the shadows. She grinned and furrowed her brow in concentration once more. Her palms flickered and with them so did the shadows. The latter grew ever so slightly. Tallulah watched wide eyed. The shadows seemed to have a life of their own as they swirled about independent of one another yet never straying far from their masters' hands.

"How are you doing that?" Tallulah asked, amazed at what she was seeing.

"I... I don't know!" Corvena shouted, giddy with excitement. Tallulah had never seen Corvena express such open glee. "I... read it somewhere... when... when I was... at the library on duty... about bones. But some... of the... tablets...were missing." Corvena struggled to keep her concentration as she spoke. The shadows fading and surging back to life then repeating according to how much Corvena could put towards them. Tallulah could see now that her friend's pale face was drained of all pink hues and her jaw was clenched tightly.

"Corv, maybe you should take a break."

"No, I've got it now. I'm fine if I could just-." Just then a shadow shot away from its kin fading quickly. Then another much larger shadow shot away like ink towards Tallulah.

Tallulah barely managed to dodge the shadow magic before swirling back to Corvena who was straining herself now.

"Corv, stop!"

"I-. I can't! If I let go it'll go everywhere." Tallulah could hear the excitement mingled with strain in her voice.

The shadows were growing out of control now. They became more sporadic as they grew and Corvena shook with the effort to tame them. The inky blackness was at her shoulders now. She remembered what the Dragon had once told them about the bones. Insourced magic like this, chaos magic, it couldn't be tamed. It was a dangerous thing to trifle with.

"You have to release it, Corv."

"I can't! I might hurt you!"

"Release the magic Corvena!" Tallulah screamed against the growing humming noise. "The bones are chaos magic Corv. You can't control it!"

Corvena swallowed and Tallulah backed away quickly. Corvena screamed as she raised her palms upward. The world around Tallulah exploded into darkness. The shadows poured from Corvena's palms at an alarming rate and encircled them. Tallulah could no longer see her own hand in front of her. She called for Corvena but was greeted only by silence.

She shivered at a horrid tickle on the back of her neck and knew somehow it was the shadows. She could feel them trying to slither inside her mind. Whatever Corvena had released had a mind of its own. Yet it didn't seem hostile, more...curious. She fell backwards onto something rod-like and hard. It burned and she cried out. It was a Dragon bone. Without thinking Tallulah grabbed the bone pulling from the sand and wincing at the pain. She thrust it into the shadows around her. She could feel the living darkness encircling her. Like an asp it struck fast and sudden. But Tallulah was faster.

She gripped the bone as hard as she could and let its chaos enter her, filling her to the brim. She wanted to vomit and drink it in all at once. She was everything and everywhere all at once, evoking a nauseous feeling. She did her best to direct the chaos. *Protect me.* She called to it. *Save me,* shield *me.* As if the chaos could hear her plea it obeyed. Tallulah tucked into herself and held the bone tightly to her chest. From her center came a new hum. A quieter noise, calming yet steady. It pushed the darkness away with such force that immediately began to drain her. Still she knew the chaos was taking the brunt of it.

She watched her shield push through the darkness bit by bit, dispelling it until at last all the shadow was gone and she was alone in the daylight. Tallulah released the magical shield and threw the bone as far as she could. She understood then what Corvena had said to her just minutes before.

She could feel that element of control that she usually possessed in her magic was almost completely gone. When she finally looked up she saw Corvena lying face down in the sand. Tallulah didn't dare draw breath as she sped over to her and turned the petite mer girl over. She wasn't moving. *No, no, no, no, please no.* Tallulah shook her gently at first then with all the violence and anger that had lived in her heart since her mother's death. Since her father had left her. Since the alderman had betrayed her trust. Corvena gasped and her gills flared in quick spasms. Tallulah let out an anxious sigh.

"Corv? Can you hear me? Are you alright?"

Corvena's breaths slowed and steadied. When Corvena finally opened her eyes Tallulah gasped. One was golden. Suddenly, she understood. They were not simply golden in name. No, it was the dragon's magic that was slowly changing them.

Chapter 21

*Brother, this world is so much more incredible than we ever thought!
Though I miss you and dear Everleigh more than I can say I would
make a liar of myself were I to deny my lust for travel. Mermaids,
beasts larger than our ship and oh the sunsets... I cannot wait to tell
you in person of my adventures at sea. See you soon.*

Prince Henry

The last known correspondence between the crown Prince
Henry and Prince Richard of Allagor

Ivara (1603 A.D.)

Yelling, cursing and threats directed towards her in a language
that was foreign to her; all while covered in stains and dirt from the
day's work. It was hell. No worse. At least in hell everyone spoke the
same language. While Ivara understood most of the things that
were said, the accents were far too thick to easily slip out of her
own tongue. She tried, she really did, but she always ended up
dashing back and forth from the kitchen to the tables redoing
orders and giving out apologies like a crook would give out lies.
When it seemed as though her situation couldn't possibly get worse;
it did. The day was overcast as the last of a blizzard blew through.

Seasons passed, and winter was in full swing now. Many of the
taverns' more familiar patrons were at home safe and warm
waiting out the seasonal storms. Or so Martha had told her. What
remained was a few drunks that probably hadn't left the bar in

days, weary travelers who for the most part were kind to Ivara as most of them hardly spoke the native tongue. And of course, the gangs. Ivara hadn't exactly landed in the best part of town. She had rather suddenly come to this realization when she went to get drinks and passed by a rather shady grouping of men. She was quickly shooed away as if she were a rat.

Ivara could tell by the walker's mannerisms that they were not the type to be trifled with. The way they fingered their knives and daggers all while glancing around the tavern as if both suspicious and overly confident at once. They spoke in hushed voices and did not like it when Ivara was near. Eventually both her curiosity and her fright had gotten the best of her. She did her best to memorize their words and then approached Martha with the information. Her employer didn't look surprised as she explained the men's occupations. They were traffickers. Stealing people from their homes only to sell them off in other areas.

"Stay clear of those men, lass. As well as anyone you may think similar. I'll serve them for now, you keep to the bar." Martha had told her. Ivara wondered why she refused to call the local guard.

She had steered clear of the table until that overcast evening when they called her over. Wiping her hands off on her apron she walked over.

"Yes?" Her vocabulary was basic at best, so she stuck to smiles.

The men smiled at her. There were three of them sitting at the booth. They had maps and books and coins spilling across the table. The looks on their young yet gruff faces covered in scars and signs of ill treatment unnerved her.

"You been a watchin' us lass?" The man directly across from her asked. He was huge. His skin tan with a long white scar running down his eye and nose halting just short of his crusted lips.

"No." She hesitated. Martha had taught her the basics of human speech, but she wouldn't be able to hold a conversation long.

The scraggly man sitting to her left grabbed his cup of ale draining it in one big gulp. "Go easy on 'er Scepious." He let the cup drop to the floor. "Well, go on pick it up." The one on the left laughed. She went for the cup, the bottom of her dress hitching up an inch. She took the stinking cup, making a note to wash it soon. Upon standing up she felt a cold hard sensation on her lower leg. The three men leered at her. She turned ever so slowly to the third man. He sat with his arms crossed and his feet propped up on the table.

"Can I help ya dearie? Yeh seem a bit startled!" He adjusted his arms so that Ivara could see the tip of his blade.

Ivara gave the man a hard look that conveyed nothing less than indifference as she pushed her leg into the blade and jerked it to the side. The cut was shallow but the pain was enough to make her grunt. The sailors stared at her. Ivara smirked, cup in hand she left them to their business.

Martha was busy arguing with a customer about her "famous home-made apple pie, it's the best of the best, don't yeh know" so Ivara swung by her tables for a final check. The tavern was dimly lit and filled with booths and tables. A bar sat just outside the kitchen, but they hadn't had enough patrons thus far for Martha to put Ivara there permanently. So Ivara watched and waited and helped as best she could wherever and whenever she was needed. She had just passed the bar and was well on her way to entering the kitchens when she heard a crash. Ivara jerked her head to the traffickers that had been giving her a hard time but they seemed just as stunned. In fact, all but Martha seemed either surprised or irritated.

It was then that Ivara realized the crashing sound had come from the far side of the room. She turned her gaze to meet that of the new and rather rough-looking patron that had just entered. The man was huge, each of his legs thick as her father's tail. In his muscly arms he held a small coin purse. He leered at the tavern's few residents. Not half a second later a man probably around the age of twenty crashed in after him. The larger man whipped out a curved blade of medium length and pointed it at his assailant. The younger, somewhat shorter man drew his sword and stuck it under his prey's throat.

"Come on Carter, give it up." The second man said to the first. The big one, Carter made a gesture of surrender which was in stark contrast to the tensing of his muscles and the twitch in his foot. Ivara saw the hit coming. Carter dropped his blade knowing his opponent would track the weapon with his gaze. So, when he took the bait and looked down Carter took the opportunity to knee him just below the stomach. Ivara winced. The man fell to his knees dropping his sword and Carter reached down, swiping it from his slim hands. His large face screwed up into a rather unflattering smirk, Carter walked to the bar. Ivara went still. The huge man flicked a gold piece at Ivara.

"I'll have some ale." He grunted at her.

Shaking, she took the dirty cup still in her hand and filled it with day old ale. She thrust the cup at him spilling a good portion. "I don't take well to people who cause a ruckus." It was the longest sentence she had said to date, she did her best to sound confident as she said it.

"Thas all well an good but ya gonna have to show me some respect if ye expect to get paid." He promptly took the ale and poured it on her. "Now, les try this again shall we?" He cleared his throat. "Miss if you'd be so kind as to fix me some-" One of the taverns chairs came crashing down on Carter. It was the man who had threatened him before.

"Was that drunk fool botherin' you miss? I'm Richard, you must be-." Another crash as Carter slammed into Richard knocking him off his feet. The two men fell to the floor, the smell of ale following close behind. While the two were hammering at each other in one giant ball of fists Ivara saw her opportunity and took it. She grabbed Richard's sword from the floor and ducked back behind the bar.

There were crashes, and a few screams from the onlookers then silence. There was a groaning in the wood as one of the men arose to claim his victory and likely his coin purse. Ivara too rose, sword in hand and eyes closed, pointed it at the man on the other side of the bar. But there was no haughty laughter or mocking remark. Instead, when she opened her eyes, it was a very drunk Richard, who'd been beaten black and blue that greeted her with a painful grin.

Entering the bar behind Richard was a ginger man covered in freckles who looked at her curiously. As he came closer she recognized him. He was the walker that had held up a spear to her throat and nearly killed her. *Jensin.* That was what the other walkers had called him. Richard, being the opposite of his lanky, ginger companion, tall and well-built with dark hair and sea-green eyes. Jensin smiled at her and whispered, "glad to know you had a backup plan."

Chapter 22

"Many believe it is their connection with the dragons that make the Golden Mer so formidable. However since the time of Ella the race of dragons has been nearly extinct. So what is it? What gives these glistening mer their edge? I would offer dear reader that it is their skin. From their golden eyes to their metallic tails these mer wear their skin like armor."

Dragons And Their Gold a book of research by Alyssa Dagny

Tallulah (1554 A.D.)

Tallulah felt a shiver run down her spine and tail, she gasped. "Your eyes." She said pointing to her friend's heterochromatic features. She'd heard of mer with different colored eyes but never before had she seen the phenomenon in person. And yet as she looked at Corvena instead of the green natural eye and the green glass eye, something different, something strange looked back at her. The green glass eye remained, filling the hole in Corvena's skull. Now though the natural eye was a glowing gold as if it was imbued with its own magical light.

"*Your* eyes! They're golden." Corvena whispered in hushed tones. Tallulah hardly had time to think as she took her friend roughly by the arm and pulled. Corvena didn't struggle, nor did she let her temper spike. Perhaps because like Tallulah she knew they had done something. Whatever it was, it didn't feel right. There was something about reaching for that power that felt new and different. It terrified her and yet... she still yearned to feel it again. That sudden sense of exhilaration.

The refraction of light off of the water cast Tallulah's attention back to her friend's new dual colored eyes. "Your eyes... they've changed." She whispered, taking her friend's face in her hands. "They were green before weren't they?"

"Are they not still?"

Tallulah shook her head. While the left eye had remained a pulsing emerald hue. Its mirrored counterpart had changed. It was now the color sun kissed gold. The hue of jewelry and coins. The color of riches and majesty. "One is golden." She informed her friend.

"Yours too. Both, it suits you well." Corvena replied. "What do you think caused it?"

Tallulah bit her lip worried that she might sound silly. Still she replied honestly. "Do you think it was the dragon bones? Or just the amount of magic we tapped into perhaps."

Corvena took Tallulah's hands from her face and gently let them fall to her side. "I'm sure it's normal." She said more to comfort Tallulah than herself. "Brina, the matrons, they all have golden eyes... it's the magic. It must be! You felt it too that push like you were breaking through a barrier. And now that *sheer energy*. We made it Tal. Whatever we did changed us. We're becoming Golden!" She said excitedly.

Tallulah took a hesitant breath. It was true she *had* felt it. She would miss the glow of her silver eyes. So far as she knew she was the last to bear the signature feature. And now that part of her life was laid to rest in the dust of history. She swallowed. The time for mourning had come and gone. She was not her people. She had not sacrificed their children to the land devils. She was no longer of the silver eyed mer. She had grown and changed. She looked up determinedly at Corvena. She was Tallulah, Golden mer of the Arkstone. And now after so long she finally had the power to fight back against the horrors of history as they worked to repeat themselves.

Chapter 23

"When one meets a member of the royal family it is imperative that said individual introduce themselves in the proper manner. Ladies should be wearing the latest fashion in court and simple finery. Pearls are a wonderful go to when one is in a rush. Gentlemen should present in equally expensive fashion. Both women and men should incorporate the kingdom's colors into their ensemble. As for manners, a steep curtsey and polite smile are imperative to a good first impression... as well as to keeping one's head."

A Commoner's Guide To Court by Gwyn Stonecrest

Ivara (1603 A.D)

After the brawl in the tavern, the young prince Richard, as Ivara would later come to know him, apologized to Martha and promised to pay for the damages. To which Ivara's boss had responded by patting his cheek. "Anytime dear, I know you need a place to settle your emotions."

It took all three of them, Jensin, Richard and Ivara but within the hour the place was mostly cleaned up. Aside from a few broken chairs and glasses that had to be disposed of, everything was back in place. Every chair, table and decoration that had been damaged was moved out back and Carter was promptly kicked out and left to care for his wounds.

Ivara listened as Jensin explained to Martha and herself why such a fight had broken out in the first place. "...So then Richard made a bet with Carter and won. Some people just don't do well with bets." Jensin explained once the trio had sat down for a well-earned rest. Many of the patrons, including the seedy types left after the fight leaving the tavern almost entirely empty. Ivara told Martha and Richard about her run in with them but didn't mention the cut as she didn't want to worry her. Finishing the last of the cleaning Ivara went to the storeroom for a clean rag. She spent a good five or so minutes looking for one that wasn't covered in grime. She plucked one off the shelf that looked as if it had been ripped off a tunic and started back toward the bar. She slowed when she heard the conversation being held between the three humans.

"He just found her? No husband? Parents?" Richard asked. Ivara peeked around the door frame to see his handsome face twisted up in a look of confusion.

"Well thas what Hubert said. Girl didn't speak the vernacular, so I been teachin her here an there. Been here a few months shy of a year. Fast learner that one is but I'll tell ya one thing. She ain't from nowhere around here." Martha replied walking around a table to adjust one of the chairs.

"How do you figure that?" Richard asked.

"It's all in the eyes, boy. There's a certain way people look at other people whom they have a connection with whether it be for good or bad. When you have that connection it's like a tether that connects yeh to the world around yeh. She don't got that tether." Martha touched her temple. "Watch boy. You'll see."

Jensin clad in a crimson coat that utterly clashed with his fiery hair clenched his fist in frustration. "For heaven's sake can we stop talking about your new barmaid, we have actual matters that need discussing!" Jensin's expression softened when he spared a glance toward Martha. "Sorry Martha, it's just..." Jensin turned back to face Richard. "A week Richard. That's it. Just one week with no bar fights or getting drunk or-" Jensin threw his pale arms in the air.

Ivara watched him nervously, sure now that it was the same man from the boat.

"Come on Jensin. Loosen up." Richard smiled at his friend. "Take a seat." Richard turned to Ivara, "Ale at table three please!"

Ivara scoffed. "That's not table three. You *broke* table three." She walked over to the tap and fixed them all some drinks. She didn't particularly like the taste of ale; it was bitter to her tongue and left her feeling strange if she drank too much. She preferred the taste of mead to anything else the tavern offered. She made the trio of humans drinks as well as a small cup of mead for herself and sat down with them.

"Jensin, have you met Martha's newest serving wench?"

"No." Jensin reached up with one very freckled hand to take his drink. "Last time I was here Martha was training that curvy brunette."

Richard sighed "What a sight that one was." He looked up guiltily at Ivara. "Oh you're nice too."

"Thanks." Ivara responded despondently. Her voice was dripping with sarcasm. She turned to get out of Jensin's view but just as soon as she turned she felt his hand on her arm. With a sigh of defeat, she turned to him. Jensin sported a strong but less bulky build than Richard along with pale skin. He looked like someone had dumped a barrel of assorted spices on him with all his small freckles. His shortly cut hair was a bright red with golden undertones.

"So, Jensin, what brings my favorite emissary to this fine establishment? I don't see you here often, had you come by any later, you would have missed the whole fight!" The Prince asked as he plopped his feet on the table. One could easily label him as rude but he wasn't trying to get attention. Ivara watched him tilt his head back and sigh and she saw something that made her smile. Contentment, he was happy here. Both men seemed to know this place rather well and Martha, who was more uptight than Ka'I even treated both men like her own sons. Ivara looked over at Jensin.

"Well I actually returned to Allagor *months* ago."

The dark-haired one raised his eyebrows as if to say, *Really?*

"Yes Richard. Really." Jensin replied shortly. "Maybe if you didn't have your head stuck in an ale barrel you would notice these things."

Richard bristled at his friend's comment and took another swig. "Go on."

"Good news, the council of Ellenward was eager to throw their support our way. With the kingdom's heirs gathering support from the lords and ladies at court, though siding with one house this early could end badly for us in the long term."

"That's good, now hit me with the bad news."

Jensin sighed, "I couldn't get close enough to tell for sure but I think they're involved in some illegal trade."

"Jensin every kingdom has a black market. Why should we care?"

Jensin sighed. "I don't know. Maybe I could go back or-."

"No, it isn't safe. The weather's gone to hell, well a cold hell. Besides we both know the sea isn't safe."

"I can tell." Jensin remarked. He sipped his ale methodically. "Anyways, the mer have gotten more *adventurous*."

"Oh?" Richard brought his feet down and leaned in.

"Apparently, they have found some way to communicate with the sailors. We were..." Jensin looked at Ivara with suspicion, "...*visited* on our way back."

"Did it attack you?" Richard asked.

It. Ivara winced.

"Do you honestly believe I'd still be here if it had? No, quite the opposite actually. It did speak though or perhaps mimic is a better word for it, whatever it was the sailors were terrified."

Richard screwed up his face in concentration. "That doesn't make sense. Nearly every report we receive of these sirens is due to an act of aggression. Why are they suddenly playing nice? We just received another report of sailors being attacked by the mer. The entire ship was torn to pieces." Richard scratched his chin in thought. "It doesn't make any sense."

"Perhaps they had a score to settle with you." Ivara chipped in. Both men looked at her. "You hunt the mer without mercy. It stands to reason that the families of the dead would want revenge."

"Ivara, Allagor banned the killing of Mer outside of battle years ago. Besides these *things* don't have families. Their savages, animals. I doubt they can even *feel* empathy." Jensin responded.

Ivara hesitated then. The Mer weren't easily killed but every few years a couple hundred would fall to human spears. In a sense it was like a long war, except all the participants had long since forgotten what they were fighting for. Sirens were taught from a young age to be wary of sailors. And despite Jensin's words the killings hadn't stopped. So the Mer continued to butcher and feed off of sailors.

"Maybe things are starting to look up for once." Richard told her.

"Sure." Ivara took a sip.

"So you look like you've been busy." Jensin said sarcastically, nodding to Richard.

"*Actually* I have been." Richard rebounded. "Remember that string of missing persons reports from a year ago?"

"Of course. My father nearly went out of his mind trying to catch the culprit, I think it still bothers him to this day that they never found the bastard." Jensin replied.

"Yes, well it would seem we are not quite out of the woods."

"Same guy?"

"I'm not sure. Amos mentioned they have found a body though so it's looking more and more like a mass murder case." Richard said.

"Traffickers?" Jensin asked.

"Not sure yet, but if it is them then there is a decent chance they'll be hiding out on the outskirts of the city."

Ivara stared at him. "I'm sorry, why haven't these people been locked away?" The more she spoke she more aware she was of her accent. Being immersed in the walker language was one thing, but having a full on conversation was another.

Richard looked over at her with a humorless grin. "Well first we have to catch them. Fortunately for us, criminals and other such low life's tend to frequent this lovely establishment and I just so happen to keep in touch with its owner." Richard drawled with a smirk. He inclined his head to Martha who was now grabbing a seat. The plump red headed woman smirked.

"I feed Prince Richard and his people information; I like to help where I can. Allagor's home ya see, but lately the streets have become dangerous after dark." Martha said sadly.

"Why not just arrest them if you know who's unsavory?" Ivara asked.

"Because—," it was Jensin who responded now, "—*everyone* works for someone in this kingdom."

Chapter 24

My dear brother,

Mother and father have bid me to write to you. They keep telling me that putting my grief to paper will in some way exercise it from my mind. But all I see is a pile of perfectly sealed, unsent letters collecting dust on my desk. I miss you. My body aches with it. My hands shake and my tears soak the parchment. The ink bleeds and the letters are hardly legible. If only you were alive to read them.

Unsent letter from Prince Richard to crown Prince Henry of Allagor.

Ivara (1604 A.D.)

Both the red head and his royal friend made frequent appearances in Martha's tavern over the course of the following months. And each time it was Ivara who would serve them.

While she found the Prince to be something of a womanizer, his copper haired friend was a different matter entirely. Stoic, and always gazing at her as if studying her every move.

Some days Prince Richard would come in late disheveled and tired and in desperate need of a drink. But more often than not he was already lost to his drink by the time he came stumbling in. Ivara for her part had begun to earn Martha's trust and was given a ring of keys to close up at the end of the night. So, when it was dark and cold and an exhausted prince would stumble in and Ivara would be waiting.

"I have your drink." She tried to smile.

Prince Richard took the goblet without hesitation. He took two huge gulps before spitting all over the floor and hacking. "What the hell was that?"

His handsome features were marred by disgust, shock, and betrayal.

"Water, because you're already drunk. That and I'm not exactly in the business of killing my friends by drugging them." Ivara leveled with him.

He laughed. It was a haughty laugh and Ivara felt conflicted as to whether she should slap the smirk off his face or admire his overly confident grin. But she let him have this one. That one moment of pride. She wasn't sure why. "Friends? You and me? Ivara I'm a Prince. I am your future King!" He stood, wobbled, and sat back down. "What are you again? A little orphan making a living-."

"No." She interrupted him. Oh, she was pissed.

"Excuse me?"

"I'm not an orphan. I have a family." Ivara whispered. It was difficult to get the words out.

He laughed again, raising his arms and gesturing to the room around them. "Then where are they? Have you run away?"

"I didn't run, I just...there were other forces at play. Now hush. It's my turn. You're upset, something in your life just changed and it really messed you up. So, you figure coming in every few days and venting to a girl you will never really know is enough to get you through this."

"How did you...?"

Ivara held up the tankard, "You can't hold your alcohol nearly as well as you think you can."

"That... can't be legal." He slurred the last word.

"What? Taking your money or listening to your sob stories?" Ivara held out her palm which contained three shiny golden coins.

"What? Where-? Did I give you those?" He stared in amazement.

"Actually yes, you did, last night right before you told me about the time you, your brother and some Princess found a secret way out of the castle." The Prince opened his mouth to respond but she waved her hand. "That aside, any idea how much they are worth? I'm still learning your currency." She smirked.

"A lot. That's probably enough to get you through the rest of the winter. Um, may I have them back now? I must have miscounted yesterday..." Richard's face warmed with shame.

"No." Ivara answered matter-of-factly. She knew the coin was far more than he owed but she hoped that taking the coin purse now would lessen his drinking when next he came. The Prince sighed but he didn't challenge her further.

"Fine. I suppose I do owe you a thank you for looking out for my health, if not my coin purse as well."

She smiled fondly. "On the house." And flicked a few of his coins to him. "Now tell me. What's wrong?"

The onyx haired prince took his time draining the goblet. When he had finished, he sighed and pursed his lips hesitantly. "My older brother, my *only* brother, went missing last year. His ship was taken down by the mer. You know how those savages can be." He shook his head. "We were supposed to go together, but I was sick and asked to stay behind."

"It's not your fault. If anything, you got lucky."

"I know." The Prince laughed but there was no humor in it. "That's the worst part though, isn't it? Knowing you got out but that the one you love didn't. It's easier to come here, I guess. Drink and forget and hope that whatever clock is ticking will tick just a bit faster."

Ivara sat down in the hard wooden seat adjacent to him. She was silent for a moment and when she opened her mouth to speak she chose her words very carefully.

"After I left my home I realized that many of my friends and family might not be there when I return."

"You mean...?"

"I mean they might be gone. But the ones that still live are worth fighting for. There is nothing to be done for the dead except to honor them and their final wishes. But for the living... we might save them still." She put her hand on his and he didn't pull away.

"I don't know if I'm ready to do that. To help people when all around me everyone just wants to move on. Even my own parents!" He pulled away as his temper again rose and tears stained his red-hot cheeks. "I've tried to distract myself. First with whores then alcohol and now this damn missing person's case but it always falls through and I'm back where I started. Alone and mourning the death of someone who everyone seemed to love in life but afterwards don't seem to give a damn about!" Richard slammed his fist on the table.

"Tell me about the missing people. Are they from the capital? Slums?"

It was a cheap distraction but all she could think of to calm him down. It worked. He sat up straighter and tried to annunciate his words better.

"Jensin's been handling the details but from what he's told me the victims seem to be random. Men, women, even a few children. He thinks we're dealing with peasants mostly but can't be sure."

"Why not? Surely the families would know their class."

"Ahh yes. And therein lies the difficulty. Most of the victims weren't formally reported. In fact the only reason we became aware of the issue at all was when a boot black in the slums complained to the guards about a customer who'd skimmed him. Apparently the kid had let the man off knowing him to be a regular. Two weeks later, no man, no payment."

"Why hadn't the man's family reported him missing?"

"Doesn't have one so far as we can tell. Anyways that's how it started. Over the next month or so similar situations started popping up. Same story every time, someone goes missing, the reporter has little to no information on the victim and whatever information is offered turns out to be a dead end, no family, wrong address, so on and so forth."

Behind him the door to the tavern swung open. Jensin walked in, his face dripping and his hair plastered to his face. The stony faced red head walked over to them, each step making a comical sploosh sound as his boots hit the wooden floor. Jensin was sopping wet from head to toe. When he reached the duo, he opted to plop down beside Richard, his expression seeming to bemoan everything about his current state.

"Looks like a storm." Richard observed doing his very best to keep a straight face.

"Ya, just a bit." Jensin said dryly as he wrung out his coat. He looked between the two of them. "Have I interrupted something?"

Ivara shook her head but it was Richard who replied.

"No, Ivara was curious about the disappearances, so I've been filling her in."

"And?" Jensin eyed her skeptically.

"And what?" She fired back. Ivara crossed her arms returning his expression.

"What do you think?" Jensin asked. She couldn't tell if he was mocking her or being genuine.

"I'm still learning your customs, much less your, your-." She struggled for the Allagorian word for 'language'. "your way of speaking. Why would you want *my* help?"

"Well it couldn't hurt. At the least I'd like to know your thoughts on the whole thing." Jensin replied.

Ivara thought for a moment.

"I suppose it is strange how none of the victims have any reliable contacts or stable points of reference but then again, if I were kidnapping or killing folk I'd go for people that would draw the least amount of attention. So I guess from that view it actually makes a lot of sense."

Jensin nodded ever so slightly. Was that approval on his face? She couldn't quite tell. Still, it was encouraging so she continued.

"What doesn't make much sense to me is the erm..." Once more she reached out for the foreign word. "shall we say storage."

Jensin and Richard exchanged confused looks but she went on.

"I mean to say that some of these people have been missing for over a year. Decomposition would begin immediately with bloating beginning anywhere from three to five days in. If your missing people have been dead for any amount of time then they would stink and most would have long since passed the beginning of their putrefaction. And that's not counting beasts that feed on the dead."

Richard made a disgusted face but Jensin lifted his eyebrows and leaned forward, listening intently. "From what Richard told me it is unlikely that whoever is stealing these folk off of the streets could afford to preserve them in any sort of way without drawing attention, but I still think you should check in with apothecaries and such. See if anything related to the process has been purchased lately even down to herbs."

Richard pursed his lips. "All this could just as simply mean they're alive." While his statement spoke of hope his tone was anything but.

"Which brings me to my second point. This is far too many people to keep in one place without drawing attention. You'd need thick stone walls and something underground like a cave or dungeon to contain the noise and resources like food and water to keep them alive. So, if your victims are still alive they're likely scattered. If they *are* all in one location they've almost certainly been drugged into silence. At least that is how it worked back home."

"How do you know all this?" Jensin asked. Richard didn't seem to notice his friend's suspicion but Ivara whipped her head around.

"What, surprised that I sport an education?" She countered. It was true. In the brief time since she had returned to Makoul her father had kept her busy with every tome and tutor available to them. He seemed desperate to catch her up on all that she'd missed while in the west.

"On matters such as these, yes. I hadn't heard of any universities in the east that allowed women to learn of such grotesqueness."

It was a game she realized. He had recognized her after all. And he wanted her to stay on edge. There was something else there too. If he had wanted to expose her he would have done so already. No he wanted the information she had to offer but he needed her to be clever enough to play along. She relaxed her shoulders quite deliberately and smiled at him.

"You live, you die... and dead that aren't attended to tend to smell quite foul with time. My older brother was an undertaker, it is his life's work. He would often bring me to work with him. I enjoyed watching him immerse himself in something that came so naturally to him." It was a complete lie; she had no brothers. But she'd heard enough from the rabble at the tavern to piece together a general idea of how the villagers cared for their dead. She just prayed that the two walker men didn't dig any further.

Jensin sat back and downed the rest of his ale. The copper haired walker considered her for a moment before wiping his mouth.

"Your brother must miss you." He said. The corner of his lips turned upward, but just barely. He knew she was lying, so why not out her to Richard?

"Not likely. He was much older than me, more likely he has his own land and children to look after now." Ivara uncrossed her arms and relaxed. She swung her head towards the door as it swung open to reveal a tall, bearded man in bright green boots.

"Show time." Jensin began to stand but Ivara took hold of his hand.

"Let me." It wasn't the deaths themselves that interested her but rather the 'markings' as Jensin had called them. Could they be related to her own marking? She needed to know. Perhaps some small part of her wanted to prove herself as well. Regardless, the words could hardly be taken back.

Jensin looked to Richard and the latter gave him a *what could go wrong* look. The copper haired young man sighed but ultimately relented.

"Fine. Remember to give a fake name. Something believable like Henrietta, Anna or Elizabeth. Do you know the docks well?"

"Sort of." She'd only traversed through there on her first day as a walker, but she'd seen much of the docks when she had still been mer. The thought of returning to the sea made her heart ache with longing, but she pushed it down trying her best to focus on the present.

"We want to lure him to a whore house near Grotumn. Also, the man's name is Ravik but I doubt he'll tell you of course. I think that's all. Got it?"

Ivara took a breath and then rose. "Got it."

As she made her way towards the man she couldn't help feeling expendable. Then again she was only a lowly serving wench to these surface dwellers.

The man was tall and muscular but not bulky. He looked older than Richard or Jensin by a good bit but his hair still retained its chestnut color, as did his beard and mustache. Ivara went to grab a cup of ale and pulled the chair adjacent to him. She slid into her seat and sat the ale in front of him. The man looked her up and down suspiciously.

"For you." She slid the ale closer to him.

"And to what do I owe the honor?" He asked dryly.

"I'm a client, or at least I hope to be by the end of this conversation." Ivara scooted her chair closer to the table that stood between them.

"Name?" He asked, his tone was bored but his posture gave him away. He was tense.

"Anna-Rose." She answered, briefly forgetting the names Jensin had given her. The Allagorian language was still so new to her. Every time she spoke it felt like she was chewing up every vowel and coughing up ever other sound.

"That's not an Allagorian name, and you don't look like one who hails from Thornhaven." *Shit.*

"Quite right. I'm not from Allagor. Neither is my target." She said with as much wit and confidence as she could muster. She knew Jensin and Richard were watching her from behind the curtain of their private booth in the corner of the room but she dared not glance back at them.

The man relaxed ever so slightly. "Alright tell me about the target."

"A young brunette woman. She goes by Heleen. I want you to kill her and bring me back her signet ring. You may dispose of the body as you see fit or keep it around if you'd like. I don't give a damn."

"The woman do you wrong?" He wasn't asking to be polite. No he was feeling her out. Looking for a slip up, any tell that she might be deceiving him.

"It's family business. I'm afraid the details would bore you."

"Try me."

Ivara didn't expect to have to give a backstory. She swallowed hard trying to pull something together.

"The girl is a cousin on my father's side. After my grandfather's passing her and her husband managed to steal the family wealth.

Now three years later, her parents and husband are dead and Heleen is the sole proprietor of a wealth that does not fully belong to her."

"Ahh, hence the signet ring. I suppose I shall be paid a healthy sum then?"

Ivara dropped her coin purse on the table. "You'll get the rest when you've retrieved the ring for me."

The man, Ravik, took a single coin from the pouch and began flipping it through his fingers. After a moment of silence he finally nodded to her. "Alright. I'll take the job. Where will I find the mark?"

Ivara sighed. "These days she frequents the whore house near Grotumn, you know the area I'm sure."

"Quite well. One might say it's my second home. Is your cousin a patron or an employee?"

"Patron." Ivara stood. "She prefers male wal—" Ivara stuttered realizing she had almost said walkers. "...male lovers. If that makes any difference. You will know her by her finery. Will you be needing any more details?"

"No, I think that is all. We will meet again in three days' time, here of course."

"Only three days?"

"I'm no novice darling. I'll have your ring back to you soon." He said, eyeing the coin. "Until then I'm sure I don't need to ask for your discretion on the matter."

"Of course." Ivara bowed her head to him.

"Good. See you in a few days then." With that Ravik got up and left. Ivara waited until the bars doors had completely shut behind him before she relaxed and let herself take a large sigh of relief. She returned to Jensin and Richard and sat back down.

"Well?" Jensin asked anxiously.

"He's going to kill a woman within the next three days, near Grotumn just like you said."

"I suppose you have a plan regarding the woman?"

Ivara nodded. "Actually I do. I'll play the mark, might need a wig and a bit of cosmetics but I think I can pull it off. When he comes for me you two and anyone else you see fit to bring step in."

Richard sat back and crossed his arms. "Not a bad plan."

"There are of course some things I'll need to buy beforehand." Ivara pursed her lips. But Richard pulled a coin purse from within his coat and dumped it on the table.

"Will that be enough?"

"I think so, yes." Ivara took the coin purse. "Anything I don't use I'll return."

Richard waved her off. "Don't worry about it."

Ivara smiled at the Prince. He wasn't all that bad looking and his chiseled jaw combined with his small smile made him even more handsome. Ivara thanked him and turned away blushing all the way back to the bar.

Chapter 25

Khipu sent to the King of Neroth by the royal families medic.

Tallulah (1555 A.D.)

"What did you say?" Brina looked at the servant with dread in her heart.

The dead eyed messenger repeated himself. "The Master has received notice that the royal family of Neroth will be arriving within the year. The Dragon has expressed his wishes for you to set your current studies aside in favor of readings regarding the rich culture and history of the Kingdom. You will be notified upon their arrival."

In a move that spoke of stress rather than Brina's normal excitement, she reached up and tore the khipu away from the servant, scanning it and rereading it over and over. The khipu was shorter than most that were found in the library and its knots were rushed.

"Why? Why are they coming here? Did the Dragon say?" Brina demanded.

"I do not know. I did not ask, nor will I. Take the khipu, keep it if you wish. I have more pressing matters to attend to." And with that the least interesting person in the Arkstone swam away.

Brina's gills flared in frustration and she tossed the khipu over her shoulder to sink to the floor.

"What's wrong? I thought the royal families of the south were relatively upstanding mer. Certainly the Prince of Neroth has a rather good reputation." Tallulah smirked. The local gentry's daughters seemed to think so.

"Well you haven't met any southerners. Their reputation does *not* proceed them." Brina huffed.

"What, and you have? Meaning no offense but are you the daughter of a Lord?" Corvena asked mockingly.

"No I –."

"Then what could you possibly know about the aristocratic side of society?" Corvena's question was rhetorical of course. She'd always looked down on Brina since they first met. "Have you ever even met anyone from high society outside of these dreadful meetings the Master forces us to attend with such individuals?"

"If you'd give me a moment to answer –." Brina began.

"You don't need a moment. It was a yes or no question." Corvena smirked as she said it. Tallulah opened her mouth to tell Corvena off but Brina beat her to it.

"Stinking sewage." Brina muttered.

"Excuse me?" Corvena said.

"I said you stink of sewage. You may think that you are so refined as the daughter of a Lord and that you're so pretty. And now of course since you have access to a bit of magic you *must* be better than everyone around you. And in a way you're right. You *are* beautiful. Your family *is* wealthy. And for all your faults you *have* improved in your magic skills over the past year. But make no mistake. On the inside you must be made of sewage grime that spills out into the sea from the walkers. I for one can think of no other explanation for your awfulness."

"I –." Corvena tried to interrupt her but Brina held up her hand.

"I'm. Not. Done. Do you honestly think that the King and Queen of one of the largest kingdoms in the south gives a damn about you? They don't even know you exist! Your only value to them is your magic. That's it. You can smirk and mouth off about how you're 'from the aristocracy' all you want. But if you try any of that around these people I promise, the *real* higher ups, the *real* aristocracy will eat you alive!"

Corvena was silent. Tallulah tried to find the words to dissolve the argument between her two friends but all she could do was sit there in shock. She'd never seen Brina erupt in such a volatile fashion. The older mer girl had always been supportive and kind to her. Going so far as to have what Tallulah had previously assumed to be something of an infinite well of patience for Corvena. It would seem the well had run dry. With a look of disgust Brina swam out of the room. Tallulah swam towards the room's exit but Corvena grabbed her arm.

"Are you really going after her after *that*?" Corvena spat.

"Don't lay that shit on me. *You* started this. *You're the one* who likes to push people as far as you can before they implode." Tallulah pulled out of Corvena's grip and followed after Brina. It didn't take her long to catch up with her golden sister.

"What?" Brina said. The words stung. Brina had always been gentle with her.

"I just wanted to make sure you're alright." Tallulah said quietly.

Brina put a single webbed hand to her head closing her golden eyes and sighed trying to master herself. Her golden tail slowly coming to a stop.

"I'm sorry. I shouldn't be taking my frustration out on you. I just..." Brina took another long breath. "I've met Neroth's royal family, and I don't look forward to meeting them again. It's put me on edge but still that's no excuse." Brina began to turn.

"Where are you going?"

"I think I need some time to cool down. Someplace where I can be alone with my thoughts." Brina offered a half smile.

"Well you're going the wrong way."

"Huh?"

"This is the way to Osirus' grotto. He likes his alone time as well." Tallulah told her.

Osirus had only been with them a year. A golden mer the same as her. Though Osirus was the only male among them. Tallulah knew the mer boy had been marked with a rune of infertility in order to join them.

For a brief moment Brina looked almost guilty. "Of course, I suppose I was so lost in my thoughts that I wasn't paying attention to where I was headed." With that she swam off in a different direction.

Chapter 26

Tallulah,

Tell your Master that Ivara is safe from Neroth's wrath. I had planned to retrieve her once this savagery blows over, however I fear there are larger problems at hand. The new king of Neroth is bold but he is not insane. He would not send his raiders this far north unless he was certain he could conquer it. Make no mistake the people still bear loyalty to the previous king's heir. You must convince your Master to release the princess... or we may all suffer the consequences.

Intercepted khipu from Scyla to Tallulah of the Arkstone

Ivara (1604 A.D.)

The following morning Ivara awoke to find a letter had been slipped under her door. Turning over in her sheets, she yawned and rolled out of bed. Martha had given her a thin white slip to sleep in. While she was incredibly grateful she still felt as if she might freeze over the second the blanket vanished from her body.

Shivering Ivara tiptoed into the golden sunlight where it streamed in through her window warming her with its rays. The sudden warmth caused her to yawn again and she stretched before picking up the letter. On the back her name had been written in Allagorian. Each letter connected in an exquisite display of elegant cursive.

She turned it over but there was nothing else written. Gingerly Ivara opened the envelope. A single piece of parchment sat snuggled inside. It read:

Dearest Ivara,

Though I find myself uneasy at the thought of placing you in harm's way, I also realize the importance of your mission. Thus I shall have my men stationed all over Grotumn for the next three days and nights. They will await your arrival and hopefully Ravik's as well. Should anything go wrong they have been ordered to tend to you immediately. Both Jensin and I will also be near. Unfortunately, I am not at liberty to give you exact locations but please know that we will not be far.

See you soon,

Richard

Ivara read the letter thrice before finally setting it down on her bed. She smiled to herself.

"See you soon." She whispered tracing over the words with her fingers.

The Prince's red headed friend might dislike her but the swoon worthy prince seemed to have taken a liking to her quite quickly, perhaps a little too quickly.

"Right then." She took out the bottle of brown dye she had purchased the previous night after her meeting with Ravik. Ivara removed the cap and got to work. She rubbed the mixture into her hair, massaging it into her roots and scalp. The dark brown mixture smelled strongly of perfume and ambergris. She held her breath through much of the process. After letting the mixture set for half an hour or so she went to her wash pot to ring it out.

Once her hair had been wrung out and she had dressed she sought out Martha who had eagerly agreed to do her hair for the next few days. Ivara hadn't realized how the different people of Allagor wore their hair so differently from one another until Jensin had pointed it out. Thankfully, they could rely on Martha where Ivara's appearance was concerned. Her ginger boss sat her down and got right to work.

White powder was applied to Ivara's face and a dark rouge cream was dabbed onto her lips. Her eyes were lined with kohl the same of which was lightly applied to her lashes. All the while her now dark brown hair sat in curls around her face. As a final touch Martha took a rosy colored powder and applied it to Ivara's cheeks.

"There, all done." Martha said sweetly as she finished wrapping an olive bow on the backside of Ivara's hair. Martha held up a looking glass and when she grinned at Ivara her smile spoke of a motherly pride.

Ivara tilted her head to either side admiring herself. Her dress was the color of sea grass. A deep green hue that demanded to be seen. At the center of her stay, however, was a pattern of olive vines and yew trees to contrast. In her curly brown hair she wore a bow to match. Her face was much paler now and her cheeks boasted a bright pink hue. Her lips had been made narrower by Martha's application of the rouge. There was a beauty in such an odd look. A sort of elegant façade that was so strange to her it was mesmerizing. She smiled and her doppler grinned back at her through the glass.

"Thank you."

Martha nodded. "Anytime, stay safe."

"I will."

"And you're sure the boys will be there as well? I don't like the idea of you alone in that area. It's known for having some unsavory characters."

"I'm counting on it." Ivara chuckled. "But yes, Richard and Jensin will both be around."

Martha waved to her as she left. Ivara's shoes clicked as she eagerly stepped onto the cobblestone outside the inn. The midday sun shone warmly on her face and she made her way towards Grotumn. Towards her mission.

When at last Ivara had finally arrived at the brothel she realized she wasn't sure what to do. Jensin had told her where to go, how to dress and so on but he had failed to mention how she might occupy herself if Ravik failed to appear. Ivara lowered her hood and decided to enjoy the sun while she waited. After all, who committed a murder in broad daylight?

She made a quick drive by of the vendors in the square. Most offered fake jewels and replica fineries from afar. A few offered to sell her food: bread, cheese, and bruised vegetables for the most part. Ivara opted for a wheat loaf and some cheese. The man thanked her, and she eagerly unwrapped the bread from its cloth realizing how her hunger had grown since she had forgotten breakfast. A grave mistake she would not soon repeat.

The first bite into the bread was anything but pleasant and she spit it out onto the street. Luckily, the cheese was a bit better. Ivara opted to feed the pigeons with her leftovers and the awkward looking birds seemed quite grateful.

She had just begun to doze, lulled into sleep by the sun's gentle warmth when a shadow cast a darkness over her eyelids. Ivara's eyes fluttered open. It was Ravik. He had dressed himself in commoners clothing and wore a cheery grin.

"May I?" He gestured to an empty seat on the bench.

"Of course." She tried to pitch her tone just a hair higher than when they had last spoken. Mimicking the way her sister Mele spoke in that honey sweet girlish way.

"I must say, the docks don't often sport such fine and dare I say wealthy beauties such as yourself."

"I've been told I have expensive tastes but if one can afford such luxuries then why hold back?" Ivara did her best to sound pompous.

"So now Allagor's wealthy come to the slums to feed the fowl?" Ravik asked.

"Not entirely, no. Actually, I have other business to attend to." When Ravik raised his brow in question she simply finished. "Certain personal matters." Ivara let her eyes drift towards the brothel for just a moment before looking back at her bench mate.

"Don't tell me you mean to go in *there*." His words dripped with a pompous sarcasm. But Ivara could tell he was fishing for information.

She stood to leave. "I don't believe that is any of your business Sir."

But no sooner had she turned that he grabbed her wrist and gently turned her around all the while eyeing the signet ring Jensin had loaned her.

"Nice ring. That's a signet ring if I'm not mistaken. Is it real gold?"

Ivara stomped in feigned infuriation as she let herself fully step into her role as Heleen. "Of course it is real gold! Do you think me some commoner?" Ivara took a long breath. "Now if you will please excuse me-." She tugged but Ravik held his grip on her.

"Heleen, isn't it?" It was not a question.

Ivara looked around. It was still light out; did he really think to kill her here? Out of the corner of her eye she saw movement, a figure with copper hair. She glanced but the figure was gone. Could it be that Jensin had really come in case things went south?

"What do you say we take this chat elsewhere? Someplace a bit more private." Ravik tightened his grip on her and dragged her toward the marina. She pulled against him but to no avail. Ivara tried to steady her breathing. She knew that her friends were near so why weren't they intervening? Ivara tried to calm herself but she was already shaking.

Ravik gripped her arm so tight it began to throb as he dragged her past several buildings and eventually onto the deck of a large ship. They journeyed below where Ivara could see two cages the size of small prison cells. Both were empty until Ravik threw her into the one closest and carefully closed and locked the cell door.

"Now, darling *Ivara, let's* talk."

Ivara froze. Her eyes widened, her mind replaying Ravik's words. "That's not-." She backed up against the curve of the hull at the back of her cell.

"It was a clever story; I'll give you that much." Ravik absently reached for his knife. Ivara tensed but he only grabbed an apple from a desk adjacent to her cell and began slowly and methodically slicing.

The pirate perched his feet on the desk and eyed her for a moment before continuing. "Don't take it personally dear, I would hardly be alive if I didn't have a healthy suspicion of all my clientele. Unfortunately for you a clever story and a bit of makeup was never going to pull it off."

Ivara swallowed hard and took a shallow breath. "What gave me away?"

"A few things actually. First and foremost, your choice of locale. I happen to frequent the fine establishment we discussed and being the observant man that I am I have never seen any clients with such a description as you gave. Secondly, perhaps you hadn't noticed, but my occupation is that of pirating and trafficking; it matters not if they are objects or people. That being the case, I'd like to think I know a mer when I see one. Especially one with such a thick accent."

"Mer?" Ivara gaped at him.

"Oh don't look so surprised. My nephew walks with more balance and he's two years of age. You're not fooling anyone who's actually seen a mer. Though I would like to know how you managed to shift into a human form. Magic like that, *real* magic, has always fascinated me."

Ravik offered her a slice of apple. She took it, it was green and tasted sour on her tongue. She made a face and the pirate chuckled.

"So on to business. We can do this the easy way or..." Ravik held up his blade, the apple juice glinting in the sparse sunlight that shown below deck as it dripped off the blade.

Ravik's terror came in part from his calm demeanor, Ivara thought to herself as she watched him. She'd always imagined villains to be ugly, chuckling big strong men and mer with huge swords and evil grins. But here was a lean man, relaxed in the knowledge that he was in control.

He did not need scare tactics. No threats or menacing chuckles. Just a man and his apple were enough. Because they both knew that every breath that Ivara took in his presence was at his pleasure. That casual control...it was terrifying. She wondered briefly how many other villains roamed the human realm wearing their mundaneness as a disguise. Ivara made herself inch towards him until she was at the bars. She cleared her throat and began.

"What do you want from me?" She tried with all her will to make the words sound casual, unbothered.

Ravik looked up towards the light at something Ivara seemingly could not see. He ignored her question before sneezing. "Apologies, allergies. Where were we? Oh yes. Don't you want to hear my terms first? Or are you so eager to spill more of your false story."

Ivara gritted her teeth. "Fine. What are your terms?"

"Simple, I will ask you certain questions, if you answer truthfully you will be released, as soon as the information is verified of course. I can hardly return to my boss empty handed after catching a mer. She'd gut me, or worse and I don't intend to be one of her little experiments."

"And if I lie?"

Ravik thought for a moment. Ivara thought she might have caught him off guard but the pirate was quick witted and fast in his reply.

"If you lie, I shall open you up and see for myself if the mer are at all similar to us on the inside. Oh don't give me that look I'm not so awful as to drug you or kill you, I shall allow you to be fully present for the entirety of my investigation. Then we can both see what a lying whore looks like on the inside."

"Alright. Fair enough." She didn't doubt he would use the knife on her. But she still tried to keep calm.

Ravik smiled. "I had thought you might agree. Let's begin with the big one. My erm *services, how* did you come by them? *Remember*." He twirled the blade in his hand.

"A friend. I've managed to make many friends near the docks. After that it was just a matter of asking the right people."

"Right people?"

"You know, the ones who know how to keep their mouths shut."

"Does this friend have a name?"

"Yes, but I can hardly pronounce it."

"*Try*." His voice was stone cold.

Ivara thought. She couldn't say Richard, he was the most well-known man for miles. It had to be someone else but she didn't know anyone else besides Jensin. When she pushed herself to recall Martha's patrons her mind drew a blank.

"Scepious." She blurted. Where were they? Jensin had promised not to put her in any real danger! Did Prince Richard's heart felt note mean nothing? Or perhaps he was just trying to assure she did not have second thoughts. Had something gone wrong? Panicked thoughts mingled in her mind.

"I knew the fool had a loose tongue. Thank you, now what was the purpose of the façade? The cousin story was too elaborate for a quick laugh, and no woman would be stupid enough to pull something like this alone."

"I owed a friend of mine a favor, so they asked me to tell the lie and get dressed up to meet you. I wasn't privy to much beyond that."

He eyed her for a moment. "A half-truth but we'll leave it for now."

As he spoke Ivara could hear the wood above them creak with the sound of footsteps and the clash of swords. Ravik sighed and put a hand to his temple. "Damn, this really was going quite well."

No sooner did the pirate stand than did the port door above them fly open and standing there in the blazing sunlight of the setting sun, covered in blood and wearing a wicked grin was Jensin. He was dazzling and absolutely terrifying all at once.

Jensin thrust his blade downward making his way down the steps but Ravik pulled out his own much larger blade. It was not an equal fight. Immediately it was apparent to Ivara that Ravik had far more experience in which his life had been on the line. When he swung his curved sword, it was like a dance. Each stroke flowing into the next with the intent to kill as the only alternative was his own death. Ravik's blade spoke of survival while Jensin's spoke of victories won amongst trainers and friends.

The accumulation of winning many practice matches and a few in the field combined with his already incredibly high adrenaline made him confident. When her red headed friend swung his blade there was no caution.

"Get away from her!" Jensin yelled in a fury.

The two danced around one another in their respective intents. Ravik struck like an adder while Jensin charged like a bull. But then, finally, the adder struck and the bull could not recover. Jensin screamed a string of words she had never before heard as Ravik, fast as ever, thrust his blade into Jensin's foot, were it not for a quick side step Jensin might have had a nub in place of a foot.

Ivara shook the barred door to her cell, even as she knew she couldn't get out without the keys. Then behind her there was a deep growling sound and she whirled around to see a beast staring at her. It was the same that she'd seen so many times both in wakefulness and in her night terrors. A hallucination, it had to be, she knew nothing so large could fit inside such a small cell but that didn't stop the great golden dragon from appearing before her.

I'm going crazy. This isn't real. This can't be real.

She thought her heart might stop beating from the fear. It shouldn't have fit inside the cell, it's head alone was much too large. Her breath was coming in short gasps now and she was shaking. Above her the door shut and when she turned around Ravik was gone. She looked back over her shoulder but the dragon too had vanished. Ivara was shaking violently now, she could feel her lungs closing up inside her. She screamed and sobbed with confusion and terror, no longer sure of what was real and what was a waking nightmare.

"Ivara!"

She looked up to where Jensin had slid down into a pool of his own blood. Seeing her acknowledgement, he threw something at her. It was only when it landed just outside the bars did she realize he had swiped the pirates keys. Ivara stood and hastily worked through the keys trying them each until she finally found a winner. She flung the door open and ran to her friend kneeling down beside him.

"I can't carry you but I will help you walk." She said to him between rasping breaths, still terrified to turn and see the golden beast lurking somewhere in the shadows of the ship.

Jensin nodded but he wasn't able to speak through the pain as she aided him to the steps. Ravik had disappeared to the top of the ship. Jensin leaned heavily on the wall while Ivara ran up the first few steps and tried to open the door. It wouldn't budge. She tried to peep through the cracks in the wood but something heavy had been placed on top of the door. However, so close to the door she was able to smell something. The smell was new to her, odd in a way.

"What is it?" Jensin muttered; his face now pale from the lack of blood.

"The doors jammed or locked or something." The adrenaline in her blood made her fumble with her words. "And there's this smell, like soot but also the inn on a cold day. I don't know how else to describe it." She said apologetically.

"That's ok I do." There was however nothing 'ok' in his tone. "It's a fire, *damn it*!"

"But if he locked us down here then the fire can't get to us right?"

"Doesn't matter, the smoke inhalation will kill us first anyways."

Ivara swallowed. "How do you get rid of a fire?"

"Water, lots of water."

They both looked at one another as the same idea came into full focus for both of them at the same time.

"Look for something sharp or heavy!" Jensin yelled but Ivara had already begun moving. She searched for any dry rot on the ship. She'd seen shipwrecks before outside of Makoul. It was always the bottom of the hull that was the most damaged. Ivara dug through the ship's cabinets until she found a large sword similar to Ravik's and wedged it into a weak spot in the wood. Jensin was silent as he pushed himself trying not to pass out from the pain. Ivara pushed but neither the blade nor wood would budge. She could smell the fire now and her eyes were beginning to burn. Ivara threw herself into her makeshift levy and there was a popping noise: a single plank of wood loosened enough to let water in.

"Ok new problem." Jensin said. "We need to get out of here before the ship floods."

"Right." Ivara swore under her breath.

"Can you swim?" She asked.

"Decently well, yes. You?"

"Not anymore!" She motioned to her legs in a panic.

Ivara shoved the sword back down and managed to pop out another piece of the rotting plank. The hull was flooding quickly now and water was coming up to Ivara's ankle. Ivara kept at her task. Out of the corner of her eye she could see Jensin slumped over on the ground.

She worked quickly until a hole just large enough for her to squeeze into was flooding the ship. She grabbed Jensin and helped him in. He yelled out when his injured foot bumped something in the water but continued to shove himself through the hole until he was all the way through and she could see his one good foot kicking him towards the surface. Ivara swallowed hard and followed after him, feet first.

When the water was at her chin she took a breath and pushed herself through. The water was cold and sent shivers all throughout her body. When she opened her eyes everything was a blur. The blue world around her no longer presented itself in perfect clarity. Another reminder that Scyla hadn't just taken her tail. The temptation to open her mouth and try to breathe was like a weight made even worse by the burning sensation in her chest as she flailed in the water. All her efforts and she was hardly rising.

The burning in her chest grew and she felt the water shift around her. Ivara looked towards the burning ship she had just escaped from. It was sinking and she was unable to swim out from under it. Ivara flailed as she sank further down. She opened her mouth to scream but instead found sea water flooding her. Her vision ebbed away but in the distance she could spot a blurry dark figure twisting its way through the water.

As the figure came into focus she could see a deep blue tail and smooth pale skin. Long dark hair and bright blue eyes reminiscent of her sea blue tale. It was Uhane. They'd found her, finally, they had come to claim her. Ivara was certain of it. Scyla had surely sent her older sister here to rescue her from this land. It was the last thing Ivara saw before the burning in her chest consumed her and her vision went completely black.

Chapter 27

"It has been said that the royal family of Neroth has a rather complex relationship with its members. Though to anyone who has been properly informed on the kingdom's history this should come as no surprise. Neroth, after all, has been known for generations as the 'conquerors of the south'."

Excerpt from *Royal Families Of The Sea* by Freya Burg

Brina (1555 A.D.)

Brina swam on, with Tallulah in tow, the water getting warmer the closer she got to the surface. She coughed; all around her the sea was getting cloudy. Confused, she let herself surface, releasing her breath. The air above the sea burned her face and upon looking around she spotted its source immediately. A ship on fire, it's occupants jumping off their sinking vessel in desperation. She sank back under the waves to find one of the walkers flailing about in the waves. He was sinking and choking. Brina grabbed him and brought him up above the waves but the fire was too much. She felt a hot stinging sensation on her hands and yelped letting go of the man. When she tried to grab him again he was no longer moving. Just sinking into the abyss. She watched the dead man sink until he was out of sight and clutching her hand resumed her journey.

"What do you think? Walker war or just a sailor mishandling explosives?" Brina asked Tallulah when they stopped to rest.

The mer girl shrugged. "I'm not sure it matters all that much. Regardless, those bodies and debris will likely find their way to the Arkstone within the coming days."

Brina sighed. "You're right." She had hoped today would be sunny and warm. A day to calm all her worries. A day without death and forlorn thoughts. Perhaps it was the turning of the seasons, or perhaps despair and misery were the price of becoming a young adult. She longed for the days of her childhood when she had no responsibilities. When she first realized her freedom from her family and when she was naïve enough to believe that such freedom would allow her to live as she pleased. She looked back at Tallulah. Still a child in many respects Tallulah had become something of a little sister to Brina in the past years. Someone to be protected. A vessel to place the love that she might have shown her twin brother had the dragon not forsworn her from visiting him.

"Swim back to the Arkstone, tell the Dragon that there is trouble brewing amongst the walkers. And tell him about the debris headed west." Brina said gently. It was safer this way, they were hardly out of the outer ring of the city so Tallulah would be able to get back quickly.

Tallulah nodded dutifully. "And you?"

"I'll head to the grotto. I need to speak to Osirus."

Tallulah smiled. "Tell Osirus hello for me." Brina nodded. She knew Tallulah felt guilty for not spending any time with Osirus. They all knew their new golden brother must feel lonely. Of all of them Osirus seemed to be the odd one out at every turn. For starters he was the only boy in the group. On top of that he had only joined their group of golden maidens the year before. And for all their duties it was rare that any of them got to interact for very long. Brina did her best to make time in between her own duties and studies.

It was some time before she reached Osirus' grotto. At first glance the grotto seemed empty but a slight movement near the sand gave Osirus away. She swam down to greet him. A genuine smile on her face.

"Don't tell me, the Dragon has another task for us." He moaned.

"Yes, unfortunately. The king and queen of Neroth will be arriving by the end of the year." She exhaled letting all her nerves and anxiety come to the surface. Osirus's brow crinkled as he looked her over.

"What happened to your hand?"

"Just a burn." She replied.

"May I?" Osirus reached out anxiously. She gave him her hand but winced when he ran his dark hands over it. He took a bone blade from among his things and began carving a small healing rune into her palm. The pain of the rune was worse than the initial burn but she did her best to stay composed. "Where did you even find fire? I never took you for someone who visits walker harbors."

"The surface, it was a ship fire."

"And you swam towards it?"

"No. I, I saw this walker drowning and I wanted to help." She looked down. "But I couldn't help him and now he's dead."

Osirus' expression was serious now. "You shouldn't go near fire; it could kill you."

Her gills flared with frustration. Osirus was only a year younger than her and aside from Corvena, was the most frank with her. Usually she enjoyed having someone speak to her without meandering around, trying not to hurt her feelings but in the moment it just angered her. "I told you I was just trying to help." It was suffocating, the pressure the Dragon put on her, the responsibility , the magic. Feeling the beginnings of headache Brina changed the subject.

"Do you ever think of your family?"

"I do."

"Do you miss them?" She asked him.

"Yes, I miss my parents and brother but most of all I miss my little sister." He sighed mournfully. "You two would have gotten along quite well. She was very kind as you are, though not nearly as patient." He chuckled.

"What happened to her?" Brina asked.

"She was born blind, which is quite common within the northern kingdoms. But aside from her sight she was a healthy child. As she aged she began to have headaches more and more frequently, first just a few times a year but slowly they increased in both amount and intensity until it became a daily occurrence. She was still just a tad and the headaches became so bad that eventually she would stuff her ears with sea grass so that no sound could make the problem worse. My mother asked our alderman about it and he sent us to the Arkstone. The medics here kept asking my parents when she first went blind. I remember being so confused by the question at the time."

"Why would they waste time with such questions, why not give her healing runes?"

"They tried. No healing rune would work—they all just brought her more pain. Until finally one of the Dragon's medics cracked it. 'The girl has a disease.' They told us. 'One whose emerging symptoms are a lack of seeing and migraines.' The runes weren't working because the disease fed on her mind."

"...and healing runes only work on flesh wounds." Brina finished.

"She passed a few months later. We were all a mess but it was my mother who was the worst. She couldn't speak, could hardly look at me or my brother. And the wailing, day and night. Screaming and wailing until her voice was raw. It hurt seeing her in so much pain.

I barely had room to deal with my own grief for wanting to help my mother. It was my brother though who came up with the idea, to help her that is. Once my father told my mother and they agreed we were once more off to the Arkstone. The mer here agreed to give her an amnesia rune, for a price of course." He gestured to himself.

"I suppose it's for the best though, I don't think I could live the rest of my life pretending she didn't exist. At least here I can miss her, and grieve for her freely." His voice was sober. Grief mingled with acceptance in his voice. "What about you? Do you have any family?" He asked.

"I have a twin brother. We were our parents' only children. My parents wanted my brother to inherit their... estate, territories, and titles. But they were afraid if anything happened to my brother that other family members might try to sweep the estate out from under them. So to avoid this they decided not to marry me away but rather to lend me to the Golden Dragon. No trade, they wanted nothing in return. I'm not angry, just a bit sad. I could happily live the rest of my days without seeing my parents again, but my brother is an entirely different matter. I miss him every day." Brina took a deep breath. She could see her brother's young smiling face in front of her. Her only memento of a life now out of her reach.

Chapter 28

Remember the prophecy. Remember your mission. Should you fail, it is not just you who will suffer the consequences. We must do anything... even the unspeakable to avoid this war. The girl must die.

.

Intercepted correspondence sent from an unknown contact to
Lady Rhea of Allagor

Ivara (1604 A.D.)

Ivara made a choking sound as water rushed out of her lungs. It was violent and every breath burned. Smooth slippery palms flipped her over so that her face was in the sand and she wretched until she could once more breathe without fear of choking. When she was finally able to breathe Ivara looked around for her savior, for her sister. Instead, she found Richard hovering over her, a terrified expression plastered to his pale face.

"Richard?" Ivara looked around for Jensin. A flash of movement in the water caught her eye and she could see two cold blue eyes outlined by long onyx hair staring at her before dipping under. Ivara put a hand to her temple and groaned at the mounting headache that resided there as she tried to draw Richard's attention away from where Uhane watched them off shore.

"Are you alright?" She nodded weakly and he put an arm around her waist and placed one of hers on his shoulders. With their efforts combined Ivara was able to stand though she still heavily leaned on the Prince.

"Where are we going? Where's...where is Jensin?" Ivara asked exhaustedly as they treaded across the warm sand. Richard must have removed her corset via knife as she could see it lying not far from them on the beach. As for her shoes, she faintly remembered kicking them off in her failed escape. Ivara let the Prince lead her up and down the mid beach slope until they reached a black mare that had been patiently awaiting them. Ivara looked around but there was only one horse.

"Jensin took the other one. He was well enough to ride so I sent him on ahead. I told him to go ahead and that I'd take care of you. Ivara whatever happened... he was terrified for you."

"Thank you but where..?"

"The castle." He answered once they were both on the mare. Richard took a moment to adjust himself behind her then reached around and gently took hold of the reins bringing the horse to a canter. "There's an infirmary there that can treat you."

"I'm... fine really." Ivara said into the wind.

"No offense but you look anything *but* fine."

"Thanks." Ivara replied exhaustedly but if the Prince had heard her he did not respond. They rode on, to the clacking sound of the horse's hooves on the cobblestone for nearly an hour before Ivara, in her deep and thorough exhaustion began to doze.

She could feel Richard's warm arms tucked around her waist keeping her from falling forward and so leaned heavily against him, letting her head fall into the crook of his shoulder. If he minded he did not say anything. Her mind drifted in that light sleep slowly coming to terms with the events of the evening. Cementing them in her memory as fact rather than some strange fiction.

She'd seen it again, in that cage that Ravik had put her in. The beast. No that wasn't the word. *Dragon.* A winged creature dipped in molten gold, and covered in glittering scales. She knew it wasn't real but not for the reasons that she should have. A more logical, evidence driven mind would point out the obvious signs. For one,

Jensin never made mention of such a creature. Though he had been preoccupied during the fight, Ivara rather thought he might have said something to her even with everything else going on. Then there was the fact that dragons were not real.

These *should* have been the thoughts running through Ivara's mind. Clear and factual statements that would point her toward a physician. Thoughts that would lead her to the direct and undisputable conclusion that she had been in fact hallucinating. But when in the history of all that has come to be have things ever been so simple?

Instead Ivara's mind swirled with thoughts she didn't quite understand and yet on one of the deepest levels of her mind, perhaps even her soul it did make sense to her. Of course it was a hallucination, dragons were much, *much* larger than that! The beast she had seen in that ship had scales the size of her hands. Far too small from what she would expect a real dragon to have. Secondly a real dragon could never have fit in any boat made by walkers much less a small cell on a pirate's vessel. To even entertain such an idea of a small dragon was laughable. Indeed in her dozing she chuckled to herself just a bit.

Thirdly, Ivara had never actually seen a dragon in her life. Though she'd heard many legends and myths. Fairy Tales and bedtime stories as a child, they were just that. A fiction told to children. Therefore, whatever she was seeing must be some result of stress mixed with her imagination. Her thoughts continued to wander as she sank further and further into that coveted relaxed state of sleep. Until she felt the horse slow and she forced herself to wake. Richard helped her down but she still landed rather hard, wincing as her knees took the brunt of her clumsy fall.

The castle was massive. One of the largest buildings Ivara had ever seen! Stone walls of grey towered around them as they made their way through the front gate. Ivara had regained enough strength now to walk on her own and so let Richard lead her by the arm up the steps toward the infirmary. Once inside they passed many guards who nodded to the prince. Walking on Ivara noticed a woman, older than Richard but not by much, reading on a bench in the hall. The ebbing sun cast her strawberry blond hair aglow and made her look like a pale angel in the light. She looked up briefly from her book and smiled warmly at both of them.

"You'd better hurry. They had to give Jensin something to calm him after he awoke to find you hadn't yet arrived." She said to the prince.

"Is he awake now?" Richard asked worriedly.

"Oh no. The sedatives should have kicked in by now. Who's this?" The woman nodded to Ivara. Her tone was curious but not at all unkind.

"Ivara, she was hurt in the wreckage, I'd like to get one of the medics to look her over before we send her back to Martha's inn."

"Of course but why bring her to the palace? Surely there were dozens of herbalists in town. And there are certainly dozens if not hundreds of medics and apothecaries between the palace and harbor, why did you not take her to one of them?"

Richard blushed; he'd been called out. "She was working with Jensin to exploit the Ravik situation and it was dangerous. She put her life on the line for us, she deserves competent medical care. Besides Jensin was... worried."

The woman put up her hands in defeat. "No need to get defensive, I'll go fetch a healer." She stood and was off.

Ivara twisted her head to look over at Richard, wincing when it was painful to do so. "Who was that?"

"Princess Everleigh, she was to be my sister in law. That was before my brother went missing, now she is to be my wife." He cleared his throat. "No more talking until you're well, come on we're nearly there. Just down this hall."

Ivara looked down at the bench where the woman had left her book. The title read, *The Prejudice of the Mer Folk*, an interesting title to find in a walker kingdom Ivara thought. Perhaps the walkers were just as curious about the mer as the mer were about them. Richard led her into the infirmary where she found an empty cot to finally sit down. The room was large and while most beds were empty the few that were taken up seemed to be by those who had fallen sick due to natural causes. A few beds down Ivara spotted a pale lanky figure with fiery red hair snoring. She smiled at the sight, perhaps the first and last time she might see a totally relaxed Jensin. His foot had been wrapped in bandages and propped up on a wooden block.

"Are you feeling any better?" The Prince asked her. Still no sign of a healer or the Princess.

"I told you before I feel fine. Just-" She yawned heavily. "...exhausted is all."

"Rest, I'll go fetch an apothecary, since Princess Everleigh seems to have gotten lost."

She smiled at him as he left. Indeed she was still tired. Deathly so. Ivara didn't remember putting her head to the freshly cleaned pillow nor could she recall falling asleep but when she awoke the next morning to the first rays of sun, and the singing of birds, the previous day's events came back to her in sweeping succession.

The infirmary was empty save for a few souls still asleep in their cots and a single young woman who sat wrapping bandages and folding cloth. Her skin was an almond color and freckles covered her face highlighting her beauty as she shifted in the sunlight. A combination of dark brown curly tendrils fell from the ribbon at the back of her head and her purple eyes seemed to glow in the sun. She looked to be younger than Ivara but not by much. The girl jumped when she spotted Ivara and hurriedly walked over.

"How do you feel?" She asked sweetly. Her voice like honey.

"Much better, thank you I, um well I hadn't meant to stay overnight." Ivara replied sheepishly.

The woman laughed brightly. "I think you're in like-minded company on that line of thought." She said gesturing around the room to the other patients. "I'm Kirsten, by the way. I assist the medics in the mornings, mostly just to make sure everyone sleeps through the night. I'm not actually a nurse though. More of a glorified servant truth be told." Despite her bright tone, and kind expression there was a certain sourness hidden in her words.

"Well, I suppose that works because I'm not actually sick." Ivara replied half smiling at the girl.

The two women laughed for a moment, then Kirsten replied.

"I heard about yesterday. Is it true you were kidnapped by pirates?" Her purple eyes were wide like a child waiting to be told their favorite story. Ivara realized the woman might be a bit younger than she had first suspected. Likely about fifteen or sixteen in terms of walker lifespans.

"Sort of. More like a plan gone astray. I was helping Jensin and Prince Richard with something." She said with a small smile.

"Oh like a spy?" Despite her excitement, the girl's smile faltered. "You ought to be careful with such work. Spies or at least those accused of such treachery tend not to last long here in Allagor."

Again, her bright smile and girlish gaze hid something darker, something far more brutal than the girl was willing to reveal.

"Sort of." Ivara chuckling at the ridiculousness of it all. She ran her hands through her hair as she explained. "I don't think I managed to get them any decent information. I suppose I'm not really cut out for such things. Perhaps my skills are limited to serving drinks."

Kirsten put a hand to her mouth to hide her giggling laughter. The sound was like a babbling brook, lithe and happy. It took her a few minutes to fully master herself. "Did you at least catch the pirate?"

Ivara shook her head. "I'm not sure. Jensin and I got ourselves locked in the hull of the ship. To be frank with you we were much less concerned with Ravik as we were with escaping."

"Ravik?" Her eyes narrowed in thought, all traces of laughter gone from her face as she thought.

Ivara waved her hand. "Yes, sorry, he was the pirate."

Kirsten's face turned serious. "I've heard the name before. Obviously, I've never met the man but I've heard talk that he might be involved in certain folk going missing." She gestured all around. "People talk."

The girl before her was strange, while her demeanor was quite childlike there was no small amount of intelligence behind her purple eyes. It was unsettling, but Ivara reminded herself, these people were not like her own. Perhaps she would never be entirely used to their mannerisms, she thought to herself as she continued on.

"Jensin's heard the same, unfortunately now we'll never know." Ivara slumped, her head in her hands.

"Don't look so glum, I'm sure you did your best." Kirsten said smiling.

"Yes, well sometimes that just isn't enough." Ivara huffed standing. She looked down at her grimy green dress caked in dried mud and sand. "Do you think I could um..."

Kirsten's eyes widened in understanding. "Oh yes! Of course." She looked Ivara up and down. "Hmm you could probably fit into one of my gowns, just be sure to return it by the end of the week." She winked at Ivara. "Stay here, I'll be right back." Kirsten said before rushing off.

Ivara looked around, Jensin she realized was fully awake, though he hadn't moved. She stood and walked over to his cot ignoring her own soreness. He was watching her as she sat down on the edge of bed.

"Ow." He said dryly. His face tight with annoyance and pain as the bed curved under Ivara's weight.

"How's your foot?" She said attempting to cut through the curtain of tension and unanswered questions that hung between them.

"Aside from the gaping hole?"

Ivara winced.

"I'm joking, don't look so concerned. Ravik didn't get too deep. Might need a cane for a few weeks though."

Ivara gave him a confused look and he sighed deeply.

"Sorry, I forgot. They are walking aids, for certain leg and foot injuries. They help the wounded to not put so much weight on, well, their wound. Don't you have something similar where you come from?"

Ivara thought for a moment. "No not really, of course if one has an injury we have splints and such. Then again everything is so much... heavier above the water line."

"You need not remind me." Jensin shuddered. "I don't wish to ever be near the sea again."

"At least you can swim!" Ivara said indignantly.

Jensin choked on his laughter. "I'm surprised you can't!"

Ivara made a face and started to reply but just then Kirsten returned. She carried a pale yellow gown with blue and gold lace. "Woah."

"What do you think?" Kirsten looked over the garment fondly. "I made the gown to my own measurements, but I don't think you'll be too far off. Just in case though, let me know if it doesn't fit and I can try and find something else." Her voice sparkled as she spoke.

Ivara took the gown and held it up to herself. It was beautiful. "You *made* this?"

Kirsten went red and tucked into herself. "Well, yes. It's a bit of a hobby of mine. When I have the time, it's also much cheaper than buying gowns from the market." She added the last part quickly.

"It's beautiful, thank you." She exclaimed. "Where might I go change?"

"Oh that's right!" A light went off behind Kirsten's purple eyes. Jensin and Ivara exchanged a curious glance as Kirsten took Ivara by the arm and led her out. "His majesty, Prince Richard asked that I show you to your room."

"My room?" Ivara raised her eyebrows at Jensin.

But her new copper haired friend just smiled and shrugged.

"What, you really thought we would let you risk your life only to throw you back to the wolves?" He said. Despite his flippant tone she could tell there was far more to the decision than was being presented to a lowly barmaid such as herself. Afterall only moments ago she hadn't been aware that she even *had* a room.

"I'm not privy to the details but my cousin, the Prince made it seem like you'd be staying with us for some time." Kirsten added brightly. Her whole body seemingly engaged in her sprightly demeanor. It was then that Ivara noticed the pearl necklace adorned with an obsidian jewel. The necklace kept twisting revealing a symbol carved into its backside that was only visible to the keen eye. Ivara gestured to the accessory.

"It's beautiful."

Kirsten quickly put a hand to her chest again turning red. "Oh it's nothing." She waved Ivara's comment off.

Ivara grinned. "Hmm let me guess, a gift from a secret lover?" Kirsten looked.

"No." The girl whispered her hand clutching the jewel even tighter now. "It was my mothers."

They walked on for a time making small talk until finally arriving at one of the castle's many guest rooms. Kirsten led her through the large wooden door and Ivara could feel her jaw drop. The room was far more grand than she might have ever suspected. A large bed all made up with layers of fine fabrics and sheets and adorned with red and purple pillows sat in the corner of the room. Beside it a dresser that she could never hope to fill. In the center a large rug with intricate floral designs. On the wall to the right of the bed, sun streamed in through the window illuminating a small white letter that lay on the bed. Ivara turned the letter over, it was indeed addressed to her in the Prince's fine cursive. She smiled tentatively as she opened it.

My Dear Friend Ivara,

It is my hope that you have recovered from your recent injuries. Ivara rolled her eyes, they both knew she was hardly injured at all, still she read on. *Assuming this to be the case I would invite you to join me on an expedition of similar purpose tomorrow morning. I have had the servants lay out appropriate garb for such an outing. I hope you won't find them too unladylike.*

Indeed beside the note there lay a cream colored blouse and a pair of leather trousers. She smiled and went back to the letter.

P.S. Don't tell Jensin about this. It may make him quite ill.

P.S.S. Wear comfortable shoes. Trust me.

Yours, Richard.

"Well? What did it say? Has my dear cousin asked you out to a pleasant picnic in the gardens?" Kirsten asked. Ivara stammered for a moment. She had forgotten Kirsten was in the room with her.

"It's just an invitation to spend the evening together." As the words left her mouth she cringed, knowing exactly how it must have sounded. "But not like that!"

Too late. Kirsten's grin grew and she snatched the dress from Ivara.

"You can try this on later. I'll put it here." She said carefully laying the dress on the edge of the bed. "You however have a date. So I'd advise you to get your beauty sleep! There's a nightgown in the dresser if you wish to take a short nap. Send for me if you need anything! I'm never far." Kirsten whisked away, with the giddiness of a child. A small smile slipped onto her face. No it wasn't a date, so why was she so excited?

Chapter 29

"I have only just returned to my home in Ellenward. My travels have shown much, but perhaps most interestingly the way the rest of the world views prophecies. It seems our sisters and brothers in the east put little to no faith in seers and such. That said, even the Allagorians, stubborn though they are, keep records of the Dolah. Perhaps we are not so crazy after all."

The Prophecies Of Northerners by Alec E. Kalith

Ivara (1604 A.D.)

Ivara was up at dawn. She got dressed hurriedly and ran down the grand staircase nearly tripping over herself as she did so. Each minute was like an eternity as she waited for the Prince to appear. When he finally did appear she was surprised to see that he had dressed quite similarly to herself. The prince wore a matching cream top and brown pants, as well a long overcoat to conceal both a knife and sword at his belt. Seeing Ivara's lingering glance Richard took her by the hand.

"Come with me." He said, leading her down a slim dark stairwell.

"Um, are you taking me to the dungeons?"

Richard chuckled. "The armory actually. Given your last endeavor I thought you might like to have something a bit more...well you'll see." He said, pushing open the heavy wooden door. There was little light in the armory as the entry of it was lit by a single window and a small number of lamps. Swords hung on either wall and racks of armor both new and old stood on mannequins throughout. Servants traveled in and out pretending not to notice either of them. Richard went to the adjacent wall returning only once he had spotted his prize. The blade was just longer than her arm. Richard held it out to her. "The blade's name is *Aurum*. It's one of the armory's shorter broadswords, but I figured it would fit you."

Ivara took the blade by its handle and swung it. "Thank you, but I've never used such an instrument."

She wished she weren't lying to him. That she truly was here to help, and not just searching for answers about Makoul and her memory in the absence of the witch.

"I'll teach you when we get back. For now all you need to know about Aurum is that it is one handed and light." He said, gently taking her second hand off the handle. "And it is very, very sharp. Oh and here's the scabbard and a belt."

Ivara, with Richard's help, managed to tighten the belt accordingly and adjust the sword so that the harness wasn't digging into her side. Though the extra weight still threw her off a bit. An hour or so later found them both atop their horses. Richard, on his mare from a few days ago and Ivara astride a tawny male paint.

At first riding on her own had frightened her. She was not used to being so high up and unlike her home, falling above water usually meant a painful injury. However as they rode on her fear turned to thrill and eventually a solemn appreciation for the gentle beast. The horse seemed to know its way and followed dutifully after his female counterpart.

They rode on at a steady trot down the cobblestone roads through the city. Together they passed hostels and taverns, trade squares and brothels. The people and their customs breathed life into the city they rode through. Eventually they arrived at a large stone building nearly the size of the palace. Columns stood on either side of the building's huge, adorned archways. Ivara stared in awe.

"What is this place?" She asked as she dismounted and followed Richard to a public stable.

"The great library of King Dameon. Most scholars date it as over five hundred years old."

"Incredible." Ivara whispered. "But what are we doing here?"

"While our last plan did go awry it wasn't a total failure."

Ivara went red with shame. "So Ravik got away?"

"Yes, but like I said, not a total failure. I have a hunch but I'll need to do a bit of research to confirm."

"And you brought me along because...?" She didn't mean it to be rude but of all people Richard knew best how poor her reading skills were.

"I thought you might appreciate a quiet place to practice your reading. If you're feeling brave enough though you're more than welcome to help me look."

They walked through the grand cathedral like archway passing men and women alike, all highborn from the looks of their custom tailored garb and fine jewelry. A sense of wonder filled her at the sheer vastness that surrounded her. Endless hallways of which she could not see the end lined with books, tomes, and scrolls. More than any one man or mer could read. She walked beside Richard and together the two entered a grand room with huge ceilings. Row upon row of shelves filled with books and in the center many long rectangular tables sat so close together that at such a distance as they stood it appeared to be a single long piece. On either side was a wide grand staircase that led to two more floors. Richard took her by the hand and led her up the steps to the top floor. Special tables stood at regular intervals sporting lanterns but thanks to the many windows and good weather there was plenty of light.

"What exactly are we looking for?" Ivara asked once Richard had settled on a shelf.

"Do you want the short version or the long?"

Ivara looked around. It wasn't even midday yet. They had time. "Long."

Richard looked over his shoulder and grinned at her. "Alright so Jensin told you that we suspected Ravik of working with local criminals." Ivara nodded. "What we didn't tell you was *why* we suspected Ravik. I've had one of the Children of Whispers trailing the pirate for the past month and a half." Seeing her confused look he explained. "The Children are peasants that work for the palace. They blend in well with the locals. They're not actually children of course."

Ivara nodded thinking how strange walker customs were. "So what have these 'children' told you? Have they found anything on Ravik?"

"Nothing. Well aside from the normal robberies and such. Nothing pertaining to our case though. No murders, kidnappings and yet, in that time at least three people went missing, one of which turned up dead two days later half a mile from their home and covered in scars and 'strange markings' as the locals put it."

She nodded. Jensin had mentioned something about markings to her. "So what was the point then? Why even try and catch Ravik at all if he's clean, vaguely speaking."

"Because it's not Ravik we are after. Never was. Most of the criminals in Allagor report to higher ups. Something like a crime lord in layman's terms. We know of a couple scattered throughout the city but the pirates mostly stay out of their way. Men like Ravik tend to keep to themselves and their shipmates. So originally our thinking was to raise Ravik's suspicions, bother him and see who comes to his aid. However when everything went to hell it wasn't just Ravik's crew that arrived to help him but members of various factions. Only twelve or so individuals in total but these weren't pirates Ivara. We passed one of the men on the way here, begging on the side of the road."

"And you didn't arrest him for trying to kill Jensin and myself?" Ivara asked indignantly. The Prince's words disturbed her.

"Ivara think about it. Individuals of no relation to Ravik came to his aid. We know they're not in the same factions, so they must be helping him in some way."

"That makes sense but I still don't see why you couldn't have arrested them."

"Have you ever heard the expression, where there is smoke there may be flame?"

"No, why?"

"I think Ravik might be working for someone. And I am of the opinion that everyone who came to help him did so because they are working for the same someone."

"Well it makes sense, but I don't see why we need a couple of books to tell us that. Can't you just find Ravik or the beggar, interrogate them until they confess and then catch the culprit?"

"Too late for that I'm afraid. Ravik and his cohorts know we're on to them. However, Jensin said the locals mentioned one of the bodies had been covered in strange markings. Strange markings, missing people...I think you know where I'm going with this."

"So say Ravik is part of a cult or some sort of secret club that dabbles in magic, do you really think there would be something here, in a library that stands open to the public on such secrets?" Ivara asked.

"In this library, there is always something to be found." Richard said confidently.

They split up, Ivara heading toward the less frequented areas of the floor while Richard took off in the opposite direction. She could recognize most of the words or at least infer their meanings but to read large texts with any sort of confidence was still beyond her. So instead she opted for the smaller texts. Sixty page copies of scholars notes or pocket prophecies. Once Ivara had a neat pile of seven or so books she found a lone table where she could work in peace.

"Ivara!" She whipped her head around so fast a portion of her braid came undone. Whoever had the gall to yell in such a quiet establishment! But that wasn't what startled her. The voice was familiar. It wasn't Richard though, that was evident. The voice was female and slightly muffled. She looked all around but could see no one. Ivara took a breath and went back to her reading, picking up the first small pocket-sized title *The Weird and the Wondrous: An Examination Of Folklore Around The World.*

"Psst. Over here!" The voice said a bit more quietly. Ivara looked over to her left where she could just make out a dark-skinned woman leaning out from behind a shelf. Ivara could only see from the woman's shoulders up but she was quite beautiful. Her eyes glowed a metallic gold and the tightest curls coiled atop her head keeping close to one another. Her warm dark ebony skin was covered in golden scales. She smiled and gestured at something behind Ivara. Ivara turned but they were completely alone. "Come on! Hurry Ives, before it scuttles away!"

Feeling a bizarre sense of comfort towards the stranger, Ivara rose and strode over to meet the enthusiastic golden eyed woman. But just as soon as she had done so the young woman turned back towards the isle that she'd been standing in. When Ivara arrived only seconds later the hallucination was gone.

"Hello?" But the young woman had seemingly vanished. "No, no. Not here." Ivara whispered under her breath, cursing her own mind as she made her way back towards her table. Though in truth she was a bit shaken. She knew it wasn't real and yet... Ivara tried her best to calm herself and sat down.

Ivara flipped open *The Weird and the Wondrous* and began skimming through its pages, most of which were crude illustrations. The book was less of an 'examination' and more the diary of a traveler as he learned about the people and places around him for the first time. With the weird being mostly drawings of creatures from the folklore of dozens of different cultures from southern Allagor, to Ellenward in the northwest and seemingly everything in between. Huge pale serpents with glowing red eyes, various illustrations of mer that were surprisingly accurate, pixies that leave gifts in the day and curse you in the night, a demon like creature dubbed the Dolah, that would summon the end times, even changelings which the text described as 'horribly ugly beings that vaguely resemble a child.' All these and more and yet nothing on runes, strange markings or the occult. Ivara sighed, moving on.

Time seemed to exist in another dimension altogether as she sat there attempting to decipher the old Allagorian writing of each book. But each time it was always the same, a few interesting factoids but nothing she was looking for. So she would reach for the next and the process would begin again. Once that pile was finished she would go fetch a new set and begin again.

Hours had passed and the fine cushioned seat in which she sat had long since begun to feel uncomfortable. Simply going through the motions in her frustration, Ivara reached for the next book. This one was slightly larger than the rest and its cover was a dark navy whose title glittered in gold font. It read, *The Prophecies Of Northerners*. Her curiosity piqued and Ivara turned to the first page. The book began with a riddle.

Dear reader, before you begin your endeavor in such knowledge as comes with prophecies you must come to an understanding with yourself. That understanding starts with a question. If you are told you will get your shoes muddy in the evening, and indeed it comes to pass that your shoes did get very dirty, you must ask yourself; Did your shoes become dirty because you felt no need in keeping them clean as a result of the inevitability that they might get dirty? Furthermore, if you had not been told about the eventual state of your shoes might that have changed the eventual cleanliness and indeed the outcome of your shoes? I would ask that you might keep such questions in mind as you read... So as not to drive yourself mad. Now, on to the prophecies.

The writer went on to recount each prophecy made by one of the northern seers, the date at which it was given, a few of its most commonly accepted interpretations and of course, the seers' names. Most of the prophecies Ivara found to be very straight ford. One reading, '...*and on the seventh day of the fifteen hundredth year there shall be fire and it shall consume any who have stood against the crown.*' Further reading confirmed that indeed the prophecy, which had been given four months prior to the fire had been perfectly correct though admittedly under suspicious circumstances. Ellenward was facing a rebellion at the time and a group of loyalists managed to take a village and set it ablaze.

Ivara kept reading. While most of the prophecies read to her as walker nonsense or obvious fear mongering there were a few diamonds in the rough, but regardless all such prophecies were entertaining. One such seemingly ridiculous fortune was that surrounding something the writer dubbed a 'Dolah' in the seventh and final chapter titled, '*Prophecies Regarding the End Times.*' Ivara turned the page. This telling was longer than the rest and much more dramatic she thought.

'*Listen good folk for the time draws near and the Dolah approaches. Clothed in righteous anger and accompanied by the three queens of the pit. Those who witness him shall see these signs and take them as a warning to his coming. First there shall be five devils that will rise from the depth. Each shall have the power to invoke a certain hell upon their victims. Second, there shall be a disruption of the monarchs in the north, south and east. Third, that being which lives and dies by the athame will find a new prey among the people of land. Fourthly, watch for the fair haired foreigner. As in the moment she is crowned, she shall inherit all the east and Armageddon shall be unstoppable. Then once all this is done you shall see a maiden wandering a dangerous wood. She shall be accompanied by a noble unicorn and you will know the Dolah draws near.*'

"Find anything interesting?" Richard's voice broke her from her swirling thoughts and Ivara realized she'd allowed herself to become so enthralled in the text that she had at some point hunched over the book.

"Not really… are there unicorns in Allagor?" Ivara asked as she pondered the end of the prophecy.

Richard chuckled dismissively. "If unicorns are real then I'd like to see one." The Prince turned his attention to her other books. "What about all these? Surely you found *something* that piqued your interest."

She stretched out and yawned. "I found a few books on cultures, ethnic groups and various religions but the strangest were writings about rituals, daily prayers, and whether or not to consume fish on the holy day."

"And that?" Richard pointed to the navy printed book she'd been reading.

"It's a prophecy book, now *this* actually does have some rather interesting predictions albeit their rather eccentric at times."

Richard took it from her and flipped the text so he could read the cover. "The Prophecies Of Northerners by Alec E. Kalith." He chuckled. "I knew the northerners were eccentric, but I would have never thought they'd be brazen enough to start publishing this rubbish."

"What do you mean?" Ivara said, crossing her arms. "A lot of these prophecies actually came true! There's even a section on Armageddon."

Richard rolled his eyes in good humor. "The northerners have their charms, but level headedness is not one of them. You can't tell me you honestly believe a vague prediction made by some old man hundreds of years ago."

"Well no, I don't know, but it might be fun to entertain the idea. Perhaps there could even be a prophecy in here about our killer!"

"Ives you're reaching. I seriously doubt we are going to find our murder suspect in a compilation of fortune telling books written on another continent hundreds of years ago."

"Fine." She put her hands up in surrender. "But you must admit it is interesting even if it's fiction. I mean '...five devils that will rise from the depth...' doesn't it just make your mind wander?"

"Not really." Upon seeing her face fall he quickly followed up saying. "Most folk learn Ellenward's history as children. There's this strange mythos surrounding the five tenants or devils as they say in Ellenward. The myths hold that each tenant will help bring about the end of the world."

"How?"

Richard thought for a moment. "It's been years since I've studied such things so I don't recall all the finer details, but I do remember something about there being an enthraller. He was always my favorite of the five. A being that could read minds and even control them."

"Enthraller? That sounds like a monster of some sort."

"It is. Well they all are of course. Ancient beings capable of massive amounts of destruction, at least according to the folklore and prophecies. But that is neither here nor there. Are you ready to head back?"

Ivara nodded and yawned once more. Once they had left the grand library and were settled on their horses she turned to him. "If you had just planned to take us to a library, why have me dressed like this? Why even give me a sword? I hardly need one in a library."

There was a half second of silence before Richard replied. "When I found you on the shore, there was a moment where I thought you might have been dead. And I had agreed to send you completely unarmed and wearing that ridiculous gown. I know what it's like to feel helpless, *to be* helpless, I felt it when the servant brought word that my brother had been declared dead. And I've felt it every day since. The sword, the blouse, the trousers even, it's so you can get away. So that if push came to shove and you found yourself in danger you could save yourself." His tone was heavy with the grief of his past. Until he lifted his head and it all seemed to fade away as he put on a cheery exterior. "Besides, you can't honestly tell me that trousers and a blouse aren't more comfortable than a corset."

Chapter 30

"The current King and Queen of Neroth have never been known for their hospitality. However, if there is one thing that even the simplest minded peasants understand, it is that our King and Queen are clever, especially when it concerns their children. Perhaps that is why no family or kingdom has dared to threaten Neroth in generations."

Royal Families Of The Sea by Freya Burg

Tallulah (1555 A.D.)

It had been nearly half a year since the messenger had arrived bearing the news of the royal visit when at last their guests arrived. The King and Queen of Neroth arrived in a rather small company for such a rich kingdom. Though for such a journey she supposed it must be faster to travel with a smaller party. They had dressed in their finest, and Corvena had even taken the time to go over basic courtesies with them, though Brina had mostly just ignored her and Osirus had little interest in the visit. Brina and Corvena got along rather poorly as of late, but especially when either was stressed. Osirus... well Tallulah didn't know the mer boy as well as she would have liked. In the year and a half since he'd joined their golden group of mishaps he'd hardly said a word to her. On the few times that she approached him Osirus was usually reading carvings or practicing runes. She wondered for some time what his magical talent would be.

They stood all four in a line together and greeted the royals upon their arrival. Each bowing then introducing themselves in turn. Brina took the lead as she always did.

"My king and queen, the Arkstone welcomes you, I am Brina, one of the senior golden servants of the Great Golden Dragon. These are my companions. We have been sent to serve you and your company. Your messengers indicated that one of your party is in need of healing?" Brina finished her greeting with a deep bow.

"When we began our journey, yes, that was what their hallowed majesties required of your kind. However as of late my master's fortunes have turned for the worse. That which his majesty the King and his Queen require is incredibly...erm specific. Perhaps such matters should be dealt with in private, young master Brina." One of the family's advisors said tentatively.

Brina bowed once more and beckoned them to follow her. All the while eyeing something long and stiff that the servants carried with careful precision.

They entered the hall, the King and Queen, Brina, Osirus, Corvena and Tallulah as well as a few guards and servants. When they'd all found their places in the room, the package was dropped in the center, and Tallulah could now see the faint outline of a mer wrapped in many layers of fabric. Brina saw it too and her eyes began to redden.

"What is it you would ask of us? Speak now." Brina began curtly. All sense of welcome now gone from her voice.

There was a long silence in the room and the water felt stale. When suddenly the King spoke, his voice a grievous sound.

"Heal him, if you can. Please my child. Whatever magic they have taught you here..." The King choked on his words. "Save him from his fate."

Slowly Brina swam toward the bundle that lay on the floor and gently she began undoing the cloth wrapped around the face. Tallulah gasped. They were identical, Brina and this mer boy.

Brina's soft features made masculine on the mer boy's face. Brina's soft expression hardened. Tallulah had never seen pure undiluted hate upon her friend's face as she saw it now. Fast as lightning she turned to face the king. Her composure entirely broken by her rage.

"You fool! He is dead! You've killed him." Her scream morphed into a sob. "You've killed him!"

Angrily the Queen took hold of Brina's wrist. "Do not play us for fools girl. We did not send you here to learn of medicines! We know well the power your master has gifted you. Do you think the rumors of the golden blooded necromancer have not reached us in the south? Surely you or one of your number can save him, use whatever magic you deem necessary. He is your brother, you must!"

"We can do many things," Tallulah began "but to reanimate those who are dead?" Her voice was a whisper. She waited desperate for one of her peers to say something but none dared to speak. Even Corvena looked horrified though she did her best to hide it by looking away.

Brina put up a hand to stop her. "I will do what I can, mother. But I make no promises. You've brought me a month-old corpse. There is little hope that anything will come of this work."

The Queen of Neroth put a gentle hand on her daughter's cheek. Both were crying now. "Thank you dear."

Chapter 31

"Thank you for your generous funds and immediate support when called upon. It was your army that saved us, and with the funds provided we may yet rebuild. It is because of the Kingdom of Colors that Makoul did not fall but rather defeated Neroth's army."

Khipu sent from Lord Nerous to the Kingdom of Colors

Ivara (1604 A.D.)

Ivara waited until night had fallen over the castle and the district below. Grabbing her boots and blouse she dressed quietly for her nighttime journey. There was something surreal about seeing the once bustling halls so devoid of life. It was off putting in a way. Ivara nearly felt as though the portraits that hung on the wall might be watching her as she tiptoed down the steps. There were of course a few dozing guards stationed here and there but none of them questioned her. She had nearly made it to the main door when the familiar click of expensive boots clued her in to the man who'd been following her. She turned.

"Jensin."

"Ivara." He nodded. "It's a bit late to be running errands. Wouldn't you agree?" His voice was terse with... was that jealousy that lined his tone?

She sighed. "I'm not a criminal. You don't have to shadow me everywhere I go."

"Actually, I do. Part of my job." She rolled her eyes. "*Also* you could have let me know, about the other day. I'd have been happy to join."

"Don't be ridiculous you were still on the mend." She tried to shove past him but he put a gentle though firm hand on her shoulder.

Jensin sighed. "Where to?"

"The beach, actually. I think I may have just found my way home."

Perhaps the walker texts and murders could offer her answers but so could the witch. And she would much rather be with Scyla than here amongst strangers.

"Oh? Straying a bit far from the Prince's bosom aren't you." Jensin said tersely as he walked up next to her. Again that distinct tone of jealousy crept in to his every word. "Do indulge me."

"I will," she paused, the question that had been on her mind for weeks now forcing it's way to her lips. "You've known I'm mer for some time. Does that not scare you?"

Ivara thought he might laugh at the question but Jensin just smirked at her.

"Not in the slightest."

"Why not?"

"Because I know, and *you know* that if you ever betray myself or my kingdom I will kill you, and throw your remains into the ocean for the sea fowl to peck at until nothing remains of you but sea foam."

Ivara swallowed hard. She knew that he was suspicious of her but Jensin had never outright threatened her before.

"What about me? Do I scare you?" He asked.

She leaned into him until she could feel his breath on hers. "No." She whispered gently. Though she couldn't quite explain why the man with a stern face and sword on his belt did not threaten her.

He should have and yet all she could see when she looked at him was his tousled red hair. The way he grinned when he thought nobody was looking. It was as though a tiny thread was constantly pulling her towards him. Ivara wondered if he felt it too.

They finished saddling their horses in silence. Together they rode on for nearly an hour before Jensin finally asked.

"So you think you've finally found a way home?"

"Oh, yes, during the incident with Ravik, I nearly drowned, Jensin. If it weren't for my sister, Uhane, we'd both be dead right now. I need to see her. Speak with her and ask her what state Makoul, my *home* is in. Perhaps she might know a solution as to my current state."

Jensin grimaced. "Those savages don't save people." He said under his breath.

"What was that?"

He sighed. "Nothing, sounds like a plan. Care for an escort?"

"Do I have a choice?"

Jensin smirked. "Not really, I was just being polite."

They rode together on a black mare so as to not attract too much attention. With Jensin coming along, walking was no longer a viable option as his foot was far from healed. Ivara had watched as with each limping step he did his best to hide his pain. Once they were on the horse Jensin's mood improved dramatically. So much so that Ivara nearly forgot that she was being babysat. They filled the time with hushed small talk and it didn't take long before they arrived for Ivara to find the spot where she had been found by Richard.

"Stay here." She said to Jensin once they'd cleared the sand dunes and were on the upper half of the beach. He returned her comment with a dry look but she explained. "If Uhane sees you may not come up to meet me. My sisters aren't fond of your kind."

"Not fond as in skittish or not fond as in she may try to kill me?"

"The latter. Besides, you wouldn't be able to understand us anyways."

Jensin huffed. "Believe it or not, Ivara, I've studied a few mer languages."

"Not this one." He gave her a questioning look. She just sighed. "My sister is mute. She signs. Most of my own people haven't even bothered to learn the language. I highly doubt you're any good at it."

"Alright, you make a decent point. I'll stay put."

She smiled. Ivara knew how much Jensin was putting on the line to let her do this alone. It meant that some part of him trusted her even if that part was small.

"Thank you."

The tide was coming in and the water was cold on her feet. Ivara couldn't see much in the dark. Her human body hindered her in many ways but the worst were her senses. Taste, touch, sound, everything was dull to her now. But sight was the worst. In the darkness of the night she could hardly see her hand in front of her. She sat there for what felt like hours. *Had she been a fool to come here? What were the odds that Uhane would come back? For that matter, had Uhane actually recognized her?* Thoughts of doubt swirled around in her mind until she had become lost in them. So caught up in such thoughts she failed to see the faint glow of the blue that whipped through the waves disturbing the bioluminescent creatures around it. Or the mop of long black hair that rose out of the sea with silent caution until Uhane was feet from her beckoning her closer.

Coming. Ivara signed once she had seen her sister. She made her way in until she was chest deep in the mild waves.

Her sister's pale skin and ice blue eyes shined in the moonlight as she put a hand on each side of Ivara's face and kissed her temple. A single tear fell from her eyes as she gazed at her sister, a porcelain figure in the moonlight.

Are you safe? Uhane signed into Ivara's palm. She nodded vigorously.

I want to come home. Ivara's hands shook in Uhane's palm.

Uhane smiled at her but there was no joy in her expression. *Not yet. Not safe.*

"What do you mean?"

Uhane dunked herself in the water and took a breath before coming back up to reply. *The city-states are in disarray. Ka'I left to try and quell unrest but the waters are dangerous Ivara.*

"Makoul?" Ivara said aloud.

Uhane nodded. *It was a bloodbath, Makoul is unrecognizable. Father has sent messengers to explain the situation but none have returned. They're saying that even the south is in ruins.*

"Maybe if I could come home I could somehow help. I could - ."

No! Uhane signed into her palm. *Makoul is not how you left it. It's become dangerous to even leave the castle. Besides, whatever sort of magic did this to you...*

"Scyla. She did this to me; even if she was only trying to help. But there may be some other way to reverse it."

Uhane thought for a moment. *Do the walkers know that you are mer? Is that why they tried to drown you?*

"It's more complicated than that. But I'm safe for now. Why?" Ivara said.

Stay with the walkers then. I'll try to track down Scyla and reverse whatever spell she's put on you. In the meantime stay put and stay safe.

Ivara took a long breath. "Alright. I'll stay... at least until we know more about the spell."

Uhane nodded and gently grasped Ivara's hand. *See you soon little sister.* She said before descending into the cold once more.

Chapter 32

"At every university that I have lectured at, and being nearly seventy the list is quite extensive, the same question is always asked. The same query that sits in so many human hearts. If magic can do all these incredible things, can it bring back one who has passed?

So what is the answer? Well I cannot answer in an official capacity but I can say this much. Such practices being of the dark arts, regardless of their validity, have been outlawed by most universities."

Practical Magic by Daniel E. Simmons

Brina (1555 A.D.)

Brina hated the darkness. Still she sat there, alone, hour by hour next to what remained of her twin. Her brother had been dear to her, a glimmer of hope during those first few days when her family had first left her here. She could still hear his voice in her mind.

I'm coming back for you.

And she'd believed him. With all of the stupid naivete of a little girl she had believed him. And every day she'd found happiness knowing that somewhere in the world her brother was planning his return. And here he was. He'd kept his promise, she chuckled a bit at the thought.

"You abandoned me." She said into the darkness. "Left me here all alone." Gently she placed her practiced hands on his cold decaying skin. "No, you don't get to leave. Not without saying goodbye." She sobbed angrily as she began reaching for the Dragon's magic that flowed through her veins. Over sixty five years of bringing people back, of struggling against the black void of death and each time she lost a bit of herself in it. She pulled and pulled, struggling against it. "Come back!" She screamed at the force that held her brother's body still. "You...can't...leave...me." She could feel the burning now. If she went much deeper into the Dragon's magic she might be lost in it, or worse she might have to use chaos magic and that would likely kill her. The burning sensation began in her hands and traveled up her arms until she felt as if her entire body was on fire despite the cool sea around her. She thought she might die in the fire, be consumed by the pain of it when suddenly a cool light hand touched her shoulder that made her cry out.

"Incredible." A male voice whispered in her ear. "It's really you."

She turned to face him and gasped. His appearance still carried the weight of his death. Skin rotted off his face, and one eye was asunder. His hair remained but his body was grey. She wasn't surprised. After all, necromancy was never permanent. But despite all that it was still her brother, he smiled at her. Tears spilled out of her salt mixing with salt. She wanted to hug him, squeeze him, but past experience as well as the decomposing body beside her told her otherwise.

"I never thought my older sister might be learning real magic. You should be proud."

"Elder?" She asked. "We are the same age, and you were born first." She chuckled.

"Yes but technically you are the elder now." He quipped. They both looked on at what was left of him.

"What happened to you? And don't lie to spare my feelings. You don't know what I've done to get you here."

"There's a sickness spreading through the southern realms. I'd be surprised if it hasn't reached Makoul and the other city states in the east by now."

"Did it claim you quickly?"

"No, mother sent for every healer money could buy but there was no healing it, only prolonging the illness."

"Well I can't truly give you life but if you want to be buried back home I can have the wounds sealed up for travel in a matter of weeks. We will have to do a cleansing of your innards, perhaps take them out completely, which may take some time. Then there is the matter of the disease itself. A good wash should do the trick."

"Save yourself the trouble. I'm not going back."

Brina looked at her brother accusingly. "You must. You are the sole heir to Neroth, the crown Prince, the only Prince. The people need their chance to grieve. And that's aside from the fact that everyone will be wondering who will take the kingdom once mother and father have passed into shadow."

"You could."

"I cannot, I am bound to the Arkstone, you know this."

"Then find another to rule in your stead. I don't care, but I'm not going back. Have them bury me here."

"And what about me? If I don't preserve you for your body's journey back south they'll thrash me and think that I have no respect for the very monarchy I was born from!"

"Let them think as they will. You said it yourself: you are bound to the Arkstone. They are not, let them leave with their thoughts as they return to that disease and war ridden kingdom. I'm not leaving you again."

Brina was silent for a long moment before she finally found the courage to speak again.

"Will you stay with me through the night?"

"Of course."

He held her hand as she lay there by him. There were no stalagmites to wrap her tail around and keep her in place so she let her golden tail swish about with the current. When morning came her brother was gone, his body still and unmoving. Silently she rose, rubbing at her red face. And though she tried, the tears simply would not halt their course. Fumbling over herself Brina swam out of the room to fetch the servants.

"Wrap him up, he is to be buried in the golden crypts on the south side of the mountains. Be gentle with him. The prince was my brother, preserve him as best you can." She said quietly. She found her parents staying in one of the guest rooms on the upper floor of the Arkstone castle. They were already awake when she arrived or perhaps they hadn't slept at all. She wouldn't be surprised if it was the latter.

"Well? What news have you? How does my boy fair?" Her mother asked the moment she spotted Brina in the archway leading to their room.

"The Prince," Brina could not bear to say his name. "is dead. He will remain so. I spoke with him last night and it was his wish for his remains to be interred here in the Arkstone's crypt." Her voice cracked with grief.

"You brought him back and did not come fetch us?" Her mother spat. It was an accusation filled with rage, venom and most of all grief. Brina's father however was quiet. He just held her mother's hand steadfast in his silence.

"A month old corpse! That is what you brought me. You might be grateful that I was able to bring him back for the short time that I did. Direct your ire elsewhere *mother*. It was not I who killed him!" As soon as the words left her mouth she regretted them. It was not her mother who had killed her brother, but a faceless plague. "I'm sorry." She said quietly.

Her father swam to her, taking her hands in his. "I know you do not wish to speak of it but with your brother gone, you have a duty to fulfill."

"The crown princess of Neroth, it is your birthright you've only to claim it darling. Claim it and come home." Her mother had urged.

"Don't call me that, princess, darling, any of it! I am Brina of the Arkstone, Servant of the Golden Dragon. *This* is my kingdom. *This* is my home."

"You are *my* daughter and you serve none but the kingdom of Neroth!" Her mother grabbed for her arm but Brina pulled away.

"You do not care for me but rather for your bloodline. A putrid stinking mess of a line that should have ended long ago. What did the Dragon give you to leave me here with him? What was the exchange? Tell me truly."

Her mother looked away. "Nothing."

It wasn't what she was expecting. There was always a price with the dragon's bargains. And there was *always* a reward. She had watched as Tallulah's father had traded her for a new start away from war. And for Corvena it was a cure for her mother's illness. Even Osirus had been traded for something.

"Nothing?" She repeated. "Then why?"

"Why not is the better question." Her father responded. "I mean the opportunity to learn from the dragon himself! You couldn't dream of a better education, and though we'd hoped it would raise your price, becoming heir will have to do until we find a good husband for you."

"My *price*?"

"So to speak. Dowries are all too common amongst mer of our status, but magic, along with all the other things you've learned. Oh the suitors would line up!"

"And that is not even mentioning the magic your children will one day wield!" Her mother chimed in gleefully.

She wanted to vomit. "Do you even realize what you've done to me? I am bound by blood to this place, to my master. I was raised as a wealthy orphan. I am forbade from romantic desires and marriage. Because of you I will never even have children!"

They stared at her in silence for a long moment. So many times Brina nearly spoke but it was simpler to let the silence hang there and let her rage and grief build off of each other. Finally she swallowed hard and spoke her voice a mere whisper. "You are not welcome here. Neither of you. The boy –." She took another breath. "*My brother* will stay. He will be given a place of honor amongst the bones of dragons. Do not ever call on the Arkstone for aid. We will not come. We will not help you."

Chapter 33

"In regard to the art of prophecy though, one must be very careful. This school of magic is rare amongst us humans, but when prophecies occur they are almost always reliable in some manner or another. The difficulty comes not from the prophecy itself but rather from interpreting and thus understanding it."

The Prophecies of Northerners by Alec E. Kalith

Tallulah (1555 A.D.)

It was late in the evening when Tallulah finally caught up with Osirus. The mer boy had ebony skin though much darker than her own. And though he'd only been with them a year he had already earned his golden eyes. His tail too had begun to turn too. He kept his hair cropped short. He'd always been friendly to her but never approached her for a conversation.

Tallulah noticed the mer boy mostly kept to himself in quiet observation, only interacting with others when he had no other options of escape. She'd intended on simply waving a hello and being on her way, but as she saw him leaving the Dragons den and she noticed the deep dark circles underneath his eyes and his exhausted expression her heart began to fill with worry.

Beside her swam Corvena, Brina was not with them, as per usual. Though today her excuse had come in the form of one of the royal families from the south. Tallulah took Corvena by the arm and the two mer girls swam over to an exhausted Osirus.

"You look like hell." Corvena said by way of introduction.

Osirus didn't even glance her way. "I'm well aware. Unfortunately, my looks are the least of my concerns at the moment."

"When's the last time you've slept?" Tallulah asked gently.

Now Osirus did look up at them. "Sleep? No, I need to..." He yawned.. "I need to stay awake. I can't go to sleep, night terrors and all. I'm sure you've had them before."

"Bad enough to keep you up so long that you forget your way home? Can't say that I have." Corvena said.

"Huh?" For the first time Osirus seemed to awaken enough to consider where he was. "Oh I suppose I was swimming the wrong way wasn't I?" He began to laugh but the sound was weak and tired.

Tallulah and Corvena shared a concerned look. Just then Tallulah felt a cold whoosh of water behind her and turned. Brina had appeared seemingly out of nowhere looking somehow nearly as tired as Osirus. Tallulah wondered how such productive individuals could run on so little sleep though it was obvious from the look of exhaustion on her friends faces that the day had caught up with all of them.

"Thought I might find you all here. Mind if I stick around for a bit?" Brina asked, her usually peppy tone made sour by her day's work though her eyes glowed feverishly gold in the light of the evening.

"Not at all, I was just on my way." Osirus swiveled, now facing the correct direction. He turned to go but Brina put a hand on his shoulder.

"Night terrors again?" She asked him.

He looked at Tallulah and Corvena apprehensively but eventually relented and nodded at her. "It's the same dream, every time. It all just seems so real, it's like I *know* her. But when I wake up she's just a stranger in the darkness."

"What did you see in the dream?" Brina asked him.

Osirus turned to them, and in his expression Tallulah could see a heavy grief that lay like a shroud over his person. His gills flared as he took a breath before he spoke.

"I saw a walker woman standing on a hilltop overlooking a vast sea. Grey storm clouds gathered in the sky above but there was no rain. Her hair fell in waves at her back and moved with each gust of wind. She faced away from me so I could scarcely see her face at first, just her back side. Her body was thin and pale, and though she bore many fresh open wounds none of them bled. She wore a thin grey dress with many tatters throughout that left her body thoroughly exposed and nearly naked. Her skin was yellow and blue bearing the hues of a corpse and when she did turn her face to me her lips bore the cold hue of one who had kissed death intimately. As she turned toward me I saw that the sea fowl had picked out her eyes and what remained were mere funeral stones, gems of great value that shone brightly in the gathering darkness. One shone a bright bloody red, a ruby. In the other eye a single golden coin which bore the effigy of a great beast. I got the sense that she saw me and it was terrifying. Then the nightmare was finished with me." As the final sentence left his lips Osirus shuddered.

Chapter 34

"Rune work is perhaps the most common school of magic amongst us humans as it is the most accessible. No dragon bone required, but instead blood, the one form of currency that every man can pay."

Practical Magic by Daniel E. Simmons

Ivara (1604 A.D.)

Ivara awoke the next morning still exhausted but with an added sense of achiness. It was as if her body was slower to recover from so many outings in such a short period of time. She wondered briefly if such a feeling was due to her change in form. That was the first thing she noticed. The second was Kirsten standing over her with a mischievous smile on her small face. Startled, Ivara twisted away.

"Good morning." Her optimistic new caretaker said by way of greeting.

"Hi." Ivara yawned.

"The Prince has requested that you attend breakfast this morning. I told him you would be exhausted but he just said, 'Kirsten at least ask' so I just said I would but I didn't expect you to wake up so soon."

Ivara groaned and pulled her sheets over her head. "Tell him I'm still asleep and I'll give you all of my wages for the next two weeks."

Kirsten frowned for a moment before mastering herself and pulling the sheets off her. They wrestled for a moment before Ivara gave in. She let Kirsten dress her and fix her hair. She even went so far as to let Kirsten lather her face in makeup and her body in perfumes. Her attendee was a golden brown woman, young possibly in her mid-teens. Ivara saw a faint resemblance to the Prince in Kirsten's features, faint but present. Not his sister, but a cousin. Her purple eyes, tan skin and dark curly hair that she kept tied back with a single purple ribbon gave her a homely and yet exotic look.

"You know at first I felt slighted that the invitation to breakfast was intended for you and not myself, given that the Prince is my kin." She swallowed down her anger and grief and for a moment the mask of joy fell. "Of course I shouldn't be surprised, my mother's crimes will likely haunt me until the day I finally leave this wretched castle. Though after considering it, I think this could prove opportune for both of us." Kirsten tried to smile as she finished Ivara's rouge.

Ivara's head shot up. It was the first time the girl had dropped her childlike demeanor since they'd met. What was even more unsettling was just how quickly she plastered it back on, but this time her smile felt a bit less genuine.

"Why?" Ivara lifted the small hand mirror to see an unrecognizably colored face. Her pale skin had been powdered to look even paler and her lips were blood red and overlined to make them look bigger. Her face had been contorted to the point of looking gaunt. Powder had been applied to her hairline to make her forehead look larger.

"The dress. My dress. Well not *my* dress, but I made it. Hmm, pink isn't really your color, next time we'll try blue."

Ivara looked down at her glittering morning gown. Unlike her makeup this was masterful work. Only an experienced hand could have pulled this off. Her eyes widened. "You made this? When?"

"Well not made, exactly, I altered it last night. While we were walking I sort of measured you. Not exact numbers obviously but you're about Princess Everleigh's size so I figured if I altered the bust and sleeves a bit…"

"Oh my…" She was speechless for a moment. "Kirsten, this is amazing work."

"Thank you. I've actually always dreamt of being a seamstress. But I never thought to take it up as a serious hobby until my mother passed. I figured if I could get one of my dresses in front of the court then maybe they might give me the chance to work on the Princess' wedding gown." She looked down. Her tone growing serious. "You would honor me by wearing my dress to breakfast."

Ivara smiled. "I would be honored to present it to the court. Perhaps I could convince the Prince that I need a personal seamstress if I am to stay at the castle for any duration of time." She winked at the maid. Kirsten smiled but said nothing. They embraced quickly then Kirsten sent Ivara out with directions to the dining area.

Ivara arrived at the dining area after getting turned around only twice. She was rather proud of that. The room was huge but rather plain. Decorated with the occasional golden angel or some other silly item painted in the king's color to look priceless; the room felt devoid of life. Or at least it would have if not for the three people sitting at the main table chatting quietly. Ivara walked in trying her best not to disturb their conversation.

She looked over to see Richard, in full royal garb for the first time since they had met. He sat at the head of the table. To his right sat a woman who looked to be nearly twenty; she wore a pale blue dress with a black veil that covered her face, though Ivara recognized her to be Everleigh. To Richard's left sat Jensin.

The woman to the Prince's right, Princess Everleigh was pale with strawberry blonde hair. She flaunted a pair of bright blue eyes that matched her blue morning gown. The woman wore her hair in loose curls that fell around her head. The look was in stark contrast to most of the women that Ivara had seen so far whom had worn their hair in tight buns or up high on their head. Ivara was startled when the woman turned her head. She was stunning. Ivara thought only sirens could be that beautiful. How odd.

As soon as they noticed her, the room went silent. She stood at the edge of the table unsure of what to say. There were so many forms of greeting in the Allagorian tongue and though she had long since learned them she still wasn't sure of each level of formality. Thankfully, the woman in blue noticed and stepped in to help.

"Oh! You're here!" She squealed, throwing her arms up in the air.

"For goodness sake Everleigh you act as if you've never seen another human being in your life." Richard mocked. At this Jensin began choking on his drink.

"Can you blame me Richard? You may be free to roam the land as you see fit but when your very existence serves to secure an alliance between the two most prominent kingdoms in the east," Princess Everleigh gestured to herself. "The King and Queen tend to keep you locked away in a stone castle." She smiled at Ivara tucking a bit of the mer girl's hair behind her ear and cusping her face.

"It will be nice to have another woman around. I mean there is Kirsten, but since her mother's death it's like all the joy has been sucked out of her." Ivara blushed at the strange comment. Everleigh walked elegantly over to her chair and patted the one beside it. "Come sit!"

Ivara looked around. Except for the four of them, the room was empty. Not even guards or servants were present. "Shouldn't we wait for everyone else?" Ivara asked, looking at the group.

"This is everyone." Jensin said rather pleasantly. "We made our own little breakfast club and if you're a good little lady I'll write you a letter of recommendation." The look he gave her held equal amounts of sarcasm and jesting. Was... was he flirting with her?

"Very funny." Ivara said shortly. She turned to Richard. He was staring at her. Ivara looked herself over. "What's wrong?"

"Nothing. Nothing at all. That dress. It fits you quite well." He replied.

"One of Kirsten's finest. Poor girl would have made such a lovely Princess." Everleigh agreed. Her voice, a whimsical coo as she spoke of times long past.

"She asked me to wear it, said her work had never been displayed before in court. And I'm sorry did you say Princess?" Ivara said. "She wants you to make her a royal seamstress."

The Prince ignored her question and looked her over hungrily.

"Well the gown hasn't been *properly* displayed yet so..." Richard said.

"You can't be serious." Ivara raised her eyebrows. He smirked at her. She walked to his seat and twirled for him. "Happy?"

He smiled; it was a less than wholesome expression. When she glanced over at Jensin, the Prince's friend had gone red and would not meet her eyes.

"Very but..." The Prince looked over and shared a knowing glance with Princess Everleigh. "...well things with Kirsten are complicated to say the least. Tell my dear cousin I'll think about it."

Ivara nodded and took a seat next to Jensin.

"Can we talk about something meaningful now? I received a report this morning from one of the guards that-" Jensin began before Everleigh cut him off.

"If I have to hear one more of these boring reports I'm going to throw myself from the highest tower in this castle." Everleigh huffed.

"They're not boring Everleigh, they're informative and important!" Jensin snapped.

"Unless they have something to do with my Prince Henry, they are boring and a waste of my time." Everleigh said. It was a moment before she relented and sighed, waving her hand for him to finish. "Go on then. Have your fun but don't expect to see me at dinner tonight."

"Drama queen." Jensin muttered under his breath. "Where was I? Oh, right, so the guards informed me this morning that well um..." Jensin stopped. He looked from Ivara to Richard.

"What now?" Ivara asked.

"You may want to stave from finishing your breakfast until I've finished." They all rolled their eyes, but leaned in suddenly interested. "So I was speaking with one of the guards this morning and he informed me that there's been another attack. It happened sometime early this morning. Only a few witnesses."

"How many dead?" Richard asked.

"Just one, but we suspect this was premeditated."

"Unlikely but do go on." Richard muttered.

"Think about it, every known attack thus far has been carried out in the same pattern." Jensin said.

Everleigh sighed, placing her hand to her head. "Here we go."

"I'm serious! It fits the pattern. Missing person of little value, and no title nor family. The timing fits too." Jensin spoke with a nervous excitement.

"Richard, didn't you tell me that you and Ivara already went by the library and came up empty?" Everleigh asked tentatively.

"Yes, exactly. So far all we have towards our cult theory is simple speculation. We need real tangible evidence."

Jensin pulled out a folded piece of parchment. "You mean like this?" Ivara leaned over to watch as her copper haired acquaintance unfolded the parchment. Dozens of poorly drawn runes had been scribbled on the page. She recognized the symbols but couldn't remember their meanings.

Everleigh glanced worriedly at her from across the table. "Are you alright? You look as though you've seen a ghost."

Indeed Ivara could feel her heart palpitating in her chest as she looked on at the symbols. But there was no recollection, only familiarity with the symbols. The language was just as foreign to her as it was to the rest of them. And yet she felt like she *should* recognize them.

"What are we looking at?" Richard asked impatiently.

"Good question, I'm not altogether sure to be honest with you. These symbols were found carved into a body we found a few weeks ago."

"Runes." They all stared at her. "Their runes, written magic. They mean something, I'm just not sure what."

"How do you know?" Jensin pressed.

"I don't know." When she reached to her memories for an explanation she found nothing. Instead her the mark on her forearm began burning and she winced at the pain.

"Are you alright?" Jensin whispered beside her.

"Fine." She took a deep breath; the pain was already fading.

"So what? Some fanatic is running around killing low born folk? Am I missing something? What does this prove?" Richard said, ignoring Ivara's small outburst.

Jensin sighed. "Yes, my friend, you're missing a lot of somethings. Firstly it proves that our killer is educated and likely has access to the library. Second it gives us something to go off of. After breakfast you go back to the library to cross reference the symbols with anything you can find, runes, exotic languages, *anything.* And this time do tell her majesty, your mother that you will be occupied during the evening. Between your fathers ailment and the recent developments with your brother I doubt the Queen needs anything else to worry over."

"Am I to assume you will be too preoccupied to come along?"

"Yes. While you're out Ivara and I will go investigate a warehouse where Ravik's associates have been seen. I've had my eye on the warehouse for some time."

"Is that safe? I mean how is your foot?" Everleigh asked concernedly.

"I'll be fine. It's actually much better with the herbs Ked lent me."

"What's the deal with the warehouse?" Ivara asked, trying not to overthink.

Jensin shrugged. "Not sure. The damn thing has sat presumably empty for over a year now. Property is in the name of a ghost and-."

"A ghost?" Ivara asked.

Everleigh giggled. "Basically, someone who has been off of our records for a while, that's what we call them. Not an actual ghost of course, just someone who's proved difficult to track down."

"Oh. Thanks." Ivara said sheepishly.

"Alright so spill. What's your working theory?" Richard asked, relaxing back in his chair.

"The missing people, Ravik's shady behavior, they're both symptoms of a much larger disease. That is to say they're connected in some way but taking care of one won't take care of the others."

"So you *don't* think Ravik is our killer? Explain." Everleigh said leaning in.

"We can assume that the individuals working *with* Ravik likely work for someone. Now whether they've been bought out from one of the factions or hired individually is yet to be determined. The missing villagers and the murders are likely being committed by this group. Given that in every case the victim is of low class and little family we can assume that this pattern was established by the group before the killings began. Which means..."

"They probably planned each kill and if they're planning then they need a place to congregate." Ivara finished. "You think it's that easy? That we'll be able to ambush them at a warehouse?"

"We'll have to find out." Jensin surveyed the table. All of them had since lost their appetite. "Well? Thoughts?"

"Be careful. Don't go rushing in. And make sure you have enough soldiers this time." Everleigh said after some thought.

"I second that. Be careful." Richard said.

Jensin gave them a wry smile. "Oh we will."

Chapter 35

My dear darling Prince, time moves slowly with you gone. It was as if the world stopped the moment you sailed away. Thoughts of your hands in my hair, your lips on mine... they fill my head day and night. I yearn for your return, my love.

Always yours,

Princess Everleigh, ward of Allagor.

Last known correspondence from Everleigh to Prince Henry

Ivara (1604 A.D.)

Upon leaving the chamber Ivara could hear the light footsteps of the blond Princess falling in step behind her. When the Princess had caught up with her, the light sunny smile was gone, replaced by a sterner expression.

Everleigh glanced around the castle halls; they were alone save for the guards who stood unmoving at equal distance. "Walk with me?"

Unsure what else to do, Ivara nodded and Everleigh took her hand. She followed the Princess down a set of stairs on which she found herself clumsily stumbling down, her legs not yet comfortable on the unevenly descending path. They passed multiple chambers before finally they arrived at a cellar.

"Pardon, but where are you taking me?"

This made Everleigh giggle. "The beach."

The grimy cellar certainly didn't *look* like a beach nor did it smell like one. What it did smell of was rat droppings, and the stink of time passing. Carefully constructed cobwebs hung at the corners of the cellar walls and loose stones sat slowly turning to dust all around them.

"I discovered this passage when I was a girl. Henry, Richard and I were playing a game and I needed a place to hide." Everleigh said, rather proudly.

"And you decided to go in?"

"Oh don't tell me now that you're afraid of dark passage ways. Come on." The Princess took her hand and they walked down the hall past various rooms. With each one they passed Everleigh counted until they arrived at a dark gated passage.

"Everleigh, I'd always been under the impression that every room in a castle served a purpose."

"This cellar *did* serve a purpose, a few hundred years ago the cellar served as servants quarters. Until a structural error was discovered in one of the rooms and one by one the rooms began collapsing. Dragon bone is a wonderful base for masonry but it is quite expensive and it's said that too much of it can weaken the stones." Ivara was so struck by the Princesses words that she nearly missed what the Princess said next. *Dragon bones? Here? On land?* Perhaps the Princess was mistaken. "Of course, once work began on the remaining rooms to keep them stable the servants refused to stay in the cellar. Today what remains is used for making and storing the wine, as the rest of the cellar has been deemed far too dangerous to enter."

Ivara looked around suspiciously. "I don't see any wine barrels. Did we pass it?"

Everleigh laughed as if at an inside joke. "Of course not! The wine is stored on the other end of the cellar."

"Wait so that means –."

"We're here!" Everleigh cut her off excitedly.

In the sea Ivara's sight had been very good, though she'd never been to the Deep, she'd noticed that the walkers lived in near constant light, even at night they had candles and lanterns to light their way. It had taken her some time to get used to it, now that she was she could appreciate the utter darkness that surrounded her and the Princess. Ivara heard a shuffling and a slapping sound.

"Everleigh?"

"Yes."

"What are you doing?"

"Feeling for something on the wall... it's here somewhere...where...oh! Here it is!"

Ivara heard a click followed by a grinding sound then the wall before them began to move. At first it was a small speck of light in front of them but slowly the speck grew and grew as the wall split in two like doors and Ivara could finally see the beach.

"How –. Everleigh your hand!"

"Oh it's just a bit of blood." Everleigh said, wrapping her long draping sleeve around the shallow wound. "The rune on the door, it only responds to royal blood."

"I'm sure that's just a rumor." Ivara said as she glanced behind them to see the stone door shift closed once more.

Everleigh shrugged and took Ivara's arm. "It very well could be, but then how is it that the banished princess would have been able to reach the village without being followed?"

"Who?"

Everleigh smiled and Ivara suspected that *this* Princess was one for stories. "When I was little the servants would tell me stories of the banished princess. The story tells of a girl who fell so in love with a boy from the nearby town that every night she would sneak out through a small opening in the cellar."

Ivara held up her spare hand to stop the Princess. "But there is no opening it without the rune."

"Exactly." Everleigh continued. "Oh the princess was *cunning* and devised a plan so as not to get caught. She would carve two runes on the wall, one to create an opening, and another to close it. Then she would seal it with her own blood. So that only those of royal blood might open it. The royal family of course has always been a bit..." Everleigh looked around, spotting no one, she continued in a hushed tone. "...Let's just say that they are quite aware, as most royal families are, of their positions."

"So the only people that could open the door were those that would never find it...."

"...And those that would find it could never open it." Everleigh finished with a smile.

"Except for you I suppose."

Everleigh giggled. "Yes I suppose that is true. In my defense I was a rather curious child. Once I moved to Allagor the King and Queen assigned me my own set of servants to raise me and educate me. Though I must say Lady Rhea was my favorite. Despite her tumultuous youth and her crimes later in life she was always kind to me. She was like a mother to me. Some days she would even set aside her own daughter to educate me and spend time with me.

Moreover, she was the first and for a while the only person who understood what it was to be a stranger in your own home." The Princess spoke with no small amount of fondness but there was a sadness to her voice as well.

"Hmm I do not believe I have met her." Ivara responded, doing her best to sound polite and mask her confusion.

"Nor shall you." Everleigh sighed. "Lady Rhea met her end less than a year ago on account of treason."

Ivara stopped. "Treason?"

"Yes. Though I attended her execution out of respect it was all I could do not to vomit afterwards. The worst of it was to do with her daughter. Poor Kirsten was allowed to attend and afterward the

King stripped the poor girl of all her titles and land and confined her to the castle as a servant."

Another piece of palace politics clicked into place for Ivara. Kirsten had seemed eager to serve the Princess and help with her wedding gown. Could the girl truly be genuine? She would have to keep a closer eye on the young seamstress. Losing a mother to execution had never engendered feelings of kindness.

They continued once more at a regular pace and Ivara asked the question that had been sitting in the back of her mind since the Princess had used the rune. "Everleigh…"

"Yes?"

"Is this safe? Wandering around without your guards near, outside the castle no less. I do not mean to question your decisions but –."

"Then don't. The guards know I come here; it was not so long ago that I would come here with my betrothed. He loved the beach nearly as much as I did." Everleigh tugged at her and they continued their walk down the beach.

"Richard told me. Prince Henry wasn't it? Forgive me but I am not as familiar as I should be with the Allagorian royal family." Ivara said as a gust of warm wind blew past them loosening both women's updo's significantly.

"Yes, Henry, Richard's older brother. He was the crown Prince of Allagor… he was *my* Prince." The Princess smiled mournfully as a single tear ran down her cheek. She wiped it away quickly. "In three days' time he is to be declared dead." Everleigh wiped the tears on her sleeve, her voice a raspy whisper.

"I'm sorry, truly." It was all Ivara could think to say. Sprinkles of rain fell from the sky and Ivara looked up to see the beginnings of a gentle shower.

"Richard is a good man, a noble man despite what some in the King's court say about him. I am certain that they only speak ill of their Prince because they do not truly understand what he has been through. Prince Henry was the life and joy of any room he walked into. As much as I would like to think of him as my own, in truth he was the peoples' Prince. Richard on the other hand has lost his brother at only sixteen and now with his father's health in decline..." She sighed. "...it's taking a toll on him."

A fat droplet of rain fell into the Princesses eye and as she wiped it away on her sleeve Everleigh looked up. Seeing the storm clouds form swallowed her grief and continued.

"Well it seems our time is waning; don't worry I'll be quick." Everleigh turned, taking both Ivara's hands. "I am to be married very soon. Once Henry is declared deceased, my engagement will be severed. I will be expected to marry. The King has already promised me to Prince Richard to maintain the peace treaty with my kingdom. The Allagorian nobles are tolerable but they are all fair weather friends if that. They would not be seen with me were I not of higher status than they. Thus I could use some true friends at court, and I would like you to be one of them."

Ivara took hold of her skirt and bowed deeply to the Princess. "I am honored by your highness but I fear I may not be in Allagor for long as I must return home as soon as I am able. My feelings of home aside, I know nothing of your customs and history. In truth I am still learning the language."

Everleigh took Ivara's hands, facing her now. "Rise, I don't want to add you to my court because of your knowledge of linguistics, history or culture. I would have you join us as a friend."

A drop of water fell into her eye and Ivara shut her eyes tightly, feeling faint. She felt herself fall. In her mind's eye Ivara could see the waves crashing against the shore. She could feel the tight corset that clung to her upper body beneath her blue dress. She could see the walls of the castle all around her. The vibrant palace colors seemed to fade to grey around her and the air felt stale. It was a familiar kind of loneliness. One Ivara had hoped to never feel again, even by proxy. She swiped at wet strands of strawberry blonde hair that had fallen from the intricate braid that held her long thick hair atop her head. Below her Ivara saw herself, laying in the sand as if in a trance. Her dirty blonde hair wet with sea water. When Ivara opened her eyes once more the honey-haired Princess was hovering over her with a worried expression. Ivara began to stand only to realize that the soft sand into which she had fallen challenged her to keep her balance. A wave splashed the two women in a cool reminder of their situation.

Another wave came rushing toward them only to fall flat in the surf just before reaching them. Ivara looked over to see that Everleigh's extensive blonde updo had begun falling apart and soaking strands stuck to either side of the Princess's face.

Ivara smiled sadly at the soaking wet Princess. "I would love to be your friend." She whispered.

The sun was high in the sky by the time Ivara had returned to her apartments, changed and found Jensin. She briefly wondered what would happen if she simply declined his offer to accompany him but she doubted anything good would come of it. And after hearing what befell Lady Rhea upon being accused of treason it wasn't something Ivara was willing to chance.

"Nothing about this 'plan' of yours sounds like a good idea." Ivara said dryly as she beckoned her horse into a trot to catch up with Jensin. She silently thanked whatever forces were at work for the riding trousers Richard had gifted her as well as her sword that hung at her hips. Though even Jensin himself had admitted the sword was more of a decoration to warn off enemies.

"Oh please. Have a bit of faith. A small group of the King's men will meet us there. If it looks like the building is occupied we simply sit back and observe."

"And if it's deserted like you said this morning?"

"Then we go in investigate a bit, take some notes and leave just as quickly as we came. The goal is to figure out where they are meeting. Hopefully, I'm correct and we won't have to look very far."

Ivara shook her head. Her nerves were on edge and she could see flashes of their last run in with Ravik and his folk. The last time they had tried to pull the wool over their enemies' eyes had ended in disaster. What made this any different? She could feel an itching sensation on the inside of her arm where lay an old scar she'd nearly forgotten she had. Only in moments such as these when her nerves were high did she swear she could feel the ache of the blade cutting into her skin many years ago. The memory was hazy, at times it was lost to her entirely.

They tied the horses up a short distance away. When they entered the warehouse Ivara was surprised to find it completely empty save for storage boxes. Before they came Jensin had made a point to inform her that the warehouse was often used for storage so she knew what to expect. The walls were empty of any design, just old rotting wood. And though the storage boxes were plentiful, the rest of the warehouse had nothing to offer.

"What now?" She asked Jensin.

He took a moment to think. "Here take this. It's a crowbar, we need to see what's inside the boxes."

"I thought you said that only the locals used the warehouse for storage." She said taking the curious looking tool from him.

"Yes but I just have a bad feeling about it alright."

"Well if you have a feeling." She said sarcastically as she turned away. The first box she checked was filled with cured leather and animal hides, the second held the same. As they searched they found boxes with grain, some with fishing equipment, and others with tools.

"Do crafters frequent this town?" Ivara asked.

"That's an understatement, last year the crown's treasury grew fatter from here than anywhere else in the kingdom aside from the capital, because nearly every man and woman's trade is crafting. They sell their goods at the quarterly market but unlike others they don't bring meat and grain but rather armor, fishing poles, clothes, and such."

"Hmm, makes sense." Ivara came upon another box marked with a locking rune. She ran her hand over it looking down at her own arm as she did so. The locking rune was similar in appearance to the marking on her own arm though the two symbols were far from twins. Something about it seemed so familiar to her. She had seen the locals make use of runes in Makoul; it was one of the only forms of magic that those without a source could make use of. Yet she had never carved a rune herself. Much less removed one. Her thoughts circled back to Princess Everleigh's tale.

"Jensin give me your dagger."

He looked over at her skeptically. "Why?"

"I want to try something. I'm not sure if it will work but I think it's at least worth a try." Seeing his hesitation she continued. "You brought me along to help right? So let me help." Hesitantly he handed her his blade. "This box has a locking rune on it." She explained as she gathered her courage blade in hand. "Everleigh told me a story about an exit from the castle that requires blood to activate the runic magic. I think this might work in a similar fashion."

"The rune Everleigh told you about requires royal blood to work. You never told me you're a princess."

"I'm not but I am the daughter of one who is linked by blood to a source." Ivara took a breath to master herself and sliced into her hand. The pain hit her first, then the familiarity. She had felt this before. Her body knew this pain, knew what it was for flesh to be sliced into at the palm. She was grateful when Jensin came over and hurriedly took the blade from her and squeezed her bloody palm over the rune. The rune glowed in a flash of gold, then she heard a click.

"Are you alright? You look dazed." Jensin asked her. There was a hint of tenderness and concern in his tone.

Ivara swallowed her pride. There was no telling when Scyla would signal for her and her Allagorian friends might be the only friends she would have for some time.

"No, no I don't think I am. It's been happening for some time now." She whispered.

"What are you talking about?"

"Visions, sights, sound, touch, taste, all ghosts of familiarity. Memories that aren't my own. But they feel so real. Just now the cut felt so familiar. And the woman in the library. I *knew* her. I swear I knew her but she was just a stranger... I feel like I'm going crazy." Ivara began rambling.

Jensin put a hand on her shoulder. "Take a deep breath. I've got you. You're not crazy. I'm sure having a cut felt familiar. You mean to tell me in your what sixteen years of life you've never cut yourself?"

Ivara wiped at her tears and chuckled. "I'm eighty-three."

Jensin's eyes widened. "Well then, point proven. Now I can't speak for you strange mer folk, but as for us humans it is normal to think you see someone you know in a stranger. It happens all the time."

"But –." She wanted to explain that there was more. The golden dragon she had seen in Ravik's ship, the way she had watched herself faint from Everleigh's eyes on the beach. Jensin cut her off.

"No more buts, you are perfectly sane. Now let's see what this mysterious box of wonders has in store for us."

They opened the box together. Inside were beautiful and expensive sheets of fabric each folded up nicely. Jensin reached in and grabbed a long folded piece of fabric and silently wrapped her wound. Ivara thanked him and began rummaging through the boxes' innards. She recognized a piece of blue fabric as matching

Princess Everleigh's dress and held it up. "You failed to mention that they supply the palace with goods."

Jensin looked over, cocking his head to the side in confusion. "That's because they don't." He took the fabric from Ivara's hands and began examining it. "What else is in that box?"

Taking the dress back from Jensin she placed it in her bag and began sifting through the fabrics. "A couple of dresses and plenty of fabric. Looking for anything specific?"

Jensin sighed. "No, not really. To be honest I'm not sure what I'm looking for anymore. I feel like I've been going around in circles with this case for months. It's exhausting." He took a deep breath. "Ready to head back?"

She nodded. "Can I keep the dress?"

Jensin looked her over as she held the dress's shoulders up to her own and twirled around in it. A small smile of endearment appeared on his face as he blushed. He turned away, hiding the expression with haste. "Sure. But be careful that you don't ruin it before we get back."

Chapter 36

"To the Dragon, master of the Arkstone,

I beg that you read this khipu. Things stir in Neroth, horrid things that I dare not speak of in a mere khipu lest it be intercepted. I do not know how much longer we have. A rot has set into the kingdom, a plague of the heart and mind. It has infected our politicians, even our family. I fear a civil war may soon be upon us. Should my brother in law succeed in overthrowing us you must know that I am pregnant - ."

Remnants of a torn khipu sent to the Golden Dragon of the Arkstone from the Queen of Neroth shortly before her death.

Tallulah (1556 A.D.)

"Argh! Stupid hair clip!" Brina tugged at her long brown hair. In recent years as she had begun to grow into herself and enter womanhood her hair and tail had seemed to race one another in length. Usually she would keep her long locs down to float about her face but today was different.

They'd been awoken before sunrise to begin getting ready. As the eldest and most senior of the Dragon's apprentices it was Brina's responsibility to keep the rest of her group in check. At least that was the task Nan and all the other handmaidens held her friend to. The reality was that both Osirus and Brina were of the same age, and even Corvena and Tallulah would begin coming into their maturity within the next twenty years. They were all four of them leaving their childhood and entering into the responsibilities of being true servants of the Golden Dragon.

Golden maidens, that was the term the locals used to describe them. Though Tallulah wondered how many of the locals could truly distinguish between the Dragon's servants and those bound to the Dragon by blood such as herself.

Brina reached for the cutting stone. Fast as lightning striking the sea, and with twice the fury, Corvena blocked her. "Don't you dare."

Brina made an impatient noise that reminded Tallulah of some of the land animals she'd seen on her rare trips to the surface.

"It's *my* hair!"

"Quiet! Come here and give me the comb."

"I-"

"Shh. Stop talking. That's why you have no friends-."

"I have friends!" Brina said indignantly.

"Tallulah doesn't count." Corvena finished, sectioning Brina's hair. Some days Tallulah was convinced Corvena was the child of whatever demons lurked in the deepest part of the ocean. That she was as hateful as she was beautiful. She certainly wasn't a pleasant person. Yet... every now and then she would show her soft side. Small things. Things that nobody but Tallulah would notice. She was beginning to think there was much more to the mer girl than her venomous exterior.

Corvena tugged ever so gently at Brina's long, chestnut waves. "The trick is to start from the bottom." Corvena replied to their silence. Tallulah watched her work, garnering only mild protest from Brina. The latter eventually stilled and Corvena began braiding. Of the three of them she was the only one who had ever been any good. Coming from a wealthy family she'd been taught young how to make herself presentable. One strand over the other, she worked until she reached the tips then wrapped them back over her head to form a crown. Tallulah handed her the pins and Corvena finished the job. "Finished."

Brina bit her lip and spun herself in the looking glass then glanced at Tallulah who smiled in return. The moment was sweet, Tallulah thought. Brina smiling meekly at her reflection and Corvena proudly looking between them. Brina reached to touch the braids but Corvena was faster and slapped her hand away. Just like that the moment fell away.

"Don't ruin it!" Corvena shrieked.

"Ouch!" Brina snapped. Brina reached up and tore out her pins leaving the still intact braids to fall at her sides. "You're not my friend! I don't need your help! And I certainly don't want it if it means you treat me like waste thereafter." Whatever Corvena's reply Brina waved her off. "Never mind, ugh just... never mind. C'mon Nan is waiting at the west end."

"We'll meet you there." Tallulah said calmly. Brina gave her a questioning look but nodded and left their room. Tallulah turned back to Corvena. "She's just stressed, didn't mean anything by it."

Corvena shook her head and her long silky black hair shuddered in the water around her. "She doesn't like me." In one quick motion she pulled her hair into a high ponytail. "Erm could you..?"

"Huh? Oh of course." Tallulah swam over from where she had been admiring the fabric of the sheer teal garment draped over her. It sparkled in even the smallest amount of light. Tallulah took hold of the mer girl's hair. "Is it right over left or left over right?"

"Doesn't matter."

"Thanks. *So* helpful." Tallulah said flatly and began her best attempt at a braid. She used the simple three strand technique that Corvena had been teaching her. It was easier on her own hair for some reason. When she'd finished Corvena turned and gestured to Tallulah's tight kinks. "Oh no you don't have to."

"You sure? It will only take a moment."

"Corvena last time you braided my hair it took *hours*."

Corvena gave her a half smile. "Still I feel bad."

"Don't." Tallulah shrugged. "Besides I rather like mixing it up it's—"

"Beautiful." Corvena whispered, completing the thought.

"What?" The compliment caught her off guard. It was almost as startling as the mouth it came from. Corvena looked away.

"Nothing, your hair I just-" Corvena was turning red now.

The awkwardness was stifling. "Thank you, um we should probably get going, they'll be here soon." Tallulah said and immediately wanted to facepalm. No wonder Corvena never complimented her.

"Right! Let's go." Corvena seemed to have completely recovered judging from her pale coloration. "Gods you're slow. Hurry!" And just like that she left and Tallulah was left wondering what had just happened.

Chapter 37

...though she has been home for nearly two years, my poor sweet Ivara still suffers intense nightmares nearly every night. Scyla bid me write to you if the problem worsened. Last night... last night was terrifying. Ivara woke up screaming in the middle of the night. She said her poor mother had been speared through the back, then she began raving about a searing pain in her eye. I've never seen anything like it.

Khipu from Lord Nerous to the Master of the Arkstone

Ivara (1604 A.D.)

The sun was waning when they left the warehouse. Ivara carefully folded up the elegant dress which she had taken from the runic box and gently tucked it away into her saddlebag while Jensin untied their horses. After which they set off back to the castle. They trotted along in silence passing various villages, inns, churches and graveyards. Ivara gestured to one such graveyard ahead of them. "I can't think of a single reason to keep your dead, they'll just rot away."

Jensin bristled, obviously uncomfortable with the comment. "It is to honor them. So you can go see them and speak with them after they have passed on to the next life. You don't have that in Makoul?"

"No, though I have heard of places in the south like Neroth for example, that have found a way to bury their dead in tight holes carved into the sides of underwater mountains. In Makoul though we simply put what remains of them in a bag and anchor it. The bags are porous so when the remains break down enough to escape they will provide food to the local wildlife." She turned to him and saw his disturbed expression. He did not hide it well. His blatant expression made her chuckle. "How much further?"

They walked on in silence. Something in the conversation had struck a chord with Ivara and she couldn't get the picture of the blood red water out of her mind. The warmth of it on her skin. And the fear that made a home in the back of her mind. She looked over at Jensin and in that moment she saw herself in the freckled walker.

"I'm sorry we didn't find what you were looking for." She offered when he went silent once more.

Jensin gave a humorless laugh. "I keep running through everything in my mind and it's like I have all the pieces of the puzzle but they just aren't fitting."

Ivara glanced down at the rune on her arm. "I know what you mean."

"Huh?"

She hesitated. *Could she trust him?* He already knew she was mer so what could be the harm. She took a breath. "You know I'm mer."

He nodded. "Well considering you *climbed onto my ship*. Yes, I caught on to that rather quickly." He chuckled. "In truth I may have pissed myself just a bit when you tried to say my name."

She laughed.

"Just over two years ago, I lost my memory."

"What, so you don't know who you are?" He asked in disbelief. When she didn't respond he became more serious. "You're serious? But you know your name at least. Or is Ivara a fake name?"

"No, no, I know my name. I know my parents, and sisters. But everything else... at best it's a blur."

"So technically, *you* could be our killer?" Jensin teased.

She grimaced.

"Right, sorry I was just trying to lighten the mood." He reached over and put a hand on her arm. "Don't worry they'll come back, your memories that is." He said it with such confidence that she nearly believed him.

She looked around just now realizing they were taking a different way back. Ivara said as much.

"Yes, well, the king's road is the fastest way back to our beds."

"Oh? Are we close to the road?"

"We're on it actually." He answered shortly, gesturing to the long road ahead.

"Why didn't we take this road when we were coming here?"

"Because I wasn't in a rush and the sun was still out. Bandits tend to attack at night."

"They do?"

"Oh please. Do they not have thieves and bandits where you're from?" Jensin asked in faux aggravation at her questions.

Ivara laughed shortly. "We have the sort. Mer that attack wanderers as they travel to their destination with little food or weapons. But attacking only at night would be foolish."

"And why is that?" Jensin said. She could tell he was bored, frustrated and tired but still she answered.

"Because we see better in the dark. Light is lost the deeper you go as is color and nearly all mer live deeper than any walker could dive."

Jensin thought it over briefly before replying. "So then how would one ambush a traveling mer?"

"A good question. The sea is full of travelers, whales, sharks, oarfish, regalecs... the list goes on. It is rare that a true traveler sits still for long and my people are no different. When I was traveling back home to Makoul my guardian Scyla suggested we spend the majority of our time in the deeper parts of the mesopelagic zone, the creatures that live there can get large and some are quite dangerous. But the lack of light protected us from any bandits during our journey home."

Ivara was so distracted watching Jensin's reaction to her words that she didn't see the man laying at the side of the road until her horse had nearly run him over.

"Help! Please!" The man cried out feebly. Ivara pulled back the reins of her horse but Jensin reached over and grabbed the reins away from her.

"No. We keep moving." Jensin said firmly.

"He's hurt!" She shouted back without turning her head. Once she was upon the man she began trying to soothe him while she investigated him for any mortal wounds but the man seemed almost entirely unharmed. "What is it? What ails you?" She asked him quietly.

"My leg, oh!" He yelled. "It must be broken, nothing else could render such pain!"

Ivara slowly lifted the man's pant leg to examine his leg then realized she didn't even know what she was looking for. She hardly understood how her own human legs worked, much less how to identify a serious ailment. Ivara heard footsteps behind her and realized that she would need Jensin's help with the man.

"Can you walk?" She asked the man before turning to berate her walker friend for taking so long. But instead of her friend she found a blade tip at her throat and Jensin, hands tied standing a few feet away in a similar position.

The man with the blade chuckled. "Yes, he can walk." She couldn't see his face due to the mask that covered it.

"What do you want of us?" Ivara said cautiously.

The bandit party crept closer and Ivara could see that their shields and weapons had all been marked with runes of protection and sturdiness. But she could not help but revert her attention back to the masked man before her with the blade. "Your bag, empty it."

"I have no gold, sorry to disappoint." Ivara replied sourly.

"The bag, *now*!" His blade pressed deeper now and Ivara could feel something warm sliding down her neck. She swallowed hard.

"My saddle bag, it's over by the horses. The black mare that one's mine."

One of the men began sifting through her saddle bags. Until he finally rose up to his feet shaking his head. "It's not here."

"What? Of course it is! I saw them leave with it! Check again." He turned his attention back to Ivara. "Where. Is. It?"

"Where is what?"

"The dress! Where is the dress dammit? I know you stole it from the warehouse down the road. I saw you myself. So where are you hiding it?"

"All this over a dress? Here, take it." Ivara tossed her shoulder back to the man. "The dress is in there, I'm sorry I didn't realize –."

"Realize that this," He pulled the dress from the satchel. "could be the key to stopping a war? No, of course you didn't know."

"What?" Ivara asked confusedly.

The man's sword arm lost its stiffness and he began talking to himself. Mumbling the same thing again and again. "Yes only the select few, only them, us, only us, only they know, the select few know."

Ivara tried backing away only to bump into the deceptive man from earlier. He grabbed her from behind and together they fell and rolled around on the dirt. Ivara kicked and screamed as she struggled against him but he was far too strong for her. He tried to silence her with a hand across her mouth but she took the opportunity to bite down as hard as she could. The man yelped in pain. With his other hand he grabbed her head and hit it against the ground, hard, before standing and assisting the other man with tying up Jensin who was raging against them. The pain echoed in Ivara's skull and she screamed. Her vision was blurry and her head pounding as she crawled away. One of the men grabbed her by her arm and she vomited at the sudden motion.

The man made a disgusted expression then seeing the mark on her arm his eyes widened. "This one's been marked! It's an amnesia rune!"

The second man finished muffling Jensin and came over to examine Ivara. "Who did this to you? Who marked you?"

Ivara shook her head. She tried to say that she didn't know but her voice was a raspy whisper and the taste of vomit soured her tongue.

The men looked her over once more then sighed in unison. "If the mistress wanted her dead then she would have killed her rather than mark her." The one on the left said.

"She had the dress, perhaps she knows. We cannot risk it." The man on the right pulled out a large dagger and held it up preparing for the killing blow.

Ivara could feel herself falling. A sense overwhelmed her and suddenly the man's knife was in *her* bulky, muscular hand. She held it steadily looking down at a terrified version of herself bloody, bruised and covered in her own vomit. She held the dagger steadily.

"What are you waiting for?" The man beside her said. She looked from him to herself and back again. She was angry. She was terrified. With a scream she sliced at the man beside her, dropping her own thin body in the process. In the back of her mind she could feel the impact, but she was too lost in her proxy's mind to pay any mind to her body. Then she felt a choking sense, a loss of breath, the feeling sucked her back into her body. She was choking on her own vomit. When she looked up the two men were each throwing heavy blows on one another.

She grabbed the knife intended for her demise and scooted to where Jensin lay eyes wide and struggling against his restraints. She took off the cloth that muffled his speech and began cutting away at the rope that held his hands together.

"Hurry!" Jensin whispered.

"I'm trying!" Ivara whispered back.

A large hand grabbed her from the back causing her to drop her blade and suddenly she was facing one of the bandits. He swung his sword at her and she held her arms up in a hopeless attempt to defend herself. The blade cut through her arm's skin like butter. She cried out in pain even as something clicked into place in the back of her mind. She cried out just as visions of those she'd known began appearing all around her.

Suddenly she could no longer tell what was real and what was her imagination. To her left a mer girl with deep brown hair, pale skin and green eyes cried out scratching at her arm and ripping the dozens of jellyfish tentacles that gripped it. In front of her a mer woman with deep brown skin and tight curly hair was smiling and giving her a concerned look, then turning to another mer woman behind her who was a shadow made flesh.

She fell back with a scream and when she looked up a great golden dragon stared down at her. Her breaths came in quick and shallow as she could not move for terror. All these faces, ghosts of strangers that had haunted her for as long as she could remember. Driving her insane. Then in a moment of clarity she realized something. The faces that surrounded her were those of family, friends, and teachers. She *did* know them. Some more intimately than others but she knew each one as well as she knew herself. They were memories, not ghosts. *Her memories* she realized. Locked away from her for so long but now they were free. Now *she* was free.

Then Jensin was there, hands freed and now holding a sword. As swift as the wind itself Jensin was upon the bandit's leader shoving his blade through the man's eye. Ivara watched as he pulled the blood soaked blade from the dead man's eye and pressed it up against the dress.

"Don't touch her! Leave us, or I shall cut this garment to shreds!" He screamed at the remaining men. "And I shall summon my witch to cut down what is left of you!" He gestured to Ivara. She did her best to give the men a steely glare but the visions that still swirled around made it difficult to concentrate.

"Only if you give us the dress." One of the bolder bandits shouted out.

"Done. Now go!" Jensin threw the dress at the bandit. Ivara's vision was fading bit by bit when Jensin ran over to examine her wound. His face darkened as he took her arm and began wrapping some cloth around it. "We need to get you to town. To the castle... do you stand?" Whatever he said next Ivara could not hear as she had already lost consciousness and the darkness found her.

Chapter 38

"The Red Mer as they are often called live deep in the sea, where there is no light. Thus the crimson color that makes them stand out so much here in the shallows, is the key to their camouflage in their home waters. This fact along with their enormous serpentine regalecs, and mysterious ancestry make them terrifying foes to face, especially when encountered in the deeper parts of the sea."

A Beginners Guide to the Kingdom of Colors by Nyra of Neroth

Tallulah (1556 A.D.)

Tallulah didn't like outsiders. Though she did her best to be kind and welcoming, everything her kin had *not* been, something about those who sought refuge in the Arkstone irked her. Perhaps they each reminded her that once she had not lived in a palace but in a system of caves neighboring a shipwreck. That once she did not have old Nan to tend to all of her personal needs, to hug her when she cried, to encourage her and to be strict with her. Instead she had a mother that did not want to be a mother.

A mer woman raised for the spear cursed with a crooked tailed child who could not swim well even now. Perhaps it was the awful truth that before she had come here she'd been unloved and powerless to change her own destiny. Now though everything was different. And every mer that swam through the golden gates reminded her of that.

They reminded her that in a matter of years for some, moments for others, power could be acquired or taken away and so could love. Some small part of Tallulah wanted to be acknowledged for how far she had come. She was a child of the Dragon now. A student of magic. How could these foreign visitors ever understand what all she had been through?

The years since she had arrived had begun to turn Brina cold. In many respects the bubbling girl that had greeted Tallulah with a warm hug and bright smile was dying. These days Brina greeted visitors with frustration, speaking only when spoken to when surrounded by strangers. Most of the strangers they greeted wanted something of them, few sought the Arkstone for sightseeing or general pleasure.

But the family that entered their halls on this day were not immigrants, nor did they seek riches. No, the family that stood before Tallulah and her golden kin appeared to be quite wealthy at first glance. The Lord floated at the far left, his hair was a light brown and his tail a deep saturated green that matched his eyes.

Beside him swam a woman of crimson skin. She wore no garments save for the rings of dazzling white cloth tied around her forearms. Her long dark red hair was tied half up on top and the rest was left to float around her. Her pale grey eyes dazzled from a distance. As did her crimson skin and tail. Her left forearm was marred with a black scar that appeared to embed itself in her veins as if her very blood had turned black. Small white blotches appeared on her chest, abdomen and tail. Other than that she was crimson in color. The mer woman placed a delicate hand on her protruding abdomen. She was expecting them.

She was an odd sort of eye catching beauty that you just couldn't look away from. But Tallulah recognized the Red Mer before her as the woman that had aided her and her father all those years ago. The sight of the mer woman's pale grey eyes surrounded by crimson skin was enough to make one want to hide away but

Tallulah knew better. Beside her a mer girl, presumably one of their children, had her arms crossed. Her expression was marred by the annoyed expression she was giving her siblings. The mer girl seemed to be an exact replica of her father, from her emerald eyes to her dark brown hair.

Beside her were two mer girls who might have been twins had it not been for their polar opposite features, but even then the similarities were striking. The first a blonde haired mer girl with brown eyes and a pale pink tail. The other dark as a storm but with skin paler than any of her sisters and both her eyes and tail were bluer than the sea itself. The first struggled not to laugh, as the second signed something to her. Tallulah wondered at their joke before turning to the last of the children. The youngest of her siblings, she looked around in awe until her eyes landed on Tallulah and she smiled. Tallulah offered a shy wave. The mer girl's eyes were stone grey and her hair somewhere between brunette and blonde, though it lacked the warmth of her sister's hair.

"Children! Bow before our guests!" Nan shrieked loudly at them. Turning to the family she said, "The Golden Dragon of old welcomes you to the Arkstone. As a show of goodwill he offers his most trusted and humble servants to aid you whenever you should find the need to call upon them."

Brina who'd been working all morning managed a bright smile. "Brina of the Arkstone." She began bowing. "The Master welcomes you Lord Neuros."

Corvena mastered her face quickly and smoothly. She gave a deep bow and a pleasant smile. "Corvena of the Arkstone, the Master welcomes you."

Tallulah did the same bowing as deeply as she dared and smiling kindly just as she'd been trained. "Tallulah of the Arkstone, the Master welcomes you."

Osirus bowed. "Osirus of the Arkstone. The Master welcomes you."

Lord Neuros smiled deeply and bowed to them. He gestured to the crimson skinned mer woman. "My wife, Lady Brizo." The Lady of Makoul gave her a small smile of recognition.

Nan bowed her head to the woman, "All the sea has heard the startling tales of your people my Lady. The Red Mer are highly revered in these parts."

"The honor is mine. In all my travels I must say I have never visited the Arkstone Palace before. I see now that the legends hardly do it justice. Though I must say I am hoping that the rumors regarding payment are not true. But more on that later, I'd like to introduce you to my children before we go before the Master."

She turned to her children, introducing them each in turn. "My eldest Ka'I Mare." The eldest of the mer girls bowed deeply keeping careful control of her features. "The twins, Mele and Uhane." The two mer girls clasped hands and bowed in tandem. "And my youngest, Ivara." Ivara, who had been taking everything in, was startled into focus via a slap from her sister's tail. She looked forward again and gave a curt bow. Tallulah couldn't help but to notice the girl was the smallest of her sisters and the shyest as evidenced by the mer girl constantly picking at her fingernails.

"Pardon, but is there a place where the children might be able to stay while the discussions are being held?" Lord Neuros asked Nan.

"Of course, though I feel obligated to tell you that hiding the children away will not dissuade the Master when it comes to your *payment*."

"Yes, yes of course. Why do you think we brought them along?" Lady Brizo replied with a nervous smile.

Tallulah and her golden sisters escorted the mer children one by one towards the guest housing that had been prepared for them. Corvena led the eldest of the girl's, neither looked quite thrilled with the other, while Brina and Osirus took the twins, their gentle nature eased all the more by Brina's kindness and motherly traits. This left Tallulah to guide the shy mer girl that had been staring at her for the past half hour. The mer girl was not very talkative but that was just as well for Tallulah.

The Arkstone was her home, and these outsiders... No, that wasn't fair. The poor girl was nervous and overwhelmed. Tallulah remembered the nervousness, the dread, the sudden realization that she may be left behind, all of it as if it were yesterday. They were halfway to the guest housing when Tallulah turned and took the mer girl's hand. The webbing was much thinner than the hands of one from the west.

"Care to go on a field trip..." Lost in her thoughts Tallulah had forgotten the girl's name.

"Ivara." The mer girl whispered not looking up.

"Alright, care to go on a field trip, Ivara?" Tallulah asked gently, letting herself sink down in the water until she was eye to eye with the girl. The girl thought for a moment before responding.

"Will it be dangerous? Mother said we were not to get hurt, she said that it could hurt the deal."

"Nothing can hurt you so long as you stick by me." Tallulah smiled. "Can you do that?"

The little mer girl nodded and Tallulah began leading her towards the outskirts of the city.

Chapter 39

Gentle folk, I come here to die. I die a sister, I die a bastard and I die a mother. And though it sickens me to place my head on such a bloody block as this... if it is my life that is the price to keep our world whole. I pay it willingly. Mortem Dolah.

The last words of Lady Rhea.

Ivara (1604 A.D.)

In her dream Ivara could see a huge ship leaving port with an ecstatic young man aboard. His presence felt familiar and comforting but when she looked upon his face she was overwhelmed with sadness and regret. Suddenly the dream twisted and changed, but she remained the same. She was in an angry crowd outside the palace. A woman about twenty three years her senior was being escorted to a bloody block while an executioner stood with a large axe at the ready.

The woman wore an ornate purple gown that matched her deep purple eyes. Her long black hair was tied in up a purple ribbon but strands of black and grey had fallen out. Her face was a porcelain imitation of Kirsten's. All around her the crowd shouted curses on the woman. Ivara stood there, frozen in Everleigh's body quietly sobbing. Terrified for the woman before her that faced execution.

She'd been in the room when the King had passed his judgment. 'Traitor' that was the word he had used to describe Lady Rhea. The same woman who had acted as a mother and close friend to

Everleigh for as long as she could remember now kneeled over an executioners block taking in her last moments alive. Moments later a guard held the twitching head high showing it off for all to see while the body lay motionless at his feet. The dream twisted and changed once more and suddenly she was back inside. As she gazed in the mirror she could see her beautiful golden locks of strawberry blonde hair and piercing blue eyes. Everleigh's hair, Everleigh's eyes. The door to her apartments opened and a young man about her age entered.

"Henry!" She greeted him with a kiss on the cheek.

He pulled away gently. The Prince cupped her face in his hands before speaking. "I'll be back within the month. And I *will* marry you. I love you Everleigh but I must do this for my own sake. I *need* this."

"But why?" She cried into his hands. "What have I done to make you leave like this?"

Henry, her prince, the boy that was supposed to be an arranged spouse had grown into the love of her life. Once a boy, now a man. Once a prince soon to be the king. Once her friend, now her fiancé. She loved him so much it drove her mad. And now he was leaving her. Even for a month, she wasn't sure if she could bear it.

"You know why, with my father's illness getting worse it won't be long before he passes and they will crown me. I won't spend the rest of my life stuck to a throne staring at the same stone walls. Please, you must understand." Her Prince pleaded with her.

She sobbed but nodded. On her forehead Ivara could vaguely sense a cool wet cloth. The feeling pulled her from her sleep and she awoke to hear two women talking to each other. When she opened her eyes the blurry vision of Everleigh leaning over her with a wet towel came into focus. The foreign princess looked frazzled and tired. Her updo had fallen out and she wore only her nightgown. Another shape came into focus behind her, Kirsten.

"Here's some fresh cloths and water." Kirsten said quietly as she handed the items to Everleigh.

"Thank you." They spoke in hushed voices.

The cool sensation on her forehead had begun to warm then suddenly it returned as Everleigh lay a new rag on Ivara's head. It took her a moment to realize that neither of her friends knew she was awake.

"Did the medics say anything about her arm?" Kirsten asked.

Everleigh shook her head. "It's rune magic, few here even know what the runes mean, much less how to heal a damaged one. They said it's best not to tamper with it. Besides Kirsten, it was carved into her skin! What if we hurt her by trying to help?"

Ivara tried to move, to speak. Let them know she was awake and alright but sleep tugged at her and she was not strong enough to fight it. Slowly she let herself fall back into the blissful darkness where nothing but dreams awaited her. The visions came once more in a smoky haze.

She was walking up the tower steps, Princess Everleigh ahead of her walking at a brisk pace when out of pure curiosity she looked out one of the windows as she passed. What she saw shocked her.

A head with dark hair slowly succumbing to strands of grey. It's eyes, her mother's eyes, were open and it lay on its side facing her. Where once there had been beautiful purple eyes now lay black holes and dry rotting flesh. Crows were taking their turns with the head and its body which lay a few feet away. She felt warm tears drip down her face, Kirsten's face. Breathing became difficult and she fell to her knees in anguish. Arms wrapped about her and the Princess's soothing voice cooed in her ear as gentle as breeze.

Then the dream shifted and she was no longer in the comforting arms of the Princess but underwater and out in the distance a great golden castle sat submerged with mer going in and out of it. Beside her was the witch Scyla and two other mer women. The first with long dark green hair, and one golden eye, the other being a common green color. Her tail shone brightly of gold and glistened in the sun alongside the other mer woman. This one had deep brown skin and her tightly curled hair swayed this way and that in the current. The first pulled out a blade but before Ivara had time to lean away in fear she awoke once more.

The room was dark, one window had been kept open and through it Ivara could see the full moon. It's light gave the floors and walls a cold eerie feeling. When she tried to sit up a piercing feeling struck her head. She tried once more pushing through her headache but had to clutch the bed to keep her balance. They were back, her memories. The Golden Mer, the Arkstone, years of trying to master this magic that she had been given at only thirty five years old. But she was a child no longer. Forty eight years later though she was far from mastering her magic. At least she knew now that running wasn't the solution.

She looked down at her arm. At the cloth that covered the amnesia rune that had been carved into her skin and since ruined by a walker blade. She cursed her own idiocy. She should have never let this happen. Questions buzzed around in her mind like bees to their queen. *Did her friends miss her? Did they know her rune had been broken? Were they looking for her?* Ivara pulled herself out of bed grabbing at the wardrobe for balance as she led herself over to the window. The sea was calm tonight, as calm as she'd ever seen it as a walker. Tomorrow she'd have to find Scyla. Beg for a way home, not to Makoul but to the Arkstone. As for tonight she was content to watch the push and pull of the tides and listen to all the land animals sing their nightly hymns.

Chapter 40

"I heard then three battle cries. Once from the north, another from the south, and finally from the east. When I looked each way I saw that their monarchs were weak and would not last long."

An excerpt from the prophecy of the Dolah as it was first recorded by the mer of the Arkstone in the year 1207

Ivara (1604 A.D.)

When morning came the following day Ivara was still gazing out the window lost in thought. A soft knock came at the door. It was Kirsten, her curly brown hair tied up in a purple ribbon. The human girl, on the cusp of adulthood, wore a white under dress with a brown leather corset and purple skirt. The only thing that remained noteworthy about her appearance was her ornately carved necklace.

"Oh good you're up. How do you feel?" Kirsten said softly.

Ivara took a long breath before answering. The air was cool and misty outside. "Better, how long was I asleep?"

"About a day. You had a pretty bad fever. Here." Kirsten handed her a cool damp cloth. "For your head. Just because you're awake doesn't mean you're not still sick. Though you look much better."

Ivara took the cloth and let out a sigh of relief as she dabbed it against her forehead. "Thank you." She said to her friend. She wondered briefly how someone like Kirsten who'd been through so much pain and loss could ever be content to be a mere servant. But mostly Ivara wondered how the girl had come out of the loss of her mother with her kind heart still intact.

"Perhaps you should rest a bit, you look pale. How long have you been up?" Kirsten said coming over to the window.

"I'm not sure. When I woke it was dark out, and the moon was high in the sky."

Kirsten gently took her by the arm and led her back to her bed. "Don't worry I won't confine you to the bed, that's the medics job, but you should definitely eat something before you take off and you should at least sit for that. I'll go fetch you some breakfast, please just rest, I won't be long."

Ivara nodded weakly and watched her friend leave the room. When she could no longer hear the clatter of footsteps Ivara began unwrapping her bandaged arm. The cloth was white and red with spots of dried blood. Once she finished unwrapping it she could see the wound all too clearly. The rune had long since scarred but the cuts remained fresh. Her memories had returned to her and yet she still had no clear way of returning home. Suddenly a thought occurred to her. Her friends in Allagor knew her to be quiet and naïve. But time told a different story.

Her time with the Golden Mer had hardened her even if it had nearly driven her insane. She would have to pretend she realized. Pretend that she was still a curious amnesiac. Pretend that she would not do anything it took to return to her sisters and brother at the Arkstone. She swallowed hard. It was deceptive she knew and yet, her small amount of peace here in Allagor would surely be jeopardized if her new found friends came to know her as a witch and a weapon rather than a young woman. That was if Jensin had not already given away her secret. It wasn't long before Kirsten returned with a tray of cheese, bread and wine.

"Eat something it will help you get your strength back." She said placing the trey on the bed next to Ivara before turning to leave once more.

"Wait!" Ivara called just now realizing how scratchy her voice was from lack of drink.

"Yes?" Kirsten said, turning to face her.

"Sorry but would you mind staying? Just for a bit?" Ivara wasn't entirely sure why she had asked. Perhaps it was a newfound loneliness that had arisen in her along with the realization of how far she truly was from her mer friends. Or perhaps she just wanted to talk. She wasn't entirely sure. Still Kirsten nodded and sat on the bed opposite to her.

"Is everything alright?" Kirsten asked gently.

"Yes, it is. I just, well I realized it's been nearly a year since I last saw my family. And just when I find myself feeling at home in your, forgive me but Allagor is a strange land... I'd just rather not wallow in that thought alone." Ivara took a piece of bread, she hadn't realized just how hungry she'd been.

"I know exactly what you mean. I lost my mother a little over a year ago. It still hits me now and again. That pang of grief and loneliness." She shivered.

"I'm so sorry. What happened?"

Kirsten took a long breath before replying. "She was beheaded on counts of treason and spying. Someone had caught her sending off letters containing descriptions of the private day to day business of the royal family... of Princess Everleigh specifically."

"How was she even able to access such information?"

"Oh Everleigh didn't tell you? My mother was the King's *bastard* sister." Kirsten swallowed hard. "She should have been born a princess, instead they called her Lady Rhea. *Lady* ugh, as if it were a gift for the daughter of a King to be given a title.

My mother used to tell me stories of her youth, of how her father gave her the title to show his love for her, without ever knowing the damage it did to her. Anytime the old king, my grandfather, turned his eye away the court saw fit to jest about her title. Then they banished her because she fell in love with a commoner. And even that wasn't enough, the poor man was executed for taking my mother's innocence. It was the first and last time they ever called her Princess."

Kirsten wiped at a tear that spilled from her purple eyes. It took the seamstress a moment to catch her breath, when she did, she continued in a shaky voice.

"I always thought family was about love. I never met my grandfather but my mother spoke of love and kindness when she told me of her childhood and being raised in Allagor. I was born in Ellenward but I can still remember the light in her eyes when she received the letter that my uncle, the King, had invited her back to court.

I never thought anyone could be so heartless as to murder their family. But they did, they took her head and left her corpse out to rot away in the sun. I was still asleep when it happened. When I awoke the crows were already picking at my mother's eyes." Kirsten said, looking away visibly shaken.

"I'm sorry it must have been awful knowing that she had mere days left."

"Oh no the whole affair was kept a secret from me, it was my mother's wish. I knew she was imprisoned on counts of treason of course, but nothing more. I didn't even know she was dead until I was walking up the eastern tower and saw her head being picked apart by fowl the same evening that she'd been killed. Only then was I told but by then it was far too late to say goodbye."

`Ivara reached out and put her hands on Kirsten's in a comforting gesture but couldn't think of anything to say to her friend. Kirsten looked down and seeing her scar pulled away. In an obvious effort to change the subject she began asking about Ivara's trip to the warehouse.

"So I heard you and our redheaded friend found something?"

"Far from it actually, the warehouse was just that, a warehouse. Nothing of interest inside it."

"Really no beautiful gowns that one might steal?" Kirsten teased.

Ivara put a hand to her temple in embarrassment. "So Jensin told you about that bit. You should have seen it Kirsten. It was the most beautiful thing that I've ever seen and it was just laying there. I know it was wrong but -."

"Relax Ivara, I'm not judging. Though you probably shouldn't take things that don't belong to you." She gestured to the cut on Ivara's arm. "That said, what happened to the dress? It wasn't with you when the two of you returned."

"Oh we ran into some unsavory folk on the way back." Ivara held up her scarred arm. "They attacked us then took the dress and left us both with some rather painful souvenirs." Ivara chuckled weakly.

Kirsten didn't laugh. Instead her face froze and she rose to leave. "I have to go. You should keep a bandage on that." She was halfway out the door when she turned. "Oh and Ivara, you really should be wearing long sleeves, at least until you leave us for good. Nothing good will come from a foreigner showing off a disenchanted amnesia rune." With that she turned and left.

Ivara sat there on the bed for what seemed like an eternity mulling over her friend's words. *Did all walkers understand runes?* No, of course not. Jensin hadn't known runes, or if he had he never brought such knowledge up around her. Richard, despite his superb education, didn't even seem to believe in magic, much less runes.

She finished off her breakfast and went back to bed seeking respite for her now pounding head. When she awoke the sun was high in the sky. Ivara dressed herself. Though she still felt a bit weak she was able to put on a simple white chemise with a teal kirtle overtop. She found an old leather corset in one of the drawers and fashioned it over her gown. The back of the corset had been laced in golden string that sparkled in the sunlight spilling in through her window. She liked it and lamented the fact that she would not be able to see it again until she undressed. Gingerly, she opened the door to her room and began walking. She would need to find and speak with Scyla as soon as possible.

Every moment she spent on land was another day that her golden sisters at the Arkstone wouldn't be able to contact her. She needed to return to them not only for their sake but also for her own. She was still untrained in her magic and had little control over it. She was a danger to herself now and to others until she fully mastered the golden magic the Dragon had gifted her.

She was also tentatively hoping that Scyla had information on her birth sisters. Had Wyntir reached their mother? Was Ka'I safe? Was Makoul intact? Had Mele and Uhane made it to safety with the surplus of citizens under their care?

She told herself that of course her sisters were safe. Why else would Uhane have returned to Makoul and thus Allagor to find Ivara? But a terrifying what if scratched at the back of her mind and Ivara knew she would not be able to rest until she had a solid answer to these questions.

In her rush she failed to notice the ginger man speaking with a guard down the hall and managed to bump into both simultaneously.

"Oh sorry." She apologized, blushing as she turned to Jensin and the guard.

"Ivara you're up, good we need to talk." Jensin nodded in dismissal to the guard. "Thank you for the update."

"Indeed we do Jensin, something's happened." Ivara said in a low whisper.

"What is it?"

"I trust this information may stay between us?"

Jensin mulled it over a bit then motioned for her to be silent. "Not here. The walls have ears, come let's go back to your room." She followed him back to her quarters. Once they arrived, he locked the door behind them. "Speak quietly." He said as he gestured for her to continue.

"I remember." She said eagerly.

"What do you mean?"

"My memories have returned, and it is urgent that I speak with Scyla, she's the witch who helped me come into your world in the first place."

Jensin's eyebrows shot up. "Scyla? As in the fabled Sea Witch that mothers use to scare their children from straying too deeply into the surf?"

Ivara looked hard at him. He really was surprised.

"The very same." She said shortly. "She is a friend of mine. She helped me come into your world, and before that she helped me leave the Arkstone and return home."

Jensin muttered something incredulous under his breath. "Alright I'll assemble a few men to escort you."

"No!" Ivara yelled in hushed tones. "I doubt anyone that you could send would take well to such a creature as Scyla. I'll go alone."

"Alone with me at least." Jensin offered stubbornly. He shook his head, his expression one of disgust as he said. "I fear what those mean might have done to you had things... not gone the way that they did." Fearing he would not let it go she just nodded.

"Fine, come along. But you mustn't threaten her or harm her. And you would do well to prepare yourself. Scyla can be a bit testy."

"You really think I would harm one of your strange mer friends? After what you did to those bandits on the King's road? I'm not daft, Ivara."

Ivara winced, she had hoped he might have forgotten what she'd done on the kings road. Still she tried to lighten the tone. "No but you are a walker, and with lack of age comes lack of experience. How old did you say you were?" Ivara teased flirtatiously.

"I didn't, though if you must know, seventeen." He straightened trying to seem taller.

Ivara was genuinely shocked. She'd known that humans had short lifespans but never realized how short they truly were. "Seventeen? I can't tell if you're joking or not."

"Really, well then how old do I look to you." Jensin said, taking her arm as they walked out the door and towards the stables.

Ivara looked him over. "Your mid-eighties perhaps."

Jensin halted and gave her an incredulous look. "What? Now it's you who jests surely."

"No, one of my sisters just celebrated her eighty eighth birthday, and you look about her age."

"Impossible, few ever even live to see their eighties." Jensin said as they turned a corner.

"Perhaps that is how it is with your people but mine often live to see four centuries."

"Alright then how old are you actually?"

"Eighty – three."

Jensin in his confusion tripped and Ivara gripped at his coat to keep him from falling.

"Thank you." He said once he was steady on his feet. They walked on through the castle until they reached the stables. It was all Ivara could do not to pinch her nose. It wasn't the most kindly of smells.

"By the way," Ivara said turning to Jensin who was saddling their steeds, "why did you tell Kirsten about the dress we found in the crate? I thought that sort of information was to be kept secret. Wasn't that the whole reason we didn't bring an escort?"

Jensin looked puzzled. "I never told her about our outing aside from the fact that you'd been wounded." He handed her the reins.

Chapter 41

"Though they are not a royal family, the Mare's of Makoul have a long and interesting history. The family have held their lordship for over twelve hundred years. The mer women in the Mare line have on more than one occasion married into royalty. While the men serve as both stewards of their water and warriors."

Royal Families of the Sea by Freya Burg

Tallulah (1556 A.D.)

The swim was longer than Tallulah remembered it to be, but then again she hadn't been to this region of the outskirts in nearly a year. Behind them swam a mer girl only slightly older than Ivara. The girl called herself Ka'I, Tallulah only needed a short glance to identify her. The elder of the mer girls kept her distance, obviously thinking that stealth was her personal strong suit... it was not. Perhaps Ka'I thought herself a spy... Tallulah hoped the mer girl didn't stake her future on it. Tallulah looked onwards, they were nearing the farm, she could see them in the distance. Blobs of iridescent blue, purple, and green swam around in the far distance.

Tallulah turned to Ivara. "I need you to trust me ok?" The mer girl nodded her head. "Alright, from here on I need you to keep your eyes closed. I'll know if you open them!"

The mer girl giggled and shut her eyes, taking Tallulah's hand once more as they swam closer and closer to the farm. The creatures slowly coming into focus as they neared them.

"Are we getting close?" Ivara said, still keeping her eyes firmly shut.

"Yes, almost there just a bit further. Remember, do *not* let them touch you!" Tallulah whispered urgently. "Ok open your eyes!"

Ivara did so and gasped at the sight before her. All around them giant capillatas danced through the water, their colors changing with every movement. Huge transparent bags of flesh floated in various directions around them. Each bag of flesh sporting hundreds if not thousands of long thin tentacles. Mer men with tan skin that sported blue dots on the arms and neck, red raised scars all over their bodies, and deep purple and blue tails swam all around them with spears and nets. They watched as each mer man took his turn trying to catch the capillatas without getting stung.

"There's so many." Ivara said aghast. "What...what are they?"

"Capillatas, that's the local term for them at least. Twice a year the farmers will herd them here once for breeding and once for –."

"Harvest." Ivara said pointing to the mer who'd managed to take down one of the great beasts. The joy had vanished from Ivara's face and she looked down. Tallulah stroked her hair and put a comforting hand on the mer girl's shoulder.

"Don't be sad, it's said that a single capillata can feed an entire village for a whole day. Though in retrospect I assume that rumor has to do with the larger varieties."

Ivara smiled a bit. "Are they always this big?" She asked.

Tallulah nodded, and the jellyfish-like beings danced all around her in the warm blue water. "All that I've seen are, but the sea is a big place so who knows."

"Look, that one there is nearly as tall as my father's castle in Makoul!" Ivara said pointing to one of the larger of the creatures. The beast's size still took Tallulah's breath away even to this day, even after years of visiting the beasts during their season. Behind them a whoosh of the water and Ka'I came swimming up to them.

"*What* are you doing here?" Ka'I asked.

Tallulah didn't hesitate to throw the girl's sass right back at her. "What are *you* doing here without Corvena?"

"I'm forty years old! I don't need some half-wit, golden eyed *freak* to tell me what to do or where to go. Especially one who's less than ten years my senior."

"Half-wit?" Ivara swam out from behind Tallulah. "These mer have been nice to us, and all you can do is run your mouth with insults! If you wanted to come along so badly why didn't you just ask Lady Corvena for permission?"

"Because I don't need her permission or your permission or anyone else's to go do things." Ka'I began pumping her webbed hands all around and her gills flared with frustration. Tallulah reached over to calm the girl but in Ka'I's excitement, the mer girl failed to notice a mid-sized capillata gently glide past her. The creature's tentacles quickly brushed the skin of her arm and the mer girl paused before crying out in pain.

"What do we do?" Ivara shouted in a panic.

"Swim back, do you remember the way?" The girl nodded. "Swim as fast as you can and get your parents. Be sure to tell Corvena and Brina as well. Do you remember what they look like?"

"I think so."

"Good. *Go!*"

As soon as the little mer girl was off Tallulah turned her attention to her other charge. Ka'I floated in place crying and clutching at her arm. In her panic she had yanked the creature's tentacles and ripped them from its body. The lone tentacle now whipped about as the mer girl twisted in pain. Tallulah dodged it as best she could praying that Ivara was a fast swimmer and that her parents were even faster.

"Ka'I listen to me you have to stop twisting around. You have to be still ok." Tallulah tried her best to sound gentle and calm but her heart was racing. Tallulah allowed herself to sink below Ka'I until she could safely grab the mer girl's tail, right above the fin and began dragging the poor soul back to the inner city.

It wasn't long before she sighted two mer in the distance. The first was nearly Tallulah's size and had pale skin and a greenish blue tail. Tallulah recognized the mer girl as Ivara. As the duo came closer Tallulah could make out the anxious look on the mer girl's face. The second was a longer figure whose crimson color marked her from the top of her head to the tip of her tail with only a few spots of white. The pair swam quickly towards them and Tallulah could see that Ivara was holding her mother's hand.

Despite the mother's crimson complexion, when the pair had finally gotten close enough Tallulah could see the ire in the woman's face. Perhaps red mer could not be flushed with anger, but anger was not a difficult emotion to spot. Tallulah took a breath of the sea water around her, and swam upwards to meet the pair, ready to take the full force of the mothers anger. But to her surprise when the red woman spoke it was not to her but rather to the eldest of her daughters.

"Are you stupid?" She screamed at Ka'I. "Have you not the intelligence of an eel?"

Tallulah, not wishing to see the girl in pain any longer spoke up. "I know of a rune to numb it, and another to heal it once the nematocysts are removed but it may be difficult to find someone to do the latter."

The red mer woman just waved Tallulah off. "No." She sighed. "Some lessons must be learned the hard way. Do you have a blade? Good, give it to me."

The mer girl's mother took the blade from Tallulah's hands, seemingly indifferent to her daughter's moans of pain. In her other hand she wrapped the loose end of the torn tentacle around her hand as if it were rope or seaweed. Tallulah watched amazed, the mer woman barely flinched at the sting. Then she leaned in and whispered something to her eldest. Tallulah could only make out the word 'weak' then the girl's mother forcefully yanked the tentacle off of Ka'I. The mer girl gave a yelp of pain, her mother remained stone faced as she let the tentacle drop off into the darkness below. Then she took the blade and gently began scraping at Ka'I's now inflamed skin. Bit by bit the stingers began to fall out of the mer girls flesh until there were none left.

"Come, it's time we returned." The red mer woman said once she had finished. They were nearly back to the palace when Ivara's mother looked over at Tallulah. "You keep staring at me, what is it?"

"Nothing, I've just never seen someone so unmoved by the creature's venom." Tallulah replied a bit embarrassed that the mer woman had noticed her stares of admiration and curiosity.

The red mer woman gave her a small smile, the first crack in her hard demeanor that Tallulah had seen since the woman arrived. "My people are well versed in venomous creatures. You are a scholar, I assume your records make note of my peoples intimate bond with our serpents, our regalecs. You've met my regalec?"

Tallulah thought of the huge white scaly serpent like creature that had arrived with the mer woman and her family. "I saw him when you arrived, yes. I have studied the regalecs, but I never thought I would see him again. I assume the creature is back at the palace?"

The Lady of Makoul paused, turning her head as if listening to something Tallulah could not hear. "No, he is hunting. Just south of here."

Tallulah swallowed, hard. The thought of such a terrifying creature roaming wild did not sit well with her. She tried to change the subject. "You mentioned your people are educated on dangerous creatures. Are regalecs such as yours venomous?"

"Oh very, you don't think I was born crimson do you? No, I was born pale as winter snow." The group turned and Tallulah could see for the first time a dark scar on the mer woman's arm. Tallulah was silent the rest of the way back, contemplating what she had learned. They arrived to a very frustrated Corvena. Together Corvena and Tallulah took the mer girls back to their sisters while their mother returned to her meeting leaving her two children behind.

After checking that Lady Brizo was a good distance from their room Corvena began expressing her frustration. "Are all easterners so *annoying*? Or is it just your lot?" Corvena said not even looking up from examining the webbing in between her fingers. They had long since left the earshot of the adults and were free to air their grievances to their younger guests as they saw fit. All senses of formality were dropped.

"Us? What did we do to -. Ow!" Corvena slapped Ka'I and she went quiet. Anger rising like lava bubbling up on the ocean floor. "Swimming off like that was stupid and you could have gotten killed had Tallulah not been looking out for you!"

Tallulah put a hand on Corvena's shoulder. "Enough she already got it from her mother."

Corvena sighed. "Fine. What about the rest of you? Can't seem to get the older one to shut up but you haven't spoken a word." She pointed to the dark haired one. Tallulah was always startled by Corvena's outspoken personality but to speak to a Lord's child in such a way...

The blonde smacked Corvena's hand away.

"Uhane is a mute." It was Mele, the fair haired, pink tailed twin of Uhane.

"Damaged goods. There's always one I suppose. What about the little one?"

"Ivara." Tallulah's charge did not elaborate. The mer girl looked anxious and uncomfortable. Tallulah turned to her. "Are you all right?"

Ivara nodded. "I don't like small rooms. Makes me feel sorta stuck."

"Ya I get that. Sometimes it helps to remember that you can swim in and out whenever you want. That way you know you can always just leave." Tallulah said.

Ivara nodded but stayed silent.

"What are you even doing here? The Lords don't usually bring their spawn." Corvena spat. Her tone was harsher than before and her words were venom. It occurred to Tallulah then that perhaps her friend's anger stemmed not from impatience but from jealousy. Corvena too had been a Lord's daughter, once upon a time.

Ivara brushed her off without the slightest hint of offense. "Papa doesn't tell us the details. Just that the plague reached Makoul a few months ago. Father mentioned your lot have researched a cure?"

"Still doesn't explain why they brought you along." Corvena pointed out without so much as acknowledging the girl's question.

For the scenery. Uhane signed sarcastically. Making Mele chuckle and Ka'I roll her eyes, hard.

"Well no sense in waiting here. Let's go!" Brina spoke brightly and her whole face lit up whenever she spoke of mischief.

"You want to listen in?" Mele said one pale hand to her mouth as if scandalized.

"You don't?" Corvena retorted.

"Alright, who's coming?" It was Brina, her voice full of excitement.

"I'll go." It was the youngest. Ivara winced at her eldest sister's glare.

"Splendid, I'll swim ahead and make sure we're clear. You two," Brina pointed at Tallulah and Corvena. "find something to do until I come get you."

Tallulah held out a hand to the mer girl and pulled her out the opening to the spare room. They swam on for a bit till they were clear of the great halls.

"Sorry about my sister. Ka'I I mean. She's not usually this awful. She's just worried, one of her friends told her that the Golden Mer kidnap little mer children. I told her that's just silly but she never listens to me." Tallulah and Corvena shared a knowing look but said nothing. Had she been stolen? Or had she been sold? Perhaps simply given up? She wasn't sure which was worse or if she even knew the difference at this point.

"Your sister mentioned the sickness?" Tallulah said gently trying to change the subject.

"Yes. Mother won't tell us much on the subject but I overheard her speaking with one of our servants one evening. She said that the sickness has been spreading much more rapidly as of late. Over the past year it has claimed nearly ten thousand mer in the Kingdom of Colors alone!"

"Would you like to see our library Ivara?" Corvena asked abruptly. Her tone was sweet, her face kind. But Tallulah knew her friend better than most, it was a distraction.

"Oh I can't read." Ivara whispered.

"Well then we shall have to find you a tutor." And they were off.

The library was a spectacle to behold. Great towering walls with shelves carved in the sides holding countless scrolls and tablets with knowledge yet to be known. Tallulah remembered when she had first come here with Brina. She'd been barely literate at the time.

Cam was the written language of the wealthy, and few had the time or resources to learn it. She'd been overwhelmed by the sheer number of volumes against the yellow walls. The engravings that led one to their desired section for reading. And the runes that floated like glowing illusions. Some runes induced silence; others focus. Each catered to a more conducive learning experience.

She had been wide eyed and almost terrified then. Now she could kill a sleeping mer from ten meters away she realized with no small amount of horror. She looked over at Ivara and saw that same innocence in the mer girl that had once lingered in her. But the mer girl seemed to thrive off of it. She let it guide her. Where Tallulah had stared in horror at the huge open space and the sheer number of volumes it held Ivara gazed on in wonder.

"Optimism." Corvena said flatly.

"Huh?"

"That look in her eyes. It's hope and one day it will get her killed."

"I think it's nice. She's had an easy life."

"No, she's privileged. And even if she's smart enough to know that things can go south for her she will always bet against it." Corvena spat.

"So?" But as the word left her mouth she spotted something in Corvena's eyes. Her friend was jealous! Corvena must have realized she was letting on because she turned.

"Look I know better than most what the day to day is for the child of a lord and I just-"

"-feel like she should have it harder." Tallulah finished. She'd never given much thought to Corvena's past, chalking it up to money and privilege but she could see now what she had initially missed. Corvena, like Tallulah, had never received proper love and care from her parents.

Tallulah grabbed her arm. "Be gentle. Just don't shatter the illusion okay?"

Corvena rolled her eyes and pulled away but, to Tallulah's surprise, swam over to Ivara with a smile so sweet nectar could drip from it. Her words were soft, her gestures warm, as she led Ivara down towards the starters section. Tallulah waited until she saw Corvena swimming back up, her act washed away with the salt of the sea.

"Right then. Let's get to work." Tallulah lifted a brow in question but kept silent. "Something stinks. Why would Lord Neuros bring his whole family just to collect research? Why not send a servant?"

"I don't know, maybe we shouldn't pry Corvena."

"Well I think you're wrong. Did you notice something about the girls? They don't really look like their parents."

"Huh? Ka'I and Ivara do. And the twins – ."

"Look nothing like their father. And the mother is almost completely crimson, eyes, skin, scales, hair. Everything, not one of the girls looks like their mother. Perhaps the mute has her father's hair texture but that is all."

"Ok I'm lost."

Corvena smirked, but there was nothing mocking in her jest. "Thought you might be." She led them over to the anthropology section. Corvena's fingers felt over each scroll, occasionally pulling one out for further inspection before putting it back and hastily repeating the process. She did this quite a few times before finding what she was looking for. The inscription on the scroll read *Crimson Twilight: The Blood People of The Deep*. "Ha! Found it! Have you read this yet?"

"No," *I didn't think you would have either.* "but make your point. Those tutors are a bore. I doubt they will keep our young friend occupied for long."

Corvena let the scroll fall open. "I was doing some light reading the other day on the ancient peoples. Most of which died out long ago except for a few factions. This scroll only covers two, The Blood People and The Dragon Worshipers. At least that's what the older scribes called them. The latter is obviously referring to us which dates these scrolls quite a bit."

"But we don't worship the master."

"Ya my point exactly. Whoever wrote this account is probably long dead."

"So you think that Lord Neuros is somehow related to the Golden Mer or the Master?

"What? No. I'm more concerned with this part." She pointed a pale delicate finger to the page.

...but regarding those people of the Blood, there seems to be no true passing of traits. This is exaggerated by the albinism prominent in the more esteemed members of the community. Often a Blood will be shunned out of the community if too much natural pigment shows itself before their first bite...

Tallulah read the words over and over again, her mind turning with the possibilities. "You think Lady Brizo is a Red Mer, a Blood."

"It would explain the girl's looks."

"Oh I'm sure plenty of siblings don't look alike."

"I was a carbon copy of my siblings."

"You have siblings?"

Corvena ignored her and looked away. "Besides, it would explain why Lady Brizo hasn't left the family yet."

"Why would she leave? Has she no love for her children?"

"The Blood mer are a race of warriors, drawing strength from the venomous bites of their sea serpent companions. However the venom is deadly to those who are not born of the red mer's blood. The Red Mer seem to have built up a tolerance. Amongst the Blood mer the gene that allows them to survive the venom is linked with albinism. The less pigment they show the stronger they will be after their first bite. Red mer only ever leave the community to reproduce."

"...And none of Lady Brizo's children show any hints of albinism. But it still doesn't answer why Lord Neuros brought his entire family just to obtain a bit of research."

"Isn't it obvious? None of the children show even hints of the albinism the Red Mer are known for. Therefore, beyond holding titles of heir's they're useless. And the Dragon isn't going to give up that cure for free..."

"He's going to take one of the children." Tallulah realized. Then another thought occurred to her. "Why are you so invested in this anyway? Why do you care?"

"I have my reasons."

"Which are?"

"Tallulah we are both forty eight, still barely out of childhood. Give me one good reason why an all-powerful entity much less a *dragon* would want us? What use would a dragon have of children? And yet he keeps collecting us like jewels."

"So you're pissed off that your parents didn't want you. What does this have to do with Ivara's siblings and the Red Mer?" Tallulah was surprised at how cold it came out.

Corvena rolled up the scroll. "I knew you wouldn't understand."

"Wait stop, I'm sorry. That wasn't fair." Tallulah looked at Corvena then. Perhaps truly seeing her for the first time. Seeing past her long dark hair and her piercing gold and green eyes. Her pale skin and sharp features. Seeing past her almost cruel beauty to what Tallulah had once thought a heart of stone. But where there is stone there is magma and a passionate heat flows below. Tallulah realized that she was now seeing this passion in Corvena.

Her friend saw a problem that needed solving, and she would solve it if only to prevent others from being ripped from their families as they had been. Perhaps she was an awful mer. Perhaps she was cruel and rude and vindictive but in this moment she was so much more. In this moment, her golden eye burned with hate at what the world had dealt her.

"I think something is coming Tallulah. And I think the Master knows more than he is telling us."

Tallulah swallowed. "Ok." She breathed. "Ok."

They spent the next few hours rummaging around for any information on the Red Mer. They managed to piece together a few rituals and Tallulah even found a map. She was in the middle of translating it when Corvena called her over.

"Shh you don't have to shout!" Tallulah chastised.

Corvena waved her off. "Ok so I think I've got something. Red Mer, as per tradition, are required to remain celibate until they've found a partner. But a few pages later it says that because the magic they use is heritable they may request time away for mating."

Tallulah thought for a few minutes piecing it all together. "Ok so Lady Brizo is Red Mer. I thought we already established that."

"Yes but what if even though none of Lady Brizo's children received the characteristic albinism they're still linked by blood, being her daughters, to the Red Mer. And considering Lady Brizo is crimson, that probably means she already went through the initiation process and has a higher capacity for magic than mundane mer."

Tallulah took a moment to ponder it. Upon taking her oath to become a Golden Mer she had been made to swear not just fealty but celibacy as well. So it stood to reason that among other things the capacity for magic was heritable. "If you are right, and I must admit I think you are, then why put the Red children through the serpent's bite in the first place? Don't they already have a capacity for magic?"

"Yes but they'd still need a source."

"The serpents!" The two exclaimed in tandem. "That would mean that even without the bite the girls could still prove dangerous, especially if the Dragon manages to acquire any of them."

"How so?"

"Well take Ka'I for example. If she has even a hint of her mother's capacity for magic then she's already one step ahead. Could you imagine what someone with both the Serpents and the

Dragons blood running through their veins could do with a bit of chaos magic. That's how you create a living weapon."

Chapter 42

"The vision continued and I saw a creature locked in a cage of crystal, it beckoned to taste new flesh, the flesh of those that walk above."

An excerpt from the prophecy of the Dolah as it was first recorded by the mer of the Arkstone in the year 1207

Ivara (1604 A.D.)

With the help of Jensin's map they set off down the kings road towards Martha's inn, their agreed starting place. As much as Ivara didn't want to admit it, she wasn't actually sure where Scyla's cave was, much less if the witch would still be there. Jensin for his part had given her a go at the map but whereas maps under the sea were reliant on the depths of cities and kingdoms in order to show locations Jensin's map mimicked a birds eye view of the kingdom. Merely looking at the map was enough to disorient her.

It was paramount now that she return to the Arkstone and report her information. Yet Ivara wondered if it would be worth the trip to return to Makoul first since after all that was why she had been sent away. Regardless she would need to become Mer again, if it was even possible. She would start with Scyla. The Sea Witch was likely to know more than she was letting on and perhaps with some bargaining Ivara could convince the Witch to be a bit more helpful.

"I'm surprised you wanted to come along." Ivara said once they were on the road.

"You really thought I'd let you, a foreigner, a mer of all things, go visit a witch without any supervision? Don't be daft. Besides after our last two outings, it's clear that with as much trouble as you attract, an escort is a necessity." His tone was flirtatious and light hearted but Ivara sensed an inkling of worry behind his words.

"So is it a matter of trust or do I just strike you as a maiden in need of saving?" She teased flipping her hair behind her shoulder flirtatiously.

"It's always a matter of trust Ivara. Anyone who tells you otherwise is likely trying to take advantage of you." Jensin replied.

"And here I was thinking that you cared about my well-being." Ivara smirked at her riding companion.

"I do actually." His tone softened.

"Oh?"

"If you must know, I find you quite magnetic. And aside from nearly getting us killed I quite enjoy our little adventures."

"Good, that means it's working." Ivara said teasingly, making witchy gestures with her hands.

Her companion's eyes widened. "What's working?"

"Oh you know, the spell I put on you when first we met." Seeing his face turn unsure she began to laugh. "Relax, it's just a joke."

Jensin looked at her strangely. "Do you know any magic?"

Ivara considered lying but then considered how much Jensin had opened up to her. Perhaps it was time the favor be returned.

"Yes, I was raised in an environment where knowledge of Sourced magic was actually quite common. Though much of my education was considered secretive."

"That sounds incredible. When I was a boy I used to pretend I was a sorcerer... much to my mother's dismay." He chuckled. "What did your mother think of you learning magic?"

Ivara thought for a moment. She hadn't seen her mother's face since the day she had first arrived at the Arkstone. What *would* she think of all this?

"I don't know. My mother was not present for most of my childhood. She and my father traded me to the Master when I was only thirty five years old."

"Your parents gave you up?"

"It was more like a trade. Makoul, my home was suffering from a terrible plague at the time. As Lord of Makoul it was my father's duty to solve the problem and look out for the wellness of the mer who lived there. My father and mother had heard of the miracles that happened in the Arkstone. It was rumored that in the Arkstone the dead spoke, shadow and light were bent as water is by a wave. But the Master of the Arkstone, the one responsible for these miracles of magic always demanded something in return. More often than not this price was a child, preferably female though once he did allow an infertile male to join us."

"So your parents just sold you like livestock to a stranger and what, hoped for the best?" Jensin's face twisted in disgust and sympathy.

Ivara was surprised at how angry and defensive he sounded.

"It wasn't so bad. Had it not been for the nightmares I probably would have stayed."

"Nightmares? You left because of a few bad dreams? What –?"

"We're here." Ivara pointed to the town as they rode up in tandem. She was not ready to divulge all of her secrets to this human, no matter how much she fancied him. Ahead of them were the houses of peasants and commoners and at the center of it all a familiar inn. And not far off Ivara could see the docks in the dim light. They steered the horses towards the village. Ivara watched delightedly as the town seemed to come to life around her. Children playing on the side of the road. Women washing clothes and hanging them up to dry. Merchants selling their wares. Each walker going about his or her life. The sight of it reminded her of Makoul and nearly brought her to tears. They hopped off their steeds and found a place to tie them up close to the tavern.

"You said you know where the cave is?" He asked. His dejected tone told her he already knew the answer.

"No actually. Not precisely. Though I remember a man took me from the cave to Martha's and it wasn't too long of a ride so the cavern can't be far."

"Damn, I was hoping the specifics would come to you on the ride. With your memory improving and all… ah it's fine. We'll just have to make do." He took a deep breath and swatted a fly buzzing around his temple.

"What's wrong?"

Jensin pointed at the sky. "See that?" Ivara nodded. "It's midday. Which means even if we knew exactly where the cave was located we'd still barely make it back to the castle tonight."

"But we don't know where it is."

"Yes, that's the problem. And spending the rest of the evening looking would be a waste of time." Jensin sighed. "Alright how about this. I'll get us a map from one of the locals, I'll see if I can find any that mark caverns or wells and such. Meanwhile you go get us some rooms to stay in at Martha's inn. Here take this." He handed her a purse filled with coins.

"What about you?"

Jensin pulled out another purse and jingled it in reply. "We'll meet back at Martha's inn in an hour or so."

She watched him walk off towards the market before turning and making her way to the inn. It seemed like just yesterday Martha had taken her in, taught her the language and helped her recover from her transition into a human. She went to open the doors attempting to calm her nerves. The interior of the inn had been decorated with flowers and furs. And though there were not many patrons given the time of day, the few that were present seemed in high spirits. Martha stood in the back filling a tankard but paused when she turned and noticed Ivara. She smiled wide and ran over to embrace Ivara.

"Ivara! How have you been deary?"

"Good, his majesty the Prince and his friends have been very kind to me. You look well, as does the inn." Ivara gestured to all the flowery decorations.

"Do you like it? We're gettin' ready for the spring festival. If there's any holiday that will get ya in a festive mood..." She trailed off lost in thought for a moment. "But you never said why you were here. Has something happened?"

"Oh no, Jensin and I are just visiting the area for a day or two."

"And I suppose you'll be wantin' to know if I have any rooms available. Well, I do, actually." The plump woman strolled over to her books and tabbed through them. "Ah here we are." She frowned. "Hmm, well I'll be..."

"What is it?"

"Seems I have one room left. With a single bed. But if you brought company I can always haul up a sleeping mat. What'll it be?"

Ivara bit her lip, her breath shortening. "I'll take it." Ivara handed her the coins and followed as Martha led her upstairs and past her old room.

"Alright here you go." The inn keep handed Ivara the keys. "If you need anything at all, don't hesitate to ask." Martha said before heading back down.

Ivara walked into her room and sat quietly on the bed. Various questions buzzed around in her mind. *What would she say to Scyla? Was it safe to return? Did she even want to return?* She hated herself for even thinking it but the longer she stayed here the more attached she grew to this world. To the realm of humans, their languages, their clothing, even the ways in which they laughed were different. Yet she couldn't remember a time when she had been happier.

Duty called her back to the Arkstone, just as family called her to return to Makoul. But here she had no duties, she didn't owe anyone anything. Here she was a commoner, trained in magic in a society that could not value such things as magic less. Her dreams as well had become much less frequent and much more manageable. Then there was Jensin. The human male seemed to be warming to her at an increasing pace. She could feel the tug of closeness whenever he was around. The quickening of her breath. The way she yearned to be in the same room with him.

"You will not know love nor true friendship. They are attracted to your blood, and though they will not know why, they will let themselves be manipulated by you and they will take to you as a bird takes to the wind." She could remember the words as if the Dragon had spoken them only moments ago. Despite the many years since they had the conversation, the words were still clear in her mind. Back then she hadn't quite understood what the Dragon's words meant. Now the truth of it made her heart ache and she wondered how all her new friends would act towards her had her blood not called to them.

Just as she was getting lost in her thoughts a quiet knock came at the door. She opened it and in the doorway stood Jensin. In his hands were two rolled up pieces of parchment dotted with outlines in ink. Maps if she had to guess.

He grinned. "Mission accomplished. Care to see?"

Ivara beckoned him to sit down, though the room was too small for a desk or table there was a wooden seat in the corner. Jensin grabbed it and laid the paper out on the bed. The first was a map of the village and nearby farms, towns, and buildings as well as their proximity to the coast. The second piece of parchment was a bit more difficult to decipher.

"What are all those markings? They can't be roads." Ivara pointed to the strange pathways inked out on the page.

"Their caves and caverns, the lines running throughout are the connecting waterways. If Scyla is mer like you then the cave has to be connected to the sea which narrows down our search a lot. Though it still leaves quite a few caves."

"Wow this is incredible Jensin! Where did you get these?"

"Some local farmers actually. I know," He said, seeing her expression. "I was surprised as well. Turns out the village farmers keep maps of the waterways so they can prepare in cases of drought. But they also marked the sources of salt water at my request. Including a few caverns that are linked to the sea."

Ivara examined the maps gleefully. "When do you want to start?"

Jensin looked outside. It was evening now and the sun hung low in the sky casting a golden hue upon the land. "We'll leave at dawn tomorrow."

"Alright then." She handed him his set of keys. "There was only one room available."

"Oh." He looked at her, a silent query in his eyes. An unspoken question hung between them.

"I don't bite if that's what you're about to ask." She meant to break the tension but her words came out nervous.

He nodded anxiously. "Right, I um... I'll be back." He said before turning and leaving.

Ivara tried to fall asleep but her embarrassment barred any rest that might have found her. Seconds turned to minutes and minutes turned to hours. All the while she just laid there as the golden light from her window faded to dark. When she could no longer take it she stood, peeled herself away from the thin, rough fabric of her bed sheet and dressed herself. She made for the tavern downstairs, the noise becoming louder the closer she got to the dining room.

The tavern was full. Young men and women sat in every booth drinking in excess. Some played cards while they drank, others watched as scantily clad women danced around their tables. The escorts wore white powder all over their faces. Green and purple eyeliner had been drawn around their eyes in thick lines and red lipstick formed a heart shape on their lips. Ivara watched them closely, a question forming in her mind.

"They're just dancers." Martha said, coming up behind her.

"What?"

"They're dancers from Madame Madeline's brothel across the way. Folk come here to eat and drink then stumble on out so the Madame's girls can take them for a whirl."

"Smart but I thought the Madame only employed a few women in such trade."

Martha chuckled. "Oh these girls aren't harlots, they're from the neighboring villages. The Madame offers to pay for their trade schools, or dowry's in exchange for a few years of entertainment. Believe me deary, few fathers would ever let their unwed daughter in the Madame's brothel. No, these girls will come when called upon and in a few years their future will be much more assured."

Ivara considered it for a moment. What to her eyes had seemed like an outrageous party with all sorts of men and women was so much more. She was once more reminded of the incredible complexities of these humans. "And you took the Madame up on her offer immediately?"

"Well to be honest with you when the Madame first mentioned it I was hesitant. 'This is a proper establishment' I told myself. Didn't want to be associated with the type that takes part in such. But the tavern was low on patrons after you left. We were struggling. To be honest, I was planning on closing shop within the year, but *now,* well suffice to say it's the best decision I've ever made."

They made small talk for a while after that. When a seat opened up Ivara gladly took it and handed a few coins over to Martha to buy some food and drink. She sat there for an hour or so watching the dancers, the drunkards, the bar fights, the card games, all of it was so different from anything she'd experienced back home.

When the tavern started to get too rambunctious Ivara took her last sip of her drink and headed outside. She could remember countless nights spent gazing at the stars and the moon as the waves moved her around. But tonight there were no waves, only a cool breeze which filled her hair making it flutter in front of her face.

She shivered and watched as a drunk patron stumbled out of the tavern, his drink still in hand. He was an older man, but even intoxicated he knew his way. He did not waver in any direction as he made his way to the brothel. Ivara watched him curiously. A beautiful blonde woman met him at the door and ushered him into the brothel. The door wasn't open long enough for Ivara to see much else.

Many of the building's windows were shut or otherwise blocked out. In one window a man stood gazing out at the patrons below. He wore only his trousers, and though he was in the top window his short red hair gave him away. Jensin seemed lost in thought as he stared out at the village below. Finally he paused, meeting Ivara's gaze. Jensin tensed when he saw her but relaxed as a naked woman with ash brown hair and blue eyes came up behind him and put a hand to his shoulder. The woman whispered something to him as she tugged him back inside.

Choking on her tears and rage, Ivara turned and returned to Martha's tavern. She felt like an intruder. But even more so she felt betrayed, though the rational part of her mind argued against her heart. Jensin only barely admitted today that he enjoyed her presence, which was a far cry from love. Besides, even if he did care for her in *that* way, which of course he didn't, there was the matter of celibacy.

Ivara had *dragon's* blood running through her veins. Magical blood that linked her to the greatest source alive. And as such she had given a vow of celibacy, swearing to never have children by anyone and never to pass on such power. She had never thought she might come to regret such a vow... until now. Overcome with emotion Ivara wiped at a tear with her sleeve.

She entered the tavern and quickly pushed her way past its increasingly drunk guests, towards the stairs and into her bed. Her brief foray hadn't been enough to induce sleepiness but rather had the opposite effect. She could not calm her swirling thoughts so instead she lay there staring at the ceiling.

Thus she was still awake when Jensin came stumbling into the room. His shirt was poorly buttoned and his hair tousled. He took a few steps into the room and froze, seemingly forgetting their sleeping arrangement.

"I can explain." He said by way of introduction.

"No, you can't. And besides, it's none of my business who you sleep with."

"Ivara it's not what you think. I didn't sleep with her!"

Her gaze hardened. "Why did you lie to me?"

"I – what?"

"You said you enjoyed my company, that you cared for me. Why say all that? It's not like I'll be around much longer. So why?" She whispered.

He tried to reach for her but she pulled away. "I do care. I just..." Jensin let his head fall into his hands in frustration. "I do care for you. That's the problem. Ever since I saw you on that boat... I yearn for you. I do not love you. I just *yearn* for you. It's unnatural."

"Say what you mean." Ivara knew his words before they left his mouth but still, she needed to hear it from his mouth.

"I just kept thinking to myself, what if it's a spell? What if I've been enchanted?" He threw up his hands in frustration. "So I shacked up with a whore thinking maybe, just *maybe* it could put me off of you. Break whatever *this* is."

"And? Did it work?" She whispered.

He looked like he wanted to scream at her. "If it worked I wouldn't be crawling back to the witch that's holding my heart captive!"

Witch. It surprised her how much the words stung. She felt several warm tears fall down her face before she mastered herself enough to speak.

"It's my blood. Something about the magic in my blood makes people care for me. It's like a survival instinct. I can't control it." She said, looking away from him. "I'm sorry."

The creek of the floorboard was the only sound as Jensin walked over and took her head in his gently lifting her chin until she was staring into his brown eyes. "Well if you can't defeat them..."

She had only a second for the confusion to register on her face before his lips were pressed against hers. Ivara had never kissed another in such a way. It took her mind a moment to realize what was happening, but by that time her body had already committed to the act. She pressed herself against him and leaned in to kiss him. Her hands counted the scars on his back as he finished taking off his blouse leaving only his trousers. For the first time in her life she didn't want to go back to the Dragon, or to Makoul. All she wanted was this moment. She wanted to capture it in a bottle and carry the feeling of his hands in her hair for the rest of her life. So she did.

Her eyes rolled back in her head and she let her golden blood take over. Her sense of touch came alive and her breathing came in quick gasps. Her mind whirled like a scribe capturing every detail and she grinned with the knowledge that for tonight at least, her dreams would be splendid.

When morning came the following day Ivara struggled to pull herself out of her bed due to exhaustion. Becoming human had been difficult and strange in many ways but she would have never guessed how tired she'd be or how much her body would need to sleep on a daily basis. A knock came at her door. Knowing it was Jensin she hastily finished dressing and opened the door. He didn't enter but instead stood at the doorway holding the two maps from the previous day.

"Ready?" He asked, offering her some breakfast.

"It's not even first light out yet."

"It will be once we set out."

Ivara followed him out and together they untied the horses and set out. While her verbal aspects had far improved, her written Allagorian was still quite lacking, as was her reading of the language. Thus it was that she trusted Jensin to lead them. The morning ride was silent at first. Neither of them wanting to bring up the obvious until finally Jensin broke the silence.

"So this spell –."

"Golden blood, from the Master." She corrected him.

"Right, so this blood. Does it put a trance on everyone you meet or just..." Jensin trailed off.

"Just what?"

"Well do you have to be attracted to them first?"

She thought on it for a moment. "I'm not sure. By all rights everyone I've met in Allagor should have been weary of me. But they all welcomed me instead. Even Ravik was far less villainous than I had expected."

"And you can't turn it off? Like with a rune or something?"

"Not so far as I know. But once I return home, I'll be able to ask." She replied.

"Right." His voice was sad. "I nearly forgot why we came all this way."

They rode on in silence and finally reached their mark once they were high in the sky. They dismounted and Jensin led their horses over to a tree to tie them up. In the distance they could hear other horses whining but Ivara didn't see anyone nearby. The cave opening was just tall enough for Ivara to walk in without smacking her head on the ceiling.

"Anything look familiar?" Jensin asked, hunching over as he entered.

"No, not really. Though I suppose it does smell familiar."

"Smell?" Jensin looked at her dumbfounded. "What do you mean?"

"It smells of…" She sniffed the air and thought for a moment, "salt water and eggs that are old and rotten."

He sniffed the air. "Wow you're right."

They walked on until it became too dark in the cavern to see and Jensin was forced to light a candle to help them see. After walking about for some time they heard something. The rushing of water, they ran into the next opening in the cavern to find a small waterfall rushing out of one side of the cavern's wall. Ivara cupped her hands together and let the waterfall in before drinking it. It was salty yet tasted cool and clean. She turned to Jensin.

"Are we near the sea?"

Jensin checked his map, running a finger from location to location. "Hmm yes it looks like the ocean empties out into this cave system but, wait a moment that doesn't make any sense."

"What is it?"

"The drawings of the cave don't indicate any way to get from where we are now to the sea. It's blocked off here at the waterfall."

"But the water is draining somewhere, it must be otherwise this whole cave would be flooded by now." Ivara looked down at the sizable pool that the waterfall drained into. An idea came to her. Jensin must have come to a similar conclusion because he quickly spoke up.

"Ivara you don't know what is down there, don't jump in."

"No, I'll go see if the hole is big enough for a person then come back for you."

"We don't even know if this is the correct cave! You said yourself you don't recognize it."

"I was also barely conscious when I came to that cave. My memories a bit foggy." She raised her hand to silence any further discussion and began untying her cloak. "If it will make you feel any better just follow me."

Jensin watched, shaking his head in frustration at her. "Be quick or I will."

The water was cold when she jumped in but her feet didn't touch the bottom though she could feel a few aquatic plants scrape against her pants. She dove down, and forgetting how her vision had deteriorated since becoming human, opened her eyes only to have her vision blurred by the water and darkness. She felt around until eventually she came upon a crack in the pool of water. Ivara followed it with her hand.

The crack led her to a significantly larger hole at the very bottom of the pool just barely large enough for a single person. Ivara entered but there was no room in the claustrophobic space for her to swim and so she found herself pushing against the walls of the underwater tunnel praying that it did not end in a dead end. The water around her began to warm and Ivara could see a light up ahead. When she was finally out of the tunnel she surfaced into the cavern from her memories. To her left the cave opened up into the sea, and to her right the wide ridge just above the water and a small opening into the outside world. But instead of finding the cave empty she swallowed as she looked around at the bloody water and the dead body that floated in the center of it.

At first all she could do was stare. Her heart began to race and her breaths came in quick succession one right after the other. She recognized the pale green skin, the purple and red tentacles and the countless scars and runes burned into her skin. She swallowed hard. It was Scyla, her scarred body floating lifeless in the shallow pool. Slowly Ivara swam over to where the body had become stuck on the shallow edge of the pool. In her shock she became deaf to the splashing behind her and she hardly realized that Jensin had entered the cave with her.

"What is that thing?" Jensin asked as he swam to the shallow edge of the pool where he could stand once more.

"Who." Ivara whispered. She tried taking deep breaths to master herself. Slowly she made her way over to the knee deep water where the corpse lay. "Her name was Scyla. She's – she was a friend."

Small sea creatures had already begun to tear at the mer woman's flesh which made turning her over even more difficult. Hands shaking she began to look around for the athame.

"Ivara what are you doing?" Jensin sounded in shock as he stood behind her.

"There is an athame, whoever killed her must have taken it. It's not here." Ivara said, throwing up her shaking hands in frustration. "Dammit!" She screamed. The sound of her anger echoed in the cool cavern.

"It's ok –." Jensin tried to put a hand on her shoulder but she shook him off.

"No it's not ok nor will it be! That athame was my only way back to Makoul, back to the Arkstone, back to my *family*. Without it I am stuck here. Cursed to spend whatever is left of this short human life pretending to befriend those that would have me killed should they realize who I am!" She fell to her knees in the stinking water and began to sob. "What am I to do?"

Jensin did not respond, instead he sat down next to her and held her. They sat there for what seemed like both minutes and hours simultaneously. Perhaps it was the constant dripping of water within the cavern's walls or the otherwise silent environment but she felt as if time itself had stopped for her. Suddenly every ounce of anger, sadness and frustration that she had been holding inside herself came rushing out in wretched sobs. Jensin just hugged her tightly.

Chapter 43

"Something that few mer understand is the nature of the Red Mer. I feel that I have met enough of our crimson cousins to say this much. The Red Mer are *not* the apathetic monsters we here in the shallows make them out to be. They are an ancient and duty bound race of mer that dwells in near complete isolation. So is it any wonder that this solitary people, calls their young to be strong even if such strength is forced upon them by magical blood, runes or even the venomous bite of a regalec? After all, such practices have kept them alive far longer than any other race of mer."

A Beginners Guide to the Kingdom of Colors by Nyra of Neroth

Tallulah (1556 A.D.)

"Tallulah?"

Tallulah looked over; they floated around in the Arkstone's legendary library. With her mind so focused on the implications of Corvena's words she had nearly forgotten their third party. "Yes?"

Tallulah offered a sincere smile. The mer girl, Ivara, had a plain beauty about her. Her dirty blonde hair combined with her pale grey eyes made her look timeless and stern. But then she smiled and the façade was shattered. The second her lips parted to giggle her age came bursting through and all Tallulah could see was a charming tad just her junior. Where Brina's energy had been that of a tad in a sweets market, the hyper energy of a child, Ivara's was different. Hers was one of introverted curiosity despite any who would try to manage her. "Hey Ivara?"

"Yeah?"

Her mind buzzed with white silence. "I...um..." Corvena raised a brow. "We should be getting back."

"Right." Ivara nodded.

"You're not serious?" Corvena feigned astonishment.

"What now Corv?"

"We have to go find out about, you know," she gave Ivara a suspicious look, "*the thing*."

"Oh for the love of-." Tallulah put her hand to her forehead frowning. "Fine. Fine, we'll do it your way. Ivara you up for a bit of fun?"

"That depends. What sorta fun?"

"The *spying* kind." Corvena whispered, then turning to Tallulah asked. "Do you think the Lord and Lady of Makoul are still in their meeting with the Dragon?"

Tallulah nodded. "Definitely." They both turned back to Ivara. "Would you like to come listen in on a conversation with us?"

"Oh yes! I'm a wonderful spy. I listen in on my sisters all the time!" They all laughed.

"All right you heard the girl Tal, she's a professional!"

Tallulah just sighed, her gills flaring and followed them up and out of the library towards the private halls. The Dragon's lair was at the heart of the city at the deepest part. Many pilgrims thought the Arkstone was an object, some sort of treasure that the Dragon guarded. It was a wild fantasy that seemed to persist even on the outskirts of the Reek. While Tallulah had never been in the lair herself she could never see the motive in hoarding treasure. Nan had taught them to shed their love of people and objects and the idea of a secret treasure didn't exactly mesh with her ideology.

There was no visible opening to the lair. At least not one big enough for a massive, winged serpent with four thick legs and scales the size of her head. Even after years of living in the Arkstone and studying the tablets on dragon history Tallulah could never quite find an adequate reason for why a creature that spent the majority of its life sedentary required wings. It was only accessible to mer through a series of highly guarded tunnels beneath the city. Looking down one perhaps not as informed at Tallulah, nor as privileged as she would just see sand and rock. A flat barren space in the center of the city where no market, nor building was erected. An absence was all that might stand out to the untrained eye. But Brina had shown her a crack in the façade. Literally. They swam down into the emptiness.

"Where *is it*? I can never find it!" Corvena half shouted, throwing her hands up in frustration.

Tallulah quieted her and began feeling at the stone. The grainy sand scattered beneath her hand to reveal rough stone sanded down by the eons. The result was something not quite smooth and yet not altogether uncomfortable to the touch. Her hand meandered against the dark blue rock following each crevice to see where it led her. Her fingers caught on a loose stone stuck deep within a crevice. "Found it!" She gasped, grabbing the stone.

"Careful don't get stuck." Corvena said mockingly when Tallulah's arm caught.

"Just when I think you can be a decent person..." Tallulah whispered.

"What was that?"

"Nothing. Come on down. Not you Ivara...not yet." Tallulah put up a hand to the mer girl. She looked down at the crevice. It was just big enough for two mer to swim down in but three? The odds were against them. Still she wasn't the gossiping type and had only come to see Corvena through uninjured. "Right ok, Corv and I will go in first just to be sure it's safe and then you and I will switch. Sound alright?"

The mer girl nodded nervously.

Tallulah wedged herself in between the rocks letting her tail curl in on itself to make more room for Corvena once she was in. It was a tight fit to be sure but not an altogether unpleasant one. Corvena was waiting for her inside, she paraded a sarcastic smirk that foretold of a smarmy comment soon to come.

"You've gotten fat." Corvena said matter-of-factly.

Tallulah was surprised at how offended she was by these words. "I – I have not!"

Corvena just shrugged and gave her attention to the small peep hole below them. "Whatever you say."

Tallulah too dulled her irritation and put her ear to the stone. She could hear a man speaking in hysterical tones. "Absolutely not! My Lady wife has only a few years left before she is to return to the Red Mer. I won't leave *any* of my children on the other side of the sea! Who would look after them? Since I shall be in Makoul and she shall be in the depths of the sea!"

"I assure you the child will be well cared for; it is the greatest honor to become one with the Master." Tallulah recognized the monotone. It was one of the Dragons' more senior handmaidens. It was the same handmaiden that had dragged a terrified young Tallulah out of her room when she had first arrived at the Arkstone and cut into her hand so that she could receive the Dragons blood.

"For your kind perhaps but on our side of the sea we actually *value* our family!"

"Nerous! Stop it! A price has been laid before us let us not throw such an opportunity back in their faces." Lady Brizo interrupted her husband.

"Your wife speaks true; this offer may be rescinded and is one of great value. The lives of all those who live in Makoul might be saved in exchange for a single child." The Dragons handmaiden replied.

"What are they saying?" Ivara whispered.

Corvena and Tallulah both turned back to her in tandem. "Shh!"

"Brizo you cannot seriously be considering this?" Lord Neuros turned to his wife pleading with her.

"I told you from the start not to get attached to them." She patted her pregnant belly. "Should this one lack pigment then she too will be sent away from Makoul when she comes of age. Just to my people instead. As for the others, Ka'I is your heir, thus your attachment to her is most understandable, but the rest are bargaining chips." It was obvious Lady Brizo was growing frustrated with her husband.

"Bargaining chips! They are our children, they –."

"No they are not. They are servants into the political system in which they were born. And now it is time for one of them to do their duty to Makoul and serve!" Lady Brizo said firmly. Then more softly so that Tallulah could barely hear the Lady leaned in close to her husband and said. "Please do not make this harder than it already is."

Tears welled up in Lord Neuros' eyes as he silently contemplated what to say next. "Only one child, for the plague's cure?"

"That is all the Master asks." The handmaiden confirmed.

Lord Neuros flared his gills and his whole body began to shake as if in opposition to his next words. "Take the youngest then. Her name is Ivara. You can have her."

The handmaiden smiled and pulled a large vile from her satchel. "Careful," She said as she handed it to the Lord of Makoul. "The cure is incredibly concentrated."

Lord Neuros and his wife examined the vial. "Will this be enough for all of the city state?" Lady Brizo asked.

"Yes. Like I said, it is concentrated. Open it above the city and the tide will do the rest."

"What did they say?" Ivara whispered, now more frustrated with them.

Tallulah couldn't bring herself to say anything so she just turned to the mer girl, a look of pity in her eyes.

Part 3 ~ Ellenward

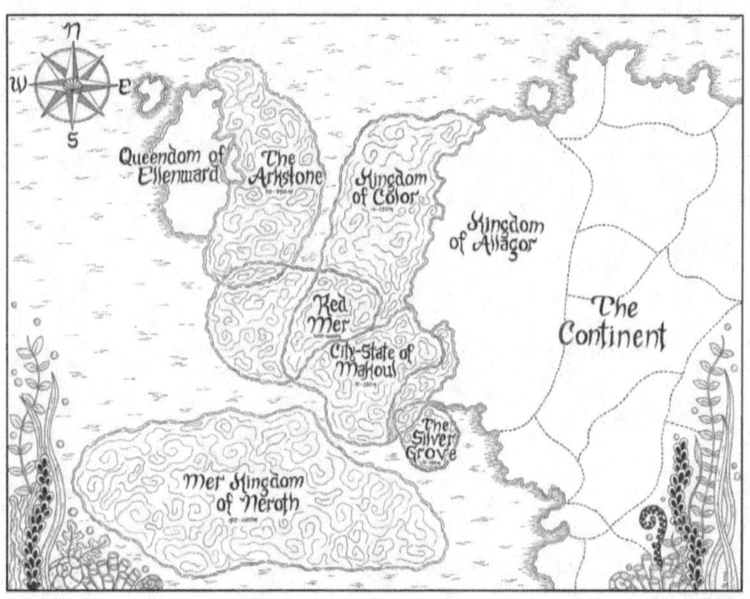

"She has given us a knife: here it is, see it is very sharp. Before
the sun rises you must plunge it into the heart of the prince."
Hans Christian Anderson

Chapter 44

"Despite its many uses, even magic cannot heal our grief. Loss and love, perhaps the only two things that are truly immune to spells and runes."

Practical Magic by Daniel E. Simmons

Ivara (1604 A.D.)

The ride back to Martha's inn was cold and wet. The grey weather did little to improve Ivara's mood as they rode back to the tavern. A downpour of rain caused mud puddles to fill in the roads and Ivara tried her best to steer her mare away from them. Ivara didn't mind the cold, nor the wet, nor the shivers. She found herself numb to nearly everything around her. She knew she should be angry, enraged even but it wouldn't bring her friend back to life nor would such waste of emotion allow her to return home. So instead she resigned herself to internalizing the bleak world around her, staying silent despite Jensin's best efforts to help her grieve.

Ivara swallowed hard. Scyla was dead, her blade Dormethius was gone and she was stranded. Not even her golden sisters could save her now. The same sisters that she had betrayed when she had given in and touched the walker man beside her. She was disgusted with herself. And yet... would it be so bad to start her life over in this strange realm? It wouldn't be the first time she'd had to begin again. Let the tenants of war paddle around in their terror of the

Dolah. The damn thing wasn't even real. Just some prophecy made to keep her in place... right?

On and on they rode, however this time the road seemed longer. They saw no bandits nor any wild life. Just trees, dirt and mud. It was as if the sky itself was in mourning. The grey clouds above her wept and the wind howled in grief that mirrored her own. The inn was packed with evening customers when they arrived. And amongst the crowded room was a familiar face.

Ivara fell into the chair that the Prince pulled out for her and slumped over, head in her hands attempting to hide the onslaught of silent tears. Richard looked over to Jensin for an explanation but the redhead just shook his head. Ivara was prepared for the Prince to question her, ask where she'd been, why she was upset but instead all she heard were footsteps as he walked away. When he returned it was with three large ales which he clumsily laid before them before sitting down at the table. There was silence and Ivara realized the two men were waiting for her to speak first. She took a deep breath and wiped the tears from her face with her already soaked sleeve.

"Richard? What are you doing here?" Ivara's voice cracked.

"Jensin mentioned you two were going cave exploring. I'd like to help. Though it might be fun, also Everleigh and I have an update regarding the runes."

"I appreciate it but we've finished. The individual we were looking for is dead." Ivara said in monotone. She really did appreciate the Prince's enthusiasm but she was far too exhausted to entertain him.

"Dead? Who could you possibly be looking for in a cave? And why would you go in alone, if you had informed me I could have sent an escort to guard you!"

"I had also considered a guard but it wouldn't have made a difference. The cavern was far too small, and besides, like Ivara said, the witch was already dead when we arrived."

Ivara cursed under her breath at Jensin's slip of the tongue. She could see the gears turning on Richard's face. "Did you say witch? Why would you seek out a witch?" He looked between them; all trace of merriness gone. "What's going on?"

Ivara couldn't take it anymore. Perhaps it was her exhaustion, or her frustration that despite her friendship with the Prince she could never truly be honest with him. She glanced over at Jensin who she could tell was being pulled in two directions. She couldn't ask him to lie to his best friend of years for her. Nor could she expect him to. If ever there was a time to come clean, this was it.

Ivara took a deep breath. "We sought out the Sea Witch. Her name is Scyla. She was to turn me back into a mer, to help me go home. When we got there she was dead, murdered." She whispered.

She watched Richard's face morph into various emotions as he processed her words. First shock, then hurt, betrayal. Then anger and hurt again. Slowly he turned to Jensin.

"You knew about this?" Jensin was silent but he gave a small nod. "You knew that she was one of those... those *creatures* that *killed my brother* and conspired with her?" Richard shoved himself away from the table spilling the drinks as he stood.

"If by conspire you mean try my best to help her return home and otherwise keep a close eye on her then yes, I have conspired. But only for your sake." Jensin rebutted. "And besides, I highly doubt that she killed your brother –."

"For my sake? How long have you known? How long!" Richard raged, throwing his fist against the wall very near to Ivara's face.

"Since she arrived." Jensin said, attempting to step between them.

"Your kind killed my brother." Richard said to Ivara.

Ivara stood and looked him in the eye now. "I do not know what befell your brother but none from my home even knew of his death! I did not kill him, I swear."

Richard slapped her across the face so hard her nose began to bleed and grabbed her by the throat. "Then *where is he*? You didn't kill him right? So why hasn't he come home!"

She coughed and her blood splattered his white tunic. Then a command from her mind to his.

Unhand me.

In an instant he had dropped her and she fell to the ground coughing and sputtering. With a look of horror, Jensin came to stand between them.

"Richard, stop this!" Jensin yelled, guarding Ivara with his body.

Ivara dove around the copper haired man and took the Prince by the front of the coat.

"If you *ever* raise a hand to me again I will reach into your little human mind and drown you in your own grief." This time she spoke aloud. "You stand before a golden maiden, a servant of the Golden Dragon of Arkstone."

Her fists balled up and tears of rage spilled from her grey eyes. She wanted to scream at him every obscenity that she knew. She wanted to *hurt* him. For withdrawing his friendship so suddenly. For accusing her of murder. For demonizing her.

The Prince stared at her now as if she were a wolf baring her teeth. Wide eyed terror shown on his face as he stumbled backward. The tavern's patrons stood watching aghast but Ivara paid them no heed. Ivara closed her eyes taking deep breaths. Each one hitching as she cried. Finally she opened her eyes, the Prince had not moved. He just continued to look at her like she was a stranger.

She turned and made her way up the stairs to the room that just a night ago she had shared with Jensin. But the man that had so recently shared her bed did not follow.

It was only then, alone in her bed listening to the rain that she allowed herself to cry. To mourn for a life she would never again live. To grieve for a friend. Her father, her mother, her sisters both birth and blood; she would never see them again. She shook and wailed and cried out in her misery. She lay there sobbing until exhaustion finally swept her away into the realm of sleep and dreams.

It was weeks before Ivara finally found the courage to return to the castle. Martha had offered her stay, and work once more. She spent the weeks in the library whenever time allowed, reading about magic, runes and prophecies. Ivara spent hours searching for anything that might help her return to the Arkstone. To her Master and her beloved sisters. Night upon night she sat in the library teaching herself to read and praying that her saving grace lay in one of the tomes that surrounded her. And night after night her work proved futile.

Each day that passed she wondered when the Prince would finally decide to behead her as his father had done with the Lady Rhea after learning of her betrayal. Had Jensin convinced him to spare her? But then if that were true why hadn't Jensin come to visit her?

Her questions were left unanswered as hours turned to days, and days to weeks. Until the day came that a letter was shoved underneath her door, Ivara nearly ignored it completely. That was until she saw the writing on the back and realized she recognized the author's penmanship.

She wasn't sure how Everleigh had known where Ivara was staying, perhaps Richard had told her. The letter was an invitation to come to court for a private audience with the Princess. Ivara briefly wondered if they meant to arrest her. Her fears were seemingly confirmed when a harsh knock came at the door. It was one of the palace soldiers, his identity concealed behind his armor.

"Come with me." His command was muffled by his metal helmet.

"Do you seek to imprison me?" She asked in a tentative whisper.

The guard ignored her. Instead he gestured towards the stairs. Ivara took a shaky breath, clutching the envelope in hand and allowed herself to be escorted outside. Rather than a tumbrel or a caged wagon what awaited her was an elegant carriage that was led by four pristinely groomed horses. The guard silently strode around her and opened the carriage door, gesturing for her to climb inside. She did so, now more confused than ever.

They took the king's road and arrived at the castle in mere hours. Neither the driver of the carriage nor the accompanying soldiers said a word to her the entire way. When they finally arrived within the castle walls the same guard that had escorted her out of Martha's inn now led her from the carriage to the royal gardens. Ivara did her best to keep her composure. After walking for some time Ivara spotted the Princess raising a white flower to her nose. Everleigh smiled and took a long breath before turning to Ivara and her escort. She waved the man away but did not approach Ivara. Ivara bowed deeply but could not bring herself to speak.

"The chrysanthemums smell so nice this time of the year. Do they keep gardens where you are from?" Everleigh asked, reaching for another flower.

"They do, though surely you did not call me here to discuss flowers." Ivara regretted the words as soon as they left her lips.

"Indeed." Everleigh sighed and squared her shoulders. "Henry has been declared dead. My engagement to Prince Richard is official. Some say it was the sea that killed my Prince. Others say it was the mer folk with their spears and bloodlust."

"What is your opinion on the matter?"

"I have no opinion, just grief. The grief one feels when they lose someone close to them. The grief that reminds you that you are utterly alone in a strange world with no true way home." Everleigh wiped at a single tear that fell down her cheek. Somehow even in her sadness her beauty remained.

"They told you." Ivara said. It was not a question.

"Yes. It was difficult for both of them to come to terms with. Richard more so than Jensin but we've all assumed for some time that the mer killed Henry. And besides, you did lie to all of us."

"So what happens now?" Ivara would not allow them to let her rot in a cell. If she was to die she would plead that it be a quick death.

"Now I have a gift for you." Everleigh said gently.

"You're not going to lock me away?" Ivara asked.

"Should I? Are you plotting against me? Because from where I am standing you are a young woman who thinks she is lost and alone in the world. And though you may be lost you are most certainly *not* alone." Everleigh pressed a small box into Ivara's palm. When she opened it Ivara found two large pearl earrings. "They were one of the few things I was allowed to bring with me when I first arrived in Allagor. It was months before the rest of my jewelry, clothes, dolls and such arrived. They are a constant reminder to me of the kingdom I was born to and the Princess I grew into."

"They are exquisite. True pearls of the sea."

"As are you, my mer friend. I want you to have them."

"Thank you." Ivara quickly put the earrings in her ear then bowed deeply to the Princess once more. When she arose the Princess embraced her in a tight hug. Hours later Ivara found herself lost in her thoughts as she walked arm in arm with Everleigh in the gardens. The princess droned on and on about the wedding preparations and though Ivara took no interest in the topic she did her best to listen as though she was tuned in now and again.

Her thoughts wondered in every direction. Where were her sisters and father? Were they safe? Had Tallulah and her friends at the Arkstone even realized that she was missing? What would the Dragon do once he realized that she had taken the form of a walker? Surely he would understand that she had only done it out of fear and had no intention of staying. Her thoughts wandered toward Jensin; did he even know that she was within the castle walls? Surely Everleigh had told him, perhaps he simply did not wish to see her. Still she felt as though something was brewing between them. Not anger but rather... frustration. He was avoiding her yet she couldn't say why. It was strange and Ivara knew they would need to talk soon.

Then there was the matter of the deaths, and the runes found on their bodies. They had made little progress aside from the discovery of more bodies and Ivara felt as if they had hit a dead end. Ravik was likely to be a dead end as well if he hadn't already fled the coast.

"Well?" Everleigh turned to her. "Were you even listening to me?"

"Yes, I'm sorry could you repeat yourself. I just got lost in my thoughts, that's all."

Everleigh paused looking at Ivara with pity. "You know if there's something on your mind, something weighing on you, that you can tell me."

"It's nothing, just daydreaming so to speak. What was it you asked?"

"Kirsten has agreed to sew the lace on the dress and veil as well as help with some of the guest's dresses such as yours." Everleigh tucked some of Ivara's hair behind her ear and touched the iridescent pearl earring. "She ordered the fabrics from Ellenward a few weeks ago and while the fabrics themselves may take a few weeks more to arrive, the sample fabrics arrived this morning. I was hoping you might help me look over them."

"Look over them?" Ivara was confused.

"Yes, Ellenward is known for their incredible fabrics and dyes, so the sample book is likely to be quite large. I could use some help narrowing it all down. Do you think you'll have the time?"

"I would love to help." The two women smiled warmly at each other. And for a moment Ivara's worries fluttered away on wings of joy. Everleigh led her out of the garden and through the hedge maze back towards the castle.

"You know when I was a child I would always get lost in the hedges and Henry or Richard would always come find me. They'd have to lead me out by hand else I would cry out in terror of losing my way again." She sighed. "These days I don't think I could get lost if I tried. The hedge is far too familiar, as is the rest of Allagor I suppose."

"Is that why you decided to go through with your marriage to Richard?" Ivara asked as she walked with the princess towards the palace gates.

"In part I suppose. Though mostly it came down to my duties. My family expects me to forge a marriage alliance between our kingdom and Allagor. That expectation did not die with Henry. So here I am." She sighed. "I miss him. So much so that I fear I may never be able to truly commit myself to Richard as a wife should. I loved Henry with all my heart, I still do." Everleigh's voice hitched. "Proclaiming my allegiance towards any other man feels like a betrayal."

Ivara put a comforting hand on the princess's shoulder. "I know what you mean." Ivara thought of Scyla, of Tallulah and her friends at the Arkstone, of her sisters, of her father and mother. All those that were lost to her. Those that could never be replaced and yet if she did not try she knew that she would find herself grieving alone in the dark until her final breath.

But that future was not yet upon her and she still had time to find them. In that moment, as Princess Everleigh led her up the marble steps towards her apartments, Ivara promised herself that she would never stop trying to get back to them.

"Oh sorry!" It was Kirsten, she had stumbled into Everleigh, which was unsurprising given the speed she'd been walking at. Kirsten kneeled down on the marble floor gathering her books and pages. Ivara knelt down to help her.

"No, no I've got it." Kirsten attempted to wave away her help. Ivara just smiled and began gathering pages. Pages and pages of runes and information regarding such symbols were scattered on the floor. Everleigh bent down to pick up a page and examine it.

"Kirsten, you never told me that you were interested in runes." The Princess said, flipping the page over to examine it.

"Well it's really just a recent hobby, something to pass the time." Kirsten gingerly took the pages from Ivara and Everleigh. "I must be on my way now." She smiled and began to turn but Everleigh grabbed her by the shoulder. "What's the rush? Come have tea with us. We were just about to look over the sample fabrics."

"Actually that is why I must go. I must fetch the most recent shipment of fabrics for the wedding!" Kirsten smiled.

"I thought you said it would be a few weeks at least before their arrival." Everleigh said, obviously confused but excited as well.

"I did, yes but that was actually, um, a separate shipment. Anyways, best to start as soon as possible." Kirsten bowed briefly and fluttered off down the steps clutching her books tightly.

Everleigh frowned watching her go. "Strange, I don't recall mention of a separate shipment."

"Perhaps with everything going on it just slipped her mind? I mean creating a wedding dress for the future Queen of Allagor is a lot to put on one woman's plate."

"True, but I have hired some ladies and seamstresses to assist her. Still Kirsten isn't the type to laze about all day when there are things that need to be done."

Chapter 45

"Are the gods real? And if so do they merely guide us or rather lead us with purpose through the gift of prophecy? Perhaps we will never know."

Prophecies of Northerners by Alec E. Kalith

Tallulah (1558 A.D.)

It had been two years since the day that they had welcomed Ivara amongst their small sibling hood in the Arkstone. Something about having the five of them all present at once regardless of the activity felt right. As if something inside Tallulah had finally clicked into place, suddenly the Arkstone was not just her home, but rather the place where all those she cared about lived. And while Brina would be off playing politics Corvena, Osirus, Ivara and herself would often find themselves playing games in order to become more practiced with the magic they'd been gifted with. Today it was Tallulah's turn to practice so she watched as Osirus and Corvena formed a line opposite to her and Ivara. The young mer looked up at her uneasily.

"Please don't let them hit me this time. Okay?"

"I'll try." Tallulah said, trying not to chuckle in response. The game was simple, offense would attack and defense would defend. First to yield was the first to lose. Corvena and Osirus being on offense would hurl shadow while the latter would throw rocks, shells and the remnants of dead coral. Meanwhile Tallulah would do her best to defend herself and Ivara. She knew that technically Ivara was supposed to help her defend their side of the unseen line, but the poor tad had only known magic for two years. And the Dragon had cautioned the girl from using magic as it resulted in terrible headaches and visions that might one day drive Ivara insane if nothing was done about it.

"Ready?" Corvena shouted.

Tallulah nodded and the onslaught began. Ivara hid behind Tallulah, she had noticed the younger mer girl never enjoyed being on the defensive team. Shadows rose up all around them and Tallulah could hear the thud as fist sized shells were thrown their way. Tallulah raised her hands to block them and felt for the magic in her veins. It was faint at first then the feeling came as it always did, that itch in the back of her mind that just needed to be scratched. And just like that an invisible shield enveloped the two mer girls and neither the inky shadows nor the assault of shells could reach them. They played their little game of assault for hours, each taking turns in the defensive team. Finally when everyone had grown so exhausted they could hardly swim they quit.

"I need a nap." Corvena yawned. "What about you three?"

Osirus nodded. "A nap, or a break at least. I think I'll just retire to my grotto for a bit."

Tallulah looked over at Ivara who was hovering close to her. "Well what do you think? A bit of a nap, rest up and then we can go grab a snack or play another game?"

Ivara nodded. "Can we just wait. I don't want to go in just yet." Ivara said shyly.

Tallulah waved for Corvena to go on ahead. Exhausted as she was, Tallulah didn't want the mer girl to feel out of place. She'd come to realize that in the two years since Ivara had joined the Golden Mer that the young mer girl had come to look up to Tallulah as an older sister. So she took extra care to be gentle with her.

"Of course." Tallulah said, gently putting her webbed hand to the mer girl's back. "Is everything alright?"

Ivara took a long breath. "I just keep having these nightmares. And I can't sleep at night. Then when we start training or studying I can't keep myself awake or focused."

Tallulah knew of the nightmares. Many times she'd been woken up by the mer girls cries. At first she'd thought the issue a trivial one but all that changed when the Dragon had personally refused Ivara's request for medication or runes to calm her. Now, two years since the girl had gotten her golden blood the nightmares only seemed to get worse. Sometimes she was willing to talk Tallulah through the dreams but most times she just kept silent.

"Would you like to talk about your dreams? About last night?" Tallulah asked softly.

She hesitated before reluctantly sighing. "Ok." Ivara sounded anything but sure. "I was in a small room and my head hurt. And there was a couple crying in the corner of the room. A medic came and poured acid on one of my eyes, and it was awful Tallulah." Ivara began to sob as she clutched at her head. "And I screamed for the medic to stop but he just kept pouring and carving out pieces of rotting flesh from inside my eye. And I could feel every scrape of the blade!" She choked on the last few words.

Tallulah gently pried the mer girl's hands from her head. And swept a calming hand over her face. "It was just a dream. And I see two beautiful grey eyes looking back at me."

Ivara hiccupped. "You don't understand." Her gills flared. "I could feel it! It was so real. Even when I awoke I could feel my eye throbbing. Why won't the master help me? What have I done wrong?"

Tallulah swallowed hard. She hated seeing the girl in such a state of anxiety but she didn't know how to help. "You haven't done anything wrong. Why don't we try this, tonight when you go to bed I will personally protect you from these nightmares."

"You really think you can?" Ivara said hopefully.

Tallulah flexed her muscles and posed jokingly. "I am a shield am I not? I can protect anyone from anything."

A small smile creeped up on Ivara's face. "Thank you." She whispered before wrapping her arms around Tallulah in a hug. Afterwards Tallulah watched the mer girl swim back towards their apartments in the Arkstone. As much as Tallulah wanted to follow her she knew the girl could handle herself. So she turned and made her way towards Osirus's grotto.

"Back again?" Osirus said by way of greeting.

"You know eventually someone's going to buy this place." Tallulah warned. "You really should pick a different hideout."

"Well they haven't bought it yet." Osirus joked before turning and seeing her expression. "What's wrong? Is it Ivara again?"

Tallulah let herself float downwards until her back hit the sandy bottom of the grotto. She sighed. "I just don't know what to do. The Master doesn't seem to give a damn, and no medic will help for fear of punishment. But it is just getting worse. Now she's saying it's not just night terrors but rather dreams where mer are cutting into her flesh! Worse yet she says she can feel it!" Tallulah shivered at the thought of a blade coming near her eye.

Osirus sighed and came to sit by her. "You are there for her. That's all anyone could ask of you."

Tallulah's gills flared with frustration. "Ya, offering empty promises is *definitely* 'being there for her'."

"Empty promises? What did you tell her?"

"I told her that I could shield her from the nightmares." She held up a hand to halt him from interrupting her. "I know ok. I know it was stupid but she was *sobbing* in my arms. What else was I supposed to say!"

"I wasn't going to call you ill of mind. The opposite actually."

"Really?" Tallulah sat up intrigued.

"Well didn't you mention last time we spoke that she's been rather unsuccessful in her attempts at sourced magic? Perhaps the dreams aren't dreams per say but rather visions."

"How do you figure that?"

"Well," Osirus swam above her in the grotto. "when I first started having visions I thought they were daydreams or just my imagination running a bit too wild. Actually it was Brina who helped me figure it out."

"So you think she's a seer like you?"

"Depends, did she tell you about her most recent night terror?" Osirus asked.

"Yes, she mentioned a medic pouring acid into her eye and then cutting it out and –. Oh my." No sooner had the words left her lips than she realized.

"Corvena!" They both said in unison.

"They aren't visions of the future but of the past!" Tallulah shouted.

"Do you think Ivara knows?" Osirus asked swimming closer to her once more.

"I doubt it. If these visions are her subconscious trying to use the Dragon's magic do you really think I could shield her from them?"

"It's worth a try." Osirus smiled at her but his expression quickly went from joy to disgust and confusion.

She took his hand. "Osirus? What's wrong?" She shook his arm but he did not seem to hear her. "Osirus!" He shook his head and shrugged her off putting a hand to his temple. "What did you see?" She asked him.

Osirus began speaking quickly. "A priest in a red and purple robe, perhaps a village alderman, stood on a stone just above a yew tree. The tree had no leaves nor did it bear any fruit. Around the tree was a meadow of wild chrysanthemum flowers. The priest took a small boar in one hand and a knife in another then he looked at me and slit the boar's throat and began sprinkling its blood on the yew tree." When Osirus was finished he looked over at Tallulah. Neither knew what such a vision meant but she grabbed him by the arm and together they swam to the Arkstone's library and began recording it.

Chapter 46

"As unlikely as it is that a commoner might be invited into the private quarters of a Prince or Princess, it is still important to know the protocol, just in case. One should never speak unless spoken to first, and never start a conversation. It is also important to remember that you are there purely for your royal friends' amusement. So do not overstep by making suggestions or giving unsolicited advice."

A Commoner's Guide to Court by Gwyn Stonecrest

Ivara (1604 A.D.)

They made their way to Everleigh's lavish apartments. The Princess's rooms were much larger than Ivara's, sporting several sofas, an ornate tea table and at the center of the main room was a raised block that stood before a tall mirror. It didn't take long for Ivara to work out its purpose, one simply had to stand upon the block in order to properly observe their reflection whilst a seamstress worked away at their garments. By the bedroom door large multicolored glass windows led out to a wide patio. The glass doors were only half open so colorful sunlight and a gentle breeze flowed into the room in equal measure. It wasn't long before the Princess had retrieved the book of fabric samples. Lush greens, vivid reds, deep purples and vibrant blues accompanied intricate patterns of golden lilies, and swirling floral designs.

"There are so many possibilities." Ivara gasped, flipping through the color samples. "Perhaps golden on the sleeves with purple embroidery?"

"Yes I was thinking the same. But then there is the veil, I'd like to incorporate my family's house colors, blue and white."

"Then perhaps a white veil with blue floral patterns sewn in? I think it would look quite dashing on you."

"Oh you can't even fathom how long I have been mulling these colors over even before they arrived! Thank you." Everleigh wrapped Ivara in a tight hug. A knock came at the door and the two women ended their embrace and turned. "You may enter."

"Sorry to interrupt but might I borrow Ivara." It was Jensin standing in the door frame.

"Oh yes, yes of course." Everleigh turned away from Jensin and winked at Ivara before nudging her out the door.

"You look exhausted. Haven't gotten much sleep?" Jensin said sympathetically.

Ivara let him lead her back downstairs and toward the doors to the garden. "I've had a lot on my mind. How's Richard?"

"Stressed, I think the news about Prince Henry shook him, it seems we are both in up to our knees. Then there is all the hustle and bustle of planning a wedding has him a bit overwhelmed."

"You don't seem too nervous." Ivara observed.

"And why should I be? It's not *my* wedding. Besides, I'm Richard's friend, not his keeper. Though when I do get married it will be a spectacle, I can promise you that."

"Oh? Then you'll need an equally stunning bride. I'd start looking sooner rather than later." Ivara smiled.

"I'm not too worried about that, I've had my eye on this one wench for quite a while." Jensin said with a pointed look at Ivara. "She's put something of a spell on me."

"Oh?" She couldn't help but blush.

"Perhaps after all this fuss around the royal wedding has passed, I shall begin formally courting her. Maybe I will bring her a fish, a symbol of our love." Jensin put a hand to his chest theatrically. Ivara, who could no longer help herself, keeled over with laughter. It was a moment before she was able to master herself and stood straight once more.

"Well, I assume you've come here for a reason, other than to declare your love for this mystery maiden, so spill."

"Right…" He took a deep breath and looked down at his feet and Ivara realized he was nervous. "Will you teach me about your magic?" He asked without raising his head.

Ivara was surprised by the question. "Alright."

"Really? Just like that? No conditions?"

"Well truth be told I was never very good with the magic side of things and I'm still recovering my memories, but I will teach you as much as I'm able to. May I ask why the sudden interest? You've known I was mer since we met. Why ask now?"

"True, it's just that thing we found in the caves-."

"Scyla?" She corrected him, slightly put off that he would call a mer a thing.

"Yes. I never knew things like that could exist. It was incredible and disturbing… And it caught me off guard. I don't ever want to be in that kind of situation again. Unprepared I mean. That is to say I don't ever want to come face to face with something that I have no understanding of."

"I understand." She offered her arm to him. "May we relocate to the garden?" He smiled and took hold of her arm. They walked in tandem down the marble hall until they came to a small set of stairs that spiraled downwards. Ivara picked up the front of her skirt and carefully tiptoed down so as not to trip.

"I must say," Jensin grabbed hold of the railing to steady himself. "You have grown quite well established on those two legs of yours."

Ivara smiled. "High praise coming from you."

Jensin shrugged and led her down another, even narrower hallway. "Eh, likely not as high as you deserve."

"What is that supposed to mean?"

He shrugged again.

They emerged side by side into a lush green paradise. The palace greenhouse was warm and the light breeze that did flow through did so with the utmost gentleness against Ivara's fair skin. She took a deep breath and smiled. A thousand different scents mingle there before her like colors from all sides of the spectrum. She smiled deeply at Jensin, her heart palpitating with excitement.

"Scared?" She asked teasingly.

"Should I be?" Ivara could tell he was only half joking.

She just laughed in reply. "Right then. Where to start?" She spoke mostly to herself but Jenson was ready with a reply.

"How about you start with Scyla and that dagger you were looking for."

She gazed at him for a moment. His intelligence was such that she felt no need to speak in layman's terms or ease him in. "Magic comes in two types, sourced and unsourced. It's like tea. The tea leaves are often just as consumable as the tea itself but one is much preferable to the other." She paused awaiting his reply.

He thought about it for a moment before replying. "Seems about right. What's the difference between the two then?"

"Unsourced is exactly what it sounds like. Pure undiluted magic. Chaotic and messy. It's difficult to manage even to someone who's trained but it's malleable. My kind call it chaos magic, when a Source dies their remains release whatever magic is left behind and anyone can draw from it."

"Even me? Humans I mean?" Jensin asked.

Ivara considered him for a moment before nodding. "Yes, I believe so. It would certainly explain the runes."

"You mentioned Sources, are those like people who sell spells? Like an apothecary?"

"Oh no. Think more like a distillery but take the walker, I mean human, element out of it." Jensin's brow furrowed in confusion so she rephrased. "Hmm I suppose it's like this. Unsourced magic is all around us, yeah? Like...the water from the river. What's stopping you from drinking it?"

Jensin made a disgusted face. "The river is dirty. Piss and shit and gods only know what, you couldn't pay me to drink from it."

Ivara smirked. "Exactly. But who will purify the water? Who purifies the magic so that it can be used by others? Sources. But only one who is bound to a Source may use their magic."

"Why give it all away? I mean if it's so valuable why just give away such power?"

"It's not that simple. We of Sourced magic are bound to our masters and to their will. That bond can never be broken. And since Sources are forced to draw on Unsourced magic they are thusly forced to give up bits of themselves.

"Why would anyone give up their freedom like that?" He looked concerned as he said, "Why did you give up your freedom?"

"Lots of reasons. For the Red Mer it's largely about heritage. Only those with vitiligo or albinism may enter their territory, much less go through the choosing process. My little sister is an albino, as was my mother before she bound herself to her serpent. For them it's a high privilege to serve alongside their serpent kin. As for Scyla I don't know much except that she has guarded Dormethius for most if not all of her life. It's complicated."

"And you?" Jenin asked.

"For me there was never really a choice."

"Oh?"

"I was a child. I can still remember the first case, of the plague that is. She was an older mer, with salmon hair and dark skin. Her eyes were the color of emeralds...And on her face... her skin was like dry rocks cracking and falling away. Just bloody red flesh." Ivara shivered. "She turned out to be the first of many in Makoul. My family and I traveled to the north western part of the sea. There were whispers of a Golden Dragon that could destroy cities with a mere thought and heal the sick and ailing with a single touch. Fairy tales to some of course but if you could have seen it... We were desperate. But when we arrived we found the Dragon to be far from myth."

"Dragon?" Jenson laughed. "Surely you're not..?"

"Serious? I am. He agreed to help. Even gave us an antidote that the Golden Mer had been using for years. It was more than we could have ever asked for."

"He didn't ask for payment?"

"Of course he did. He wanted one of my father's daughters. He chose me."

"They just left you there? How old were you?"

"I was only thirty five years old." He looked puzzled so she tried again. "I believe that is about seven years of age in your terms. I wasn't the only one he had traded for. In fact, so far as I know I was one of the last. The bonding ceremony was bloody. But what could I do? I had no family, just a Dragon and two mer women dragging me around giving me orders."

"That sounds so...lonely." Ivara and Jensin turned fast as the wind to see Richard standing awkwardly at the entrance of the garden. He swallowed hard and gestured for himself to approach. "May I?"

"How long have you been standing there?" Ivara questioned feeling her chest tighten.

"Long enough to work up the courage to apologize." Ivara could see in his eyes that he meant it. "I'm sorry." He whispered.

"Me too. I shouldn't have lied, I just – " But she had nothing she could say that would make him understand. "I just wasn't ready to lose one of the few friends I had here."

"And now?"

Ivara took a long breath and put a hand to her temple. "And now, I know losing you was inevitable. So what's the point in keeping up a façade?"

He snorted and handed her a flask of rum from his pocket. "To the inevitable then." She took a swig wondering if the Prince always had alcohol on him. The liquid burned and she welcomed it. His hand brushed her fingertips as she returned it to him. There was a new sort of intimacy between them and yet she hadn't felt so far from him since that very first night in Martha's. Not love, but rather a compassionate bond built on shared grief and understanding. They stared at each other for a moment and she took in all of him. Not just his perfect smile, or attractive build but the bad parts too. For the first time she saw him not as who she wanted him to be but for the flawed, incredible, grieving, brutish, kind, and utterly human being that he was. From his expression she could tell he was making a similar assessment of her. He cleared his throat. "Well, go on. Let's see some magic."

"I'm out of practice if you were here just a half an hour ago-."

"But I wasn't. So let's see it. Impress me."

Ivara rolled her eyes but smiled still. "Alright. Magic is like any other skill. Anyone can do art but some make better painters, others work more with charcoals right? Technically speaking talents are just a well-honed skill, something someone has a natural affinity for that they worked at and honed with time and practice."

Richard made an impatient motion with his hand. "So what was your talent?"

"Dreaming, that's the general term for it. I doubt you have a word for it in Allagorian, perhaps oneiromancy."

"So interpreting dreams then?" Jensin furrowed his brows. "I must confess you have utterly lost me, Ivara."

"It's like if someone's whole life was painted on a pane of glass and the glass was utterly shattered. I can go in and live those small fragments as if I was the person I'm dreaming with."

"'Dreaming with?" Jensin asked again, still skeptical.

"Yes, sharing a dream is a very intimate form of connection. When you experience another's dreams they are often tied to memories with significant emotional weight and I get to experience it just as the one I am dreaming with experienced it."

"That doesn't make any sense - ." Jensin began but Richard cut him off.

"Show me."

"What?" Ivara was taken aback.

"Show me the mer." Richard repeated. She hesitated but eventually slipped her hand into his.

"Let me know when you want to leave."

"How?"

"You'll know. Ready?"

He swallowed and Jensin looked between the two of them nervously. "Oh hell." He said rubbing his temple. She felt the tingle at the back of her neck and the rush down her spine just as before. He twitched so she knew he felt it as well. Fast as lightning she reached for his mind and grabbed it before it had the chance to twitch away from her. There was a falling sensation and Ivara did her best to open her mind and let Richard in. Some small part of her vaguely remembered that she was in a lush green garden standing opposite from the Prince and next to Jensin. But when her eyes opened it was not Richard that stood before her but Everleigh. Young, probably twelve or thirteen. Her hair had been pinned up and her sun dress had been hiked up so she could run. Behind her a boy just a few years her senior by the looks of him with a face similar to Richards but sporting deep brown eyes was counting off. Ivara immediately recognized him to be Henry.

"Three, two, one. Go!" Henry yelled into the wind.

Ivara as Richard took off into the garden's maze, racing Everleigh, Henry and Jensin. She ran as far as her legs would carry her until a large root made her trip and Ivara fell face first into the mud.

The memory shifted and Ivara was looking through the eyes of her younger self though she could still feel Richard's presence in her mind. Then a young man was reaching to help her up. "Thanks." Her voice, Richard's voice, was deeper. Perhaps fourteen years old? It was hard to be sure. The boy that stood before her was very tan, his long hair so dark she nearly thought it was black. Richard's memories identified the teen immediately as the young Prince Alaric of Ellenward.

"Sure thing. Thanks for giving me an excuse to get away from my sisters." They both laughed.

"Aleric! You'd better come quick!" A young tan girl called from atop the staircase. Her face marred by scars and her hair white as snow. "The Allagorians asked about succession, Tanith and Ada look like they're going to kill each other!"

Ivara as Richard laughed. "Your sisters sound...interesting."

"Terrifying is more like it." Alaric laughed. "Come with me? As back up?" Ivara smiled and took his hand and together the two ran up the steps feeling the warm sun beat down upon them. But she wasn't halfway up when the memory shifted once more. She was taller now. And it was pouring. Ivara continued to run up the steps, she could hear Jensin behind her. Both of them soaked when they finally burst into the grand hall just in time to see Everleigh snatch a piece of parchment from Amos's hands.

"Your majesty - ."

"No Amos. No more waiting. It has been months since Henry's last letter. I am done waiting." She eagerly began reading. Ivara watched through Richard's eyes as Everleigh read the parchment, then re-read it, a silent hand going to her mouth. She let out a gasp.

"No." Everleigh whispered. Tears pricked at her eyes as she dropped the parchment and fell to the floor. Her sobbing grew louder and louder into screams. "No!" Ivara ran to comfort her. Everleigh grabbed her and she could feel her shake with grief. But it was Jensin who picked up the letter and read it aloud. Ivara didn't hear the words, but she did feel them. She felt each syllable tear at a piece of her. The grief made her want to vomit. And when she could no longer bear it, like a light in the dark there came a tug at the back of her mind. Gentle at first, then more desperate, and finally a yank. Ivara pulled herself away from the memory. Navigating through Richard's mind she eventually began to feel the warm breeze of the garden. She could feel long soft strands of hair brush her face. Her hair. The transition from Richards mind back to her own took mere moments but seemed like a lifetime. When she finally felt steady on her feet Ivara opened her eyes and looked around. Richard was staring at her. His face was red and tears were streaming down. She realized she too had been crying. Ivara pulled away to wipe at her own eyes.

"Well?" Ivara asked.

"I had no idea... the mer...they're beautiful."

"What did you see?" Jensin asked, walking up to them. "I mean you're both crying so it can't have been anything too wonderful."

Richard took a shaky breath. "I was in a spherical room of sorts. Except underwater, it was almost like a cave. To my right a tan mer girl, only about twelve or so. She had long brown hair and the sweetest smile. But her eyes. They were golden! Nobody said her name and yet I knew it, Brina. There were other girls too though their names are escaping me now."

"Golden eyes as well?" Jensin asked.

"Yes!"

"Corvena, she was the one with the different colored eyes. Tallulah was the other one." Ivara clarified.

"Yes, yes, and we were all playing this game. It was fun."

Jensin looked disappointed. "Is that all?"

"No, no, I saw another memory. A Dragon."

Now it was Ivara's turn to look surprised. "You saw the Master?" When she had opened her mind to him she had only expected him to see surface level or otherwise superficial memories.

"He's so big. I never knew any living thing could be so huge, Ivara!" Richard said.

"Oh so now you believe in dragons too?" Jensin muttered under his breath.

"I heard that and yes! You should have seen it Jensin!" Richard retorted.

A small smile grew on Ivara's face as she watched them go back and forth teasing each other. She may never be able to return home but perhaps she could make a home amongst friends here. Maybe one day she could learn to call Allagor her home.

Chapter 47

"Perhaps the most practical of magics is that of friendship. As silly as it may sound, friendship and love can often be stronger than any spell or rune. Unfortunately, they can also be just as deadly."

Practical Magic by Daniel E. Simmons

Ivara (1604 A.D.)

Ivara shifted uncomfortably in the gown that Everleigh had lent her. It was just a hair too small for her in the waist and the Allagorian custom of dawning stays and corsets on top of everything else only hindered Ivara's breathing all the more. Still it was quite beautiful she thought to herself smiling at her reflection. It had been a full week since she had returned to the palace. Yet in the days since, Ivara had come to truly understand what she had lost the night she left Makoul. Two years. It had been two years since she had left the Golden Mer. Osirus had been right about one thing at least. There had been a shift in power. Unfortunately, the details of the matter still evaded her while she remained with her new found walker friends.

Fortunately, her more immediate issue was to find a way down the spiral staircase to the private room Everleigh had described in her note.

To the most elegant and gracious Lady Ivara Mare,

The Princess Ward of Allagor and his Majesty the Crown Prince of Allagor cordially invite you to a private luncheon to be held Thursday at noon. The couple kindly asks that you dress in your best attire and grant you to bring a plus one from within the court's most intimate advisors and their families only. All guests must show this letter upon entry.

Signed, their royal highnesses the Prince and Princess of Allagor.

The signatures had been written in crimson ink, as was the custom of the royal family here. Great broad strokes and looping curves formed Everleigh's signature whereas Richard's seemed rushed. There came a knock at her door and Ivara turned and carefully placed the letter in her pocket.

"Come in."

It was Jensin. He wore a deep green suit complimented by gold buttons at the center.

"It compliments you." Ivara said, gesturing to the elaborate garb.

"Thank you but I put my dignity in a drawer whenever I'm called to play dress up... so there is really no sense in trying to salvage it." He chuckled.

"I was being serious. Green is a nice color on you." Her hand grazed the side of his face and together they took a moment to simply enjoy each other's presence.

He shivered at her touch then took her hand in his. "You look like you can't breathe."

"I can't." She said flatly. "It seems we will both have to suffer the rich today." Ivara said sarcastically.

"Can't you just loosen it? The corset I mean."

"What and lose face among you walkers?" She feigned offense even as she held out her hand to him. "Shall we?"

He smirked. "I thought you would never ask."

They arrived to find a line of guests also awaiting entry. Jensin peaked around to get a better look.

"And?"

"There's a woman at the head of the line who arrived without her letter." He sighed. "How difficult is it to-. Ugh never mind. Have you made any progress getting back home?"

"So eager to see me leave? I'm joking! But yes though it is very slow going. I'd like to take another look at that book on runes once time allows, I suspect it may contain information on shifting."

"Oh?"

"Don't act surprised."

"I thought you couldn't go back without the blade?"

"I can't. But that's the least of my problems where Dormethius is concerned. The legendary blade is immensely powerful; whoever stole it likely has no idea what they're truly wielding."

"What about your Dragon?"

"A dead end. A spell this complex will likely have to be reversed by either myself or the athame. I'm sure the Master would help if he could but I have no way to get to him. What about you?" They moved up in line and Ivara watched the woman stomp off with a scathing look in her eyes. "Have you learned anything that could help us find the killer?"

"Not much. I handed the information we managed to collect to Amos and the guards who have been doing their own, albeit less discrete, investigation." He took a deep breath and put a hand to his temple. "Apparently when they returned to the warehouse it had been burnt to a crisp. Whoever it was knows we're onto them. It also means that most of the evidence is gone."

"Wow." It was all she could say. They had been so close. It felt like a slap across the face. "Were you able to identify any more of the victims?"

"Yes but there's little correlation. They were all of low birth, little money and only a handful of family members between them all."

"So the killer doesn't want money, they're not interested in playing politics and it's unlikely that they are out for revenge." Ivara pondered aloud.

"Like I said, not much to go off of."

They moved forward a few paces in line.

"Or perhaps it is! Jensin remember how the bodies were covered in runes? What if whoever drew the runes those men and women chose them because nobody would come looking for them? What if while they were living at least, they were practicing!"

"Our killer isn't a psychopath..."

"...he's a scholar. And he was using the book to learn basic forms of magic."

"Then testing the runes on living people. Oh gods it was right in front of us this whole time!"

Jensin's eyes glittered with the realization. He leaned over and kissed her. Beside Ivara a man cleared his throat.

"Letters please." The man was tall, broad and his voice was gruff and old. Ivara handed the parchment to him. "This way please."

Ivara and Jensin were led in by a female servant with a very pleasant smile. Ivara found herself seated at the end of the table next to Everleigh who sat beside Richard and opposite to Jensin. Everleigh dropped her conversation with Richard upon seeing Ivara and immediately reached over and offered her a hug. Ivara reciprocated the warm greeting. Ivara did her best to make conversation with the people at the luncheon. Thankfully if anytime a conversation got to be difficult for her still limited vocabulary Everleigh would swoop in on her behalf. It wasn't until all the guests had arrived that Richard and Everleigh finally rose from their seats hand in hand.

"Thank you all for coming." Richard spoke to the thirty odd people in the room. "As many of you here know, it was not long ago that I lost my elder brother and the best man I have ever known. However this loss was not only felt by the people of Allagor and myself but perhaps it was felt deepest by his beautiful fiancé Princess Everleigh." Beside her Everleigh tensed. "Now it is with great excitement that I can finally announce to you all the long awaited Allagorian wedding shall take place mere weeks from this day!" Richard held up his glass and took a long swig. "To Allagor!"

"To Allagor!" The lords and ladies hooted before gulping down their wine.

Once the chatting had regained its regular volume and all the guests were occupied, Everleigh turned back to her. "Jensin tells me you're looking for a way back home?"

Everleigh did her best to make the question seem casual and conversational.

"Hopefully. I have a few things to take care of before I leave though."

"Stay." Everleigh blurted out.

"What?"

"Don't go. Stay and I'll make you my lady in waiting, grant you the title of Allagorian Lady with land and servants all to your own. You'll be able to live comfortably to the end of your days. No more running. Let Allagor be your forever home."

"I-...don't know what to say." She couldn't accept of course because...why? Because she still needed to report back to the Master? Likely Scyla had already informed him in the weeks following her transformation. But what about her sisters? They'd managed most of their lives without her, surely they could last a while longer. Then there were her fellow maidens, her sisters in gold. It suddenly hit her that through all this none of them had come looking for her. Perhaps they simply didn't need her. It wouldn't surprise her. The others were far more powerful than she would ever be. Her gifts had only ever been a hindrance to her.

"You don't have to decide right this second of course. Just promise me you'll stay till the wedding and we can speak on it after that." Everleigh's eyes were bright and hopeful. It occurred to her that the petite blond woman likely hadn't had too many female confidants given her status.

"Alright. I'll consider it."

"Oh I nearly forgot! I bid Kirsten to make your gown for the ceremony! She seemed rather thrilled at the prospect. I know how much you loath fittings but she has shown me the sketch for your gown and I promise you it will be well worth it." The Princess said, smiling with anticipation.

The day was waning when Ivara took her leave of the luncheon-turned-dinner party. Multiple guards offered to escort her back to her quarters but she declined them all. She needed the quiet of the long empty hallways to think on Everleigh's offer. Ivara stopped next to one of the many large windows and sat on its ledge. Outside she could see carriages arriving to pick up various gentry. Servants and bootblacks walked among them.

"Permanent home." Ivara whispered to herself echoing Everleigh's words.

"Hmm?"

She turned and was greeted by a curious face. Kirsten smiled.

Ivara sighed. "Just thinking aloud."

"What about?"

"Moving actually, though I'm torn." She waved the topic off. "A problem for another day. Everleigh mentioned you're taking on her wedding dress?"

"Yours as well. It's a lot of work but I'm sure you'll both look dazzling. You'll of course have to show me how the ball gown fits ahead of time."

"You'll not be attending the ceremony?" Ivara asked, surprised.

"Oh no. Weddings aren't my thing. I'm not quite sure what it is but I always feel a bit overwhelmed. Too many people perhaps." There was a nervousness to her tone that did not match her words.

"Then I suppose I shall have to save you some mead."

Kirsten forced a laugh. "I suppose so."

Ivara got up to leave.

"Ivara?" She turned.

"Yes?"

Kirsten suddenly became fidgety. "Do you ever question yourself? I mean your morals; do you ever wonder if you're doing the right thing?"

Ivara was struck by the sheer randomness of turn in the conversation. "I do, yes." She answered, Everleigh's offer still heavy on her mind.

"How do you know then? If what you're doing is right?"

Ivara thought on it for a moment. "I guess I do my best to consider who would benefit the most from my decisions." As the words left her lips her mind seemed to make its decision. "I'll stay." She said aloud. If she stayed in Allagor she could advise the royal family and mend their relationship with the mer. All her time here would be for naught if she returned to the Golden Mer. In Allagor she could do the most good. If the Dragon saw fit to contact her then she might reconsider but until then this was her home. Her permanent home. Her forever home. She smiled at Kirsten. "I'll stay."

Chapter 48

"Dragons, the envy and fear of all who reside in the sea. Though the race of dragons dwindled to near extinction long before I was born, it is said that once, Dragons roamed the entire sea. That they were so large they would cast a shadow for days when they swam above a city. Intelligent, and ferocious they were. So what, dear reader, could have killed them?"

Toren's Bestiary, Volume 1: Creatures of the Sea by Toren Dagney

Tallulah (1558 A.D.)

When they had finished recording Osirus's vision they gathered the others and swam towards the Dragon's chambers. Osirus was still a bit disorientated from his vision but the time spent going over it again and again seemed to help him, if ever so slightly.

"Can we slow down? Please Tal I think I'm going to vomit."

Tallulah huffed in frustration but stopped and let him recuperate. "Better?"

His nod was all the confirmation she needed. Corvena and Brina had gone ahead of them to inform the Dragons maidens of an immediate audience and Ivara stayed behind to swim with Osirus and herself. Now Tallulah could see her friend panting as she sped to meet up with them. The mer girl was the youngest of them all and thus her tail was the shortest, she was also the only one who hadn't yet turned golden. Together the three of them raced to the Dragons hall.

When they could finally see the entry hall and the maidens guarding it Tallulah let out a breath. If her friends had already been granted entry then there was no time to waste. The maidens ushered them in and down to the great room where the Dragon dwelt. After so many years in the Arkstone the Dragons quarters still took her breath away. Huge archways and domes covered in etchings with no part of the walls larger than her fist left uncovered. Then there was the Dragon himself. He was huge and when he knelt his head down to them all and his gills flared it was enough to push them all back.

You have witnessed a prophecy?

He spoke in all their minds with a booming voice. Tallulah opened her mouth to repeat the now memorized words Osirus had spoken to them all but the Dragons voice entered her mind once more.

Let the Seer approach so that I may read his thoughts and see that which he has seen.

Tallulah peeled Osirus's arm off of her own. He hesitated before gulping down water and mastering himself.

"Master I don't remember the words that I spoke. Tallulah though, she committed them to memory and wrote them down!"

The Dragon ignored him and the room was silent save for the hum of the current. It took Tallulah a moment to realize what was happening. Osirus was having a conversation with the Dragon that she simply was not privy to. The moment dragged on for what felt like ages. None of them dared interrupt the silent conversation. Finally the Dragon raised his head and acknowledged them each in turn.

Come, he spoke in their minds. *It is time we spoke of the future and how you might overcome it.*

With that he turned and led them out the back way towards a large archway that led out of the huge castle. Tallulah followed with baited breath, Corvena at her side, Osirus and Ivara not far behind, tablets still in hand. Brina for all her experience with the Dragon did not seem as surprised as the rest of them.

This way. And they followed him into a massive hole carved into the stone floor. Tallulah felt uneasy as she gazed into the inky darkness below. The Master dove straight down and they followed close behind. Ivara stopped just at the edge.

"Oh no, that's too dark. I don't think I can-"

Corvena grabbed her arm. "Sorry Ive's. Time for some tough love." The younger mer girl squealed as Corvena pulled them downward into the deep abyss. They swam on for what, to Tallulah, felt like hours in the dark. Until eventually they came upon a light. The Dragon paused his downward motion before curving into the cylindrical wall of darkness towards the light. They followed quickly after him, none of them eager to stay in the dark any longer than was necessary. Tallulah too felt uneasiness in the dark and rushed towards the light.

The light it turned out was simply a scattering of *Luma* runes within a large study room whose multiple halls and entry ways likely led to a much larger complex beneath the city. Perhaps another city altogether. Tallulah gasped at what she was seeing. She could hardly believe it! It *was* an underground city. Or at the very least what was left of such a place. Truthfully 'ruins' was more apt to describe the place but this was no place for mer. No this was a city for *dragons*. The archways were much too tall and the smallest runes were the size of Tallulah herself.

Her breath left her as she realized she was swimming in the ruins of-.

The Arkstone. The true *Arkstone, the last city of Dragons.* As the Dragon confirmed her realization she knew his words to be true.

Giant gemstones embedded themselves in stone walls that glittered with flecks of gold. Stone etches on the walls and floor carved out rich histories in a language long since forgotten. She felt like a minnow in a great vast sea as she gazed around at the massive houses, libraries... all of it sat desolate, alone and forgotten, until now.

"I thought this place was a myth." Ivara whispered half to herself.

Their Master chuckled aloud. *Many have come to that consensus. Unfortunately, they're only half wrong. The city was once populated. We were many... now I am the last of my kind. The Dragon's face tightened with the pain of loss.*

Tallulah ran a hand over the runes that ebbed with light. They were so large she could fit her whole hand into the carvings. "It's incredible."

"But what does it have to do with us?" Brina asked.

Look around you. Touch the walls and feel the hum of sadness, the echo of loss that these halls have borne witness to. That is what awaits you, each of you, in the year of the Dolah. I had hoped that you might serve myself and the Arkstone for many years still but the years are waning and the signs are coming to fruition. The next Great War is coming.

His tone made Tallulah want to break into tears. She felt it then. Whether in the Masters voice or in the very walls around her, she didn't yet know but she knew she felt it. That hollowness that had been left after the Great War. Halls shouldn't be empty and homes shouldn't be quiet, not like this.

"What can we do to stop it?" Corvena asked.

There is no stopping this.

"How can you be sure?" Osirus asked from the corner of the room.

Come. The Dragon beckoned them to the far side of the room where images had been carved out likely many centuries before even their Masters time. There were five such images carved into the wall and each of them had been outlined in a script that even Tallulah didn't recognize. She swam up to better study the images, as did her friends.

The first depicted a man with three eyes. Two of them in the normal placement and the third in the middle of his forehead. She went on to the next image. It was a mer woman whose hair draped messily over her naked body. Thankfully, this one had only two eyes though one had been blocked out by shadow so it appeared darker than the other. The third figure, once again a mer woman, seemed to be slightly larger than the rest. She had no eyes, nor a mouth or nose but held in one hand a skull and in the other a newborn babe. Tallulah continued on; growing more and more unsettled.

She was nearing the last two figures now and as she came upon the second to last she saw a figure in armor. The sex was difficult to tell due to the lackluster style of carving but she could tell the figure was mer. He or she held a large shield that covered most of their chest. She moved on. To the right was the last figure. A mer child looked up to the sky as her skull split open to reveal dozens of tentacles. The image was haunting.

Tallulah shivered with disgust. "Whoever made these..."

Died a very long time ago.

"Who are they?" Ivara asked.

The Dragon rustled as if to speak but Corvena beat him to it.

"Their us. Aren't they?" She looked to him for confirmation.

In a manner of speaking...yes. The gift of prophecy is an ancient one and yet still we know very little about it. These are the five sentinels of war. An old prophecy that has been repeated by many seers. We have very few records of the five sentinels coming to fruition, but when they do it is a marker of great bloodshed to come.

"What are they? The five sentinels I mean." Tallulah interrupted, still staring at the last figure of the mer girl.

The first is the Seer. Indicated by the third eye. He gestured to the wall then to Osirus. *Next is the one who binds shadows.*

Tallulah didn't dare look over at Corvena. Could her friend be so powerful? The Dragon moved on.

The speaker for the dead. He looked pointedly at Brina and she stared back. *One who touches the veil between this realm and the next. Then the Shield.* Tallulah realized immediately he was speaking of her. The rest of them knew as well. All those times he had failed to call her by her name she had thought him being rude and awful...yet, he had been calling her by a title. She took a breath and turned to the final figure. *And the Enthraller of minds.*

Ivara gasped and began shaking her head.

This is the true purpose of the Arkstone. To analyze prophecies and to prepare for the next great war. These are the signs that the time of the Dolah is nearing: A gathering of the five sentinels, a disruptions of power across the world especially in the south, a source will make a home amongst walkers, and the final indication, a fair haired female shall establish herself as Queen in a land not her own.

"So the Dolah is a war then?" Corvena mused.

The Dolah will be more powerful than any of us. It shall be borne by a culmination of the three sources. This is why your vows of celibacy must be kept. The golden blood that has been given to you is a powerful gift. It must not be allowed to mix with the venom of the red mer, nor should you allow yourselves to be influenced by the creature that calls itself Dormethius. And finally you must never lay with a walker. If you do, you risk one of your own blood bringing about the war.

"What would you have us do then if not work to prevent such things?" Tallulah asked, returning to the prophecy.

Wait, watch and prepare. Whatever fate awaits us, we shall not go into it empty handed.

Chapter 49

"Family is a strange thing, and its value changes from culture to culture. In Neroth, family is a weapon, a political dagger. In the Silver Grove, family is a heavy weight in an already difficult world. In Makoul it is a warm comforting feeling of comradery. And in the Arkstone, family are those mer that find you when the world is at its darkest."

Royal Families of the Sea by Freya Burg

Tallulah (1588 A.D.)

Tallulah stared blankly at the stone tablet in front of her, not truly seeing anything in her exhaustion and frustration. It had been seven years since she'd promised to help Ivara, since she had tried and failed to shield her, and still, nothing in the scrolls or tablets showed any sign of curing the mer girl of her ever increasing madness. She'd skimmed through every stone tablet she could find. Then she moved to the scrolls. When the scrolls yielded nothing she would gather her things and swim down a level and repeat the process, hoping, praying for an answer.

She was nearly ready to give up and throw in the rag when she found it. The tablet was old and its weaker corners had begun to crumble to dust. So it was no surprise to her that the Cam was of an ancient dialect. She would need assistance in transcribing it. Still there were a few words she could pick out. *Memories And Those That Read Them.* Those six words were all she needed. Tallulah clenched the tablet tight to her chest and began swimming upward. As she swam higher light poured in above her from the top of the library's huge grotto and she could feel the warmth of mid-day. Tallulah yawned, thoroughly exhausted and feeling quite triumphant. She lazily made her way back to the room she shared with her peers. She arrived expecting to find her friends waiting for her, but instead it was one of the Maidens. Her jaw was tight and there were dark circles under her eyes.

"Shield, come over here. I've a message for yourself and the others."

Tallulah nodded and sat down her tablet at the edge of stalagmite then swam over. The Maiden offered her a skinny scroll with the dragon's acid seal still hot on its edges.

"One of your peers, the Seer, has foreseen a power shift in the coming years. The Dragon has asked that you deal with it and report back."

Tallulah could tell the mer woman meant the five of them.

"Where?"

The mer woman nodded to the scroll.

"The details are in there. All the Arkstones resources have been made available to you and your peers. I am at your disposal; you need only ask." The servant who was easily twice Tallulah's age bowed deeply. Tallulah did not need to see the look of disapproval on her face, she could feel it. Of all the golden servants none still lived that had received the Dragons golden blood. None save for Tallulah and her peers. Due to their magical blood and incredible abilities the five of them had risen quickly through the ranks. Each taking on more and more responsibility as they grew. Now it was them that servants, generals, commanders, and city leaders would go to especially if they sought an audience with the Dragon.

Tallulah nodded and the mer woman turned to leave just in time for Corvena to show up. The two had an awkward exchange at the entry way before the Maiden sighed and shimmied past Corvena.

"Oh wow! You um..." Corvena tripped over her words upon seeing Tallulah.

"Go on, get it out."

"Yikes, well you look absolutely..." Corvena put an arm around Tallulah's waist. "...positively..." She took the clip holding Tallulah's hair down and caressed Tallulah's soft cheek. "awful."

Despite herself Tallulah chuckled. "You really have some work to do on your flattery." She smiled as she said it. She reached for Corvena's braid, slowly undoing it with one hand and pulling her close by the small of her back with the other. "These derogatory one liners are getting worse by the day."

"Oh?" Corvena's mouth was inches from her own. But instead of kissing her, Corvena, with infuriating slowness let her lips travel upwards. The feel of her chapped lips on Tallulah's smooth skin was like the first touch of stone. But with a warmth only she knew. Corvena's breaths were quickening now as she neared Tallulah's ear. She could feel the heat from both their faces as they savored the exchange. Corvena hovered just barely touching her ear as she whispered.

"Come with me."

"Hmm?" Tallulah answered, trying to pull herself out of her daze.

"The Master has given me a task. Shouldn't take long, I'm to coordinate a trade between one of the wealthy families in the upper tier."

Tallulah pulled away slightly. "Actually I've been given a task of my own. But that aside, why do you need my help?"

Corvena pulled her back in. "I don't. But recently I find myself getting quite out of hand in your absence. So do us both a favor and come along to keep me in line."

Tallulah snorted and rolled her eyes. She kissed her lover briefly on the lips before pulling away. "Of course I'll come. What's the address?"

Corvena handed her a rope with a series of complex knots. Tallulah looked the khipu over. The residence was much closer than she had assumed. They gathered their things in small satchels and were on their way. Upon their arrival they were greeted with the Arkstone staple of cavern openings stacked one on top of the other. Around them small reef sharks and colorful fauna gathered.

"It's the top one." Corvena pointed. Her voice short and scratchy.

"How do you know?" Tallulah asked, the address in the knotted rope had only listed the area and the title of the couple.

Corvena's gills flared. "Because, I used to live there." Tallulah had never seen her friend cry before. But there was no denying the tears that seamlessly left her single golden eye and became one with the sea. Her green glass eye being the only part of Corvena that wasn't beginning to shake. Tallulah put a calming arm around Corvena's shoulders and together they waited until Corvena had mastered herself and they swam to the top level. The couple was waiting for them. The mer woman had dark skin and pale blonde hair and a purple tail. Her husband was similarly colored but with a bright green tail.

"Corvena! Oh, you're all grown up." The mer woman wiped a tear from her face. "What brings you here?"

Corvena offered them each a curt nod. "Mother, father. My Master has sent me. I was told you were looking to make another deal." She said formally.

"Oh! We were expecting well um –." Corvena's father looked behind them.

Her mother waved her father off. "Doesn't matter who we were expecting. We're glad to see you dear."

Tallulah opened her mouth to introduce herself but Corvena smacked her with her tail and cut her off. "Not going to invite us in?" Corvena said sarcastically. Tallulah was surprised at how little Corvena looked like her mother and father. Where the golden mer beside her sported deep green hair, and a light skin tone, her parents were both of a pastel pink hue in the skin and her mother's curly blonde hair floated in loose ringlets all around her.

"Oh um why don't we just stay outside for now." Her mother's smile faltered for just a moment.

"Fine. My reports mentioned you need money. How much?" Corvena spoke in monotone.

"Oh just enough to get by." Her mother flitted.

"How. Much."

"Two hundred." Corvena's father spoke up.

Corvena laughed, Tallulah looked between both parties not sure what to say.

"Two hundred? What are you trying to do, buy a child?" Corvena laughed. It was then that a young mer girl swam out of the home. Her hair was long and so deep green that at first glance it looked onyx. Her eyes bright green, she was identical to Corvena in every way except her tail. The tad's tail had an abnormal bend to it which made her swim slowly. The girl tugged on her mother's fins.

"Mother?" Her small tad voice whispered. She noticed them then and lurched back. "Mother, who are these people?"

"Nobody darling, go back inside like mommy told you." The mother replied gently.

"But."

"Now, I shall come retrieve you in a moment." The mother turned back to them. "Two hundred, and you can take the girl. She has an abnormal fin and your father and I simply don't have the time to care for such a child."

Tallulah turned to see Corvena doing a rather poor job at trying to master her rage. "And the money, you intend to use it to buy her replacement don't you?"

"What we do with our money is our business but, yes." Corvena's father replied.

"You got her from the same seller didn't you. She's my sister, isn't she?" Corvena was shaking now.

"Yes, we love you dear and the seller continues to have decent prices so we thought why not? But we now realize that perhaps the couple we usually buy from is not as attentive to genetic abnormalities as we previously thought. In truth the poor tad should have been put to sleep before such a defect could have come to fruition." The father replied. "It seems we will have to shop elsewhere."

Corvena shook with rage and disgust. It was all Tallulah could do to keep herself calm and not interfere. Finally after minutes of silence between the two parties. Corvena took her blade and fast as lightning cut one of her mother's fins in half. Her mother wailed in pain but Corvena's face kept steady as she spoke in a horrifying whisper.

"I expect that will take some time to heal. Perhaps in your newfound downtime you can find time to care for your daughter as well as your wound. Your request has been denied."

Tallulah turned to the angry mer beside her. Squeezing her hand as she whispered gently in her ear. "Careful, that's your family Corv, don't throw them away."

Corvena halted, but she did not turn around. "No." She said. "They're strangers. You're my family now."

Chapter 50

"'Mortem Dolah,' a common phrase in my home kingdom. In Ellenward prophecy is sacred, especially the prophecy of the Dolah which was brought to us by our first Queen, Ella the Conqueror. The phrase takes it's meaning from the prophecy of which it is derived. Death to the Dolah. Death to the Great War. And death to the five devils of the pit."

Prophecies of Northerners by Alec E. Kalith

Ivara (1604 A.D.)

"Too...tight!" Ivara squeaked out between breaths. The maid fitting her loosened the corset ever so slightly. "Moore please." Ivara pleaded. Through the mirror she could see Kirsten enter her room with a horrified look on her face!

"What are you doing? Do you know how *expensive* this fabric is? Shoo! Out before you ruin it!" Like a moth to a flame Kirsten was by Ivara's side loosening the stay and helping her shrug it off.

"Thank the gods." Ivara said once she could breathe again.

Her friend looked frazzled. Deep circles showed under eyes and her hair was unkempt.

"Goodness Kirsten, when was the last time you slept?"

"Ha! Very funny, anyways you're welcome for heroically rescuing you but unfortunately that is not why I came."

"Oh?"

"Your dress came in." Kirsten handed her a large box tied in twine. "Try it on. I'll have the ladies mark it for adjustments and I'll come and collect it in a few hours once I'm finished with Everleigh's bodice." Before Ivara could respond she was gone and the seamstresses were making their way back into her chambers.

Ivara opened the box hesitantly. She ran a hand over the red and gold fabric feeling the richness of it.

"Expensive. You must have the king's favor." One of her servants said, looking on with envy and wonder.

"Hmm?"

"Ahh excellent craftsmanship. Likely from Ellenward." Said another gingerly lifting the skirt from the box. "This cost a pretty penny, dear. You've certainly earned someone's eye."

Ivara smiled. It was beautiful and the fit was near perfect. Minor alterations in the shoulders and hips and it would be a perfect fit. She waited patiently as her maids marked the areas to take the dress in. Occasionally they would make small talk until the final pin marked the last alteration.

"Anywhere else my lady?"

"No, I think we've reached an end."

Ivara twirled one final time admiring herself in the blur of gold. For a moment she was transported away. She was no longer in Allagor, but instead in the Arkstone hand in hand with Tallulah. It was so easy to be humbled by Tallulah's beauty, her golden eyes and scales contrasted her deep ebony skin and hair. There was a time when all Ivara had wanted was to be golden, just as her friends in the Arkstone had been. Perhaps now as she twirled around in a haze of golden fabric, she had finally had her wish fulfilled.

Then just as quickly as the memory had come, it left her. She took a deep breath and wiped a reminiscent tear from her eye before allowing her maids to assist her in undressing after which they promptly left. Ivara changed somewhat unceremoniously into an old cream colored blouse and trousers. Not the most feminine thing but it was certainly comfortable. She carefully took the golden ball gown and began gently folding it the way Kirsten had shown her. The top was the easiest so she did that first. Next the skirt. Ivara began by laying it out on her bed as best she could while doing her best not to alter the pins. She tried folding the skirt as it had been in the box but after multiple failed attempts reconciled to simply waiting for Kirsten to return and help her.

Frustrated, Ivara flopped down on her bed. She could read minds! How could she not fold a skirt! The bed shifted with her weight and a portion of the skirt fell into sunlight revealing a small dark rectangle the length of her finger. Ivara stood up to get a better look but, no longer in the sunlight, the rectangle disappeared.

Ivara pulled the skirt over towards her pillow so that the rectangle was once again visible to her. She squinted then reached out to touch it. There was nothing. As if it were a shadow. But a quick glance around her chamber revealed nothing of the shape or size that would grant such a shadow. Perplexed, Ivara once more began toying with the fabric. This time she could feel a small rise where the shadow began, and a dip where it ended. So it was stitched inside then.

Curiosity overtook Ivara and she cut at a small section of seams at the bottom of the layer and inverted the skirt. Inside where the rectangle had been was a small piece of fabric stitched into the layer. On it were written six words. It was enough to make her blood run cold.

All is in place, mortem Dolah.

Chapter 51

This will be the last letter I write as the time for talk wains and the time for action hastens toward us. Do no waiver on your task. Do not disgrace your mothers legacy. Mortem Dolah.

Letter from an unknown source found sewn into the hem of a dress in Allagor

Ivara (1604 A.D.)

Ivara sprinted down the hallway, the fabric note clenched tightly in her fist. She slammed hard into Jensin.

"Ive's you look like you've seen a ghost. Are you-."

"No time." She half panted; half whispered, shoving the fabric into his palm.

His brows furrowed as he looked down and read the words. Jensin shook his head with disbelief and ran an anxious hand through his copper hair.

"Dolah, that's the legend of the war spirit. This is a *mer* legend! Where did you get this?" He asked anxiously.

"It was sewn into the skirt of my dress, my gown for the wedding."

"Shit."

"Kirsten mentioned the skirt and Everleigh's fabric might have arrived in the same shipment."

Jensin nodded. "Alright. You go check it. I'll go find Everleigh and warn the guards. Here." He handed her a short skinny dagger. "Tear it apart if you have to but be discreet until you know you're alone."

Ivara nodded. "Where?"

"The servant's quarters downstairs."

They parted and it was all she could do to keep from running. Once she had reached an empty hall she blew through, tripping over herself to get down the steps. Ivara walked with sure footing and rapped on the door. A plump brunette woman opened the door.

"The wedding dress, where is it?"

"Miss I'm going to have to ask you to lea-."

Ivara pulled the dagger Jensin had given her and held its shining tip to the woman's throat. "Where. Is. It."

The woman gasped at the flash of silver and nodded vigorously. "This way." Ivara followed her to a large box where the dress had been carefully folded up.

"Out now." The woman did not hesitate and Ivara could hear the skittering of shoes on the wood.

Ivara's hands shook as she opened the box and ran her hands over the fabric trying desperately to feel for any change in texture that might be a note. She began to relax when after minutes of combing through there was nothing to be found. Ivara let out a breath she hadn't known she'd been holding. A sparkle from the other side of the room caught her eye. It was Everleigh's corset. It had been covered in finery and jewels and plenty more sat beside it in a box yet to be sewn on.

Curious, Ivara walked over and delicately picked up the corset. There was nothing odd about it at first. However a second look granted her what she had come for. On the inside of the corset lay a smooth layer of fabric that hadn't been fully sewn in. Oh it was just the corner where the seams failed to meet one another but it was enough. Ivara ripped at it. The fabric came free easily and Ivara nearly dropped the bodice upon seeing what had been sewn into it. *Runes.* Hundreds of them had been meticulously stitched into the corset. *Morta.* The death rune stitched over and over. Marking its wearer for death.

It all made sense. The rune book, the bodies. It was all practice. Ivara gripped the corset until her palms went white. But who...her body shivered in disgust as it reached the answer moments before her mind did. Ivara took a breath then another. She didn't hear the door creak open but she *did* feel the blade as it gently pressed into the back of her neck.

"You really can't keep your nose clean can you Ivara?"

Ivara could feel Kirsten's hot breath on the back of her ear as the seamstress whispered to her. Ivara dropped the bodice and fell forward. She made a run for the door but found it locked from the inside. She turned, pulling her blade on her former friend.

"You were going to hurt her." Her voice shook.

"No, I was going to *kill* her. I'm still planning on it actually." Kirsten smirked and with one swift movement had her blade pressed into Ivara's arm as Jensin's dagger clattered to the ground. A blink and Kirsten's long curved dagger was at Ivara's throat. "I'll be quick. One final favor in the spirit of our friendship."

"Why?"

"You said it yourself. It's for the greater good."

Ivara screamed and shoved Kirsten against the stone wall. There was an audible thud and when the seamstress touched her fingers to the back of her head they came away red with blood. Ivara lunged for her blade but Kirsten was faster. She tripped Ivara and the mer woman fell face first on the ground feet from her only defense. Kirsten picked up the blade shaking her head and walked over. Ivara felt for Kirsten's mind, but instead found an impassable wall.

Kirsten laughed dryly. "Tough luck getting through *enthraller*. What, you thought I wouldn't recognize a tenant of the Great War."

Ivara looked to the girl's neck and noticed for the first time that her necklace also bore a single rune. *Protea.* The protection rune. Ivara swore as Kirsten knelt down and began. The first touch of the blade on her throat was like that of a needle. Cool and sharp but not for long. The blade's descent was slow at first as Kirsten painted the *quiesce* rune over Ivara's chest with the blood that had begun to flow from her throat. She tried to scream but it was just silence all around her.

Now Kirsten moved more quickly. Blood was pooling up around them and a darkness was crowding Ivara's vision. Kirsten pulled the blade out with vigor.

"Don't worry I'm not like these imbeciles. I don't kill without a cause." In her fading consciousness Ivara could hear footsteps approaching. So could her killer. Panicked, Kirsten dipped her index finger in Ivara's blood and hastily scribbled a marking on Ivara's arm. She knew the curves of the symbol as surely as she knew the curves of her own palm. She was being cursed to die, slowly and painfully.

She looked up and it was Kirsten who stared down at her with a smirk on her face. "All you eastern folk make the same mistake. You could have betrayed the royal family, let them hate you at the least. Maybe then they wouldn't come running to find you, to help you even as you choke on your own blood. Because they will come for you, Ivara. And by the time they find you, I will be gone." With that the seamstress' face disappeared from Ivara's view.

Suddenly blood was welling up in her throat and lungs. Darkness closed in around her and she could feel the hot agony within her slowly being replaced by the cool stillness of death. In the distance a voice. Familiar and angry. Shouting and footsteps... but that was the last she was aware of before darkness claimed her.

Chapter 52

"The mer folk are quite difficult to kill, however that does not mean death for such a people is not possible. If one intends to kill a magical being, one might consider the use of blood magic."

Prejudice of the Merfolk by Willmont Anderson

Jensin (1604 A.D.)

Jensin was running. They had all heard the scream, him, Richard, Everleigh and the captain of the guard Amos as they spoke in hushed tones about Ivara's discovery. Each of them had shuddered at that first scream. The first sign that things had gone very, very wrong. So now he was running. As fast as his legs would take him towards the servants quarters. Towards Ivara.

Skipping every other step and nearly tripping over himself at the speed he was going yet he refused to slow down. Behind him Amos and multiple castle guards followed, occasionally splitting off to block off exits or go a different route. When he finally reached the bottom floor it was to find the servants rushing upstairs in droves. Behind them a loud thud. Jensin grabbed one of the men by the arm to ask where but he quickly pulled away. Jensin shouldered past anyone in his way until he finally came to a long hall and a set of doors. They got to work and every second was an agony. It felt like they might never find her until one rather tall guard yelled hoarsely for Jensin.

"Over here! This one's locked!"

Jensin didn't think, he just rammed into the door. It budged but not by much. The screaming had stopped now and there was just silence. Jensin pulled his sword and slipped it between the door and the wall and pushed. There was a popping sound and the lock broke away. The door swung open. Blood coated the floor and splattered the walls. And there, laying still in the crimson pool was Ivara. The young woman shuddered with death lingering close by. Jensin saw the rune immediately. He ran to her and fell hard onto his knees. Jensin was quick, he immediately ripped at his shirt and began rubbing but the bloody rune wouldn't come off. So he picked her up and ran. Jensin was running. The bond that had constantly beckoned him to her, to her bed even now twisted his stomach in fear. So he ran, praying that there was still time.

Chapter 53

"Many believe that humans were never meant to possess magic, much less study it. Perhaps that is why dragon bones burn and runes require blood. Maybe these sacrifices are the natural consequence of defiling the natural order."

Practical Magic by Daniel E. Simmons

Ivara (1604 A.D.)

Her sense of smell came first. The smell of alcohol and bandages. Next came the coo of birds as they flitted outside her window singing songs of spring. She felt a warm breeze over her skin. Her body shuddered. She tried to open her eyes but the effort exhausted her so she opted to lay in solemn darkness. There were footsteps as someone walked on the other side of the room.

"...and you bid her go into harm's way without *any* protection?"

Even in her state of twilight she recognized Richard's panicked voice. A chair creaked closer to where she lay and from that spot another voice answered.

"Don't speak to me like that as if you give a damn about her! As if you would have done any differently. Everleigh's life was on the line! As was yours and mine! All of us could have come to harm were it not for quick thinking on *both* Ivara and my parts. So there, you're welcome I suppose." Jensin's words dripped with annoyance.

"Thank you? You want me to *thank you?* A girl almost died Jensin!"

"You think I don't know that! You think I don't care? I love her!" He paused to collect himself. When he spoke once more his voice was a mere whisper. "I'm not having this discussion with you. Either shut up or get out." Jensin barked.

Ivara heard a door slam and listened as Richard's footsteps faded away. She gasped when she felt a cool liquid on her neck as someone, likely a healer traced a rune there. It worked and she immediately tensed as the liquid warmed and her skin began healing at an accelerated rate. The pain of it forced her eyes to open and she could see Jensin standing over her, pen in hand.

"Do you want me to stop?"

She shook her head, *no*. It was healing magic alright. But it was *brutal*. He drew another rune on her collarbone and this time it was all she could do not to wail.

"Last one."

Ivara nodded and prepared herself. Jensin took the pen, dipped it in a crimson ink and began drawing the symbol on the side of her head. She shuddered. It was like being slammed on the stone floor all over again and Jensin handed her a rag to muffle her cries. Ivara shut her eyes and took deep breaths, calming herself until the pain had passed. When it was bearable once more she let them flitter open to see Jensin's worried expression staring at her from where he sat next to her bed.

"Any better?"

"A bit." She croaked.

Confused, she put a hand to her throat. Last night's events came upon her at the speed of light. Immediately her memories thrust her back into what she had thought at the time to be her last moments. Her breaths came in quick rasps. Panicked, she reached for the place on her chest where Kirsten had drawn the *Morta* rune. But Jensin put a gentle hand on hers.

"It's okay. We got it off of you."

"*We?*"

Jensin tilted his head to the healers behind him. It was then that Ivara realized they weren't alone. They were in the infirmary.

"How?"

"Blood actually. Took a fair bit of digging through that damn book but apparently runes can be dispelled with the same base with which they were drawn. The only other solution being to slice through them which as I'm sure you know can be fatal."

"Whose..."

"Whose blood? Mine." He glanced down and she followed his eyes to a white bandage on his right hand. Each breath she took was an exhausting challenge. Jensin looked her over, concerned. "Sleep, we can speak again when you've rested."

She nodded and succumbed to the darkness.

...

She awoke hours later to find Jensin beside her, his arms covered in fresh bandages as he continued his bloody work.

"Did you catch her?" She asked, her voice far more stable now.

"Kirsten? Oh yes." Jensin spoke with a tad too much delight. It disturbed her if she was honest with herself. Ivara attempted to sit up but a throbbing pain in her head created spots in her vision and she cried out in pain. "Take it slow and let the runes do their job." Jensin said gently.

"Everleigh's dress...she can't wear it."

"I know, Everleigh's fine and I'll be damned if she ever wears anything that Kirsten's hands have touched again. That woman has a lot to answer for. Did she clue you into why she might have targeted the Princess?"

Ivara shook her head. "No... none of this makes sense!" Ivara moaned as another wave of pain washed over her.

"Actually..." Jensin looked off.

"What?"

"If Kirsten was the one sewing the runes into Everleigh's gown then it stands to reason that she is our killer."

Ivara nodded, the action sent tingles all over her. "Makes sense. But why? I thought Everleigh and Kirsten were good friends."

"As did I, there is one explanation but you're not going to like it."

"Go on."

"Kirsten made a few notes about a 'Dolah.' The war spirit I mentioned to you. I did some digging and according to Richard and a few texts we found, it is widely held in some regions around the world that in the end times a figure will rise up. The figure had a few different names depending on where you go but its earliest mentions are in Ellenward's scrolls. Can you guess what they called it?"

"Dolah?"

"Yep. Now here's where it gets interesting. Ellenward has a rich history with the Mer as I'm sure you know. They also trace much of their knowledge of the Dolah back to their first Queen, Ella who may have actually been mer."

"Ella?"

"Don't tell me you knew her." Jensin teased.

"Of course not. She is or was, I suppose old enough to be my great grandmother's great grandmother! But I do remember learning that she was once a Golden Mer too." Ivara said, putting a hand to her throbbing head.

"Really? What happened."

Ivara shook her head, taking a breath to calm the ache in her head. "She left, became human and disgraced the Dragon by propagating with walkers. It's why all the Goldens that came after have had to swear to celibacy." Jensin gave her a questioning look. "All of Ella's line have ties to the Golden Dragon. Each of them have a slightly higher capacity for magic than regular humans. But that aside, back to your point it would make sense that much of

Ellenward's knowledge on the Dolah is traced back to Ella's heritage. Unfortunately, that means that their information is likely incomplete." Speaking was exhausting and Ivara found herself out of breath.

"That's what I was afraid of." Jensin sounded exasperated.

"Chin up. I happen to be very familiar with the Dolah prophecy." She said weakly.

"How familiar?"

"Enough to know that Kirsten wasn't going after Everleigh as the Dolah. Everleigh doesn't fit any of the supposed qualifications."

"So back to square one then." He slumped in his chair.

"Maybe not. If I could speak with her, no, I know. If, once I've recovered, I could enter her mind as I did with Richard in the garden."

"Not a bad idea though I doubt she'll let you get close enough to touch her."

"Leave it to me." She did her best to sound sure of herself.

Jensin snorted. "I will but this time I'm coming with you." He stood up and rubbed his eyes. There was a look of relief on his face when he offered up an exhausted smile. "I'm going to get some rest. I suggest you do the same."

Ivara let slip a small smile. A wave of sudden exhaustion crashed over her and suddenly her eyes felt heavy. She let herself yawn and when the warm embrace of sleep came once more she leaned into it.

Chapter 54

"If there is one simple thing that all myths, legends and schools of magic share, it is hope. The want for a better tomorrow and the need for everything to be alright."

Practical Magic by Daniel E. Simmons

Tallulah (1602 A.D.)

The water was murky at best and Tallulah could hear the booming of thunder above. Spring had come in full swing. Yellow pollen clouded the surface waters on good days and heavy storms ransacked the highest levels of the cities on bad. Tallulah sneezed and her gills flared. Ugh she absolutely loathed the springtime. Still it wasn't *all* bad. Last spring? Maybe. But this year would be different. Tallulah shook herself out of her reverie and turned to face Ivara once more.

"Are you alright?" Her friend asked gently.

Tallulah nodded. "Just don't want to mess this up. That's all."

For over twenty years they'd been at it. Trying and often failing to put a block in place on Ivara's memories. They spent days, weeks even sifting through scrolls on unsourced magic, runes, even ancient texts on the subject. Occasionally they would get close, but then they would eventually run into a small hiccup and they were back to square one. Until the day that they had come upon the amnesia rune. It was Corvena who had found it. At first she was hesitant, but after going through the details of the process and running it by their master Ivara finally agreed.

Though none of them said it aloud they all knew that eventually Ivara would go mad if she continued to tap into their memories. Tallulah could already see the edges of the madness. The mer girl had little sense of self and rarely acted her age. Some days she seemed wise beyond her years, other days she was just a little mer girl. Even the Dragon, the same master that had warned them all against leaving the Arkstone so long ago, agreed that something had to be done. So they set to creating a plan.

Ivara would receive the amnesia rune, and afterwards would be escorted back to her home in Makoul for a time. They all knew that the amnesia rune wouldn't stop the visions, nothing could. The hope, rather, was that Ivara having no knowledge of the Arkstone would be able to more easily dismiss such visions as strange dreams, whilst also focusing on re-establishing her own sense of self while surrounded by her family. The plan was far from foolproof, but it was the best they had managed to come up with.

Tallulah looked around the open ocean. A large finned beast of grey color passed them but paid them no heed. She could feel the current of water behind her and knew that Corvena had arrived. Purse in hand she was followed closely by an older Mer. This Mer was different from the rest of them, in place of a singular tail she possessed many tentacles. Her pallor was that of seaweed in the sunlight and on her skin were carved many runic symbols. Her many tentacles were red at the ends as if dripped in blood. On her waist she wore a crystalline dagger that shone brightly in the light of day. Tallulah did not need to be told what, or rather who the athame was. It was Dormethius. But despite the blade's evil reputation its handler seemed rather calm. The Sea Witch offered Tallulah and Ivara a curt smile.

"I brought the money, just as you asked." Corvena held up the purse. "And our mutual friend has agreed to help us."

"Scyla." The Older Mer said by way of introduction, smiling warmly. "Corvena tells me I'm to chaperone?"

"Yes." Ivara answered. "I need guaranteed safety and discretion for the duration of the journey both to Makoul and back here when the time comes. I assume Corvena has told you the rest?"

"I believe so. I'm to escort you across the sea. Your friend told me that once there it may be a few months before our return. Is there anything else I should know?"

"Yes. Before we leave I will have a block put on my memories. Which means I may seem disoriented at times."

"I think I can handle a slightly foggy teenager, eighty? Ninety?"

"Eighty – one, but close enough." Ivara smiled.

Scyla turned to Tallulah. "What will be our cue to return to the Arkstone? Will you send for us?"

"No, our seer has foreseen a shift in power in the south. We suspect the effects will reach the Kingdom of Colors, but we can't be sure. If anything of the sort happens you must come back immediately. *That* will be your cue."

The witch nodded. "Are you ready then?" She said turning back to Ivara.

"Not quite." Ivara's gills flared and her tail flickered nervously. She looked over at Tallulah.

Tallulah looked over at her friend, swallowing hard as she reached for Ivara's arm. "Are you sure about this?"

Ivara nodded but wouldn't allow herself to make eye contact. "I can't go on like this Tallulah. I...I'm afraid I'll lose my sense of self." Her friend said in a hushed voice.

Tallulah squeezed her friend's hand tight. "We'll be waiting here for you."

Ivara took a deep breath and turned to Corvena. "I'm ready, start carving."

Corvena took Ivara's arm and flipped it over. Ivara's inner arm was wholly unblemished, no scars, nothing but scales and skin. The one eyed mer took her blade and began to carve the amnesia rune. Though the blade was mundane, the rune was anything but and Tallulah could feel the chaos magic lingering around the wound as the blade burned the sigil into Ivara's arm. Ivara squirmed and squeezed her eyes shut but Tallulah couldn't look away. It was incredible and horrible all at once to watch someone's past be burnt away. Blood hovered about in the water but all parties simply waved it off. She watched, enthralled by Corvena's attention to detail as the mer woman guided the blade around the arm making small individual markings attaching each to the main piece.

"There, all finished." Corvena said once she had finished. "How do you feel?"

Ivara examined her arm, then noticed the intricate carved burn marks in her flesh and the blood coming from her wound and mixing with the water began to look around at them. Panic seeped into her face. Panic and a severe lack of recognition.

"What –?"

"Don't be alarmed dear, we're headed home." Scyla said gently.

"Wait but I –. Who are you?" Ivara said to no one in particular as she stumbled over her words.

Scyla turned Ivara away from Tallulah and began leading her away all while introducing herself. It was only then that Tallulah noticed the athame on the witches belt. It was quite beautiful but Tallulah felt a bit of unease when she looked at it as if the blade was alive and staring back at her.

It was Corvena who quietly came up behind her and entwined her hand with Tallulah's. They watched as Ivara took the witch's hand and swam off with her without a second thought. Tallulah and Corvena watched them as they swam away, fading into dark blue dots in the distance. Tallulah swallowed hard and it wasn't until they had returned to their shared room to find Brina's ever warm welcome that Tallulah was able to speak.

She hardly remembered her family. Even her father who'd delivered her to the Golden Mer was less of a memory these days and more of a story, a story which she repeated to herself to keep from forgetting. Intrusive thoughts swam freely within her mind, racing with the beating of her heart. *What if the rune doesn't hold? What if they were never able to reverse it? What if she doesn't come back?*

Corvena, likely sensing her anxiety, pressed her lips to Tallulah's. "She's a tough tad. She'll be alright."

Tallulah hadn't realized how much she valued her sisters in gold. How much she loved them even. Not until she'd lost one. It wasn't death...but the inaccessibility of it all, not having any means to reach out to Ivara, to check on her friend and see how she fared. It was too similar to death, too close to permanent. The realization that all she had, friends and family alike, were temporary weighed on her. Perhaps Corvena realized it too. Perhaps that was the reason for her sudden kindness.

Chapter 55

"...I saw a fair haired maiden confined to a foreign land. They put a crown upon her head and smeared oil on her temple. And as she rose I could feel it, the unstoppable force of Armageddon. I knew then that the maiden was the catalyst."

An excerpt from the prophecy of the Dolah as it was first recorded by the mer of the Arkstone in the year 1207

Ivara (1604 A.D.)

It had taken her a few weeks to fully recover and for her and Jensin to devise a solid plan. Ivara stared at the rusted metal bars that barred their entrance into the dungeon below. The hall smelled of mold, piss and rust. She could hear the dripping from the walls. It was abundantly clear that the palace dungeon hadn't been used in quite some time and had since fallen into disrepair. That or perhaps the King simply did not care for the wellbeing of those who had betrayed him.

"Ready?"

She had nearly forgotten that her copper-haired friend was standing beside her.

Ivara took a deep breath and squeezed Jensin's hand tight. "Yes. Let's get this over with." Her heart beat loud in her chest. Was she really ready to see a former friend chained to the walls of a rusted cell? No, she wasn't. And yet she found that as she rubbed the fresh scab on her neck her heart had no room for forgiveness.

"Are you sure about this?"

"I think so." She answered. "Let's go... before I change my mind."

Jensin nodded to Amos and the tall guard turned a key to open the dungeon. They walked in, side by side. Ivara's shoes clicked against the stone steps. The light was low in the dungeon and the air smelled of rot and mold. She squared her shoulders and walked in. The royal dungeons were not large. The room, if one could call it that, was round and consisted of five cells in total. Kirsten sat in the corner of the one furthest from them. She wore a cream slip and her hair was down. Time and mistreatment making her once beautiful ringlets appear disheveled and unkempt. She knew Kirsten could hear them but still the woman kept to herself.

"Kirsten?" Ivara called hoping the seamstress turned assassin would at least acknowledge them.

She hardly moved. In point of fact Ivara would hardly have known Kirsten could hear her had it not been for the echoes of her voice against the stone.

"Kirsten?" She tried being gentler this time. Invoking warmness in her tone.

"What?" She responded, her voice like an asp, quick and full of venom. Still she did not turn.

"We- *I* have come on behalf of the royal family. To speak with you regarding your actions and imprisonment thereafter."

"And pray tell what does the King want from me Ivara? Does he wish to behead me as he did my mother, his very *sister*?" Kirsten spat in mocking tones as she turned to face them. Ivara gasped when her face came into the light. She was battered and bruised and a cut on her lip was red and swollen with infection. Seeing Ivara's horrified expression she laughed but there was no mirth in it. "Does my appearance offend you? Take it up with the guards."

Ivara walked closer until she was inches from the cell that held the monster on the other side. "You've been sentenced to death Kirsten."

There it was laid plain before all in the room. Kirsten's face crumpled and all the color drained from her face. "Is that why you've come so you might be the one to tell me of my fate? Such sweet revenge I'm sure, but you don't scare me, enthraller." Her voice wobbled on the last few words. But Ivara continued.

"I need you to listen to what I'm about to say very closely. In three weeks' time you shall be beheaded in a public display, just like your mother." Ivara cleared her throat and kept going as best she could. "As it stands you have made mortal enemies of the Allagorian royal family and their supporters. There is no one in all of this kingdom that will not want you dead as soon as the information surrounding your crime is published."

She paused to look for the girls reaction but Kirsten kept her face steady. Ivara continued, reaching through the bars as she spoke to take Kirsten's hand.

"None save for me. I'm mer Kirsten."

Now fascination and fear came to light on her face.

"I am a servant of the Golden Dragon, which means I know of the Dolah prophecies. I also have modest influence with the royal family."

"What are you getting at?" Kirsten asked tenuously.

"Let me help you. Tell me everything. In exchange I will speak to Richard about your sentence."

Kirsten bit her lip clearly thinking it over. When she finally spoke it was only a whisper. "Why? I tried to kill you."

"I'm well aware. Even have the scar to prove it."

"And you're not mad?"

Mad? *Mad?* Oh she was furious. Positively livid. But... perhaps some part of her simply couldn't reconcile the shy, kind Kirsten she knew with this thing that stared at her from within its cell.

"Your answer. Now."

Kirsten took a deep long breath. "I'll tell you this much. Everleigh *is* my friend and I never want to see her come to harm. But the Dolah...the prophecy..." She sighed. "That's bigger than me or you or any of this. Everleigh cannot be allowed to ascend to the throne. We must do everything in our power to prevent the Dolah from being born and that starts with the fair haired maiden. Ivara if what you say is true. If you know the prophecy then you know that when the Dolah comes about, so will a great war. Millions of lives will be lost, but we, I can stop it. It is a sacred mission."

"Who is 'we'?" Jensin asked angrily. "Everleigh has nothing to do with this you piece of-!"

Then it clicked. Suddenly Ivara realized. Words she had heard long ago. Kirsten seemed to see the realization on her face because she smiled mournfully.

"The fair haired queen..." Ivara whispered.

"...will rise in the east." Kirsten finished. "There, now you know my reasons. When they behead me, remember what I was fighting for. Remember that my mother tried to solve the prophecy without bloodshed, it was she who arranged Henry's disappearance and for that they beheaded her."

Ivara went still, not daring to gaze at Jensin. "You know where the Prince is? All this time you've known..." She whispered in disbelief.

"Is he alive?" Jensin asked.

Kirsten hesitated. "I only found out from reading my mother's letters after they cut off her head. She had hid them where she thought nobody would find them, and for a while none did. None save for me. Her correspondence wanted Henry dead in order to prevent Everleigh from taking the throne, but she saved him. Wherever he is, he's alive."

"Who has him?" Jensin yelled.

"I don't know! The letters I exchanged with my mother's correspondence were short. I never asked about the Prince, nor did they tell me anything. All I know is what I have told you. They are coming for the Princess, you *must* understand, if Everleigh is allowed to take the Allagorian throne as Queen Consort, the Dolah will rise and thousands will be in danger. Please! Don't you see she is the fair haired maiden that the prophecy speaks of. If she is allowed to gain power we are one step closer to the coming of the Dolah!"

There was silence in the room as Jensin tried to master his temper. At last Ivara spoke as she turned to leave the room.

"I will speak to the King on your behalf." Was all she said as she walked quietly out of the dungeon and back into daylight.

Just as the door behind her shut she could hear Kirsten's weak cry. "You can't stop what's already in motion!"

Her breath came in shallow and short as she tried to tame herself. When they had finally reached the gardens they found Richard and Everleigh waiting for them as planned.

"Well?" Everleigh asked carefully.

"She's trying to prevent the Great War." Ivara looked over to her fair haired female friend. "And you're the first sacrifice."

Chapter 56

"So, was it all for naught? When all is said and done, the prophecies in this book are just words. Many of which have not yet come to fruition, and those that have, well some would argue it was mere happenstance. When we look forward to the future, who or what do we let guide us? Gods? Spirits? Magic? Prophecy? Are we predestined to follow a path not of our choosing or is every action we take vital to the act of *determining* our destiny? I choose to believe the latter."

Prophecies of Northerners by Alec E. Kalith

Tallulah (1604 A.D.)

The stone etchings laid before her were rough and old. It had been many years since she had first seen the ancient carving in the underwater Dragon city and she still couldn't make sense of it. *Tenets of war*. Those three words awoke something in Tallulah each and every time she came here and read the ancient text above the carving.

Lazily, she traced her fingers along the mural's curves, dipping into its stone edges and valleys. A hero. That was what the Dragon really wanted from her. A soldier to cut down doers of evil. But Tallulah had played the part of the hero once before and it had cost her everything. It was not a mistake she was eager to repeat. She closed her eyes and put a hand to her temple. Memories of that night flooded her mind as they did more and more these days.

Perhaps it was the lack of sleep or maybe she just missed her friends.

She still saw them every few days, but it was clear that each day brought new stressors to each of them. Tallulah could see Brina's health was in decline. It had been for a while yet none seemed to notice. Her friend was hardly eating and grew thinner by the day. It was clear that the necromancy was taking its toll. After all, how many times could one run their hand over the soft veil that divides life from death without slowly leaning into its touch?

Then there was Osirus. He had yet to produce any more prophecies of grandeur and so was allowed to spend his days with his prophetic kin. She was happy for him, in truth. She longed for a life outside the pressures of the city's walls. Corvena too had expressed such a longing to her once. But even she would never leave such a tremendous responsibility to others.

"You seem to come here a lot. I'm beginning to think you're a narcissist."

Tallulah swiveled and startled. Sure enough Corvena sat on one of the desks high above her. She swam down her onyx hair billowing in the current.

"Honestly, Tal that doesn't even look like you. The physique is all wrong."

"Oh?" Tallulah asked dryly.

"Yes. The waist doesn't cinch hardly at all! Then there's the shoulders and well you know." Corvena gestured to her chest. "It's all out of proportion. You look much nicer than this." Corvena gestured to the carving.

"Corv you can't tell what she looks like because of the armor and shield."

"Exactly! If I had a waistline like yours you couldn't pay me to hide it in some old clunky armor!"

Tallulah let slip a small smile but her mood was not much helped by the banter. Corvena, ever quick on the uptake, picked up on this.

"Contemplating how to save the world in ugly armor then?" She said more seriously.

"How not to actually."

"Oh? Interesting strategy though perhaps a few revisions before you go forward with that particular plan." Corvena quipped.

"I'm serious. This whole thing is too much. Too strange. I believe in prophecies, you know I do, but *this*?" Tallulah shook her head. "Corv every scroll and tablet I can find on these mer is practically hero worship."

Corvena came to float beside her, staring at her own figure. "So you don't think you are hero material?" Corvena asked, looking her in the eyes. "Because I do. I think of all of us you're best suited to it actually."

"What do you mean?"

"Exactly what I said. Brina pushes herself beyond her limits, always trying to be the best. She's trying too hard if you ask me. Ivara has a heart of gold but if push came to shove my money's on the other guy. I love her like a sister Tal but a few nightmares nearly drove her to madness. Osirus tries his best to hide it but we all know he wants out. It's probably why he hardly comes around anymore. Then there's me and, well that should be obvious. I'm not exactly a shining example of character. But you try Tal. Not for yourself, for everyone around you. You're the glue. A protector."

Tallulah laughed dryly. "You don't know me as well as you think you do. There are things about me that would...scare you." The last words were a whisper and she struggled to force them out. Corvena moaned.

"Oh gods here we go. Alright, let's hear your sob story."

Tallulah was taken aback by the sheer lack of empathy. Her face fell in dismay and annoyance.

"Can't you take me seriously just once!"

"Why? So you can moan on and on about your dark past? About how your awful childhood shaped you and you *just can't move on.* Tal I don't give a damn."

"I killed someone, Corv." Tallulah said in a low whisper.

Corvena's eyes widened and her face went through a hundred expressions in half a minute.

"What?"

"The alderman in my village. He was like a grandfather to me; he practically raised me. And... I killed him in cold blood."

Corvena took a deep breath before replying.

"You must have had a decent reason."

"At the time I thought so but looking back...I'm not so sure." She shook her head. "The alderman and his predecessors upheld a treaty with the walkers in the area. All our dead would go to them. For what reasons I'm still not sure but in return they wouldn't fish in our waters nor would any vessel except the ones to collect the cadavers sail over us."

Corvena looked like she was going to be sick.

"I was a tad at the time. I wanted to fix it. Rectify it, it all just felt so wrong. So I killed him, and when they came to collect the next time it was with spears. They killed my mother first then the rest of them. A few of us managed to escape though. But in the end it was my fault. I broke the treaty when I killed him. All that blood, *my mother's blood*, it's all on my hands. I'm the reason my people are dead. In killing one mer I damned hundreds!" Tallulah began shaking and glanced down at her palms half expecting to see the crimson haze of blood swirling around them.

Corvena was silent. Seconds turned to minutes as they sat together before their heroic alters. Corvena pursed her lips then replied, still looking down. "Good for you." She whispered.

"What did you say?"

"I said, good for you. All the adults around you knew, your parents, aunts, uncles. They had to have known what the alderman was doing. And they likely understood the cruelty of it. But they did *nothing*. It's disgusting." She spat the last part, and the room darkened. "Dead or alive, you don't treat children like something to be sold."

"Still, I –."

"No Tallulah, no 'still.' Stop grieving for these people who hurt you!"

They sat there in silence for a moment before Tallulah finally asked the question that had been wandering around her mind for quite a while. "Why do you care so much about them? Children you don't even know."

Corvena began tracing her outline in the carving as she replied. "When I was a tad, I lived in a small sunken ship on the outskirts with over twenty brothers and sisters. Then when I was thirty winters into my life a young mer and his wife came to our home, picked me out of the bunch and brought me home with them. My father and mother didn't even say goodbye. I watched the money enter their palms, before I left.

The young couple were kind and wealthy. They adorned me in fineries, they even gave me a name, something my former parents had neglected to do. Having a family... it filled a vacancy in my soul. Then one day I became ill. You see I had a growth here, on the side of my temple. It was small at first but within the year it had covered my left eye. The growth was getting worse by the day so my new parents resorted to having it removed completely. And though they were very wealthy, the cost of the operation still managed to put them in debt. As for me, well I only lost an eye. So when, in the summer of my forty-fifth year, my mother became ill we simply couldn't pay to help her. My parents had just recovered their debt from my surgery, they couldn't take another financial blow. So we went to the Dragon. I had heard the tales, the stories about how parents would offer their children as payment for miracles. Still I half expected they might back out at the last moment." Corvena laughed. "I still thought they loved me."

Tallulah didn't know what to say. So she said the only thing she could think of. "I'm sorry."

"You go through something like that and a thought so miniscule you hardly even notice forms in the back of your mind. 'You're unlovable,' it says. And over time it begins to grow, that voice. That awful idea. Until one day you simply accept it as truth. It may rain today, the water is cold, and I am unlovable. You think about every single sin you've committed. And the faces of those you've let down haunt you at night."

"But we aren't unlovable." Tallulah said quietly.

"No we're not." Corvena stopped tracing and looked over at Tallulah.

"So what are we then? Unlucky?"

"Does it matter? No amount of luck will bring your mother back. And no amount of luck could make my family keep me. Don't let your past keep you locked away in a box. Because people who love you enough to let you grow are the ones you grow for. You taught me that, actually." Then Corvena leaned over and kissed her.

They swam back up to the city hand in hand in gentle silence until they had left the darkness of the underground city far below them. It was a beautiful day. The summer sun warmed the waters above the Arkstone and lit up the peaks of the castle. She looked over at her love. Corvena's hair was like fine stalks of seagrass in the current and her heterochromatic eyes swept the city. One gold, one green, the latter being the fake one. Her pale body had grown elegant over the years while still bearing the muscle necessary of a maiden. And her tail burned with a golden fire that had now completely consumed all of its former purples and reds.

Tallulah looked down at her own tail. She too had become completely golden though she wasn't altogether sure when the changes had finalized themselves. She knew that for her it began with her eyes and went downward. It had been the same for Brina though for Corvena and Ivara she wasn't sure. Especially since neither of Ivara's eyes had yet begun to turn, they remained ever grey.

She was lost in these thoughts for some time as Corvena led her along and the two enjoyed the warm water and one another's company. It was some time before Tallulah realized the culprit of their intense serenity.

"Corv?"

"Mmm?"

"Where is everyone?"

She looked around. The castle was nearly empty save for the lowest level where the servants lived but even they seemed... tense.

"You don't think something happened, do you?" Her voice was tense, unsure, and paranoid.

Tallulah thought for a moment. If the Dragon's personal guard had left then there was likely a council meeting. She looked up. Sure enough one of the larger rooms was alight with runes and one could hear the soft speak of people from such a distance.

"Come on." She grabbed Corvena's arm and they began rising once more. They swam hard, Tallulah's tail whipping this way and that until they arrived and quietly swam in through one of the entry portals. Sure enough the Dragons finest Brina, and even some of the city's leaders were hunched over the stone table in the middle.

"Nice of you two to finally show up." Brina said by way of acknowledgement.

"Nice of *you* to give us a heads up." Corvena shot back.

"I might have if it wasn't an emergency and I could have found you."

"Emergency?" Tallulah asked, trying to break the string of tension.

"We received reports that Scyla's body was found on the outskirts of Makoul near the Walker settlement known as Allagor."

Tallulah felt her jaw drop. Who could have killed the sea witch? It was only by Dormethius, the final source and athame that one could kill its owner. Scyla had been Dormethius' only keeper for ages.

"Who killed her?"

"We're not sure. The problem was made all the worse when the Dragon sensed Dormethius' presence on land."

"Dormethius is in Allagor?" Tallulah said breathlessly.

"Fortunately no, Ellenward. It's a small victory but at this point... one I'm willing to take."

"What about Ivara, Scyla was supposed to be our contingency plan." Corvena asked tersely.

Brina's gills flared. "So far as we know the two arrived in Makoul as planned and she disappeared shortly after."

Tallulah wanted to vomit. Ivara had been gone for nearly three years but to think that she had been missing for part of it... she knew what that meant. The chances of her showing up again were slim to none and without her memories she was more vulnerable than ever. Tallulah had done that. She had stripped Ivara of any defense she might have needed. And now her friend's corpse was likely floating about somewhere in the blue.

"So you're telling me that one of the Sources is loose on walker territory? And one of the Dragons' assets has gone missing?!" One of the mer men at the table half screamed at Brina.

"Yes but the good news is we can retrieve the athame if we act quickly." Brina replied, turning her attention to the boisterous nobleman. "As for Ivara... for now all we can do is hope that she is alright. We need to direct all of our attention and resources towards the athame at the moment."

"Retrieve it? This is a blatant act of war! I say we stomp out the walkers like the pests they are. For too long their populations have grown out of control!" The mer screamed.

"He has a point," Another mer with spectacles said. "They could use some.. trimming. The walkers have abused our hunting grounds for generations now. As well, village populations beyond the outskirts have dropped dramatically in the past thousand years or so with many of the western sea's epipelagic groups becoming all but extinct."

"But how do we know it was they who stole Dormethius? And even if they are the guilty party, who shall we make war against? The walkers in Ellenward or the so-called Allagorians? The later would require help from our kin in Makoul, who I will remind you is wholly focused on defending themselves against Neroth's attacks." An aristocratic mer woman quipped.

Brina tried to speak but the older mer paid her no heed, simply raising their volume every time she began a sentence. Finally Corvena shoved a shadowy fist down. Tallulah watched her magic suck all the ambient light from the room, casting haunting shadows on Corvena herself.

"We are *not* going to war. Not without the five tenants, one of whom is missing or dead. Whatever we do the first step *must be* retrieving Dormethius. Even if we were to make war on the walkers it would be more bloodshed than it is worth so long as he remains hidden among them."

"And who, pray tell, shall retrieve the ancient blade? Or perhaps you were planning on growing a pair of legs and fetching it yourself." The aristocratic mer woman asked. Her pompous tone made Tallulah want to slap her.

Tallulah took a breath to speak but Corvena beat her to it.

"I will. I'll go to the Dragon and request that I be able to leave, and I'll be back within the year."

Tallulah looked over at her, her mouth agape. "But-."

"You don't seriously expect us to send some young mer after such a blade?" The aristocrat mocked.

Corvena rolled her eyes. "Fine then, send some of your friends. Or hell why don't you send a whole army after Dormethius oh wait you've no way of actually getting to the walker kingdom!"

"I am an elected official of the people! *I* shall tell your dragon to work his magic on the mer that *I* shall choose to send! You golden maidens think that you're above it all? You're not. It is high time you three learn your place."

Tallulah could feel Corvena's frustration building. Brina glanced her way. She felt it too. Even before the room began to dim and the shadows poured in like ink. Corvena's voice rumbled in the darkness of the room and her golden eye glowed. But before she could say anything further a deep gravelly voice boomed in the maidens' minds.

That's quite enough Shadow.

Within seconds the inky darkness retracted its onyx tentacles. Corvena's hands fell to her side as the light returned and she stared down the terrified aristocrat.

"Do not *ever* disrespect me or my kin again or I will gut you." Corvena's voice was like venom and her tone like a whip that dug deep into the skin of each terrified witness. Even Tallulah was shaking. The weight of seeing Corvena's magic...it was like watching a nightmare come to life. Tallulah took a deep breath, mastering herself and offered Corvena her arm. Brina nodded at them both and began closing the meeting.

They swam back towards the Dragon's lair in silence. The meeting was quick, with minor adjustments to their original plan. Corvena's specialties were far from the realm of memory magic so the adjustment of her memories wouldn't be needed. It was also decided that she would go alone. Tallulah, Brina and Osirus would stay in the Arkstone until her return the following year in case Neroth decided to set its eyes on the Arkstone.

"It's only a year, don't look so nervous." Corvena cautioned Tallulah when they had returned to their room to help her pack and tidy up. "Really Tal, I can handle myself."

Corvena offered up her signature smile but Tallulah's uneasiness just grew in the pit of her stomach.

"Just be careful." She cautioned. They hadn't spoken about Corvena's terrible show of power mere hours earlier and Tallulah feared upsetting her. For though they tried to hide it she could tell Corvena's nerves were just as high as her own. Corvena turned to face her fully, her satchel now full. There was a grief in her golden eye matched only by her own.

Before she could say goodbye the Dragon's maidens came in to sweep Corvena away. Tallulah followed them to the surface Corvena squeezing her hand tightly the whole way. When they could finally feel the warm breeze on their cheeks they began swimming inland.

"The walker country is a short distance from here, its locals have given it the name Ellenward. You will take human form until the completion of this task. Your memories will remain intact as will your capacity for magic."

Corvena's face remained fixed in stone as she listened to her to the Dragons' servants.

"The average human lifespan in Ellenward is forty- three years. You shall retain your current physical maturity in your human form placing you around twenty years of age relative to the other walkers. Human women begin to physically deteriorate around the age of twenty-five. Once you transform you will begin aging very rapidly. Thus you will be on a clock to find the dagger and return it to the Arkstone."

Tallulah was surprised to see tears flowing down Corvena's face. "This is cruel." The former whispered.

"No." Now the Dragons hand maidens spoke to her directly. "This is what you were trained for. You are not housewives, you are soldiers, you are scholars and above all you are sorcerers. If you had followed the rules laid out before you, this would not need to be an emotional event."

"I suppose I'm to simply walk to shore once I'm granted legs?" Corvena asked after a moment of calming herself.

"Yes." Corvena looked around confused but one of the maidens came to grab her.

The Maidens regarded her. For a moment before speaking to her alone.

"Shield, you will stay. If the Seer's visions are correct then it would be foolish to allow such an invaluable resource to leave the Arkstone. You will await the Enthraller's return."

Tallulah nodded, not bothering to wipe away the salty tears that fell to her cheeks. A million thoughts raced through her mind. All the things she could say and all those she couldn't. Instead she took Corvena's face in her hands and kissed her before watching as they dragged her love in the direction of a distant shore that Tallulah could not make out. It wasn't long until she was all alone drifting in the sea.

A sense of despair began to wrap itself around her. Alone. For the second time in her life she was alone. For the second time in her life, her family was in peril. Because that was what Corvena, Brina, Ivara and Osirus were to her. They were her family and she would not sit around and let them die. As much as she loved Corvena she knew her well enough to know that the only ones in danger were those who sought to anger the mer woman. It was Ivara who needed her help now. She had a mission of her own, and Dragon help those that blocked her path.

Chapter 57

"Finally I saw a maiden, near death wandering a dangerous wood. By her side walked a noble unicorn. This was the final sign. Then the vision ended."

An excerpt from the prophecy of the Dolah as it was first recorded by

the mer of the Arkstone in the year 1207

Ivara (1604 A.D.)

It was the wedding of the century. The great room was alive with laughter. Skirts whirred this way and that in a haze of color. Bards strummed their instruments and drunken lords and ladies cheered them on. Clapping and dancing was all one the unwary eye would see on a first pass. Ivara's gown was golden with white lace. A corset beneath the gown helped to hide her scars and recent obsession with jelly tarts. The dress was adorned in pearls and patterns had been traced to make it eye catching. Everleigh had bid her wear it to the celebrations and they had had the dress altered. Now her majesty Everleigh, the future Queen regent of Allagor sat at the head of the table with her new husband Richard. The two were a fitting couple and their closeness made Ivara smile.

"Enjoying the festivities?"

Ivara turned. Jensin, clad in red and gold stood before her in apparel so flamboyant it had to be purely ceremonial. She giggled while sipping her wine. Jensin glared but there was no ill intent in his look. Instead he took her by the waist and kissed her. He smelled of spiced cider. She wished with all her heart that they could stay in that moment forever. One kiss simply wasn't enough. When they finally untangled themselves she was breathless as she looked him over.

"Care to dance?" She asked. He took her hand and they waltzed away into the crowd. The music changed and the dances asked more of her. Turning this way and that she spun through the crowd going from one dance partner to another. A blue dress lined with gold lace and red gemstones that shined in the dim light caught her eyes. She smiled as Everleigh moved toward the dance floor with Richard. Time fell away as they stomped and clapped and spun.

They drank and laughed and drank some more and when all that was done they would stumble back to the dance floor and begin again. Perhaps it was the wine, or maybe she had spent too long keeping to her small group of friends here, but Ivara looked around as if seeing her friend's palace for the first time. New faces coming into focus. A woman passed her. Her dress was a deep red like dried blood with accents of purple that contrasted her dark skin and hair. She might have stood out were it not for the countless Lords and Ladies dressed in the same hue, Allagorian red. The woman smiled at Ivara and the two clasped hands and spun about until the song shifted and they found other partners. Ivara excused herself from the woman and went to calm herself by a pillar to let the dizziness fade.

When she looked up her smile began to fade, replaced by unease. There were a *lot* of new faces here. Had she really drunk so much that now her memory left her? Had she really been so wrapped up in her own dealings that she hadn't given the nobles of Allagor the time of day? Perhaps. Once the dizziness had faded she threw herself back into the whirl of cloth and wine and laughter. Her unease faded and elation came to take its place. Everleigh was working her way through the crowd toward her. Her smile and giggly response to nobles as she passed them was enough to warm the entire hall. Ivara smiled back and reached for her once the Princess was in reach.

A new partner oblivious to their friendship, no doubt, took Ivara's hand and they spun. Ivara laughed and saw Everleigh stop to giggle as Ivara struggled to explain her intentions. Still they spun ever on. The man was in a state, grinning from ear to ear as his hand clasped Ivara's waist and he twirled her without care. When Ivara turned she saw the woman in red pass her and take her friend's hand and soon they two were laughing and smiling and dancing. Ivara didn't see the flash of silver; just her friends face the moment the fear and panic seeped like blood into her chest. Everleigh fell to the floor and Ivara threw her partner off of her, running to her friend's aid. Everleigh had gone pale and her breath shallow as she clawed at her throat and spat blood. Ivara looked up but the woman garbed in red had fled.

It was as if everything was happening in slow motion. Goblets clattered to the floor, women and men alike screamed. Husbands and guards ushered the guests of lesser status out of the way. Ivara looked up for Richard but could not find him among the crowd. A firm hand pulled her away. Blood soaked the marble floor. Everleigh's body gave a final deathly shiver and became still. *No, no, no, not her, not Everleigh.* Ivara felt frozen in place. She broke her shock and ran to her friend's body but a firm hand held her back.

"Come on!" A male voice ordered. In her confusion she could barely place it until she looked up and saw Jensin fighting through the panicked crowd. Ivara tugged away from Jensin with a ferocity.

"Get off of me!" Ivara screamed at him. She wouldn't leave her. Her vision was a blur as she watched Jensin check the princess's pulse. He cursed under his breath and grabbed Ivara by her gown now dragging her across the marble floor. She kicked and screamed until her head hit something cold and hard. He let her go and she stood only to be half dragged up the stairs. *She's dying. She's dying.* Over and over again it repeated in her head. *She's-.*

"Dead. She's dead, Ivara. Whoever did it had it planned. Come on, this way." They turned and something cool seeped into Ivara's blood as the realization began to sync in. Jensin dropped her hand and soon they were running in tandem. Ivara's dress was heavy and she kept tripping over it but there was no time to cut it away or take it off. The halls darkened as they ran on. A set of steps spiraled into darkness and Jensin took her hand gently leading her down.

"The wine cellar." Jensin whispered before she could ask. Indeed a cool draft reached her almost immediately. A large hallway led them to a wide room. They sat down and Ivara sobbed, falling to her knees. Jensin closed the door but the lock was rusty, likely Allagor's last war had been before his time. They sat there together in the dim light.

"The attacker. Did you see him?"

"Her, and yes. Her dress was red like...like blood...and purple. She...she smiled at me just before..." Ivara trailed off. She tried taking a few shaky breaths to calm herself. Everleigh's laugh, they'd never hear it again. The princess wouldn't smile again. The thoughts made her shudder. She pursed her lips. Her nerves overtaking her head. "Richard?" She asked, realizing that her entire body was shaking, it was not from the cold.

"With his guards in the tower. Don't worry he's well protected. I was meant to go with them but, well you can guess." He gestured to his shoulder where a long shallow wound bled profusely. She watched him tear off what remained of his uniform and wrap the wound.

"Does it hurt?"

"Not too badly. I suspect it's shallower than it appears. What about you?"

"I'm fine. I mean I'm not *fine* but..." She ran her shaking hands through her hair and let out another tried to take a deep breath. She felt a hand on her shoulder and leaned into his touch. They sat there for what felt like an eternity but was more likely an hour. Ivara dozed off once the adrenaline left her system and exhaustion replaced it. When she awoke Jensin had dressed his wound and was looking through barrels. He had just found his drink of choice when a knock came at the door. Two knocks at first, a pause, then one, another pause then three in quick succession. Ivara looked to Jensin and he gave her a curt nod but held his finger to his lips and motioned her to move.

Just in case. He mouthed. She tiptoed behind the barrel stand and peered through a hole in the wood. She watched Jensin knock in rapid succession, stop then repeat. This went on until both parties seemed pleased and Jensin beckoned her forward in the same motion opening the large wooden door. A silver blade caught his shirt and gently forced him backwards, careful to only cut the fabric. Slowly the woman in red and purple entered the room. Kirsten stood behind her arms crossed.

The assassin had changed and now wore a white blouse and leather trousers, her various daggers sitting on a belt at her hips. Kirsten still wore her pink gown, now brown with grime and filth from her time in the prison cell. Her wet hair framed her bruised face and frail form. Her posture spoke of mistreatment during her imprisonment. She looked from Ivara to Jensin and back again. Her face twisted with disgust and pity.

"This the witch?" The female assassin asked Kirsten.

"Are you stupid? Of course that's not *the witch*." Kirsten spat. She pointed to Jensin. "He's the son of the King's advisor."

"Old or new?"

"Does it matter?"

The woman with the sword gave Kirsten a curt nod and brought her blade back, preparing it for the killing blow but Jensin was faster. He dove to the side, the blade only barely missing him. Fast as lightning he pulled out his own and the two clashed in a deadly duel. They swung at one another fast as light. Ivara made no movement towards Kirsten. Her hatred, as brightly as it burned, was somehow at odds with seeing her so broken. Kirsten for her part just watched. Ivara briefly wondered if their swords would hit some invisible string and the tension might fall away. Ivara tried to pull herself up but the world spun. Jensin spun, knocking down an old glass bottle, perhaps left by some guard or passerby. The bottle shattered its contents covering Ivara in a sticky putrid smelling liquid. Ivara's breath hitched in her throat and breathing became increasingly difficult. She forced herself to look away from the conflict in a feeble attempt to calm herself.

When she did look back she saw that Jensin had taken another blow. He wretched in pain and stumbled back. He was losing this fight. Fear and exhaustion made him stumble over himself. Even so he wasn't dead yet. Instinct and fear took hold of Ivara and she reached for the glass shards on the ground, scraping them to her. The glass was cold and yet is still burned as it cut deep into her skin drawing golden blood from her palm. Her head was whirling and she still couldn't stand but she was close enough to the cellar wall to crawl towards it. There was a whoosh of metal beside her and a bit of her dress had fallen away.

Ivara pulled herself the last few inches and reached out her arm for the wall when Kirsten's foot came slamming down on her hand. She screamed in agony as the woman put all her weight on Ivara's cut hand forcing it into the shattered glass on the ground. Fast as lightning Ivara swung her other hand around and slashed at Kirsten with the shard until she met flesh. Kirsten yelped and jumped back. The adrenaline was ebbing away now leaving only the sober reality of the pain in her hands and the throbbing in her mind. It was all she could do to press her palms to the wall of the cellar. At once she could feel the chaos flowing into her, it was blazing hot, and sweet. Dangerous, this was dangerous.

Richard. Her mind called him through the walls. The castle was a maze of stone and dragon bone. *Richard!* She screamed into the chaos. Searching for what felt like an eternity. Until finally she found him. He was huddled against one wall quietly sobbing and praying. *Richard!*

His head shot up, and he looked directly at her somehow. She realized he could see her.

"I don't understand... what's happening?" He said with astonishment.

Ivara could feel her energy leaving her. *Wine cellar. East Tower... Send a medic, he's hurt. He's...*

It was all she could manage before she came too. She was back in the cellar. Her blood was drying. Behind her metal clashed on metal and the woman's sword was at Jensin's chest.

"The Black Sails of Ellenward send they're tidings." She smirked and with a mirth that terrified Ivara, drew her blade across Jensin's chest and he stumbled back, falling to the ground. The assassin turned to Ivara. "And you..."

"Wait!" Kirsten put herself between the assassin and Ivara. "She's a magic user, don't kill her!"

"I hadn't noticed." The woman said, rolling her eyes in annoyance.

Kirsten examined Ivara silently for a moment. "Let's take her with us."

"Doesn't the Princess already have a puppet?"

"Yes, but imagine how displeased Ada will be when she hears that you've killed this one!" Kirsten stood up a bit straighter and her expression hardened with resolve. "I have been through *hell* and I am *not* going back empty handed."

The woman looked Ivara up and down. Her face marred by disgust. "Fine. But she's your charge. If one of those fish scaled bastards so much as swims by my ship they are getting speared, along with your little friend."

"Of course." Kirsten bowed but her expression showed neither submission nor gratitude. This woman had just won at something. When she turned around to face Ivara there was no softness in her eyes. Whatever her reasons for saving Ivara, kindness was not on the list.

"Where are you taking me?" Ivara sputtered crawling away on her back.

"Home. *My home.* Ellenward, maybe someone there will find some use for you."

Ivara tried to reach into Kirstens mind but her foe's runic necklace blocked her way. Before she could say another word the pommel of a smooth well-crafted sword came smashing against Ivara's head and all was dark.

Epilogue

Uhane (1604 A.D.)

Uhane was cold, wet, and miserable when she came crawling out of the sea and onto to the sandy shores of Ellenward on pale wobbly legs. Even more so when the voice began speaking to her.

So close now... We are nearly there.

The creature called himself Dormethius, and he had infested her mind, but it was a small price to pay for all that she had gained. Still the journey here had been bloody. She had never considered herself evil, even now with Scyla's blood on her hands. Uhane looked up to see the huge castle looming over the beach and shoreline. She smiled, years of living in her sister's shadow might finally come to an end. And slowly she pulled the athame out of its sleeve to study its crystalline blade in the moonlight.

A young couple out for a nightly stroll passed her on the beach. She eased her way into their minds, ignoring the pain of the chaos magic and bathing in the power of her newfound control. Then she spoke.

Go. She spoke in their minds. *Go and fetch your masters. Tell them the Sea Witch walks among you.*

Acknowledgements

What are mermaids, if not beautiful and magical individuals that inspire and appear to those whom they meet, as the human embodiment of a wish come true? It is why we become so obsessed with them and their lore. And while for better or for worse mermaids remain solely in the world of fiction, the world still remains blessed by beautiful and incredible souls. So allow me to take a moment and extend my deepest thanks to my personal mermaids. The people in my life who remind me on a daily basis that dreams can and do come true.

First and foremost will always be my parents. My father in particular, for years he both encouraged and instructed me in writing all the while providing me with a wide variety of wonderful books to read. Thank you Olan Prentice for sharing your vast knowledge of storytelling with me even as you were finishing your own book. And thank you to my cousin Jackson Branton, who created the incredible cover for this book. Thank you to my cousin Emma Dees, an aspiring author who somehow found the time in her busy schedule to give me honest feedback and encouragement on A Clash Of Tides.

Next I want to thank T.D. Frost, who spent hours going through this book and tediously giving feedback. As well to Claire Ashgrove, my incredible editor, for teaching me so much about writing. For those who have never taken on the role of a beta reader or editor this is no small thing, which makes me all the more grateful. Thank you.

A large thank you is owed as well to the incredibly talented Cassandra Lynn for creating the lovely map. I never thought I'd see the world from my imagination so elegantly drawn out. The excitement she showed throughout working on the project was as encouraging as it was inspiring.

Finally, thank you to my friends who have helped me promote this book, Claire Koleske, Jessica Nandi, Rachel LaChanse, Meghan Hinson, Stephanie Drew, Mackenzie Jordan, Savannah Chandler, Adele Marie, Liz Wilson, and Sofia. Thank you for your support, and for helping me make this dream a reality.

Dear Readers...

A special thank you is owed to you, the reader. Whether you picked this up on a whim or purchased it when it first released, thank you. It is readers like yourself that breathe life into characters like mine that only exist as mere ink on a page. It is you and your spectacular imagination that bring this fictional world to life. It is you who has made this little dream of mine into an incredible reality.

If you would like to see more from this series, please consider leaving a review. For indie authors such as myself reviews are the lifeblood of our work. It is reviews like yours that can make or break an author's career. So if you can find the time, please let me know what you thought.

For those of you who are interested in becoming a beta reader for the next book in this series please reach out to me at aliviamaar.author@gmail.com I would be honored to get your feedback!

For any communication that is business related please reach out using the same email. Likewise if you would like to connect you can find me on Instagram @livsbookshelf and on TikTok @authoraliviamaar, I am always looking to make new friends!